PRAISE FOR JOSEPH FINDER AND HIS NOVELS

The Switch

"Seemingly ripped from recent headlines, Finder's latest . . . whizzes by so quickly and suspensefully. . . . A master of what might be called the 'man in over his head' thriller, Finder delivers a tense, uncannily relevant tale about government secrets falling into the wrong hands."

—*Kirkus Reviews*

"[Finder] once again shows his knack for crafting an engaging thriller." —*Publishers Weekly*

"Finder has written another compelling thriller that demonstrates his strengths of mixing corporate themes with mayhem. . . . The perfect summer read."

—*Library Journal*

"Propulsive. . . . Ripped from the headlines."

—*The Washington Post*

"If Alfred Hitchcock were alive and working today, this is the kind of story he would direct."

—*Star-Telegram* (Fort Worth)

"Perfect for fans of *The Fugitive*." —*The Boston Globe*

"*The Switch* is a dazzling political thriller, a kind of *Advise and Consent* postmodernized for the 24/7 news cycle world. Perfectly timed and wondrously prescient, this is summer reading of the highest order."

—*Providence Journal*

"[A] much-needed shot of adrenaline sure to shake up the waning late summer days." —*The Oklahoman*

"[A] master of the corporate thriller. [Finder's] novels infuse fast-moving plots with well-researched business minutiae and impressively current tech details."

—WBUR Boston

Guilty Minds

"Nick Heller is a breath of fresh air in the world of private investigators as he will go to any lengths to succeed for his clients. His background and skills are an asset, making him almost a superhero. . . . *Guilty Minds* is a compelling thriller."

—Associated Press

"Smooth and polished—and classy enough for troubled characters to pause and make a big deal about the relative merits of rye whiskeys like Old Overholt and WhistlePig."

—*The New York Times*

"Finder shows off his top-notch storytelling skills, moving with ease from high places to low in the nation's capital."

—*Kirkus Reviews*

"Finder really knows his way around a thriller, and his sensibilities about Washington, scandal, and the immediacy—and threat—of digital publishing and electronic surveillance seem chillingly plausible. This is an exciting, insightful thriller with finely sketched characters."

—*Booklist* (starred review)

"[A] tight plot, sharp dialogue, and a cast of intriguing characters keep the story a cut above the genre pack."

—*Publishers Weekly*

"Finder shows off his clever storytelling skills by packing action, politics, and modern detective techniques into a complicated plotline that leads to murder."

—*Library Journal*

"This is a dark tale of intrigue and underhanded politics. . . . If you're a Finder fan, this book will not disappoint you. If you're not, you might become one after this read." —*Suspense Magazine*

"The plot of *Guilty Minds* . . . is taut, rapid, and tensely recurving." —*Harvard Magazine*

"Finder is one of the best contemporary thriller writers." —*Connecticut Post*

"*Guilty Minds* crosses the finish line a winner—suspenseful, swift, surefooted, and entertaining to the end." —*New York Journal of Books*

"*Guilty Minds* balances its thriller tenets with solid characters . . . razor-sharp dialogue, and a breathless plot that careens from one realistic twist to another."

—*Mystery Scene*

The Fixer

"A master of the modern thriller." —*The Boston Globe*

"If you're in the mood for tense, witty angst about closed-down career opportunities and dirty money cleansed by family redemption, *The Fixer* is the way to go."

—*The New York Times Book Review*

"Joe Finder moves from action to psychological thriller in his scintillating, Boston-based new novel. . . . There's a wondrous noir aspect to *The Fixer* that also recalls Dennis Lehane at his best. But Finder, thankfully, isn't nearly as dark or bleak and remains a storytelling maestro whose latest hits all the right notes." —*Providence Journal*

"*The Fixer* is [Finder's] most personal book. . . . A lively page-turner with smart, tight dialogue."

—*Houston Chronicle*

"Joseph Finder takes a familiar story and gives it a unique spin in his latest page-turner." —Associated Press

"Finder returns with another thriller that will have you . . . turning the pages to find out what happens next."

—*Kirkus Reviews*

"Finder can make reading about someone walking across a room excruciatingly suspenseful. . . . This is a thriller that is as much about redemption as it is about escape. A remarkable exciting read." —*Booklist* (starred review)

"Joseph Finder has written a tense, fast-moving thriller bearing the warning that there may be things you don't know and should know about your family."

—*The Washington Times*

"Adroitly told with a riveting cast of three-dimensional characters and enlightening reveals aplenty, Finder's latest standalone should be on everyone's summer reading list."

—*Strand Magazine*

"So many surprises, this book is a definite page-turner and a whole lot of fun to read. A thriller that will keep you up late to find out what will happen next. Five stars for this one!" —*Suspense Magazine*

"*The Fixer* is a page-turner with deep emotional resonance as it explores the mysteries between all fathers and sons." —*CT News*

"Engaging, easy, and quick reading, along with a practiced blending of action and dialogue."

—*San Antonio Express-News*

Suspicion

"A can't-miss thriller . . . *Suspicion* is arguably Joseph Finder's best novel to date, and he's one of the best thriller writers in the business. He's a master at making the reader feel every emotion, jump at every shock, and squirm with every twist that Danny must overcome."

—Associated Press

"[*Suspicion*] sets the suspense level to a pitch that will keep even the coolest readers sweating."

—*The Boston Globe*

"Lock yourself in a room with *Suspicion* and don't come out until you've read every last word. Completely original, emotionally satisfying, expertly twisted, and genuinely entertaining. *Suspicion* is the thriller to read this year. I loved it."

—Lisa Gardner

"Joseph Finder has always been out there on the front edge of things. With *Suspicion* he does it again, giving us a novel that is as timely and cognizant of contemporary society as it is a startling seat-of-the-pants thrill ride. In Finder's hands one man's fight for survival becomes an everyman's journey to the light."

—Michael Connelly

"*Suspicion* is Joseph Finder at the absolute top of his form: a heart-pounding, sweaty-palmed, utterly terrifying ride."

—Tess Gerritsen

"Is this Joseph Finder's best thriller yet? It gets my vote. So many twists and shocks. It kept me reading all night."

—R. L. Stine

"Finder fans as well as devotees of action-packed suspense have a great read ahead. The taut pacing, staccato chapters, and ingenious plot, especially Finder's characteristically creative use of digital surveillance techniques, guarantee a literary thrill ride." —*Library Journal* (starred review)

"There are many authors who take a reader 'slowly into that good night.' However, the real genius knows how to create the ultimate lead-in. They are the wordsmiths who can, in one page or one paragraph, grab the reader's attention and never let go. . . . A true genius wordsmith, this is one author who has created solid suspense gold."

—*Suspense Magazine*

"[A] lean, crisp thriller—a zipping Jaguar of a ride . . . The plot turns—three major ones—are as shocking as they are believable. . . . His spare, laminated style is several cuts above that of most thrillers."

—*Publishers Weekly*

"Thriller veteran Finder merits applause for this streamlined story made believable by Danny's everyman character; readers will find his palpable guilt and fear instantly relatable." —*Booklist*

"Full of intriguing characters, squirmy, fast-paced action, and a nifty, convoluted plot, Finder's latest is a real keeper. It's likely to keep you flipping pages until you reach the final, unexpected conclusion." —*Lansing State Journal*

BY JOSEPH FINDER

FICTION

The Moscow Club

Extraordinary Powers

The Zero Hour

High Crimes

Paranoia

Company Man

Killer Instinct

Power Play

Suspicion

The Fixer

The Switch

NICK HELLER SERIES

Vanished

Buried Secrets

Guilty Minds

NONFICTION

Red Carpet: The Connection Between the Kremlin and America's Most Powerful Businessmen

The Switch

A NOVEL

JOSEPH FINDER

DUTTON

DUTTON
An imprint of Penguin Random House LLC
375 Hudson Street
New York, New York 10014

Previously published as a Dutton hardcover.

First Dutton premium mass market printing, 2018

ISBN 9781101985809

Printed in the United States of America
1 3 5 7 9 10 8 6 4 2

In memory of my mom, Natalie Finder
1921–2017

1

The security line snaked on forever, coiling around and through the rat maze of stanchions and retractable nylon strapping.

Michael Tanner was in a hurry, but LAX wasn't cooperating. Usually he went TSA Precheck, as well as Global Entry, and every other way you could speed up the security line hassles at the airport, but for some reason his boarding pass had printed out with the word "precheck" ominously missing.

Maybe it was random. Maybe it was just a personnel shortage. They never explained why. His flight was about to board, but he was near the end of a crawling line of harassed travelers trundling roll-aboard cases and shouldering backpacks.

"Shoes off, belts off, jackets off, laptops out of your bags," one of the TSA agents, a large black woman, was chanting from the front. "No liquids. Shoes off, belts off . . ."

Tanner traveled constantly for business, and he was

good at it. He glided through the lines, a travel ninja. But this time? Shoes off! Belt off! He realized he was out of practice. How long had it been since he'd gone through the whole indignity? He yanked his belt off, slid off his loafers, put them in the gray plastic bin, and shoved it along the roller conveyor, padding along in stocking feet. He took his laptop out of his shoulder bag, put it in a gray bin of its own, watched it disappear into the maw of the X-ray machine. His jacket, too, he remembered. Pulled it off and shoved it into another gray bin. Tried not to slow down the line.

He glanced at his watch. His flight to Boston was boarding, had to be. If he re-shoed and re-belted and grabbed his stuff quickly, and raced to the departure gate, he'd make it onto the plane before they closed the doors.

He patted down his pockets, found a few stray coins, took them out and put them into a plastic bowl and onto the conveyor belt, to the apparent annoyance of the well-dressed middle-aged woman just behind him.

Tanner passed through the metal detector without a hitch, and he was on his way.

Until one of the X-ray attendants on the other side of the conveyor belt picked up his shoulder bag and said, "Is this yours, sir?"

"Yeah," Tanner said. "That's mine. Is there a problem?"

"Can you pick up your things and meet me over there?"

Shit. Something in his shoulder bag must have looked

funky in the X-ray machine. He couldn't afford this two or three minutes of scrutiny. But there was no questioning authority. He grabbed his stuff—belt, laptop, shoes, change, jacket, and shoulder bag—and met the TSA guy at the metal table. The man pulled out a wand of some kind and ran it around the edges of Tanner's bag. The wand was connected to a machine that was labeled SMITHS DETECTION. It was obviously designed to check for traces of explosives. He waited patiently for another minute, suppressing the urge to make a crack, until the guy finally said, "You're all set," and handed the bag back.

Tanner unzipped the bag, slipped his MacBook Air into it, zipped it back up, then slotted his belt into his pant loops while stepping into his shoes, resisting the impulse to glance at his watch again.

He arrived at the gate to find no one waiting there, just a couple of airline personnel, a man and a woman, the man behind the counter and the woman next to it. "Flight three sixty-nine?" the woman said.

"That's right."

"All right, sir, you're the last to arrive." She said it disapprovingly, like she'd caught him smoking in the lavatory.

Finally he took his seat on the plane, sat back, exhaled.

He'd made it; he'd be fine; he'd get to Boston around nine thirty in the evening, and the next day he'd be back at work.

He wasn't sure whether the LA trip had been worth it. He'd had a pitch meeting with a famous celebrity chef,

Alessandro Battaglia, star of the Food Network, master Iron Chef, part owner of six restaurants. Chef Battaglia had said he cared about the quality of the coffee they served. Most restaurateurs didn't. When it came to coffee, they tended to care about cost and profit margins more than anything, even in the best places.

Their restaurants brewed generic swill from cheap blends, mostly Brazilian and Costa Rican, and their customers, sated from dinner, usually couldn't tell the difference. But Chef Battaglia knew what good coffee tasted like.

Tanner had brought a couple of different single-origins, a Kenyan, an Ethiopian, and a Guatemalan, each roasted differently three days ago. All ground fresh in a Baratza, in front of the chef, each poured over, each distinctly different, and each delicious. Tanner had come to LA himself—the founder and CEO of Tanner Roast—instead of sending Karen, his sales director. Battaglia was too big a deal.

Standing there in his green Crocs, Alessandro waited for the coffee to cool, knowing that the best way to sample it is at room temperature. He took a loud aerating slurp, like a pro. He liked the Kenyan best of all. Tanner agreed that was the brightest, best structured, most balanced.

Battaglia seemed particularly interested in Tanner Cold Brew, which was a coffee concentrate Tanner was proud to have invented. It could be used for iced coffee, for nitro, and for hot coffee, too, and without any of the usual bitterness. They sold it by the keg.

A lot of people made cold brew, but it was never quite right. It didn't work very well as hot coffee when diluted with hot water. But Tanner's did. He'd devised an original process. The result was a clear, bright flavor, fruity and floral and chocolaty. Not roasty and heavy like everyone else's cold brew. Way better than Stumptown's—no comparison, really.

Battaglia wanted that too. All systems were go. A deal was at hand.

But he wanted to talk to his partners. Which really meant further haggling over price. He was no better than the manager of an Applebee's. Tanner Roast coffees cost more than institutional coffees, but all specialty coffee did. Chef Battaglia knew he was paying for individually sourced, impeccably produced, meticulously shipped green beans, roasted carefully in small batches . . . the whole deal. A cup of coffee from the Big Green Chain usually tasted burnt. Compared to the Technicolor taste of a Tanner Roast, theirs was a black-and-white photograph. The expense was worth it.

Easy for him to say, of course.

Tanner was operating on a few hours of sleep. He was exhausted, so tired that he didn't need to take an Ambien.

He arrived at his South End house raw eyed and headachy and punchy.

The house, five floors including the basement, seemed

echoey with Sarah gone. He switched on some lights in the kitchen and, standing at the island, opened his laptop. He'd made some notes on it he wanted to e-mail himself. The computer was off, which surprised him, because he rarely powered the thing down. Had he shut it off in the cab on the way to LAX? Maybe. Maybe he'd spaced out. It was no big deal. He pressed the power button, and a minute later an unfamiliar screen came up: a globe and the name "S. Robbins" and a blank for the password.

He stared at the screen for another minute or so until the realization sank in: this wasn't his laptop. In the rush to grab his possessions in the security line, he'd taken someone else's identical MacBook Air. Belonging to one S. Robbins.

While S. Robbins probably had his.

The perfect glitch to cap off a frustrating day.

There was a faint perfume smell to the laptop, a good and familiar white floral scent, a woman's perfume he'd smelled before. S. Robbins was probably female.

He closed the laptop a little too violently, got up, and went over to the dry bar in the sitting room to pour himself a scotch. Then he remembered, glancing at his watch. It was Thursday, which meant beer night at the Albion with a couple of friends. Which he'd been planning to skip, figuring he'd be too tired from the flight.

He was tired, yes, but even more, he needed a drink.

He took out his iPhone and punched the speed-dial number for Lanny Roth.

Lanny answered, music blasting in the background.

"Tanner! You still in LA?" For some reason, Tanner's closest friends, including his wife, Sarah, called him Tanner, and only strangers, or his employees, called him Michael or Mike.

"Just back," Tanner said. "Sounds like you're at the Albion."

"Coming over? I just got here. Brian already got dinged trying to pick up a BU girl, so the night is young."

"Save me a seat," Tanner said.

Something tickled at the back of his mind, and he picked up the MacBook Air. He'd remembered right: on the bottom of the laptop was a tiny pink square, a Post-it note. He'd put it back where he found it.

Now he peeled it off the metal case and saw a jumble of letters and numbers: 342Hart342.

He wondered . . .

He opened the laptop again and entered the characters in the password space, and sure enough, the screen opened up with the default Apple background photo of a mountain peak.

"Got it," he said aloud.

Then he closed the laptop and grabbed his car keys.

2

The baby had just fallen asleep on his mother's nipple. Will Abbott lifted little Travis slowly from Jen's breast and carried him carefully, gingerly, across the darkened room toward the crib as if he were transporting a hand grenade with the pin out. It could go off at any second.

Because little Travis, six weeks old, hardly ever seemed to sleep. A few hours here and there, never more than that. And when he didn't sleep, his parents didn't sleep.

Travis had just had his last feeding for the day, or at least until he woke up at two in the morning desperately hungry again. Right now he was the angel baby, flying through the clouds, making tiny fussing sounds in his sleep. At two in the morning, or maybe three, he would awake, ravenous and loud and beyond comforting.

Jen always got up and fed him, since the baby wanted her, not him. And because Will had to go to work in the morning. Will could roll over and put a pillow over his head and fall back asleep while Jen nursed him. It was colossally unfair. Will, who worked on Capitol Hill as chief of staff to a senator, had the easier job. But it was also the job that paid the rent on their Stanton Park apartment.

Will was always tired, always sleep deprived, since the baby was born. He'd taken a month-long paternity leave—most chiefs didn't get that—during which he tried to take the baby as much as possible so Jen could catch up on sleep. But Travis always wanted his mother. Will tried putting the baby in his car seat and driving around, but that didn't quiet him down.

Jen's mom thought that Travis might have colic, but their pediatrician said "colic" was just an old-fashioned term for an inconsolable baby without any other obvious problem. It was probably abdominal pain, but he wasn't sure. He might just be a fussy baby. He was hungry a lot, but he wouldn't take a bottle, so they couldn't augment his feeding.

The room was filled with the whooshing of the white-noise generator in the corner near the baby's crib. The white-noise machine was Jen's idea. She thought it would mask traffic noise from the street.

Anything to keep the baby asleep a little longer.

Will walked back to the bed, avoiding the floorboard that always squeaked. When he reached the bed, his BlackBerry rang. His work phone. He kept it beside the bed, in its charger, because it rarely rang past nine at night. And if it did, it was the boss, which meant it was important.

As soon as the ringtone sounded—he'd forgotten to put it on vibrate mode—Travis awoke and started to squall. From the number readout he saw it was the boss. It had to be something urgent. Otherwise, she'd just text.

"Hi, Susan," he said.

"Will, listen, I screwed up."

An ominous start. The boss was never self-critical, never self-blaming. She had a big ego and a maddeningly serene confidence.

"Okay," he said, switching into I-can-handle-anything Mr.-Fix-it mode.

"I grabbed the wrong laptop."

"I don't—"

"At the airport. I grabbed someone else's laptop. In the security line. And someone got mine."

"Okay. You flew American, right? I'll call their lost and found at National. Whoever took it probably brought it back—"

"This was in LA."

The baby was wailing now, so Will went out into the hall, one hand over his free ear.

"No problem, I'll call—"

"Did I wake you? You're not thinking clearly. The security line at LAX, Will. That means it could be anyone, on any flight, who took my laptop. Any of a thousand people. And"—she sighed heavily—"and you know damn well we can't call law enforcement."

For a moment he didn't know what she was talking about, and then it came to him. "Oh."

Icy tendrils gripped the pit of his stomach. "Oh my God. It's—it's password protected, right? I mean, no one can get onto your laptop without your password. Right?"

There was a long silence. Over the phone, Will could

hear the distant clamor of airport announcements on speakers. He was about to repeat the question when she said dully, "Yes, it's password protected."

"Great. We don't have to worry about it, then." The icy tendrils began to melt away. In the background he heard loud babble, people talking loudly, close to her.

"No," she said. "We have to assume the worst. We have to worry about everything as long as that computer is out there."

"Well, maybe whoever took it realized it wasn't hers and brought it to the lost and found at LAX."

"Yeah," she said, sounding unconvinced. "How early can you get in tomorrow morning?"

"How early do you need me?"

Little Travis let loose with an ear-shattering, gut-churning yowl. Will glanced at his watch. Ten minutes after ten. Putting the baby down might take another half an hour, and he knew it would be his job, not Jen's. If he was lucky, he'd get three and a half hours of sleep before the inevitable two A.M. awakening, and then another two or three fitful hours. Five or six broken hours of sleep, he calculated, before what was probably going to be a long and arduous day.

"Will, are you off the phone?" Jen called, voice taut with annoyance. That meant diaper duty.

"See you tomorrow," he said into the phone, then hit the red button to end the call. "Yep, I'm coming."

3

The Albion was a subterranean pub on Beacon Street on the edge of the Boston University campus. It was dimly lit, except for the stroboscopic flicker of the TV sets mounted high on the wall, both tuned to the Red Sox game. The place was meant to resemble an English pub, but the décor—a couple of British pub signs and some brass rails—was halfhearted. It looked like a college bar, which was basically what it was.

The guys were in their usual booth, the first one on the left. Carl Unsworth and Landon Roth he'd gone to BU with. Brian Orsolino, a sales manager at a tech company who was ten years younger, played in a basketball league with Carl. Thursday nights at the Albion was a ritual and had been for years. Tanner would join them occasionally, off and on, though recently he'd been more on. Since Sarah had moved out.

"Glad you could make it," Carl said. "Was your business trip cut short or something?" He was a mixed martial arts instructor, ran a small studio in Newton where he taught Krav Maga. He was tall and, of course, fit, and balding, and colored his remaining hair an unfortunate orangish brown. The poor guy was also going through an interminable divorce, the Bataan Death March of matrimonial dissolution.

Tanner shook his head. "Flight got in on time and I figured why not."

"No wife there to stop you from having fun," said Carl.

Tanner just heaved a heavy sigh. They all knew Sarah, and they liked her. Even he couldn't bring himself to hate her.

Still, when she'd moved out, they'd reacted predictably. Carl had congratulated him, pleased to have company in the lonely-guy game. Now they were all single guys, all four of them. Lanny had offered genuine condolences. A metro reporter for *The Boston Globe,* he was single and embittered, prematurely wizened, and he dated desultorily. Women usually figured out pretty quickly that he was damaged goods. He was professionally single and probably would always be. Brian attempted to cheer him up by telling him about all the awesome new dating apps and the hundreds of women available with a mere swipe of his iPhone.

"I think I'm going to break with tradition and get a glass of pinot noir," Brian said.

"But it's beer night," said Carl.

"Wine's supposed to make for healthier sperm," Brian said.

"Heh, if you believe what they tell you," Lanny said. He was always saying that. Tell him they say we should all eat more kale, and Lanny would say, "If you believe what they tell you." That was his reflexive rejoinder. It fit perfectly with his jaded, cynical reporter attitude. He was incurably skeptical, trusted no one, took nothing at face value. "You sell some coffee?"

"I think so."

"I'm telling you, you should have sold your company to Starbucks. You'd be a rich man and you wouldn't have to fly all over the place, hustling for business."

Tanner shrugged. "That's what Sarah kept telling me."

"I saw Tanner Roast at Whole Foods," said Brian. "Fresh Pond."

"Yeah, they're a customer," Tanner said.

"In the coffee aisle. But on the bottom shelf. What's up with that?"

"Hey, they order four cases a week; that's all I know," said Tanner.

"Well, yours is the best, dude," Brian said.

"Thank you."

"Says the guy who spends half his time in Dunkin' Donuts," Carl said.

"I like Dunks," Brian said. "So what?"

"Why are you even here?" Carl said to Brian. "Shouldn't you be screwing some chick?"

"A guy's gotta take a break once in a while," Brian said. "Recharge the batteries. Replenish the bodily fluids."

Some weeks, according to Brian, he had a date with a different woman each night. Brian, a beefy blond, was not particularly good-looking, but he was a closer. Better with women than with the database software he sold, though.

"You should try Tinder, dude," Brian told Tanner.

"Yeah," Tanner said, "not yet. It's only been a month."

"What are you waiting for?" Brian said.

Tanner shook his head, sighed. It was odd, he reflected. He'd told his buddies all about Sarah moving out but not about the trouble his business was in, how it was on the bubble. Business problems he preferred to keep to himself. He'd always been the successful one in the gang, the guy who'd founded this coffee company that Starbucks wanted to buy, once, and he didn't want to correct their image of him.

The subject needed to be changed—too unpleasant—so Tanner told them about what had happened to his laptop.

"You have no idea where yours is?" Carl said. "Nobody called?"

"They can't open it without a password."

"And you didn't leave it on a sticky note like an idiot," Brian said.

"Shit, what are you going to do?" Carl said.

"It's no big deal," Tanner said. "Not urgent. It's all backed up. And I rarely use my laptop anyway, except when I travel. At work, I mostly use my iPad and my phone and my desk computer."

"There's something called Find My iPhone. Ever hear of it?" Lanny said. "I think it works on laptops too. Find My Mac or something."

Tanner shook his head. "It only works when the computer's online, and it's locked with a password. So it's not going to be online."

"So you can find out who the guy is by poking around on his computer."

"Sure," Tanner said listlessly. "When I've got a minute."

4

The faint trace of L'Air du Temps in the outer office told Will that the boss had arrived.

She was early.

Normally she didn't get in until nine or nine thirty, leaving him a full hour at his desk, undisturbed, to prepare for the day. Because every day was a battle in an extended military campaign. He started preparing as soon as he got up, cup of strong black coffee in hand. A general in the war room.

In his little home office he'd glanced over the press clips that came in the e-mail from media services, sifted through e-mails (more than three hundred a day, not including the junk: he'd once counted), looked at the *Post* and *The Hill* and *Real Clear Politics* and *Politico* and *Drudge*. Read about the bills that were coming up. Sent out notes asking staff members to stop by his office and see him. Then into the office by eight thirty, girded for battle. *The commander must decide how he will fight the battle before it begins.* He'd read that somewhere and remembered it verbatim. *By failing to prepare you are preparing to fail.*

There was always a lot going on, which he appreciated; he liked being at work, in the grown-up world, away from squalling little Travis. But today the calendar seemed more crowded than usual. The legislative director wanted to fire one of the legislative assistants, who was always late. But you couldn't just fire a staffer. Politicians never want to have a disgruntled former staff member out there grousing and bitching and threatening. So he'd have to meet with the LA, give her an off-ramp, help her find a new job. He also had to sign off on some press releases. He had a ten o'clock videoconference with the state director and staff. A lunchtime fundraiser at Bistro Bis.

And there was the boss's laptop mix-up. Which could turn out to be no big deal.

Or it could be a nightmare.

In a way it was strange that Will was a chief of staff to a prominent senator. There was one all-important relationship to manage, and then there were the forty-five people who worked under him, if you counted the fifteen in the district office in Chicago. He was a boss. He had to manage a lot of different personalities. Yet he'd always been a guy who never really fit in anywhere.

He'd been a nerdy kid at a jocky college. He'd gone to Miami University of Ohio—*not* in Miami, Florida, and boy, did he get tired of telling people that—because of its great poli-sci program. On Saturday nights, when everyone was heading over to the Goggin Ice Center to watch the RedHawks play hockey, or drinking Natty Light in cans at a frat party uptown, he'd be studying at King Library. Most lunches or dinners he'd sit by himself at Harris Dining Hall while seemingly everyone around him was sitting at a crowded table talking boisterously, laughing and hooting and having a great time. The truth was, he was sort of a grind.

His father had passed away when he was fourteen, and his mother, a receptionist in a dentist's office, didn't make much money. After his dad died, his mother sold real estate on the side. But it didn't bring in near enough. So in college he did what he could: he had a work-study job at the admissions office, and he wrote term papers for some of his fellow students for cash.

Freshman year, in a fit of lunacy, he ran for class treasurer and was soundly defeated by some jock, a very public humiliation. When the election results came in, he went to his single in Swing and closed the door and ignored his classmates' knocking.

It was a great embarrassment, but a useful one, he later decided. He loved politics but learned, that night, that some people aren't meant to run for office. Some people get their picture taken, and some stand off to the side. He was the guy off to the side. He was the political junkie who could advise the simpler, denser, popular kid how to run and win. The popular kids, the charismatic, attractive ones with that hail-fellow-well-met gift that he so lacked, realized that he could be useful.

Will had been given a nickname, but it was not one he would have chosen. Freshman year, some hateful frat bro, noticing his slightly waddling gait, started calling him Penguin. As in, "Where's Penguin?" And "Let's get Penguin to do it." He wanted to be liked, more than anything, but the best he could do was be the guy you have to be nice to.

He didn't rush a frat; he knew better. When, during the fall of his junior year, a popular guy on his floor in Dorsey decided to run for student president against another popular kid, Will approached him and offered his services to "manage" his campaign. The kid, Peter Green, at first thought Will was kidding, then thought it over and said sure. Peter won, and when he gave his victory speech—really more like rambling, semicrocked ad-libbed remarks—he said, "And, hey, I owe you big, Penguin—I mean, Will." It was nothing but a slip of the tongue on Peter's part, Will told himself, and he pretended to laugh along with everyone else.

By senior year Will became president of the debating club, the Forensics Society—because no one else wanted the drudgery of the job. Which was something to put on his résumé when he applied for jobs on Capitol Hill. Along with dean's list all eight semesters.

He knocked softly on her open office door. Senator Susan Robbins was sitting behind her glass-topped wooden desk, on the phone. She held up an index finger, gave him an even gaze as she said, "Yes, Chuck. Can do. Will do."

Will waited in the doorway. She was a striking woman, with her auburn hair and cobalt-blue eyes. When she was in her twenties and thirties she must have been a knockout. At sixty-two she was still beautiful.

She was wearing her cerulean-blue suit, the one she wore when she was in combat mode. She always wore jewel-tone suits, whether skirts or pantsuits. Turquoise meant she was in a conciliatory mood. Emerald was for high-visibility hearings, when the TV cameras were there. Ruby was for evening functions and fund-raisers. He was probably the only person in the world who knew what Susan Robbins's suit colors signified. He was probably the only one who cared.

She toyed with the coiled cord, swung it like a little lasso. "I understand," she said. "Uh-huh. Uh-huh. Bye."

She put the phone down. "Come," she said.

He entered and sat in the chair beside her desk. The senator had twenty-five years on him, and sometimes he felt like one of her sons: the good son. She had a fraught relationship with her older son and practically no relationship at all with her younger one. He wondered what it must have been like to have Susan Robbins as a mother. It couldn't have been easy. As a boss she could be, well, *a lot,* but he felt toward her a fierce protectiveness, an abiding loyalty, as sticky as epoxy.

"Isn't there some clever way to find my laptop?" she said. "Online, I mean."

She was talking, he assumed, about Find My Mac, a feature on some Macs that allows you to use iCloud to locate a missing or stolen computer or iPhone. He was moderately surprised she knew about this. Unfortunately, their IT guy had disabled it on Susan's MacBook, at her insistence, for security reasons.

"In theory, but it's turned off."

"So there's no way to find it online?"

"Right. Our best bet is to contact whoever must have taken yours and arrange a swap."

"But I have no idea whose computer this is." She pointed to the laptop flat on the desk in front of her, a shimmering silver oblong. "It's locked. How do we find out who it belongs to?"

Will reached out for it. She lifted it from the desk and handed it to him.

"I'll take care of it," he said.

"I don't think you realize how sensitive this is." In a quieter voice, she went on: "If anyone finds out—it could be a felony. Not 'it could be'; it *is* a felony."

Will felt queasy. "But you'd never get prosecuted."

"Don't be so sure. The atmosphere today, it's a career ender for sure. There must be some way to hack into it, to find out who owns it, right?"

Will put a palm up like a traffic cop. "Don't worry about it," he said. "It's *handled*."

5

Tanner Roast occupied a large warehouse space on a side street in Brighton, Massachusetts, a working-class suburb of Boston. On one end were the loading bays and on the other a door marked only TANNER. As you entered, you smelled the coffee roasting.

Roasting coffee smells nothing like a coffeehouse. The air in a roastery could smell like wet straw. It was an organic, often not a pleasant smell. Tanner loved it.

But a single bad bean can spoil a whole lot, and you wouldn't know until you started cupping. Which was what they were doing this morning, Tanner and his crew, which included his roaster, Sal Persico. Sal, a tatted giant of a man, was daintily removing small glass tumblers from a dishwasher. He had multiple piercings and full-sleeve tattoos and hands as big and ungainly-looking as baseball gloves but which were in fact precision instruments. He was an ex-con and looked like it.

When he'd first applied for work, he handed the employment application to Tanner with a kind of hangdog look. Tanner quickly discovered why: Sal had checked the box—the one you tick if you have a criminal record. Tanner asked Sal about the incident that had gotten him imprisoned for three years. Sal told him about the armed robbery he was dragged into as a teenager and sounded not just contrite but embarrassed at his own stupidity. "Well, you'll find our coffee is better than the swill they serve at Cedar Junction," Tanner had said. He told Sal he didn't care about the felony as long he was as good at roasting as Tanner had heard.

They never again talked about the armed robbery. Sal was deeply grateful to Tanner. But Tanner wasn't being magnanimous. He really didn't give a damn about Sal's conviction history. Tanner trusted his ability to size people up, and Sal was a good person. He also turned out to be the Mozart of coffee roasters, a true genius at it.

"Just six today," he told Tanner, placing the cups in a line next to the Mahlkönig EK 43 grinder. "All Guatemalans."

"I need to check something," he told Sal. "Ready in ten?" Sal nodded.

His office, off the adjoining room, was decorated with a cheaply framed poster of red coffee berries growing and a map of the world with pinholes all over it. On another wall was an antique café mirror advertising Maxwell House coffee, which he used sometimes for shaving and sometimes just to sneak a glimpse at whoever was sitting in the visitor chair. He was a sales guy; he always studied his customers closely.

He'd been a top salesman at EMC, a big data-storage company in Hopkinton, Massachusetts, before he and Sarah had taken the plunge and invested their entire nest egg in a start-up venture called Tanner Roast. He loved coffee, loved the people he worked with, and counted himself lucky to be in a business he found so cool.

Atop a pile of papers on his desk sat the laptop, the wrong laptop, the laptop belonging to S. Robbins. It was nagging at him. He wanted to root around in the files, find the full name, an address, maybe a phone number. Give the man, or woman, a call and arrange a swap.

Tanner opened the MacBook Air. He heard a throat being cleared. He looked up and saw his sales director, Karen Wynant, a petite, worried-looking dark-haired woman in her late thirties. She had her contacts out, since she wasn't on a sales call, and wore her oversized unfashionable red-plastic-framed glasses.

"Michael, you have a minute?"

"Uh, what's up?" He closed the laptop.

Karen was a worrier of the first rank and tended to borrow trouble, to worry about things there was no point in worrying about. She could be exasperating, but Tanner found it reassuring, almost moving, how seriously she took the business, how committed she was. This wasn't just a job to her.

"How'd it go in LA?"

"Like I said, he wants to talk to his partners."

"I thought we agreed on the price."

"Yeah, well."

"He wants to negotiate some more?"

"He knows we want the sale. Battaglia Restaurant Group looks good on our website. He didn't have to say it."

His intercom buzzed, but he ignored it.

"Which one did he go for?"

"The Kenyan."

"Really? I'm surprised."

"Why? It's the best one we've got. Guy's obviously got a sophisticated palate."

"A little acidic, no?"

"Maybe it's not for breakfast, but it's fine for after dinner, and it's different. It's bright."

"He said he likes dark roasts—that's why I sent him the French roast Colombian."

"Maybe he'd never had a light roast before."

"Alessandro Battaglia?"

"Who knows."

"Should I follow up, or should you?" His intercom buzzed again.

"Me first; then he'll hand me off to his beverages guy and you take over. I told you all this in my e-mail. Everything okay?"

She cleared her throat again. She seemed to be working up to something. "I haven't seen a contract from the Four Seasons, have you?"

"It'll come. Don't sweat it." He tried not to sound annoyed. She asked daily. If anyone should be nervous about the Four Seasons deal, it was Tanner himself. He and Karen had flown to the Toronto headquarters of Four Seasons Hotels & Resorts three times, pitching a deal to provide all the coffee to a half dozen of the Four Seasons hotels in North America. They made it through round after round, until it was just Tanner Roast left.

What had done the trick was Tanner Cold Brew. The Four Seasons people agreed it was the best-tasting concentrate around. They complimented him on having the ingenuity to add cold brew to the tastings. None of their rivals had offered that.

So Tanner Roast won the bake-off. It was a handshake deal, the contracts being drawn up over the next few weeks, but it was a deal nonetheless. What no one apart from Tanner and his CFO knew was that this would save Tanner Roast from going under. The finances were that tight.

He stood up to encourage Karen to leave, and when he turned he saw Lucy Turton, the office manager, standing in the office doorway. Lucy was tall and outdoorsy, with short blond hair and a permanent healthy flush in her cheeks.

"A minute?" she said. Karen excused herself and left.

"Sure."

Lucy came in, closed the door, and perched on the edge of the visitor chair. "It's about Connie again."

Tanner rolled his eyes. She was talking about an office employee, the bookkeeper, Connie Hunt. Connie was out of the office a lot. She always conjured up one reason or another why she had to miss work. Last year, she was suddenly gone for a week, and when she returned, Lucy had asked her if everything was okay. Connie had replied that her dog had had puppies—so that, really, it was like maternity leave. For several years, Lucy had been begging Tanner to fire Connie. But he always insisted on giving the woman another chance. "Now what?"

"All right, so last month she was gone for almost a week because of carpal tunnel in her right arm. But when she came back she said it was in her left wrist. She was out last week because of a death in her family. Her aunt, she said. But today she just said it was her uncle who died. And I'm like, 'Which one died? Make up your mind.' Michael, you've got to fire her ass."

Tanner shook his head, heaved a sigh. "I get the sense that life's not easy for her. She left a good job to come here."

Lucy snorted. "Or so she tells us."

"We need to give her another chance."

"We've given her, like, five last chances, and it doesn't make a difference. Plus, she's always late with the monthly. She spends most of her time on Facebook or selling stuff on eBay. Don't we have a way of monitoring what she's doing on a company computer?"

"If we do, that's like Big Brother stuff. Not for me. Sorry."

When Lucy left, Tanner opened the laptop and entered the password again, from the little pink Post-it note he'd found stuck underneath. S. Robbins. He found the

Documents icon and double-clicked it, and a column of folders came up. They had names like:

Book Project
Chicago House
D.C. Condo
Correspondence
Donor Thank-yous
Briefing Memos
Press Releases
Op-Eds
Speeches
SSCI
Staff

Tanner glanced at his watch, saw that he had about three minutes before the cupping started. He opened the "Book Project" folder and then opened the first document he came to, labeled "Proposal 3.4." It began:

HONOR BOUND: Life in the Public Eye

By Senator Susan J. Robbins

After twenty-four years in the United States Senate, I've learned a few hard lessons. The food in the cafeteria in the basement of the Hart Senate Office Building is—

He looked up. *Senator Susan J. Robbins.*

"S. Robbins" was Senator Susan Robbins. He'd heard of her. A longtime US senator from Illinois.

He had a computer belonging to a US senator.

Huh.

A knock on the jamb of his open office door.

"Boss," Sal said. "We're ready."

6

Twelve small glass tumblers were arrayed in two rows. Six different Guatemalan coffees they were considering buying, two tumblers for each. There was a whole elaborate ritual to "cupping," as it was called. And scientific accuracy. Tanner dipped a spoon into the dense crust formed by the water-infused coffee grounds, put his nose right down in there, an inch away from the surface, and sniffed. He got the fleeting floral aroma, from the most volatile molecules escaping. He did that for each of the six coffees. Meanwhile Sal sniffed the other six. Any non-coffee person watching the proceedings would think this laughable. But you didn't skip step one in the cupping ritual.

Tanner nodded at Sal, who then began removing the grounds from the tumblers, using two spoons. Then his mobile phone rang. He pulled it out. Sarah. "Will you excuse me?" he said to Sal.

"We should let it cool a couple degrees anyway," Sal said, busy with his two spoons.

Walking away from the long table, toward the office, he answered it.

"Sarah." He was standing in a far corner of the warehouse, amid boxes of grinders and brewing machines, equipment they'd lend new customers, an incentive.

"Listen, Tanner, I'm sorry to bother you at work."

"That's okay. Good to hear from you. Where are you?"

"I'm at an open house." She sold real estate, houses and condos. She became a real estate agent in the impoverished days when they were just starting Tanner Roast, all expenditures and no income, and hadn't stopped. She liked it. "I can't really talk long."

"You still staying at Margaret's?"

"That's why I called." Her sister Margaret had a small one-bedroom apartment in Central Square in Cambridge. Sarah had to be sleeping on the couch, and it had to be an annoyance to her sister. In the best of times they had a contentious relationship. "You're going to be getting a call today from a company, a real estate company. They're going to need you to send them a couple of my 1099s. Proof of income." As one of the two original investors and an officer of the company, Sarah was given a salary, which wasn't a lot of money.

"What's this about?"

"I can't stay at Margaret's any longer. We're driving each other crazy."

"Come on home, sweetie."

He looked back at Sal, bent over the tumblers, removing the crust. He wondered if his voice carried. He hadn't told anyone at work about Sarah moving out. It was none of his employees' business; he liked to keep work and home separate.

"I'm renting an apartment in Cambridge."

"Come on, Sarah, that's ridiculous. Come home and let's talk. We can sleep in separate bedrooms, if you want."

"I've already signed the lease. I gave them a deposit."

"You can stop the check. You're a Realtor—you know people in the business."

"Tanner, I've gotta go," she said, and she was gone.

One night a month or so ago he'd unlocked the front door, sniffed the air, and smelled nothing besides the faint odors of the lemon furniture oil and the Murphy's Oil Soap Sarah used on the wooden floors. The slightly musty smell of the old house. But the strange thing was what he didn't smell. No food cooking. No dinner. The house was still and quiet. The kitchen lights were off. Maybe she'd ordered out and it hadn't arrived yet.

"Sarah?" he'd called out.

No answer.

"Sarah, you home?"

Nothing. She wasn't home. Strange. He looked around a little longer, bewildered, until he was sure she was gone.

He knew why.

They'd had a fight, sort of, the night before. "Sort of" because Tanner didn't actually fight; he was incapable of it. His parents had had a turbulent relationship, fought constantly and loudly. When Tanner was little he'd run upstairs to his bedroom and put a pillow over his head so he wouldn't have to hear it. He vowed never to be like them. He didn't argue or fight with people, never had, didn't know how. He let his aggression out in sports, but that was it. He avoided conflict whenever possible.

Whereas Sarah tended to be volatile. She was a highly flammable substance. She and her sisters argued all the time. Occasionally she'd try to goad him into an argument, but it was like trying to strike a damp match. There were no sparks. He wasn't combustible. He had dozens of prefab anger-dampening responses: *Well, then I guess we just disagree. You may be right. I get why you feel that way, and I'm sorry.*

So they'd had a disagreement the night before, a semi-argument. She wanted kids, and he wasn't ready. This was an argument that was probably playing out in ten million other homes around the world at any moment. She liked to use a code word, a euphemism for having a kid: "expansion." As in: "When are we going to talk about expansion?" Tanner would explain to her that he wanted to get Tanner Roast stabilized and on a steady path before he committed to starting a family.

But Sarah's biological clock was ticking. She was thirty-three, and she wanted to have several kids, and if they didn't do it soon it probably wouldn't happen. Whereas he kept insisting he needed to know he could keep the company solvent without having to lay anyone off. Sarah said that was his way of avoiding committing to the marriage, to *her.* And so on.

She'd gone to bed angry.

The night she didn't come home, he called her.

"Michael," she said when she picked up. Being demoted from "Tanner" to "Michael" was already disconcerting.

"What's going on?" he said. "I don't understand."

"I'm staying at Margaret's."

"Why?"

A long sigh. "So what is it with you? Is the company, like, your child? Is that it? Is that why you don't want to have a baby with me?"

"I never said I don't want to have kids. Sarah—"

"No, you said you're not ready. You're never ready."

"I just want to get the company on its feet. In the black. Right now it feels like it's going down the tubes." Why did she not understand this? "I want kids. Come on back, we'll try."

Is the company your child? Actually, Tanner Roast was like a family. And he was the dad.

Now he wandered back to the long table and the tumblers of coffee.

"Everything okay?" Sal asked.

"Absolutely," Tanner said. "So what do we have here?"

7

It wasn't until after the morning videoconference that Will was able to return to the matter of the missing laptop. He had a stack of phone calls to return, most important being a major donor who wanted to talk about an aviation bill. That was someone whose call you returned quickly.

He got up and shut his office door. The MacBook Air was sitting on the corner of his desk, gleaming, waiting, a reproof. He pulled it in front of him and opened the lid. In the middle of the screen was a little oval containing a headshot of some guy, obviously the owner, and the name "Michael Tanner." Below it was a space that said "Enter Password."

He entered the word "password" and hit Return—some people who couldn't be bothered to memorize a password tried to be clever. In response the little icon shook. Uh-uh.

He entered "1234" and hit Return and the screen shook no again. He tried "12345678," and still no.

He tried "99999" and got the shake.

He tried a couple more common default passwords—"987654" and "1111111"—and each time got the shake.

There had to be a way to hack into the laptop without the password, but he didn't know it. And maybe it wouldn't be necessary. The computer belonged to someone named Michael Tanner. How many Michael Tanners could there be in the United States?

He swiveled his chair toward the keyboard tray and opened a new browser window. In WhitePages.com he typed "Michael Tanner" and hit Return and found 710 matches around the country.

So much for making a few phone calls to track down the owner. Not remotely feasible.

So there was no choice: somehow he had to hack into the MacBook. Find out whose it was and ask him to return Susan's.

That called for someone with computer chops far beyond his. They shared an IT specialist with a couple of other senators. The guy was good enough, so far as Will could tell, but he wasn't going to ask him to hack into someone's laptop that wasn't the senator's. And if they did find some way to remotely access her laptop, that could be deadly. These guys weren't priests or psychiatrists. They weren't bound by an oath of confidentiality.

No, he needed a computer guy who could be trusted, and that meant finding someone—anyone—who knew nothing about the circumstances, who could be trusted because he was ignorant. Tell him what happened, how the laptop ended up in the senator's hands, and he'd be intrigued and might tell someone.

But if Will Abbott brought in a MacBook Air and sheepishly admitted he'd forgotten the password . . . well, that was benign enough, right? It couldn't be terribly complicated to reset a computer. He Googled computer repair places and found a place that looked reputable on C Street on Capitol Hill. He called and waited through the prompts and then pressed 5 to talk to a "specialist."

"Yeah," he said when a guy answered, young sounding and with a nasal voice. "I've got a MacBook Air and I forgot my password. Can you guys crack into it?"

"Uh . . . is it a new machine?"

It certainly *looked* new, but maybe it was just well cared for. He couldn't admit he didn't know. "Yeah, pretty new. Does that make a difference?"

"Well, what operating system is on there?"

"Looks up-to-date."

"The new Apple operating system, you can't crack into it. It's like the iPhone. Can't do it. Used to be, you could do a password reset, but not with the new system."

"Oh." There was a sharp knock at the door, and then it opened. The boss. No one else would just barge in. Sure enough, she entered, closed the door behind her, and stood with arms folded. The appropriations committee meeting must have just gotten out.

"Do you have it backed up?" the specialist said on the phone. "We can wipe the machine and restore it to factory fresh."

"No, I don't have it backed up."

"Then I don't know what to tell you. Can't be done. I'm sorry."

"Thanks," he said, and disconnected.

Susan said, "The laptop?"

Will nodded. "I thought it would be easy to crack the password, but it's not."

"You weren't just talking to Carlos, or whatever his name is, our IT guy, were you?"

"No, an outside repair place on the Hill."

"Good. I don't want to use our in-house guy. People talk."

"Ahead of you on that."

"Can this place do it?"

He shook his head. "But there's got to be a way. I just don't know it. Maybe we should tell the Senate Security Office what happened."

"Are you *kidding,* Will? And set off a whole investigation? No, thanks."

"You're right."

"Morty has a guy he says is really good. Some Russian or something. Supposed to be a genius. I think he's in DC."

Morton Nathanson was a real estate tycoon, a billionaire, and Susan's biggest donor.

"I don't know about bringing someone else in. If it gets out—"

"Morty is the most secretive guy I know. If *he* uses this guy, he's guaranteed to be discreet."

Will hesitated. It sounded like a bad idea to him. "Well, of course, we *could* go that way. Absolutely. But—"

"We're *going* that way," Susan said. "Is that a problem for you?"

"I mean, obviously we want to keep this thing maximally siloed, and—"

Susan gave Will her famous over-the-reading-glasses death-ray stare. "Is that a problem for you?"

"I'm on it," Will said.

8

Robert Runkel, the CFO of Tanner Roast, was a good-hearted mesomorph, a pear-shaped, ruddy-cheeked man of around forty who wore black nerd glasses unironically. His glasses would have looked hipster cool on Elvis Costello, or Gregory Peck as Atticus Finch, but on him they only exaggerated his nerd persona. He was the only Tanner Roast employee who wore a suit and tie. Most people took one look at him and saw only a dork, but Tanner got his quiet, dry sense of humor, even enjoyed the way he unabashedly geeked out on *Star Trek*. It was kind of adorable. There was a good heart there. Plus, he was an extremely able accountant.

"How would you feel about going for a walk?" Runkel said.

"That serious, huh?"

Runkel nodded.

"I'd love a walk."

It was a small office, and everyone heard everything.

When they were on the street, Runkel said, "I'm sorry to be the bearer of bad news."

"It's your job, man."

"We're not going to meet payroll next month."

"So we take out another loan." They walked past a pudgy middle-aged guy with a mustache who was replacing a broken window in the brick building on the corner. "*Como vai?*" Tanner said to the guy. "*Tudo bem?*"

"Hey, how you doin', Mr. Tanner?" the man said in heavily accented English, lighting up.

Runkel went on. "That's the problem. We've maxed out our line of credit. And here's the bad part."

"That wasn't the bad part?"

"Our line of credit has what's called 'covenants.' We're in violation of the terms and conditions of our line of credit. That means the bank wants their money paid back in full by the end of the year."

"Not possible, and you know it. What about all those private equity guys who were circling us last year, wanted to invest with us?"

"Sure. I give 'em a call, they'll happily invest with us, but that's gonna mean handing over the company to them. It won't be yours anymore. Then there's our friends from Kiev."

"The Ukrainians?"

"Right. Those scary Ukrainian 'private equity' guys will lend us money at fifteen percent interest and they'll take two board seats and charge a stiff management fee, like half a million bucks, and control most of the decisions we make."

"Meaning they'll own it."

"For all intents and purposes. If you take their money, it will not end well."

"Okay."

"You don't want to cross them; that's for sure. One of them—this guy with a big stake in some confectionery business, I think—he was telling me about some fight they had with a competitor. He threatened them. Said, 'You kill my dog, I kill your cat.' At least, that's how the interpreter put it. They don't play."

"How about we just stop paying my salary for a month?"

"That won't come close to covering payroll. We also need to reduce, uh, head count."

" 'Head count,' huh?" Tanner said. He wasn't ready to fire people, or lay them off, or whatever. Not yet. He shook his head.

"I know, I know. It's not 'head count'; it's people. I see numbers; you see people. I get it. I mean, it's great. It's wonderful. It's a beautiful thing. But it's lousy business."

They came to the end of the block and stood there for a while on the corner near the lock-and-safe company. "Don't get me wrong," Runkel said. "I have beaucoup respect for you. It's like . . . that guy you said hi to just now? I must have walked past him a thousand times, and he looks kinda familiar, but you wanna know the truth? I don't see him. I barely even notice he exists."

Puzzled, Tanner said, "You mean Joaquim?"

"Oh Christ, you even know his goddamned name?"

Tanner shrugged. "He's the handyman for the building next door. Great guy. Anyway, when the Four Seasons deal is inked, we'll be fine."

"When's that going to happen?"

"Any day now."

"It's not money in the bank."

"It's happening. In the meantime, I can mortgage my house."

"What? Who does that? You can't do that!"

"It's my house."

"No, you're not going to do that. That's insane. I mean, it's beautiful, sure, but that's the whole point of a corporation—limited liability. So when a company fails, it doesn't drag the CEO down with it."

"Yeah, well, this captain goes down with the ship."

Appalled, Runkel shook his head, eyes wide. "I'm—I'm speechless."

Tanner smiled. "Can I hold you to that?"

9

Will was editing a press release in his office, door closed, when his intercom buzzed.

"Send him in," he said.

The Russian guy had arrived more quickly than Will expected. He could see him through the glass panel in the door. He got up, opened the door, extended a hand.

The Russian gave him a limp handshake. He didn't look like a hacker. He was too well dressed, in a charcoal suit and expensive-looking tie. He had jet-black hair, combed straight back. He looked to be in his early thirties. He had the pointy face of a rat, narrow brown eyes, a pronounced overbite, a receding chin.

Will showed him in and closed the office door. He didn't want anyone else in the office to know what was going on.

"Where's the computer?" the guy asked, the first thing he said.

Will pointed to it, charging on top of the desk. "What's your name?"

"Yevgeniy. You can call me Gene."

"How long you think it'll take you, Yevgeniy?"

"It takes what it takes." Yevgeniy shrugged. "Interesting shoes for this weather." He was staring at Will's brand-new suede wingtips.

Will flushed. He couldn't help it. He'd just taken the shoes out of the box—they wafted that musky new-leather smell—this morning, having waited for the right day to wear them, and decided today was as good a day as any. He hadn't bothered checking the weather forecast, just glanced outside, and it looked like a sunny day. Somehow it had turned into rain. Which would ruin the shoes.

"Are we talking hours or weeks?"

"It takes what it takes. I need office."

"You're going to work here?"

"I can go away and come back couple days if that's what you want. But I was told this is rush job."

"I'll find you a place." The legislative director was flying back to Springfield for a couple of days; her office was empty.

The Russian had lifted the MacBook Air from Will's desk, spun it around, and opened it. "Michael Tanner," he said.

"You think you can get past the passcode?"

"Look, you just show me to office and let me do what I gotta do. And if this doesn't work, there's always other route."

"How so?"

"I don't know what you are told, but I am security consultant. I happen to have hacker skills, but my firm does more than this. If for some reason you need more."

"Like what?"

He shrugged casually. "The senator's laptop got switched with someone else. Maybe you need other kind of help getting it back."

Will went still for a moment. The boss must have actually revealed why they wanted the laptop hacked. A serious mistake. Not that he would dare reprimand her. The more people who knew about this, the greater the risk.

So he tried to walk it back. "Well, obviously this isn't the senator's computer, but if we can reach the guy who owns this one, we can make the switch."

Yevgeniy smiled and nodded. Like he didn't believe a word Will was saying. Like he knew better. "You know how to reach me," he said. "And you—you just go spray *silicone* on those suede kicks, yeah?"

10

Got a second?" Karen Wynant asked. Tanner could hear the anxiety in her voice.

"Come on in."

A sigh. "You know that breakfast place with the funny name?"

"Egghead?"

"Right. I thought we were locked in. And now they're not returning my e-mails or my calls or anything."

"It was in the *Globe.*" *The Boston Globe* had recently run an article about a very hip, new breakfast-only place called Egghead that had started as a food truck in Portland, Oregon, and now had brick-and-mortar shops in LA, New York, and Boston. They wanted to be the Shake Shack of breakfast joints. They served egg sandwiches on brioche buns along with sriracha this and Wagyu that and everything with gray salt. In the article, the founder and co-owner had mentioned that they would serve Tanner Roast coffee.

"Right? I've got a bad feeling about it."

She had a bad feeling about most of her potential sales until the deal was inked, and then she had a bad feeling the deal would fall apart. Sometimes she was right. It happened.

"You want me to talk to someone?"

"Could you? I think it'll make a difference if you call the CEO, Ryan whatever. He likes you a lot."

"Text me his number. I'll take care of it."

"Still no contract from Four Seasons?"

"It'll come."

"I heard Blake Gifford was in Toronto."

"Meeting with Four Seasons?" Blake Gifford was the clownish founder of City Roast, another specialty coffee company, one of their competitors. Blake particularly got under Tanner's skin because of his TV show on the National Geographic Channel. Also because of his man bun and single earring. The show was called *Roasted,* and it starred Gifford, who traveled to a different foreign country in each episode, pretending to shop for coffee. On his show, danger was everywhere. He crept through jungles and playacted negotiating coffee deals with brigands. He crossed the Serengeti and turned up in Uganda and Haiti and Yemen, hoisting burlap sacks of coffee. It was all total bullshit. In reality he bought almost all of his coffee through brokers, large lots of mediocre Brazilian or Sumatran, not much better than Maxwell House in a can.

She shrugged. "I can't help but wonder."

"The deal is ours. Relax. The cold brew did it."

"Well, I'll believe it when I have a contract in my hand."

Owning your own company could be brutally hard sometimes, Tanner knew. But it had long been his dream, since he was a kid.

Since the time he'd found the Box.

He had a vivid memory of the day he followed the family cat, a tabby named Tiger, up to the attic. Tanner—at the time called Mickey; he was eight—remembered how hot it was up there, the dust motes dancing in the light, the neatly organized boxes of stuff, decades old. No one ever went up there. It was declared off-limits by his parents for games of hide-and-seek. It was the place in the house where you didn't go. But when he followed Tiger into the attic he accidentally tipped over a tower of boxes. Scared, he began restacking the pile until he noticed an old cardboard box labeled TANNER Q. It had been sealed with brown paper tape that was buckling, most of it loose. It didn't seem like much of a transgression to peel off the rest of the tape, easily done, and open the box.

Inside he was excited to find a big, colorful menu for a restaurant called Tanner Q that listed barbecue stuff, pork and beef ribs and pulled pork, along with sides like coleslaw and corn bread. The menu was beautiful, heavily inked in red and green, with wonderful illustrations of the house specialties done in a woodcut style. Underneath the menu was a stack of booklets that said something about a "business plan for Tanner Q barbecue restaurants."

He'd never heard of a Tanner barbecue restaurant and wondered why his parents had never mentioned it. Maybe it was old; maybe it had gone out of business. He took the menu with him, Tiger under his arm, down to the kitchen, where his mother was cooking dinner and his father was seated at the kitchen table talking to her.

"What do you have there, Mickey?" his father had said. His face was suddenly flushed. He and Tanner's mother exchanged a wary glance.

"Oh, that's old," his mother said, taking the menu from him—not to look at it but to get it out of his hands. She put it down on the counter. "That was a long time ago."

"Did you used to own a restaurant?" Tanner asked his father.

"No," his mother said, "that was just an idea he had, a long time ago."

"Idea for a restaurant?"

"If wishes were horses," his father said.

"Cool!" Mickey had exclaimed.

"Throw that crap away," his father said. He looked uncomfortable, downright embarrassed, which surprised Mickey. He might as well have brought down a girly magazine. Neither of his parents seemed pleased about his discovery.

Later, when he asked his mother for more information about Tanner Q, she shook her head. "Don't ask your father about it," she said. "He doesn't like to talk about it."

"But what happened to it?"

"It was just a silly idea Daddy had that he decided wasn't very realistic."

"It's not silly," he said, feeling protective of his father.

"Well, it's over and done with," she said.

11

"Any progress?"

It took Will a moment to realize what she was talking about. The amendment she was cosponsoring that entailed twisting a lot of Democratic arms?

Then: of course.

"The Russian guy is in Samantha's office right now working on it."

They were sitting in the back of the senator's car, a black Suburban, as it crawled along First Street. Jerry, the senator's longtime driver, was at the wheel.

"Morty's guy?" she said after a beat.

"Right."

The rain was drumming a ragged tattoo on the vehicle's hood and smearing the windows. It was raining so hard that it would have to let up soon. Susan alternated between peering out the tinted window and glancing at the BlackBerry in her right hand. That was her personal device, the one she got fund-raising messages on. You couldn't do political business on government property or using a government-owned phone, so senators drove around the streets outside their offices making calls and sending e-mails they weren't supposed to address inside.

"How long's that going to take?"

"He doesn't know."

"But he can do it?"

"So he says." Then, because that sounded uncertain, he added: "Not to worry."

Now she was looking at her BlackBerry again, absently scrolling through messages. When he was sure she wouldn't notice, he looked over at her, regarded her for a moment. Fund-raising was always a grind, but the money for her reelection was coming in surprisingly easily. The calls weren't hard to make. A lot of donors seemed to consider contributing to the Susan Robbins campaign a down payment, an investment in someone who might very well become president. He'd joked about it with her, never discussed the possibility seriously. But other people did. He knew she'd had meetings at the DNC to plot strategy for the upcoming election cycle.

What if she did decide to run for president? He imagined sitting on the plane with her going over a speech, deciding whether or not she should meet with the governor of the state they were now campaigning in. All that unpleasantness involving the lost laptop computer is behind them. He'd handled it expertly, deftly, and she's forever indebted to him. *The Washington Post* has a front-page article on SUSAN ROBBINS'S RIGHT-HAND MAN. He's called "elusive" and "enigmatic" because he refuses to talk to reporters, or at least most of them. He doesn't play that game. The boss knows he can be trusted implicitly. His office is right next door to the Oval Office. He calls her "Madame President," or sometimes "boss," just like the old days. She appointed him the White House chief of staff because he'd proven, with that laptop disaster, that he could deal with any crisis that arose, that he was discreet and peerlessly loyal. The president is interviewed over the phone by *The New York Times* and is asked about her chief of staff—he's in the Oval, silently participating in the interview, there in case the president needs him, and not talking—and she says with a proud smile, "Will Abbott? He's the man with the golden touch. When they made him they broke the mold."

Yeah, they broke the mold and then issued a product recall, he thought now.

"Uh, Will."

Will, yanked out of his reverie, turned his head. He didn't like her tone of voice. Also the direct address. When she used his name, especially with that intonation, that invariably meant that something was wrong.

"If this guy . . . this Tanner fellow . . . got into my laptop and tells, you know, CNN what he found . . . well, it's a shark in the water; it really is." She stared at her BlackBerry. Will wondered what she was looking at so fiercely. "Taking classified material out of the SCIF is a felony." She pronounced it "skiff," for Sensitive Compartmented Information Facility.

This again. She was really stuck on it. "Theoretically,

maybe, but you're a United States senator. No one's going to prosecute you for it." *Me, on the other hand,* he thought.

Now she turned to look directly at him. "Are you forgetting about Hillary?"

"FBI never charged her."

"What about Petraeus?" She was talking about David Petraeus, the retired four-star general and former CIA director who leaked classified information to his biographer, who was also his lover.

"Petraeus was charged with a misdemeanor."

"The FBI wanted to charge him with a felony. He got lucky—the attorney general reduced the charge. Look, it doesn't even matter whether I'm charged—this'll be something I drag around for the rest of my days like a rotting horse carcass."

"No one knows you took the documents out."

"Except this guy Tanner."

"No way. He's got a password-protected computer, just like we do. He doesn't know who it belongs to."

"What if he got the password somehow?"

"But how would he? He's stuck like we are. And I'm sure he doesn't have the resources we do. He doesn't—" His phone burred. He glanced at the caller ID. "Would you mind if I take this?"

She shrugged.

He clicked the Accept button and said hello.

"I am finished," the Russian said.

"We're on our way." He hung up and said, "Good news."

* * *

Fifteen minutes later he stopped into Senator Robbins's office.

"The owner's name is Michael Evan Tanner," Will said. "He lives in Boston and is the CEO of a coffee company called Tanner Roast."

"So you should be able to find his phone number easily," the senator said.

"I'll just call the company and ask for him."

"I wonder if I should call instead."

"No. Better if you don't. Right now he doesn't know whose laptop it is, because it's password protected. But if he gets a call from a United States senator, who knows what he'll do."

"Yeah."

"He might try to get some hacker to break into the computer and then blab to the press. Or even just post something funny on Facebook—*Guess what happened to me! I ended up with a senator's laptop*. All of a sudden, it's out there that you lost track of your computer. No . . . we want to keep things chill, make it seem like it's the laptop of just some boring shmo."

"All right. Your call. Whatever. I just want to get that thing back *now*."

12

The phone trilled, jolting Tanner, waking him abruptly out of a troubled dream.

"Michael, it's Karen."

She didn't have to say; he recognized her taut, constricted voice.

"Something—wrong?"

"We lost it."

"Lost what? What time is it?"

"Five something. I got an e-mail late last night from my guy Kent, at the Four Seasons."

He massaged his eyes with his hand. "An e-mail."

"I'd asked him, again, where the paperwork was, and he said, quote, I don't think it's happening."

"I don't think *what's* happening?"

"The Four Seasons deal."

"We had an agreement. You're saying we lost the Four Seasons deal?"

"That's what I'm saying. I told you I was feeling funny about it."

He sat up, his eyes blurred, crusty. "We didn't lose Four Seasons. That's not even possible."

"No, it happened. It did. He said another bidder got the account."

"Did he say—"

"City Roast."

"Blake *Gifford*?"

"Right."

He uttered an expletive. "I'm going to call Liam." He exhaled. "I need coffee." And then he remembered that, like the cobbler's shoeless children, he was fresh out.

It wasn't until he got to the office and fired up the Bonavita, using beans pilfered from a prepacked bag of French roast, that he was thinking clearly enough to call Liam, his contact at the Four Seasons in Toronto.

"Michael," Liam said when he picked up. Tanner could hear it in his voice, the bad news, the dread. "I'm so sorry."

"So what happened?"

"I got bigfooted."

"I don't get it."

He sighed heavily. "I should have called you, but I was just so pissed off. I'd already submitted the paperwork, and this Blake Gifford asshole reached out to my boss and snagged the deal."

"But . . . the cold brew concentrate thing . . . ?"

"I know. He—Gifford learned about your pitch and said he could do the same thing, only for slightly less."

"But it—it was my idea!"

"I know. I know. Plus he said he'd plug the hotels during his show."

"Which no one watches."

"Still, it's TV, and it's National Geographic, and, you know, there's the glitz factor. The name-recognition thing, it being Blake Gifford and all."

"Nobody else was doing the concentrate. I don't even think City Roast makes it."

"I guess they do now. I'm sorry about this, Mike. I mean, your product is great and you're a really good guy. But this is above my pay grade. I'm really sorry."

He grabbed lunch from a Japanese noodle place down the block where the owner, Kenji, always greeted him with a cheery "Tanner-san!" He needed to be out of the office for a while, mulling over what he was going to do now that the Four Seasons deal was dead.

He ate at the counter while going over new package designs by a freelance artist they'd hired. He spent the rest of the afternoon in his office on the phone, with a grower in Costa Rica (bad cell phone connection; the call must have dropped ten times) and then with a coffee-shop owner in Harvard Square who wanted him to train his new-hire baristas but didn't, it turned out, want to pay for it. He called his CFO, Robert Runkel, into his office to tell him the bad news about the Four

Seasons. Runkel insisted on going over some numbers and projections that almost made Tanner lose his lunch.

His phone made a text alert sound, and he picked it up. A text from Sarah. Free to meet today?

He wrote back: Sure, after work. Now what? She'd just told him she was going to rent an apartment, which was as sure a sign as there could be that she wasn't coming back. Now she wanted to meet, what, to discuss something yet *more* difficult?

Then came the question of what "after work" meant. He had no meetings or calls scheduled for after four thirty. Normally he stayed until six or seven, most days worked out afterward, and then got home for a late dinner. He wrote: 5 OK? The reply came: 5:00 at The T Room on Newbury St.

OK, he wrote. It didn't escape his notice that she'd picked a tea place to meet with her coffee-guy husband.

As Runkel was standing up to leave, Lucy Turton loomed in the doorway. "Excuse me, Michael. But you weren't picking up. You've got a personal call. He says it's important."

"Which line?" he asked Lucy.

"Three."

"How do you know it's a personal call?"

"That's what the guy said."

He furrowed his brow. "Okay."

He picked up the landline phone. "This is Michael Tanner."

"Oh, Mr. Tanner, I'm so glad I reached you. My name is Sam Robbins, and I think you may have my computer. I'm pretty sure I have yours."

13

"Sam?" he said, confused. Sam, not Susan? He'd done his Googling, and he knew that Senator Susan Robbins was single. She and her husband, Jeffrey Schwarz, had divorced five years ago, and she hadn't taken her husband's name.

So who was *Sam* Robbins?

"Sam Robbins," the man said. "It must have happened at the LA airport. I think I took your MacBook Air by accident, and you ended up with mine."

"I'm sorry, what's your name again?"

"Sam Robbins. It probably says 'S. Robbins' on the sign-in screen, but that's me. I'm a lawyer in DC, and as you might imagine, I was getting a little frantic. It's got all my work stuff on it."

"Hold on." He opened the laptop and entered the long password in the blank. "S. Robbins," it said. When he hit Return, the home page appeared.

He wasn't imagining things; this computer was full of speeches and amendments and memos and correspondence, to and from *Senator Susan Robbins.* The "S. Robbins" the computer belonged to was a United States senator.

So who the hell was Sam Robbins?

Tanner prided himself on being a shrewd observer of people. That was one of the things that had made him a good salesman. He was a better judge of people, it seemed, than of business opportunities.

And there was something in "Sam Robbins's" voice that set Tanner's antennae quivering. The caller was trying to sound casual, in a way that was totally strained. Tanner could hear it: a kind of stage fright. It was subtle but detectable.

In high school he'd once been seized by terrible stage fright when he was playing Peter Quint in a production of *The Innocents,* the play based on Henry James's story *The Turn of the Screw.* It had been a disaster. He'd managed only to croak out his lines. Ever since then he'd gotten far better at performing. But he knew what stage fright sounded like.

"You're 'Sam Robbins'?"

"Right."

"Sam T. Robbins?" he said, making up a middle initial.

"Exactly."

Tanner's heart began to thud.

The guy is a liar.

"I don't have your laptop, Mr. Robbins. I'm sorry. I don't know what you're talking about."

And he hung up.

He sat back in his chair and stared at the ceiling. In this part of the warehouse, the pipes and wires were hidden by a drop ceiling, discolored and mottled. What the hell was going on? Who would do something like this? Was it some guy who'd somehow found out about the switch and was trying for some reason to intercept the laptop? To steal a US senator's computer?

After a few seconds he sat upright, looked at his phone's LCD display. The call had come from a phone number in area code 202. Washington, DC.

He tapped at his keyboard, typed "Senator Susan Robbins" in Google. The first result was her official Senate website. The letters were purple instead of blue, because he'd clicked on the link before. He clicked on it again. It opened a page with a big photo of Susan Robbins and a little green triangle at one corner labeled "Contact." When he clicked on that, it took him to a page listing office locations: one in Springfield, Illinois, one in Chicago, and one in Washington.

He looked at the DC phone number on the website. It was nothing like the number of the guy who'd just called, this bogus "Sam Robbins." The number on his caller ID wasn't even a Senate phone number.

So was someone trying to scam him? Or had the senator for some reason directed some flunky of hers to call and lie about whose laptop it was?

And how'd they gotten his number anyway? Yes, the sign-on screen on his MacBook said "Michael Tanner," but there must be a thousand Michael Tanners in the country. There were four or five in the Boston area alone. How had they known which one to call? They couldn't look on his laptop, because it was password locked. So had they called every Michael Tanner in the country until they hit on the right one?

Or had they somehow hacked into his computer? There was definitely something funky going on, and he didn't understand it. Tanner felt more exasperated, more short-tempered than usual. Today had been colossally bad, as if it was open-season-on-Michael-Tanner day.

The fact was, he didn't care if he never got his laptop back. There was nothing on it he needed.

If the senator wanted her computer back, she knew where to reach him.

14

Will's heart was still pounding, and he could feel the flop sweat running down his neck, behind his ears. That had been a complete, utter disaster.

He covered his face with his hands for a few seconds.

I don't have your laptop, Mr. Robbins. I'm sorry. I don't know what you're talking about.

Was there something in his delivery, his tone of voice, that had given him away?

It *had* to be the right Michael Tanner. Otherwise, he would have said something like, *Laptop? I don't know what you're talking about.* Instead, Tanner had outright lied, denied having it, for some reason.

What a screwup.

Now what was he going to do?

He definitely couldn't have the boss call Tanner now. There'd be no way to explain why the senator had just had someone call him pretending to be "Sam Robbins." That bell couldn't be unrung.

The Russian security consultant answered on the first ring. "Yes?"

"It's Will Abbott from Senator Robbins's office."

Sharply he replied, "Is there problem?"

"No. Well, yes."

The Russian was still on Capitol Hill. He returned to the office in less than twenty minutes.

"You said there was always another route."

Yevgeniy tipped his head to one side and arched his eyebrows questioningly without speaking.

"You said, 'If this doesn't work, there's always another way. Another route.' " Will explained about the disastrous call to Michael Tanner.

"So man who has senator's laptop refuses to return it."

"Pretty much."

"Why don't we make things easy and simply retrieve object? We know where he lives."

Will blinked a few times. He wasn't sure what the Russian meant, exactly, or maybe he did and he didn't want to acknowledge it to himself. But even thinking about it, and discussing it, felt like crossing some kind of a line. He didn't know how much he should ask about it. Finally he said, "What would that involve?"

"We know people in Boston area. We ask and they retrieve."

"Without . . . Non*violently,* right?"

"Of course. He will never know."

"Let me think about it."

A casual shrug. "As you wish, but I thought this was matter of urgency."

"It's just a damned inconvenience," Will said. "No big deal."

Yevgeniy turned away, a man with far more important things to do.

Will's phone announced a text message with a tritone. He pulled it out. It was from the boss.

It said only, Well?

15

That disturbing phone call preoccupied Tanner for most of the afternoon. That strange, discomfiting call from a man calling himself Sam Robbins.

He had the caller's phone number. He typed the number in Google and found out only that it was a Sprint mobile phone number. He pulled up a bunch of scammy websites that said things like *Have you received a text message or phone call from (202) . . . ?* and offered to look up the owner of the number for a fee.

He clicked on one of the websites, entered the guy's phone number, and hit Enter, and then a progress bar popped up and zoomed along, growing, and when it reached the end, another message came up offering to sell the "full phone search report" for ninety-five cents with a trial membership.

This was the kind of black hole the Internet was full of, "offers" that could turn into phishing attempts that fritzed your computer.

And so what? Did it really matter who "Sam Robbins" was?

The important thing, the major point, was that "Sam Robbins" badly wanted the senator's laptop, so much so that he had attempted a clumsy subterfuge to try to get it. He had lied. He had tried to trick Tanner. That just pissed Tanner off.

He cleared a space on his desk and opened the senator's laptop again. He entered the password in the start-up screen and watched as the desktop emerged out of the dark screen. He opened the "Documents" folder and scrolled through the list. "Tahoe Pics" and "DC Appearances" and a couple of folders labeled "SSCI," whatever that meant.

He clicked on one of the folders, and it opened a column of documents. Some of them looked like PowerPoint slides. Some were PDFs.

He chose one, in the middle of the vertical column, and double-clicked on it.

The top of the page said, "TOP SECRET//SI/TK//NOFORN" in white letters on a red band across the top.

Holy shit.

Top secret documents? He skimmed the document, but all he could deduce was that it was from the National Security Agency. The document swarmed with bureaucratic verbiage. It was near impossible to read. It might as well have been in Serbo-Croatian.

He picked up his phone and called Lanny Roth at *The Boston Globe.*

They arranged to meet for dinner.

* * *

Tanner remembered that he had Blake Gifford's mobile number somewhere. He seemed to run into Gifford on every sales trip, at every convention. Gifford had been on the cover of *Barista* magazine, and he swanned around the floor of the Global Specialty Coffee Association Expo, trailed by a camera crew. They'd had drinks together. They weren't friends, but they were friendly. Cordial. Gifford was semifamous and never let you forget it, whom he sailed the Mediterranean with, whom he skied in Aspen with. The one thing he wouldn't brag about to Tanner was the bogus "buying trips" filmed for his show. He knew Tanner wasn't fooled by them.

Eventually he found, in a desk drawer, the crumpled business card on which Gifford had scrawled his mobile number.

Gifford's cell phone rang and rang until it went to voice mail. Tanner disconnected the call and, a minute or so later, hit Redial. This time it rang five times and then Gifford picked up.

"Yeah?" A hoarse bark.

"It's Michael Tanner."

A sudden shift in tone. Gifford abruptly sounded cordial, even effusive. "Oh, hey, dude, how's it going?"

"Not really going so well at the moment, Blake. I heard about the Four Seasons contract."

"Oh, hey—"

"Not cool, man. Not cool. That cold brew idea was mine. You just came in and grabbed it."

"Whoa, whoa, whoa there, big guy. You didn't invent

cold brew. That was invented in Kyoto like a thousand years ago."

"The deal I put together for Four Seasons—"

"We came in at a lower price point, dude. Simple as that."

"But you ripped me off. That was mine. We had a deal."

"Verbal. Are you really gonna make me tell you a verbal agreement isn't worth the paper it's written on? You know that as well as I do. Come on, dude."

Tanner was so angry he couldn't find the words. "It's—not right," he finally blurted out.

"Listen, I'm sorry, dude; that's just how the game is played, my friend. It's nothing personal. It's just business."

He didn't want to admit it, but he knew Gifford was right. It was just business. He shouldn't take it personally.

When he didn't reply, Gifford said, "I hear you're *awesome* on the squash court. I'm going to be in Boston next month. I'll bring my squash racquet—we should play. Cool?"

Tanner was silent for a long moment. Finally he said, "You know, Gifford, I look forward to that."

16

The senator had a vote on the floor of the Senate, so Will power walked the half mile with her through the tunnel. Senator Robbins was wearing her sneakers.

"Did it work?" she said.

"Uh, no, it didn't, not really. But we've got other options."

"I don't understand."

"The less you know, the better."

She gave him a long, hard look. "What are you up to?"

"Better if we keep that compartmented," he said.

"Well, the longer this Tanner fellow holds on to my laptop, the more time he has to spend looking through my documents. So you want to do everything you can to get it back."

"But he can't access your files. Not if it's passcode protected."

She was quiet for a long moment, as if thinking about it.

"You do have to enter a passcode every time you use

it, right?" he said. They'd set it up that way; Will was almost certain. She didn't know enough about how to use her computer to make any changes to it.

"Oh . . . yeah. I might have, uh . . ." She waved and smiled at the senator from Oregon, who was passing by on the electric trolley. "I might have left the password on a little sticky note."

"Left it where?"

"On the case."

"I thought you don't have a computer case."

"No, I mean on the laptop itself."

"You left the password on the laptop? Like, right on the top?"

"Well, on the bottom."

She left the password on a Post-it note on the bottom of the MacBook Air? That couldn't be. No one could be that careless with a password.

No, actually, *she* could. Susan had an adversarial relationship with technology, which was a little ironic for a senator on the intelligence committee. Computers were mysterious and vaguely threatening black boxes used mostly by the young, who deliberately made things impossible for older folks to understand. It was like her attitude toward cars. She was willing to drive the car, but if a red light went on in the dashboard display, it was straight to the service station. And she certainly wasn't going to be jump-starting a dead battery.

He almost groaned but checked himself just in time. The last thing he was going to do was chastise his boss,

Senator Susan Robbins of Illinois. That wasn't exactly how you advanced your career.

"You might have, or you're not sure, or what?" he said. He felt a little queasy. This couldn't be happening.

"I usually do. Sometimes the note comes off in my briefcase and I have to dig around for the password. One of those little pink sticky notes."

"Can you check your briefcase and see if the sticky note is there? If it is—"

She abruptly handed him her briefcase.

But it wasn't until they reached the Capitol Building that Will was able to take a seat on a bench in one of the anterooms outside the Senate Chamber. He opened the briefcase on his lap and looked for a misplaced little pink adhesive square stuck somewhere.

After going through it several times, minutely, he didn't find anything. His queasiness had grown stronger, the longer he looked. Now he felt sick.

If Michael Tanner had realized he had the wrong laptop and the passcode was stuck onto the bottom of the laptop, there was no question the guy would enter the code to unlock the computer so he'd know whom to contact.

Oh Jesus. No wonder Tanner was so obviously lying, saying he didn't have it. He must have gotten into Susan's computer and realized it belonged to a US senator and looked through it.

Which meant he had quite likely found the top secret documents. They were right there on the computer's desktop, its opening screen.

And maybe that was why he didn't want to give it back. What if he didn't like Susan's politics and posted something about it on Twitter or Facebook? What if he got in touch with *The Wall Street Journal* or *The New York Times*?

His face was hot and prickly. He stood up and walked out of the room and hit Redial.

The Russian answered, "Yes, William?"

"What we talked about before—about, ah, retrieving the object?"

"Yes?"

"I've decided. I'd like to pursue that option."

"Got it."

"Wait. This doesn't lead back, right?"

"We do all the time. Routinely. Our people are good. No, is no possible connection."

"I need absolute assurance on that."

"I am giving to you. Is no way to connect to you."

"Okay," Will said thickly. He wanted to sound decisive, but his mouth had gone dry. "Let's do it."

17

Tanner needed to get some exercise, blow off steam. He called a friend, Scott, who worked downtown as a home theater installer and belonged to the same gym Tanner did: SportsClub Boston, a midrange fitness club, part of a network of gyms in the Northeast and mid-Atlantic. Scott was an excellent squash player, and Tanner didn't mind losing to him; he enjoyed the game. The gym didn't sell bottled water, and the water he got from the sink in the locker room tasted metallic, so he always stopped on his way in at the fruit stand outside the gym run by a pleasant, plump Nepalese guy. He liked giving the guy his business.

"Good afternoon, Mr. Tanner," said the fruit-stand guy.

"Good afternoon, Ganesh."

Tanner and Scott played a best-of-three match. Tanner won one and lost the other two.

Then he quickly showered and went to meet his wife.

* * *

Tanner liked tea just fine, considered it a pleasant drink, but didn't get all the hoopla. The thousand different kinds of teas, the subtle distinctions, calling herbal tea "tisane," buying loose-leaf tea in bulk, blah blah blah. To him, tea was, even at its best, two clicks away from scented hot water.

The place she'd chosen for their postwork meeting, the T Room, was a couple of white-painted rooms on the second floor over Newbury Street, minimally furnished with tatami mats on the floor and shoji screens and hanging scrolls on the walls. You had to take off your shoes. You couldn't even hear traffic. The windows were double glazed.

It was peaceful and serene. Not a good setting for an argument. Maybe she wanted to borrow some of the tranquility of the Japanese tea ceremony.

She was wearing a simple white tube dress with a thin suede jacket over it. Her light brown hair tumbled down her shoulders. She didn't appear to be wearing any makeup, except for lip gloss. And she looked terrific, better than ever. Which was not a good thing. She should look disconsolate, out of sorts, desperately missing her husband.

"I'm guessing I'm not gonna be able to get a double espresso here, right?" Tanner said when she sat down on the mat across from him. She didn't kiss him, but that didn't seem to be significant.

"Tanner, they won't allow coffee near the place. It makes everything smell."

"Smell great."

"It's like having a cigar smoker at the next table when you're dining at a fancy restaurant."

"Not exactly. So since when did you become a tea lover and defect to the dark side?"

The waiters and waitresses were dressed in kimonos. There was a complicated ritual involving boiling the pure spring water and using a tea scoop and a bamboo whisk. Tea was served in large primitive-looking bowls you held up in two hands. The tea was a beautiful green but it was bitter and seaweedy. It was accompanied by mochi desserts, sort of sticky buns filled with not-very-sweet dark pasty stuff. The bitter and the sweet. Maybe the elaborately choreographed rituals of the Japanese tea ceremony weren't so different from the rituals of estranged spouses. They were meeting in a no-coffee zone, neutral territory.

"The forms you wanted—they're in your e-mail inbox," he said.

"Thanks for doing that."

"No sweat. But I wish you wouldn't."

"Rent an apartment? It's a short-term rental."

"Should I find that reassuring?"

"Do you want it to be?"

"Do I want you to come back home? Of course I do."

She sighed. "I don't have any money, Tanner. I hate to say it, but it's true."

"Tell me what you need and I'll give it to you."

"I want to cash out."

He didn't know what she meant and wondered if she was actually talking about divorce now, in some sarcastic way. He said, "Wait, are you talking about—" He didn't want to actually say the word "divorce," because that would make it suddenly real. They'd had a fight, she'd moved out, she didn't want to talk, they were temporarily separated . . . That was all tolerable. As long as things got patched up and she came back.

"I'm talking about my equity stake in Tanner Roast. I need it back. I haven't had a closing in two months, and I'm running out of cash." They'd each put a hundred thousand dollars into Tanner Roast when it started eight years ago. That meant they each owned fifty percent of the company's stock.

"Sarah, why don't I just lend you whatever you need? You don't want me to buy you out now; you really don't. You know what kind of shape we're in? You might not even get your original hundred K back." It was worse than that, but Tanner didn't want to tell her: her hundred grand was probably worth zero right now.

"With that Four Seasons deal? Don't kid a kidder." He'd been talking about that deal at home a lot before she left, probably out of nervous energy.

"That's not— That's off."

"Four Seasons?"

"Yeah. Not happening."

"I don't understand. That was a done deal."

"Apparently not."

"Oh, wow. That's too bad. Look, let's just go our separate ways, Tanner. You don't need me as an equity partner. It's time."

Separate ways. "Sarah. How about you just move back home?"

"I have the right to cash out anytime I want. You know that."

He sighed. "Well, do what you want to do. But you get a valuation done, you'll see, we're in the red."

"We'll see about that." She said it matter-of-factly, not threateningly. "I'll send you a formal e-mail tomorrow."

She could *force* him to buy her out. Require him to come up with a hundred thousand dollars or whatever the stock was worth. Which he could maybe squeeze out somewhere, but it would be ugly. He might have to start selling off equipment.

"Sarah, can I apologize?" Tanner said.

"For what?"

He thought: *For whatever you want me to apologize for. Just give me a list.* He said, "For that big fight we had. I was a jerk."

"You weren't even in the fight."

"What are you talking about?"

"You don't fight. Everything is"—she held her hand out, palms down, flat, and gestured a perfectly flat line—"smooth. You never get upset. You never get pissed off."

"I get pissed off plenty, and you know it."

"Only when you tell me. There's no other way to know."

"Because I don't throw heavy objects or scream like a loon? Believe me, I'm pissed off about . . . well, the Four Seasons thing."

"You know what you're like, Tanner? You're like those

giant heads, those statues on, is it Easter Island or Christmas Island? You know, those huge, expressionless, impassive heads. That's you."

He smiled. *Just let the balls whiz by. Don't swing at them.*

He had a fleeting memory of one of his parents' fights, one of many that woke him up in the middle of the night and made him feel like he wanted to throw up. He was squatting on the staircase, on the step from which you could see into the kitchen without being noticed. His father's roars—"God*damn* you! God*damn* you!"—had awakened him.

His father could be terrifying. His face was dark red. Tanner saw his father pick up the ceramic pumpkin that he'd made in art class and hurl it at his mother, who screamed and dodged and just missed being hit by it. The pumpkin smashed against the wall and exploded into a hundred jagged pieces. He was upset about seeing his pumpkin break, of course, but it felt as if something else had shattered then too, something bigger and more important: that basic feeling of trust a kid has that his parents are the grown-ups, the rational ones. He'd never forget the look on his mother's face. It wasn't anger, and it wasn't regret. It was fear.

"Listen," he said calmly. "You talked about counseling before—I think that's a good idea. Let's give it a try."

"Who says I'm interested any longer?"

"Oh."

"That was a joke, Tanner. As if anything gets a rise out of you." She took a sip. "I bet your friends are lapping this up. Especially Lanny and Carl."

"Misery loves company, I guess."

"You're all just yukking it up about your shrew of a wife."

"No way," Tanner said. "Are you kidding? They all love you."

She shook her head, gave a rueful smile.

"Sarah, sweetie, I miss you. It's lonely without you at home."

"You? Lonely? Don't play that violin for me. God, you've got more friends than . . . I remember walking across the quad with you when we were undergrads. It was like walking through water. Every ten steps someone was accosting you, wanting to say hi. It was nonstop. You knew *everybody.* I don't know how you got to your classes on time. You were like a walking Facebook."

"While you were studying, I was partying," he said with a smile. "I admit it."

"And our wedding—remember, your original invite list was like five hundred people? I made you cut your list down to the size of mine, and I felt bad about it. I mean, you ended up inviting like a tenth of the people you wanted to. You're, like, the least alone person in the world."

Tanner shrugged. "I find most people interesting once you get to know them."

"It's so easy being your friend," Sarah said. "Maybe we should have stuck with that."

"With what?"

"With just being friends. More tea?"

* * *

Tanner couldn't help but think about the Box. The one that contained the menu for a restaurant, Tanner Q, that never was.

His father always had a few scotches after work, and by the third, he was usually pretty well plastered. Tanner knew to stay away from him when he was drunk. Not that he'd get mean—he usually didn't—but it embarrassed Tanner. It was a side of his father he preferred not to see. One day he'd wandered into the TV room where his father sat in his BarcaLounger, a glass of scotch in the cupholder, watching the Sox. He asked about the Box.

"It's nothing," his father said. "It was just an idea."

"But why didn't you do it?"

Fred Tanner gave him a watery, unfocused stare over the rim of his rocks glass. "Why?"

"Yeah, why?"

He gave a strange, bitter smile. "Because of you."

"What do you mean?" Tanner said, alarmed, confused.

Then his father's face became clouded and inscrutable. "I'm kidding," he finally said, but he didn't look like he was kidding. In any case, the conversation was over. His father turned back to the Red Sox.

"What'd I do?" Tanner asked, but his father didn't answer.

18

Will Abbott was on the phone arguing with the chief of staff to the senator from Indiana when another call came in. He noticed the 619 area code on the caller ID. The call was from San Diego. The only person he knew who lived in San Diego was . . .

He got off the line with Caitlin, the chief of staff, and picked up line two.

"Hello?"

"Mort Nathanson." That gruff voice.

"Oh, Morty, nice to hear from you. Susan's in a vote, but I'll have her call you back the instant she gets off the floor."

"No, actually, I called for you."

"Oh. Well, what can I do for you, Morty?"

"Man-to-man. Tell me. Do I have anything to worry about?"

"Worry . . . ?"

"Level with me. Is she still investment grade?"

"Susan, you mean? Of course, why would you—?"

"Yevgeniy told me something interesting."

Will gulped. "Oh yeah?"

"Little slipups in her line of work can be fatal."

"I don't think I understand—" Will felt his face grow hot. Had Yevgeniy told his boss, Morty Nathanson, about the missing laptop? Did Morty know more than that, know what was going on? *Jesus Christ.*

"See, when a company seems to be in trouble, I don't just talk to the CEO. I reach down a layer. I'll call the CFO, or the COO, directly. Know why? *They're never as good at lying.*"

"There's nothing going on, to the best of my knowledge—"

"Listen to me," Nathanson barked. "I've put a lot of money into Susan Robbins, and I want to know if my investment's in trouble. I'm hearing things that concern me. Don't let me be surprised by any bad news, you get me?"

19

Tanner met Lanny Roth at a restaurant in the South End, not far from where Lanny lived. It was loud, louder than Tanner remembered from the last time he'd been there. They could barely hear each other. The waitress came and recited the specials without stumbling. She was in her early twenties, skinny and small busted, pretty. Black hair, gray eyes, Goth-style eye makeup, heavily applied liquid eyeliner giving her upturned cat eyes.

"Can you repeat the appetizer special?" Lanny asked her.

"Oysters en brochette," she said.

He leaned forward, resting his chin in his hand, judging. "I just wanted to hear you say that again."

She smiled uncomfortably.

"You took French, didn't you? You have an excellent accent."

She nodded, now smiling faux graciously. "I'll be back in a while." She couldn't leave fast enough.

"You just wanted to hear her say that again?" Tanner said.

"I'd do her," Lanny said.

"Sure, but *would she do you* is the real question."

"There's that."

"You're old enough to be her father."

"Beauty knows no age limits."

"I think you might have creeped her out."

He shrugged. "Maybe she's a journalism major at Emerson looking for an in at the *Globe.*"

"She's going to spit in your gazpacho."

"Then I won't order gazpacho."

Tanner pushed aside his charger plate and silverware, took the laptop from his computer bag, opened it on a corner of the table. He entered the password—by now he had it memorized—and then handed it to Lanny. During the handover, a water glass clinked against a corner of the laptop and wobbled and nearly toppled.

"This the senator's?"

Tanner nodded. He'd already told him about the bizarre call from "Sam Robbins."

Lanny gave a wolfish smile and shook his head. "Amazing."

"The folder all the way on the right, at the top. Marked 'SSCI docs.' "

He clicked and swiped and double-clicked and squinted at the laptop screen. He pulled out a pair of cheap reading glasses from his jacket pocket. "Huh."

"You see it? All those PDFs and PowerPoint slides?"

"Huh."

Tanner waited, took his napkin from the table and

folded it in his lap. A lanky dark-haired young guy placed a basket of bread covered with a red napkin on their table. He put down a white plate and poured greenish olive oil into it.

Lanny waited for the waiter to leave, and then he said, "You know what the hell you have here?" His widening eyes hadn't left the screen.

"What?"

"Top secret documents. I mean, this is serious shit. Top secret government intelligence. This is amazing! From what I can tell, they're all about something code-named 'CHRYSALIS.' That's a secret project or program or something."

"Okay . . ."

"They're NSA documents—you got that much, right?"

Tanner nodded.

"These are classified, like, up the wazoo. Top Secret / SCI. I forget what that means, like 'security classified information' or something. It's like a subset of Top Secret."

Tanner's stomach went tight. He'd suddenly lost his appetite. Lanny wasn't telling him anything he hadn't already noticed, but somehow it was now confirmed, validated. Made more real.

"What am I supposed to do with it?"

"Let me make a copy."

"For what?"

"I'll do some digging. See what this is all about."

The cat-eyed waitress approached the table. "Have you made some decisions?" she said.

"Hey," Lanny said.

"Give us a couple of minutes, okay?" Tanner said. He hadn't made any decisions. It felt like decisions were slowly being made for him.

"I've got a . . . doohickey," Lanny said. He produced a thumb drive from his pants pocket, held it up, waggled it around.

"Okay," Tanner said. "Just—keep this between us."

"I'll see if I hear anything out there," Lanny said. "Don't worry about it. I'll keep it on the DL."

20

Driving home, he could feel the pressure of everything—the financial troubles of Tanner Roast, the loss of the Four Seasons thing, and now Sarah's demand—weighing down on him. He felt, momentarily, as if he were trapped in an avalanche, tons of earth and rock sliding down on him and burying him, crushing him.

When he arrived home, he unlocked the front door and stepped inside to the cool, dark foyer.

And he knew something was off.

He knew it instinctively, in his lizard brain, before he knew it rationally. There was some kind of change in his sensory field, and it took him a moment to realize that he was smelling something different. The faint rotten stench of food garbage overlaying the normal, regular house smells, the odors of lemon polish and old wood and must and a trace of mold.

Had something happened to the garbage in the kitchen? But it couldn't be: he didn't have any food garbage anyway. Anything food related went down the garbage disposal.

Then it was the slight movement of air that drew him toward the back of the house, to the sitting room and the pair of French doors that opened into the small city garden. He kept the doors locked, of course—this was urban Boston, after all—but as he approached he realized that one of the panes of glass was missing. Had it somehow fallen out or— He came closer. He felt the colder air from outside flow in, carrying that foul, overripe garbage scent. His next-door neighbor had put out his trash a day early. Mildly annoying, but ordinarily he wouldn't have smelled it in here.

Except for the missing pane of glass.

The glass hadn't broken. It looked like it had been cut out, sheared neatly, by a glass cutter.

And then he wondered . . .

He pulled up one of the door handles and the door came right open. *But I locked the French doors; there is absolutely no question about it.*

His heart began to thud. He could see what had happened. It was obvious: someone had cut out a pane of the French door, reached in, and unlocked the doors.

He looked around slowly for evidence of the intrusion that must have happened today. He didn't immediately see anything. His giant eighty-inch flat-panel direct LED Samsung TV, which had cost some big bucks, was still there, and he didn't notice any of the audio components missing. He didn't own jewelry, besides cuff links, and he didn't keep a stash of cash around the house. Sarah had taken most of her jewelry with her when she moved out. What did he have that was valuable enough to be stolen?

Could it possibly be . . . ?

He left the sitting room and took the steep stairs to the second floor. This was a South End Boston town house, a row house four floors high. Vertical living. It wasn't always convenient. You want a drink of water in the middle of the night, you either go to the bathroom sink or go down two flights to the kitchen.

On the second floor was his home office. *This is where they'd look first.* Nothing appeared to be missing. The laptop wasn't here; he'd stopped off to leave it in the office safe. The computer here was a Power Mac, a tower on the floor next to the desk, a big monitor, a wireless keyboard. All of that was still there.

He clicked the space bar to wake the computer, rouse it from its groovy psychedelic screen saver. He didn't password lock this computer the way he did his laptop, so it came right to life.

He grabbed the mouse and found that he couldn't get the cursor moving the way he wanted. Something was screwed up about it. He moved the mouse around the mouse pad and the cursor danced awkwardly across the screen in a way seemingly unrelated to his hand movements.

Ah.

The mouse had been inverted. The faint gray apple logo was at the top, not at the bottom. Someone had moved the mouse around and put it back wrong.

Which meant that someone had been searching for something on his computer.

He quickly looked through the rest of the house and saw no other evidence of intrusion. Maybe evidence was there, but he didn't notice anything missing.

They'd determined that the easiest point of entry was at the back, the French doors. They must have entered the back garden through the side gate, which didn't have a lock, decided that cutting a pane out of the French door and reaching in would be quicker and easier than picking the door lock. Which meant they didn't care about leaving evidence that they'd been here.

But nothing in the house was trashed, no scary "messages" left for him, no horse's head in the bed. They'd searched the house, focusing on the home office, searched the computer.

They were looking for the laptop.

The office had a decent security system with an alarm; it would not be easy to break into, and you'd have to blow up the safe to get it open, probably. At the house he had a basic alarm system, which he set only when he was going out of town. Making it fairly easy for "them," whoever they were, to break in.

And then he remembered that the home security system included a couple of hidden cameras, disguised as smoke detectors, at the front and the back of the first floor. They were set to go on at eight in the morning and go off at seven P.M. You could reset the system to record at different hours, but he'd lost the stupid booklet that came with the system. Sarah had insisted they have it installed after reports of a couple of burglaries in the neighborhood. It was old-school, used a digital video recorder, didn't record to the cloud the way the new Nest cameras did. Tanner usually forgot it was on. He'd never had a break-in; it just wasn't something he thought about.

He trotted down the stairs to the closet next to the kitchen, which had been converted to a pantry with shelving. The top shelf, though, had been given over to the security system's components. He opened the stepladder and climbed up to the DVR. After pressing a few buttons, he figured out how to rewind the recording. The odd thing was that there didn't seem to be a recording with today's date. Did that mean the thing had stopped working? He found a recording for yesterday and the day before.

They'd disabled the recording.

21

The shirt was tight at the neck. When Will tried to button the top button, he pinched the loose neck skin and could barely breathe. Was it possible he'd gained half a shirt size in the three weeks since his last formal event? Couldn't be. Though, come to think of it, he'd probably gained fifteen pounds in the last half a year. Probably gained twenty, twenty-five pounds in the three years since he'd become Susan Robbins's chief of staff. Maybe more; he'd stopped weighing himself. He had a definite potbelly now. He was looking more and more like his father every day. It was terrifying.

Jen was lying in bed, watching him dress. They were speaking quietly. Travis was asleep in his bassinet, in the bedroom, and they both wanted him to stay asleep.

Will gave up on the top button, for now, and started inserting the fake-onyx studs into the little holes in the shirt placket, or at least trying to. He kept fumbling. His fingers felt too fat. He hated formal wear, thought tuxedos—*or, excuse me, dinner jackets*—were ridiculous relics out of *Downton Abbey*, and was dreading tonight's event, the White House Correspondents' Dinner, which was being held at the Washington Hilton. The only reason he was going was because the boss was going, and he had to escort her. Which meant he had to schmooze and smile at his fellow Senate staffers and senators. And he was a lousy schmoozer.

And there was the goddamned laptop, that disaster in the making. He was totally preoccupied with it. The Russian guy had called a few hours ago to say that the break-in hadn't yielded anything. When Will had heard that, his stomach sank. But at the same time—and this was the weird thing—he was secretly almost happy to hear it. Because the arrogant Russian (he thought of him as Igor, though his name was Yevgeniy) had screwed up.

"Let me help you with those," Jen said, getting up.

"Thanks."

"Such a stud," she said as she deftly pushed a stud through the shirt hole. For some reason that made him think about sex. He could feel her hot breath on his chest, which turned him on. He'd forgotten when the last time was they'd had sex, but it was during her pregnancy. Now she was uninterested. She spent most of the day in pajamas, and her hair made her look like a madwoman chained up in the attic, but he knew better than to complain about that. She had by far the harder job, spending all day with Travis.

Jen knew about the missing laptop—she'd been there

when Susan had called—but he hadn't told her anything about his retrieval efforts. It was better that way; the fewer who knew, the better. The efforts had already crossed the line into illegality.

"Hey, someday can you take me?"

"To Nerd Prom?" That was what all the insiders called the Correspondents' Dinner.

"Yeah."

"Sure," he said, though he didn't mean it. Tickets cost three hundred dollars each, and they were hellishly hard to get.

"And while you're gliding around in your tux like James Bond, I'll be watching *Law and Order* reruns."

"Believe me, I'd much rather be at home watching *Law and Order*. Or *House of Cards*."

"Oh, loosen up, Will. It'll be fun. Now, where's your cummerbund?"

"It was on the hanger. Ah, there it is, on the floor of the closet."

"Shh."

"Sorry," he said in a much quieter voice.

He flipped his collar up and tried once more to fasten the top button. Jen retrieved the cummerbund from the closet floor and put it on the bed. "Let me try."

Just then Travis started fussing, crescendoing quickly to a loud bellow. She went right to the bassinet and lifted him out. "Someone has a poopy diaper," she said. "Oh, you poor thing."

She swung the little baby up to her shoulder, and as the two of them passed by, Will caught a foul whiff.

"Thanks," he said, meaning *Thanks for doing what I know is normally my job.*

He struggled a bit more with the collar button and managed to cinch it closed. It pinched at his neck and he felt the blood pool in his face. Then he grabbed the cummerbund from the bed. "Do the pleats go up or down? I always forget."

"Think I know?" she called from the changing table in the next room, where Travis would have his bedroom when he was a little older. "My daddy didn't exactly wear black tie or anything." Her father had recently retired after forty-five years as an auto mechanic.

"I think it's up, to catch the crumbs," he said. He put it around his belly, fastening it at the back. He turned and looked at himself in the mirror. It sort of concealed his potbelly.

"You look good," Jen said.

"Everyone looks good in black tie."

"Let me take a picture."

He looked at his watch. "Jerry's going to be here any second." Jerry, Susan's driver, was always punctual. "We've gotta go pick up the boss and then head over to the Hilton."

"Oh, come on, Will. Just one picture."

He hated having his picture taken. He was always the guy who stood to the side when pictures were taken.

* * *

They drove in silence. Will couldn't think of anything to talk about with Jerry. He realized that there were guys who were skilled at making idle conversation, equally adept with senators and limo drivers. Schmoozers. But Will wasn't one of those guys. He wasn't a schmoozer. Jerry probably thought he was arrogant, another snot-nosed Hill staffer who was full of himself.

They pulled up before Susan Robbins's Georgetown house, a redbrick Georgian town house on N Street, and they waited.

The boss came out ten minutes later and entered the Suburban in a cloud of L'Air du Temps. She was wearing her ruby gown and her Tahitian pearl necklace, the strand of marble-sized cream and gray pearls she was so often photographed wearing.

She asked Jerry about his daughter's confirmation, and they chatted for a few minutes. Then she turned to Will. "Morty said he's not going to be here tonight."

"One less ring to kiss."

She smiled.

He thought about telling her that she looked great, because she did, but that felt too personal. "Remember to shake Tim O'Connor's hand." O'Connor was the junior senator from New York.

"My new best friend." In a lower voice, she said, "Do we have it?"

Will glanced to the side, at Jerry.

"Jerry, could you raise the . . . thing?" she said, and immediately the glass partition powered up between his compartment and theirs. Will remembered hearing somewhere that the president's limousine, the Beast, had a powered glass partition with a videoconference screen built into it.

"Is it handled?"

"It's a work in progress."

"What does that mean?"

"The Russki's plan flamed out, but don't—"

"Flamed out? What do you mean? No, don't tell me."

"Not to worry. We're done with him." He enjoyed saying that. She had foisted Igor, or Yevgeniy, on him, and the Russian had screwed up.

"The longer this thing is out there . . ."

"I'm running . . . this *thing* . . . myself, and it will be taken care of. So long as I have full operational control." He paused, and the senator nodded. "This *will* be handled."

"It can't get back to me."

"It won't. Trust me."

She nodded again. "I do," she said. "I know you won't let me down."

He bit the inside of his cheek to keep from smiling with pleasure. The ball was in his hands again, and he knew just what to do.

The Suburban pulled up in front of the Hilton. C-SPAN's cameras were there for the "red carpet" arrivals.

Susan was kind of a celebrity, in Washington circles anyway, but a bunch of real Hollywood celebrities were supposed to be attending. Harrison Ford and Morgan Freeman, a Kardashian, the great singer Judy Collins, whom Will was hoping to meet. The chief presenter was to be a woman from Comedy Central.

But most important, he had to get the senior senator from Massachusetts alone for a minute. He needed to ask for a very confidential favor.

22

At a few minutes after ten, Tanner was about to pour himself a scotch and watch some TV or read a good thriller. And go to bed.

Instead, he glanced at the cardboard where the missing windowpane had been, took out his iPhone, and hit Lanny Roth's cell number.

After a couple of rings he picked up.

"Hey." Lanny sounded urgent, breathless.

"Am I calling you too late?"

"So you got my message?"

"Message?"

"No? Jesus, okay—talk to me."

"Can I buy you a drink?"

"I'm on my way to Manchester."

"Mass.?"

"New Hampshire. Just for overnight. On some damned election story. What's going on?"

"I had a break-in at my house."

"Oh Jesus. I told you they were coming for that computer."

"No, nothing taken, as far as I can tell."

Lanny took a breath. "How'd they get in?"

"Looks like they cut out a pane of glass and reached in to unlock the door. I didn't set the burglar alarm, and somehow they knew it was off."

"I'm not surprised."

"And get this: I have this old surveillance camera on the first floor of my house that's always recording, and somehow they got to it and turned it off without being captured on film."

"Yeah, they've got resources. Did they . . . ?"

He was surely talking about the laptop. "It wasn't there. It was—"

"Don't tell me. Um . . . listen, about that . . . ?"

"Yeah?"

"I talked to a guy, an old intel source of mine from when I worked in the DC bureau."

"Okay . . . ?"

"What you—we—have is something big. I mean really big. Scary big. It's up there with the Snowden stuff."

"Seriously?"

"Dead serious. I'm talking—I'm gonna get a Pulitzer; I can smell it. That's how big this story is, Tanner. It'll take me some time, maybe a week or two, maybe longer. But I'm gonna get it."

"What are we talking about?"

But Lanny didn't seem to have heard him. "My worry is—remember when that *New York Times* reporter got this huge scoop on the NSA wiretapping American citizens without a warrant?"

"I remember the story. Like ten, twelve years ago."

"Right. The reporter, this guy named Risen—who, by the way, won a Pulitzer for it—had this amazing scoop, but when the head of the NSA heard he'd gotten it, he called Risen's editors—I think he went all the way to the top of *The New York Times*—and persuaded them not to publish it. He told them it would damage national security. So the *Times* sat on it for over a year. I can't let that happen. If I get that kind of heat from the *Globe,* I'm just gonna quit and give it to, like, *The Guardian,* in the UK. The way it happened with Snowden. That way the story gets out and gets back into the US, too."

"But what *is* it?"

"It's this terrifying program code-named CHRYSALIS that—oh shit, Tanner, you know what? I'm already saying too much. We need to take this offline. I mean, they monitor our phone calls. That's an established fact."

"Monitor whose phone calls?"

"Everyone's, man, you know that."

"Nobody cares about my phone calls. Yours, maybe."

"I think they're always searching for certain keywords or phrases. Listen, I've got to file something for tomorrow on this damned election thing, but I'll be back in town tomorrow. By then I should have more on this. Do me a favor and don't talk about this over the phone anymore, okay?"

"Okay," Tanner said. "I won't."

"I mean it. Don't say a thing."

Tanner fell silent. "You know what?" he said, suddenly resolved. "I can't have this in my life."

"What do you mean?"

"I'm giving it back. I'm going to call the senator's office and send the laptop back. I have to do the safe thing."

"No, man, you don't get it. You give it back, that's the opposite of safe."

"Huh?"

"That laptop is the only reason you're still alive."

"Oh Jesus." Tanner laughed. "Come on, man."

"I'm deadly serious. These people just broke into your house. They'll stop at nothing to get that laptop. But as long as it's out there somewhere, they need you alive so they can find it."

"Are you for real?"

"Once you give it back, you're this guy who's seen a stash of top secret files about a secret program no one's supposed to know about. You're the man who knew too much. And do you know what happens to people who find out deep-cover intelligence secrets in this country? They commit suicide. Or they get into convenient car accidents."

"Oh, come on." Lanny had a paranoid streak. He believed all sorts of nutty conspiracy theories—Princess

Diana was murdered, Bush knew 9/11 was going to happen, there were alien spacecraft hidden in Area 51. He believed there was this secret government inside the government—all sorts of kooky ideas. But Tanner never took him seriously. He'd heard that reporters, especially investigative ones, often had this type of personality bent.

Once, when Lanny was reporting a story about the chemical conglomerate W. R. Grace, he had a tire blowout driving along the Mass. Pike, went into a skid, and was lucky to have come out okay. Tanner pointed out that Lanny's tires were bald; he hadn't replaced them in ten years. He'd warned Lanny repeatedly that his heap was an accident waiting to happen. That was all it was. Nothing conspiratorial.

Roth had shrugged. "Maybe that's all it was," he said at the time. "And maybe there was more to it."

Now he went on: "There was this investigative reporter for *The San Jose Mercury News* who was writing about the CIA's involvement in running drugs—the cocaine business. So what happens to him? He's found dead, with not one but two gunshot wounds to the head. Allegedly a suicide. Ever hear of anyone shooting himself in the head *twice*?"

"Lanny—"

"Then there's this guy who wrote for *Rolling Stone*, a reporter, started investigating the CIA director, and he dies in a suspicious car accident. True story, Tanner. The government has people who specialize in this kind of thing. They can make it look like you had a heart attack. They can remotely hack into your car and sabotage it."

"Okay, okay. So tell me something: Why would you risk publishing this big story? I don't get it."

"Once it's published, once it's out there, I'm safe and so are you. There'll be too much public scrutiny. It's like, they can blow out a candle but not a fire. It's before the story gets *out* that you're at risk. Unless you have leverage. Unless you have that laptop. That's your life insurance policy. Listen to me, Tanner. Do not let anyone else have that laptop, and make sure it's well hidden. Okay?"

After a long pause, he said, swallowing hard, "Okay."

23

The noise of the crowd, the babble, was nearly deafening, everyone yapping at once, spirits high. People were clutching flutes of tepid champagne, getting buzzed, and letting loose. It was also way too warm, approaching hot, an already overheated room jammed with warm bodies. And smells: competing penumbras of perfume, the marine scent of shrimp piled high on melting ice.

He overheard snatches of conversation. A woman next to him was saying, "So I told him, your *dick* is never getting out of committee. Not with me."

A guy was saying, "So I'm, like, you don't have the votes, why are we even having this conversation?"

Another woman: "The difference between God and a US senator? God doesn't think he's a senator."

His collar still pinched, and he had that vertiginous feeling like blood was pooling in his head. Sweat ran down Will's forehead into his eyes. Luckily he'd remembered to bring his handkerchief. He blotted up the perspiration on his forehead and around his eyes and on his neck, and then he sidled up to the senior senator from Massachusetts, Owen Sullivan.

"Senator."

Senator Sullivan was in his sixties, spoke with a heavy Boston accent, and had teeth that hadn't been orthodontically straightened and a pockmarked face, evidence of a long and losing struggle with teenage acne. His dinner jacket looked frayed. It looked like it hadn't been dry-cleaned in the last ten uses. He looked like what he was, a working-class guy from Charlestown, which was next to Boston. The only discordant note about him was his glasses, which were horn-rimmed and professorial-looking, sort of preppy.

Will could see the expression on the senator's face morph quickly from the initial faux friendliness underscored by wariness—*What crazy person is accosting me now?*—to relaxed and genuine—*I know this guy; he's part of my everyday world; I can trust him.* Senator Sullivan had dealt with Will plenty of times and, Will believed, respected him too.

"Hey there, Will."

"Can I have a minute? I promise, no more."

"It's not the best time. Can it wait till tomorrow?"

"Wish it could." To his surprise, his heart was thudding. He realized then that he was about to cross another line, taking the hunt for the laptop in a potentially dangerous direction.

The senator shrugged. Reluctantly, he said, "All right."

"Susan is quite intrigued by your energy-storage incentive bill."

"Really?" Senator Sullivan looked suddenly pleased. He took a sip from his highball glass, which he clutched with a paper napkin.

Will nodded. This was blatant, crude horse trading, but that was the currency of the realm. "More on that to come. For now, I need a—I need a name. You had someone who, uh, helped you out last year, when you had that stalker problem."

Now the senator's eyes narrowed. "I'm not sure I know what you're talking about."

"The guy from Charlestown."

Sullivan just blinked uncomprehendingly.

"The kittens. The, uh, 'problem solver.'"

A couple of years ago, Sullivan had had a stalker problem. Someone kept leaving dead kittens outside the front door of Sullivan's brownstone in Charlestown. Sullivan took out a restraining order, but it didn't deter the stalker, who wasn't much concerned with legal niceties like restraining orders. Sullivan's family was terrified. The stalker even broke into Sullivan's house once and disfigured the senator's daughter's American Girl doll. Nothing could stop the sicko. And the dead kittens continued.

Finally he made the problem go away. The story had been passed around among senate staffers, always in whispers, with the illicit thrill of an urban legend, though everyone swore it was true. Sullivan called in someone he knew in Charlestown, an ex-Marine who had done time in prison and had once been in the Charlestown Mob. A guy known as the Problem Solver. Apparently the Problem Solver staked out the house and captured the stalker and then broke pretty much every bone in his body. The problem went away.

Now Senator Sullivan spun away abruptly, and Will realized, with a sick feeling, that the guy was ditching him, probably furious at being asked about this in such a public setting. God, how he'd screwed up! He should have been less impatient, should have waited until tomorrow, not asked him about something so sensitive in a place crawling with journalists, a place where the senator was watched closely. What an idiot he'd been!

Then Sullivan looked back at Will and gestured with his chin to follow him. Will had misunderstood. The senator was just taking precautions. He led Will to a deserted alcove outside an unused function room, away from the crowd.

"I don't want to hear any details, but what's this for?"

"It's for Susan. She has a real serious problem. I should probably leave it there."

"Understood. All right, look." He set down his highball glass on a nearby table. He took out a ballpoint pen and wrote a number down on the rumpled napkin. Then he handed the napkin to Will.

Will took it and, with one fluid motion, suavely went to slip it into the front flap pocket of his dinner jacket, which unfortunately turned out to be sewn shut. Then, recovering quickly, he jammed it in the back pocket of his pants.

"I don't want to hear about this ever again," Sullivan

said. "Not by e-mail or text or phone call or anything. This guy— Let me put it to you this way: this isn't a water pistol I just gave you. It's a goddamned M16, you understand? You don't go there, you don't go to this guy, unless you've used up every other option. So just make sure you know what you're getting into."

Will swallowed with effort. His mouth was dry. He nodded. "I understand." With raised eyebrows, slowly and deliberately, he said, "Thank you. I won't forget." Then he immediately regretted saying that. That was how people of power talked to each other. Not someone who merely *worked* for someone powerful. For him to say it to a senator was presumptuous and silly, maybe even offensive. He added at once: "I mean, *Susan* won't forget."

24

Lanny Roth didn't want to talk over the phone, so he'd arranged to meet Tanner, the next day, at a diner in South Boston not far from the *Globe* building. The diner, a sort of greasy-spoon joint but entirely authentic in its greasy spoonness, was on West Broadway. Tanner had been there before and liked it. It smelled of bacon and coffee, two of the best scents ever. The coffee was generic diner coffee, though, which meant it was just okay, but even bad coffee brewing smells great.

Tanner looked around for Lanny, walked up and down the length of the diner, looked in all the booths, and didn't see him. Most of the booths were empty. It was after the lunchtime rush.

So he sat at a booth, and when the waitress came by with her Bunn carafe of coffee, he asked for water. He waited, occasionally checking his iPhone for mail. The waitress came by with her carafe again, and he shook his head, told her he was waiting for a friend.

After twenty minutes of waiting, he called Lanny's cell.

He reached a voice-mail message. At the beep, he said, "Lanny—did you forget? I'm at the diner."

Next time the waitress passed by he ordered a grilled cheese sandwich, just to justify taking up a booth. Then he tried Lanny's landline at the *Globe* and left a similar message. He waited another ten minutes, then e-mailed Lanny and tried his mobile phone again.

Still no answer. Had he left? He was returning to Boston from New Hampshire. From Manchester, it would take around an hour, no more. Maybe he'd gotten a late start. Maybe he'd lost his cell phone, was driving back without it. Or left his phone in do-not-disturb mode. That seemed the likely explanation. It was funny how nervous we get when someone goes off the grid, even temporarily. We all had to be reachable at all times. That's what technology had done to us.

So maybe Lanny had gotten distracted—he did space out from time to time, partly a function of how fractured his work was—and busy and forgot about the meeting he'd requested last night. Whatever the election story was in New Hampshire, some aspect of it had detained him. He was reporting somewhere, talking to someone, not answering his mobile phone because that was rude when you were talking to someone.

That was all.

The grilled cheese arrived quickly, on a big white plate. It looked perfect. The bread grilled golden brown and glistening with butter from the grill. The cheese was something bland and pale orange like so-called American cheese, maybe Velveeta, perfectly goopy. He thanked the waitress and checked his phone. Then he put his phone down and enjoyed his late lunch.

Without meaning to, he struck up a conversation with the waitress. Hard to imagine, but she'd been working there fourteen years. Once, when Stenopoulos, the owner, had pinched her bottom, she had spun right around and pinched his. That put an end to the fanny pinching. Tanner had to laugh.

He ate his lunch unhurriedly, occasionally checking his e-mail, thinking about work, about the damned Four Seasons deal and how Blake Gifford had snatched it. He composed in his head an e-mail to send to Gifford but kept it in his mental outbox. What was it Gifford had said? *It's nothing personal. It's just business.* He knew Gifford was right. But despite himself, he was really pissed off about it.

He thought about revenues versus expenses and how deep in the red Tanner Roast was operating, and if it kept going that way for another three months, he was going to have to think about shutting down. Maybe he really wasn't cut out to be an entrepreneur. He was a great salesman; he knew that. And he loved coffee to an extent that most people didn't, and he knew a lot about it. But he didn't have the—the what? the bare-fisted aggressiveness, the cold-bloodedness—that starting up a successful business seemed to require. He was too uncompromising, too obsessed with selling the best instead of the most.

But if he shut it down, if he gave it up, then what? Go

back to selling enterprise hardware? Admit defeat, tail between his legs?

He missed having someone in his life he could complain to, talk to, reason with. More to the point, he missed Sarah. He missed having her next to him in bed. Had she dressed up for him at the tea place? He wondered. Maybe some part of her wanted to come back home, end the separation. Be a part of his life again.

He glanced at the time on his iPhone. He'd been waiting a full hour. Just to be thorough, he called Lanny's cell one more time, his home landline, and his office landline, and in each case got a recording.

He wasn't too far from the *Boston Globe* building. He figured he'd drop by the newspaper and ask there.

So he paid up, thanked the waitress, left her a big tip, and headed out to his car. He remembered what Lanny had said on the phone last night. The almost paranoid-sounding stuff about how everyone's phone calls were monitored.

Do me a favor and don't talk about this over the phone anymore, okay?

Lanny had said he'd talked to an intelligence source in DC. That what "we" had was *scary big*. That it was *up there with the Snowden stuff,* the revelations about massive NSA spying on US citizens. A story big enough to win him the Pulitzer Prize. Something explosive enough, damaging enough to our national security, that some American newspaper editors might be afraid to publish it; he might have to publish outside the country.

Could Lanny have gotten into some kind of legal trouble? Maybe being in possession of those damned classified documents was breaking the law.

The one person Tanner knew who stayed in close contact with Lanny on a regular basis was Carl Unsworth, the martial arts instructor and beer-night regular. He found Unsworth in his phone's contacts and hit Dial.

As it rang, a dark thought popped into his head. He recalled all those tall tales Lanny had told about reporters who'd died in suspicious accidents or staged suicides. Could something have happened to him?

The phone rang a couple more times, and he came to his senses. Maybe it was contagious, Lanny's conspiracy-mindedness. Hang around him too much and you'd end up wearing a tinfoil hat.

It rang long enough that Tanner expected it to go to voice mail, but then he suddenly heard Carl's voice.

"Tanner?"

"Yeah, Carl, I was supposed to meet Lanny, but he never showed. I was—"

"Tanner," Carl interrupted him. "I'm—I'm standing in front of Lanny's house right now. It— He— Jesus, Tanner, they just rolled him out on a gurney."

"Did something happen to him—?"

"Oh man," Carl said, his voice high and choked, "Lanny's dead."

Tanner went cold and numb. He fumbled for words. "What— Carl, I don't understand—"

"Tanner, he—" And then Carl's voice got muffled. It sounded like he was crying. "The guy killed himself."

25

Will got home a little after nine at night. He kissed Jen and immediately took Travis—squalling and bucking—from her. He didn't need to be asked. He didn't change out of his dress clothes first. Jen looked strung out, at the end of her tether.

"He's been like this all night," she said, collapsing into a kitchen chair.

"Have a glass of wine."

"I can't, Will—I'm breastfeeding!"

"Dr. Blum says one glass of wine is totally fine."

"Dr. Blum? Dr. Blum says just put the baby in the bassinet and lock the door and plug your ears." Dr. Alain Blum, their pediatrician, was French. He had told them the secret to getting your baby to sleep was to feed him, put him in his crib, pour a glass of wine, and come in to get him in the morning. If he's going to cry, let him cry until he's tired of it. They were horrified. But recently Will had begun to think they should give the French method a try.

Jen opened the fridge, moved aside a carton of Lactaid milk, and pulled out a bottle of Yellow Tail. "Oh, what the hell," she said.

"Okay, now, big guy," Will said in his best soothing voice, while bouncing him up and down rhythmically and patting his back. It didn't calm him down at all; he just kept yowling. "Poor kid. Why are you so unhappy, little Travis? What can we do to make you happy?"

Jen poured the chardonnay into a wineglass, glugging it out until it was almost to the rim. Will quickly came over, holding the baby with his right hand, and with his left he took the wineglass from her and dumped out half into the sink. He handed it back to her, smiling, blinking. "But let's not go overboard," he said cheerfully.

Jen took the glass with visible annoyance, rolling her eyes. "Why do I always feel like I'm being *handled*?" she said. She took a long sip. "Was the fund-raiser okay?"

He nodded and didn't elaborate. She no longer asked for details about his many fund-raisers; it was mind-numbing. He glanced at his watch. It was too late to call the Problem Solver, probably. Or was it? Maybe it wasn't too late after all. He imagined that a guy in his line of work didn't go to bed especially early.

"Okay if I zone out, maybe watch some TV?"

"Sure, go ahead."

After ten minutes of bouncing and patting, Travis finally dozed off, a warm lump on Will's left shoulder. Will could feel Travis's damp face against his neck. As he carried him into the darkened bedroom, he wondered how much longer his son would be portable. There'd probably be a time when the boy would be too heavy to pick up. And wouldn't want to be picked up, wouldn't want to be hugged. Will's father hadn't believed in parental displays of affection. He shook hands as if Will were his stockbroker, not his son.

Will set Travis down gently in the bassinet, and the little hand grenade didn't detonate. He padded out of the bedroom and saw that Jen was watching some reality show, probably the one about a competition between food trucks.

"You've got the magic touch," she said.

He smiled. "I'm going to do a little work."

"Sure," she called out distractedly.

Will's "home office" was a small guest room that they both used—Jen for paying bills and such, Will as a place to park his laptop and do e-mail. It smelled faintly of lavender, from the potpourri Jen had left in a dish on the empty dresser. The last time they'd had guests in the guest room was when Jen's sister came to visit, more than a year ago.

He took the crumpled napkin from his pants pocket, smoothing it out carefully, as if it were a scrap of the Dead Sea Scrolls. The senator had jotted down the numbers in a hand small and dense, with pressure heavy enough to rip the napkin in a few places. It had a 339 area code, which he didn't recognize. He decided to call from his iPhone, not the landline.

He looked at his phone for a few seconds, depressed

the Home button to bring up the phone's home screen—or was it "wallpaper"?—a photo of Travis not crying (because asleep). He thought about the step he was about to take. It was serious, yes, but this was a serious situation. Somehow they had to retrieve Susan's MacBook from this guy, who for some reason refused to give it back, refused to even acknowledge he had it. He'd probably stashed it somewhere, maybe at his workplace. Or maybe given it to someone for safekeeping. It all depended on what this Michael Tanner wanted, what he was up to. And whether the guy had discovered the classified documents. Because if he had . . . the boss's troubles were just beginning.

He was about to make a call that he knew would demarcate the beginning of one phase of his life and the end of another. He'd already hired a guy to do something illegal, but now he was about to take it to the next step. To point a gun and make a threat, maybe. Or maybe even hit him, beat him around a little.

Whatever happened, Will was about to hire a guy to get a job done, and the less he thought about what happened behind the scenes, the less he knew, the better.

He just wanted the damned computer back.

He took a deep breath, let it out, and then called the Problem Solver's number.

After one ring, the phone was answered: "Yeah?"

Will introduced himself, and before he could say anything else, the guy said, "Where'd you get this number?"

"Your cousin from Charlestown." That was how Senator Owen Sullivan wanted to be identified. Will had no idea whether the Problem Solver actually was the senator's cousin. It seemed unlikely.

"Get off this line. Call me from a burner."

There was a click.

A burner.

He stepped into the living room, which should have been called the TV room. "I'll be back soon—I need to pick something up."

Jen turned. "What do you need, this time of night?"

"Long story. It's for work. Shouldn't take me more than twenty minutes."

She heaved a sigh. "I'm not waiting up."

It was about a ten-minute walk to the nearest CVS, where he found a revolving rack of disposable phones and phone cards and such. A bunch of phones in colorful blister packs—TracFone, GoPhone, Boost Mobile—a confusing array. He stared at them for a good five minutes before he just grabbed one of them. After he'd paid for it, he took it out of its bag and popped it out of its plastic bubble. By the time he was halfway home, the phone was operational.

The crumpled napkin was in his back pocket. He slid it out carefully and, standing in the cone of light directly beneath a streetlamp, he dialed the Problem Solver's number again.

He answered again on the first ring. "Yeah?"

"Will Abbott again," he said.

"Disposable phone?"

"Yep."

"Give me your e-mail, your personal e-mail."

Will gave the man his address at Gmail.com.

"What's your social?"

"My—what?"

"Social Security."

Will gave him the nine digits, wondering why the guy needed it.

"Check your e-mail in ten minutes." Then there was a click, and dead air. The man had hung up again.

When he got home, Jen was still watching TV. He went right into the guest room and opened his Gmail account. One new e-mail, from not a name but a long number. He opened it.

It contained a long link:

https://onetimesecret.com/secret/pnoughfhrrlhsrjpco2il5b . . . The link went on and on. He clicked it, and it pulled up a page with a red oblong that said *View Secret* and beneath it *(careful: we will only show it once)*. He clicked again, and a message came up, written in all caps, as if the man was shouting at him.

> DO NOT CALL MY NUMBER AGAIN. FROM NOW ON CALL ME ONLY USING THE METHOD BELOW.

There was a long list of instructions, starting with something about "layer 2 tunneling protocol" and "secure VPN" and "DOWNLOAD THIS SOFTWARE."

He clicked on the hyperlink. It took him to a page where you could download something called a Tor browser. He vaguely recalled hearing or reading somewhere that people used the Tor browser when they wanted to conceal their identities, to hide from government surveillance.

He was surprised by the measures taken by the Problem Solver. He'd imagined the guy as a sort of thug, a low-life mobster out of *Goodfellas* or *The Sopranos,* a guy who wore a windbreaker and a pinky ring. Instead, he was techno-savvy. More techno-savvy than Will; that was for sure. A lot more.

He was prompted to create and enter a password (at least eight digits, including a number and a capital letter), and then a message came up, from an e-mail address at ProtonMail.com that was all numbers. The message said something about VPN and PGP and Tor-enabled VoIP. Something about "killing Java" and avoiding "leakage." It was like a video game.

Will's heart began to pound. This must be the thing they called the dark web. For a long stretch—almost five minutes—odd messages were popping up on his screen. *Finishing handshake with first hop . . . bootstrapped 85% . . . establishing a Tor circuit . . .*

As he waited, he glanced at his watch. It was late, but he was so amped with adrenaline that he didn't feel tired.

After thirty minutes, he had a newly created e-mail address. Something called "Mumble.com VoIP" had been installed on his laptop. It used his computer's built-in microphone. It took several minutes to configure. The application checked his sound level. He clicked a link and a minute or so later he heard a voice. But not a human voice. A computer-generated voice that sounded as if it were filtered through a mouthful of potato chips.

"What's your problem?" the voice said, like Darth Vader on Auto-Tune.

Will explained about Tanner, who he was and where he lived and worked. He explained that this Boston businessman had something that didn't belong to him. "You need to find out where it is," he said, "and you need to get it. And just know that he's not going to be very co-operative."

"When I ask people questions, they usually answer," the voice said. The robot voice talked some more, and Will talked. There was a long delay, like five seconds, as if their voices were traveling to the moon and back. The voice told him what his services would cost. Payment would be in Bitcoin, the untraceable digital currency. Will would be sent instructions on how to purchase Bitcoin. He'd be sent the man's "BTC wallet address," a long string of characters.

When he obtained the laptop, the voice said, he would notify Will via e-mail at his new ProtonMail address. Will would send the payment. Then the laptop would be sent via FedEx.

The Problem Solver seemed to have everything under control. Something occurred to Will, and he said, "What are the . . . limits?"

The pause that ensued was longer than the usual five seconds. "What are you asking?"

"I mean . . ." He didn't know how to put it, exactly. "How far do you think you'll have to go?"

"Listen good. I don't work on a leash, okay? I do what I do. You tell me what you need. You don't tell me how to get it. I do whatever I deem necessary. You okay with that, Will?"

Will was silent.

"Still with me?" the voice said.

"Yeah," Will said at last. "I'm okay with that."

"You can still pull the plug," the voice said. "Right now. You can do it. But after this conversation? It's game on. So any second thoughts? Have 'em first."

"That's okay," Will said. His voice shook a bit. "Let's do this."

26

That's not possible," Tanner said.

"It's true."

"When I last talked to him, he was excited. Nervous, scared, but also really determined to meet with me today. He did not sound suicidal at all."

"Well, he did it."

"Did they say—how?"

"The EMT guy I talked to said they found him with a plastic bag over his head and a bunch of pills. Ativan, I think, which is a sedative. Ativan and booze. I guess that did it."

"You knew him well. Better than I did. Did he strike you as suicidal?"

"I don't know. No, probably not. I mean, he could be moody."

"He was talking to me about winning the Pulitzer Prize," Tanner said. "He was making plans, future plans, and he was excited. He was in New Hampshire last night on some *Globe* story. He said he'd talked to an old source of his in the intelligence community and that—" Tanner had told Carl about the top secret files he'd found on a senator's laptop. "He said he had a huge story. Something 'scary big.' Up there with Snowden."

"That's the whistle-blower guy who's living in the airport in Moscow or something?"

"Yeah, that's Snowden. Here's the thing. Lanny was excited about the story but scared about whether he'd live to tell it. He also didn't want me to talk about it on the phone." He paused. Strictly speaking, he wasn't talking about what was in the documents. "He told me stories about journalists who'd been killed working on big stories."

"What are you saying? You think he was murdered?" Carl's voice rose in disbelief.

"Yeah."

"But why? For *what*? Who the hell would do that?"

"I don't want to talk about this on the phone," Tanner said. "You free tonight?"

The laptop was in the office safe.

The safe was built into a section of the kitchen cabinetry that lined one corner of the great open space where everything happened, the roasting and the degassing and the packing. The corner where they did the cupping. The safe had been an afterthought during the renovation of the old dry-goods warehouse. That was the only place to put it, since digging into the poured-concrete floor would be a big hassle. Tanner had thought they'd be keeping a lot of cash around, to pay farmers in Central America who didn't take credit cards. But it turned out that everyone had a bank account, and you wired money in; that was how it worked. So the safe went mostly unused. Until a few days ago.

Obviously no one had figured out there was a safe at Tanner Roast, or at least not where it was. Otherwise "they" would have tried to break in—"they," whoever they were—and there was no evidence of that. The alarm hadn't gone off, but maybe that didn't indicate anything. Because "they" had proven skillful at circumventing security measures.

When he'd come in that morning, inhaling the complex bready smell of roasting coffee, he'd noticed a subdued mood around the place. Everyone said "hi" or "morning," but they all had a furtive, uncomfortable look about them. It took Robert Runkel, his chief financial officer, to disclose what everyone was being evasive about. "Sorry about the Four Seasons," Robert said. The word had gotten around.

"We'll talk later," Tanner said as he passed by.

"Yeah, we will," Robert said, and Tanner was surprised by his insinuating tone.

Karen was waiting for him in his office. She wore jeans and a white button-down shirt and looked mournful and grim. She was sitting in the visitor chair in front of his desk.

"Karen," Tanner said, dropping his briefcase on the

chair by the door next to the coatrack. "You know and I know it's not your fault."

"What's not my fault?"

"Four Seasons." He hated even saying the name. Once he'd seen a bleak comedy film in which Albert Brooks plays a husband who forbids his wife to say the words "nest egg" because she'd gambled away the couple's nest egg in Vegas. He was beginning to feel that way. "It's all on me."

"Oh," she groaned, "that's not why I'm here."

"Then—why?"

"We've just lost the Graybar." The Graybar Hotel was a fashionable new hotel located in a converted jail at the foot of Beacon Hill. It wasn't a very big account, but it was useful to brag about.

"You're kidding," he said.

She shook her head.

"When it rains, it pours. Don't tell me: to City Roast."

She shook her head. "Cortado."

"Shit." Cortado Coffee was an ultrahip third-wave single-origin specialty coffee company out of Pittsburgh. People talked about them in the same sentence as Stumptown and Counter Culture and Blue Bottle and Intelligentsia.

"Hey," Tanner said, "it happens. We'll get 'em back, or someone bigger."

"What pissed me off was, they're insisting on keeping the coffee equipment we loaned them. The Fetco brewer."

"They can't keep it. It's a loan. We lent it to them."

"I told them that. It's worth, like, thousands of bucks, right? They said, 'Where's the paperwork?' "

"We had a very clear understanding. It's never been a problem with any other client."

"So Kirk indicated he'd heard about the Four Seasons thing, and he wanted to drop two bucks a pound, to the intro price, and I told him no way. That was when he said, 'Then we're going with Cortado Coffee.' And he still insists on keeping the Fetco."

In his peripheral vision he noticed a looming figure, and he turned to see Robert Runkel standing there, an index finger in the air. Presumably the finger meant just one minute or one moment, but the way he held it up made him look imperious, like Julius Caesar or something.

"All right. I'll give him a call later, or I'll have the lawyers do it. Karen, I need to talk to Robert. Robert, I'll be right back. I'm getting a cup of coffee." Karen got up and traded places with Robert, while Tanner went to the warehouse. He poured himself a mug of the coffee of the day, an Ethiopian, and then opened the cabinet door where the safe was. He punched in the combination and it beeped open, which was when he saw that the laptop was still in there, along with a folder of important Tanner Roast papers, share certificates, company charters, shareholder register.

He closed the safe and glanced around. No one had seen him, he was pretty certain.

He decided it was safer not to move it.

Now that there was a chance people were watching him.

27

Tanner thought about his friend Lanny.

Landon Roth, from Westchester County, New York, came to Boston to go to college, wrote for *The Boston Phoenix* for a few years, then took an editor/reporter job at *The Boston Globe*. Until the layoffs, he had been on the national desk. He was an excellent reporter. And one of the funniest people Tanner had ever known. He was the kind of person who had to be an expert about everything, a human Wikipedia.

His stubborn insistence on pushing forward on this story about the classified documents on the senator's laptop—that took balls.

Tanner knew nothing about intelligence agencies or anything of the sort, not beyond what you read in the newspapers and online. But he kept thinking of that young guy Edward Snowden, that contractor who worked for the National Security Agency who downloaded a bunch of totally top secret information and gave it to a couple of reporters. And turned up on the run in Hong Kong and then Moscow. Imagine fleeing to *Moscow* to feel safe? That couldn't be a good life.

And then there were Lanny's paranoid-sounding stories about people killed for finding out about secret government programs or whatever. They didn't sound so paranoid anymore.

Because Lanny Roth wasn't suicidal. Tanner had known him long enough to have witnessed Lanny depressed (over breaking up with a girlfriend, or missing out on a promotion at work), and last night Lanny was far from depressed. In any case, it wasn't coincidental that he'd been reporting on these documents, talking to sources in the intelligence community about them, the night before his alleged suicide.

Tanner thought of the creepy way someone had broken into his house, somehow both sophisticated and brazen. Forget about the fact that "they" hadn't found what they were surely looking for. It was a way of saying, *We can find you anywhere. We can get in anywhere. We're watching, and we don't care if you know it.*

He had a stray thought, a worm of fear wriggling in his brain. If Lanny Roth had been killed to keep him from reporting on this top secret program—which was a good assumption—and they knew where he'd gotten the documents . . .

He didn't want to think this way.

He thought about his friends, wondered what they were up to. Brian Orsolino was surely at dinner with some chick, pretending to be interested in her job in the nonprofit sector but actually wondering what kind of panties she was wearing. Carl Unsworth was probably teaching an evening martial arts class. (He often showed up late to beer night because of a class.) Tanner glanced at his watch. This was around the time that Carl went out to Subway to get his grim lonely-fit-guy's dinner (roast chicken sub, with mustard instead of mayo, on a six-inch whole wheat sub). He found Carl's number in recent calls on his phone and clicked it.

He picked up right away. "Tanner. You okay?"

"Yeah, sure."

"Anyone try to break into your offices?"

"Not that I can see. But we've got a decent security system here."

"Good. You know what? You're staying with me tonight. Forget Pembroke Street. You haven't even replaced the glass in your window, and you could have pigeons flying around the goddamned place. Or rats running around. And I've got a guest room with a supercomfortable—well, it's a futon, but it's a *great* futon."

Tanner thought again about Lanny Roth and decided it was smarter to take Carl up on his offer than spin the roulette wheel by staying at home.

Though he'd never admit as much to Carl.

28

Tanner picked up dinner at a Chinese restaurant near the warehouse—General Tso's chicken and moo shu pork and some kind of green beans—enough for Carl too. Just in case he hadn't had his abstemious lonely-guy's dinner at Subway.

"Great," he said unenthusiastically as Tanner announced the dinner selections, handing him the white plastic take-out bag.

"You already ate."

"No. Moo shu pork is like a thousand calories a serving, and that General Tso or whatever it's called, that's like fifteen hundred. It's, like, a neutron bomb of calories."

"There's veggies."

"Deep-fried in oil. No, thanks."

"Okay," Tanner said, amused.

"Sorry if I sound like your wife."

"Sarah never nags me about stuff like that. Anyway, you don't mind if I eat it in your presence, do you? I mean, I've got bigger problems than my cholesterol right now, know what I mean?"

Carl smiled grimly. He was wearing a T-shirt tight enough to display his eight-pack. Tanner knew that Carl, who was the protective type by nature, was genuinely worried about him. He also knew that Carl wasn't going to admit that. It was easier for them both.

Tanner looked around the kitchen. It was compact and neat and generic-looking, with plain blond blocky Scandinavian furniture. The old 1950s sparkly Formica countertop, with aluminum edging, looked almost new. The house was a small, suburban-looking colonial on Commonwealth Avenue in Newton. Carl had bought it after he and his wife started divorce proceedings, when he had no money and was unhappy and impatient with everything, and he furnished it in a couple of hours at Ikea.

"The kids aren't here this week, are they?" Tanner asked.

"They're never here during the week. I have them every other weekend."

"That's it?"

Carl looked pained but just nodded. Tanner had a wrenching thought that Sarah might want to formalize their separation, file for divorce. God, he hoped not. He still didn't understand what had provoked her to move out in the first place. He'd told her he wanted kids too, just not quite yet. Right? Unless he was missing something.

"I assume you're not okay with that."

"No, I'm not okay with that. I love having them here. Even though they're not all that excited to spend time with me."

"Your wife gets them during the week and every other weekend?"

Carl nodded, scowling.

"Well, you got ripped off."

"Oh, you don't know the half of it."

"Yeah?"

"The judge gave Stephanie half my assets and none of my liabilities. She overinflated my income based on one boom year, five years ago. She assumed I was lying all the time. It's not even close to being equitable. I mean, I look at her the wrong way and I'm held in contempt and fined."

"Jesus."

"That's Massachusetts for you. Anti-male, anti-husband, anti-father, whatever it is. They're famous for that."

"After ten thousand years of patriarchy . . . ," Tanner put in.

"All right, don't get me started or that's all I'll talk about."

Tanner popped a fried ball of General Tso's chicken into his mouth. After he finished chewing, he said, "Do you know anybody in the Brookline police?"

"Brookline? Sure I do. I've trained some of those guys. Why?"

"Because I want to know if Lanny—if it's really suicide."

Carl shrugged. He looked weary. "The EMT guy said

it was probably an overdose of pills. Which means he killed himself. Alcohol and pills."

"So you don't believe Lanny was murdered."

Carl took a deep breath, then expelled it noisily. "You think he was murdered because he was—asking questions about the classified documents?"

"I do."

"I remember how he talked about that kind of thing—he told me about some journalists who died in suspicious circumstances. But he could be kind of paranoid sometimes."

"Right."

"Anyway, I don't believe that the US government would do something like kill an American reporter. I think that's nutso. That's like, I don't know, something out of the Jason Bourne movies."

"I don't know, man. You think you can get to someone in Homicide?"

"Probably. But these investigations probably take a couple days at least. There's toxicology results and stuff like that."

"Lanny had a thumb drive, a USB drive, with documents on it. He might have copied them to his own laptop, but I really doubt he'd put it on the *Globe*'s computer system. He was too careful."

"Paranoid, you mean?"

"So I want to know if they found that among his stuff. Was it stolen? Is it missing? And I want to know if they can tell whether he was suffocated."

"Tanner," Carl said, his voice quiet. "I knew the guy pretty well. Known him for years. And I say it's definitely possible that he committed suicide. He wasn't the most—stable, centered guy around. He lived alone, worked all the time, you know."

"Let's see what you find out from the Brookline police."

"Sure. I think you're a little on edge, T-boy."

"Well, you did invite me to stay here, right?"

"Your house is a goddamned crime scene, Tanner; that's why."

There was more to it, Tanner knew. Carl wasn't a muscle head, or wasn't just a muscle head. He'd once been a vulnerable kid who eventually learned how to defend himself and protect others. That was probably why he loved teaching kids. "Okay, well, I appreciate it."

"What about the senator's laptop? Do you still have it?"

"Yeah."

"Keeping it somewhere safe?"

Tanner nodded. "Somewhere safe."

Carl smiled a crooked smile. "Thought about giving it back?"

Sure, he almost said, he'd considered just calling Senator Susan Robbins's office in Washington and telling whomever he could get on the phone, no doubt some twenty-four-year-old intern, that he had the senator's MacBook Air and they could have the damn thing back; he didn't want it.

And then he remembered what Lanny had said. *That laptop is the only reason you're still alive.*

He shrugged. "So where's the famous futon?"

* * *

Tanner lurched awake in the unfamiliar darkness.

His phone moaned and then trilled. He reached out to silence it, couldn't find the bedside table, suddenly remembered there was no bedside table in Carl's guest bedroom. Why the hell was his alarm going off in the middle of the night?

It took his eyes a moment to focus, his brain a much quicker instant to realize: this wasn't an alarm. This was someone calling.

The numbers at the top of the display were a 617 area code, which was the Boston area, and a number that ended in two zeros. Some kind of company.

A junk robocall? At whatever the hell time it was in the morning?

Underneath the phone number, in smaller type, it said "Brighton, MA."

The warehouse was in Brighton.

He grabbed the phone, swiped it to answer.

"This Mr. Tanner?" a man's gruff voice said.

"Who's this?"

"Mr. Tanner, this is Lenehan in building security at 50 Mayfield Street. There seems to be a fire in the rear of the Tanner Roast offices, and you're on the contact list."

"Oh shit. What about—?"

"Fire department's been called; they're on their way."

"Thank you. How—bad is it?"

He got out of bed, swung his feet around to the floor. The room was unaccustomedly dark.

"It's hard to tell, but, well, just based on the smoke, it looks pretty bad. I don't know what else to tell you."

By now he was fully awake. "Oh my God."

"Any special instructions you want me to give the firemen?"

"No, I—oh God—I'm on my way."

Carl was out in the hallway outside his bedroom already, wearing a Red Sox T-shirt and a pair of boxer shorts. "Everything okay?"

"There's a fire at my company," Tanner said.

"Oh shit. You need help or something?"

"Fire department's on their way. Go back to bed. I have to get out there."

29

Tanner felt the first droplets of rain, a faint drizzle, as he was getting into his car on Comm. Ave. in front of Carl's house. The asphalt pavement gleamed under the yellowish sodium light, speckling with water. His stomach clenched at the thought of Tanner Roast being ravaged, maybe destroyed. He wondered if the rain might help slow down or extinguish the fire, and he hoped the rain increased.

His car, a six-year-old Lexus GS 350, a silver four-door sedan, was a mess. Empty plastic bottles of spring water cluttered the floor on the passenger's side. He rarely had a passenger, so he felt little need to keep the car clean, until it got to be too much to tolerate. Tonight he paid no attention; he drove almost mindlessly. He flicked on the windshield wipers when the rain started smearing the windscreen.

Centre Street at three thirty in the morning was empty except for a few cars, people going to work or returning home from a late shift, maybe a guy returning home after a late-night assignation.

And he thought: *Could the cause of the fire possibly be entirely accidental?* Could one of the roasters—say, the older one, the Probat—have had some sort of electrical malfunction? Could someone have left the heat on? It could get up to a thousand degrees, easy enough to start a fire. The chaff, the skins that slough off the coffee beans as they roast, was light and dry and combustible. A single stray spark would be enough to ignite it.

But none of these was the cause of the fire, he knew. The cause would be arson. He'd been targeted, and with him went everyone whose livelihoods depended on him. Now his own creation had been targeted, the company he had built over the last eight years ruined. The equipment costs alone would be in the seven figures. His insurance policy was way insufficient. If he lost the Probat roaster, he was screwed.

And maybe he had gotten lucky. He was alive.

Lanny Roth had made phone calls, set off some kind of alarm deep inside the secret government, and was killed because of what he had found out.

Maybe this was a warning? Was that too twisted a possibility? *Here's what we're capable of doing, now give us what we want?*

So Lanny was right: that laptop was his life insurance.

They—the faceless, unnamed "they" who had killed Lanny—had somehow found out where Lanny had gotten the documents he was asking about. Whom he'd gotten them from. Then they'd placed a call to Tanner, who'd refused to cooperate. So they'd broken into his house. Breaking into his place of business was harder because of the security system . . .

Suddenly he wondered. Was it possible they'd set off a fire in order to provide cover for a break-in at the warehouse? Or was that just paranoid thinking?

The rain had stopped; the windshield wipers slowed and then stopped. He accelerated onto the ramp that led to the Mass. Turnpike, then slowed at the E-ZPass gate. The only vehicles on the Mass. Pike were long-haul trucks and a VW convertible weaving erratically in the fast lane, no doubt someone coming home from a party.

He found himself driving faster and faster, and when he realized he was going over eighty, he took his foot off the accelerator. The last thing he needed was to be pulled over for a speeding ticket while his entire business, his investment, and yes, his nest egg, went up in flames and smoke and ash.

He reached the exit and then went through the complicated series of turns and switchbacks that led him to Brighton. Then he spotted the Tastee Doughnuts, the beacon that told him he was in Brighton. (Great doughnuts, not-bad cheap coffee.) He turned left, then made two rights and then a left onto the long one-way that was Mayfield Street.

On the right was a chain-link fence and then the tracks of the T, the Boston subway system, which ran aboveground in some places. On the left was the block-long redbrick building that housed the offices of an old-time safe and lock company. The redbrick warehouse buildings continued, one after another, all of them the size of the entire block, for a couple of blocks, and then came 50 Mayfield Street, where Tanner Roast was located.

And just up ahead, maybe half a block away, some guy was waving him down. A big man in a soiled sleeveless T-shirt, a so-called wifebeater. Bald, but shiny bald, and a goatee dyed black. On his neck and every exposed inch of his arms were tats, like he was a walking ad for a tattoo shop. He wasn't old; he wasn't young; he just looked powerful and all business.

He continued to wave with his left hand, wave him over to the side of the street, and then his right hand came up. In it was an immense black weapon, a veritable hand cannon. Tanner knew nothing about guns or calibers, but he knew it was a semiautomatic pistol, and it was huge.

The man locked eyes with Tanner.

They were the basilisk eyes of someone used to getting his way. It was the look of an apex predator ready to pounce.

The man was going to kill him.

And in a sudden cascade of knowledge, all became clear to Tanner.

There's no fire.

No fire trucks racing through the streets, no smoke, no flashing lights, no traffic blockades.

Just this one guy with a gun.

Someone had called his cell, pretending to be with building security. Middle of the night, when the illogical can seem logical. When you're disoriented and gullible.

Knew he'd have to drive out to the scene.

Flushing him out from wherever he was staying, which wasn't home.

To kill him. On a street where there were no eyes, no witnesses.

The man-mountain was walking closer, his gun pointed. He shook his head, stepped right into the path of the Lexus, his left hand up, palm open, pointing the pistol in his other hand.

This was an ambush. He'd walked—driven—right into it.

And he did not want to be taken.

His right foot hovered over the two pedals: gas and brake. *Do I pull over, submit to his request like a lamb to the slaughter?*

The man with all the tats waved again, repeating the gesture as if Tanner was a slow child who hadn't heard his instructions.

He expected Tanner to obey, to pull over because he was told to.

Tanner had read somewhere about a scientific study in which neuroscientists using an MRI discovered activity in the human brain indicating that we make decisions whole seconds before we're consciously aware of making them.

The man is trying to kill me. I can't let him.

His lizard brain then made a decision his conscious mind would never have made.

He floored the accelerator.

The car leapt forward mightily and struck the bald

man with a sickening thud. He slammed his foot on the brake. The car screeched to a halt. He glanced in the rearview. Behind him, the man lay crumpled on the asphalt, his head canted at a strange angle to the rest of the body. He wasn't moving.

He'd probably killed the man.

The rain was coming down in sheets, the wind picking up.

Tanner floored the Lexus and sped down the block and the next one, past the Tanner Roast building, which was dark, no fire trucks in view, then turned left and pulled over to the side of the road. He opened his car door and stumbled out onto the deserted street, into the hard, driving rain, the torrential downpour.

He doubled over and vomited onto the road, gagging and retching.

He had killed a man. He had killed a man.

The rain immediately sluiced away the vomit along with the road grime, as if everything could be washed away, washed clean.

As if anything could.

30

The damned Problem Solver had gone dark.

For much of the day, through meetings and phone calls and teleconferences, Will fretted. Finally, in midafternoon, he closed his office door and fired up Tor, the anonymous browser. It took a few seconds to establish a secure connection, and then he was in the darknet. He opened ProtonMail and signed in. Once he was in, it asked for a second password to "decrypt mailbox." He entered it. It took a few seconds more.

The inbox was empty. Just the old message from yesterday. No new message.

It had been more than twenty-four hours, and he hadn't heard anything. A lot could happen in twenty-four hours. A lot could happen to the boss's laptop.

The Problem Solver had said he'd e-mail Will at the ProtonMail e-mail address as soon as he had the laptop. But he'd never said Will couldn't contact him. So Will opened the old message and hit Reply and typed, "Anything?"

Encrypting . . . sending . . . and it was gone.

He checked his regular e-mail and found a few messages he could deal with—"Got it" and "OK." He looked back at the ProtonMail account, and still nothing. But everything took a while in the dark web, encrypting and decrypting and so on, and the Problem Solver probably didn't live on his e-mail the way Will did.

There was a knock on his door. "Come on in," Will said. It was his legislative director, Samantha, with a budget requisition. Senator Robbins's default answer on budget requests was usually no. She was, as she liked to say on the campaign trail, "tightfisted with the people's money."

"What's up?" he said, and he tried to sound interested.

Later he went through the whole ritual again, opening the Tor browser, signing in to ProtonMail . . . decrypting . . . and there was still nothing new there.

He had two phone numbers for the Problem Solver. The first was the one Senator Sullivan had scrawled on a napkin. But the Problem Solver had told him never to use it. The second was the number on Mumble.com. The Problem Solver had never told him not to use that number.

So he signed into Mumble.com, and twenty seconds later he clicked on the phone number and he waited for that robot voice.

And waited.

And there was no answer. That left the number the Problem Solver had told him never to call. The number on the napkin. He pulled out the cheapo burner phone and looked at it for a moment. What would happen if he called it? He'd risk angering the high-tech hit man known as the Problem Solver? So what, at this point?

He bit his tongue and thought about it another moment, and then his desk phone rang.

He picked it up.

"This Abbott?" a man's voice said.

"It is."

"It's Owen Sullivan."

"Oh, Senator. Nice to hear from you."

"Listen to me," the senator said angrily. "When I was a kid I had a G.I. Joe I was totally obsessed with, and one day I lent it to a classmate. Know what happened?"

"Uh, no."

"The kid twisted its head off. And that was the last time I ever let anyone borrow an action figure."

"Okay . . . ?"

"What the hell did you do, Abbott? No—don't answer that. I don't want to know. Just don't ever ask me for any more favors, you get it?"

There was a click, and the line went dead.

Will sat there for a moment, his heart hammering. What was Senator Sullivan so furious about? A G.I. Joe whose head was twisted off? The point being . . . ?

Will had a bad feeling. Something unfortunate had happened.

He Googled "Boston police blotter" and pulled up the Boston Police Department's public website. This was much fancier than the old "police blotters" in newspapers that just listed local crimes. There were headlines and photos. The lead story concerned a drug arrest, a suspect in custody after a search warrant led to the recovery of large quantities of ammunition, drugs, and cash in Mattapan. He scrolled down through the photos of hundred-dollar-bills and guns and bullets and Ziploc bags of some white substance. Next item was a statement from the police commissioner regarding community policing. Then an item about body-worn cameras.

Then there was a small item headlined DEATH INVESTIGATION IN THE DISTRICT D-14 AREA OF BRIGHTON.

> At about 4:05 AM, officers assigned to District D-14 responded to a call for a person injured in the area of Mayfield Street in Brighton. On arrival, officers located a male victim suffering from injuries apparently sustained in a motor vehicle accident. The victim was pronounced deceased. The victim has since been identified as Dennis Hurley, 52, of Charlestown.
>
> The Boston Police Department is actively reviewing the facts and circumstances surrounding this incident. Anyone with information is asked to call the Homicide Unit at (617) 343-4470.

Charlestown.

He swallowed. His throat was parched. He entered

"Dennis Hurley" and "Charlestown MA" into Google, and he pulled up an article.

POLICE INVESTIGATING DEATH OF CHARLESTOWN MAN, the headline said.

There was a photograph of an odd-looking bald man, vacant blue-gray eyes spaced widely apart, sunken cheeks, tattoos visible on his neck.

> Boston area police are investigating the motor-vehicle-related death of a Charlestown man well known to law enforcement. Dennis Hurley, 52, of Charlestown, was a person of interest in connection with at least a dozen homicides. A veteran of the US Marine Corps, dishonorably discharged, Hurley was believed to be associated with the Charlestown Mob. In 2014, Hurley was arrested and charged with cruelty to animals in a particularly gruesome incident in which he sprayed lighter fluid on a neighbor's dog and set it afire.

Will read the article over twice. *Hurley had to be the Problem Solver.* A bad guy from Charlestown with a dishonorable discharge, an ex-Marine associated with the mob: this was the guy. He had a sinking feeling.

Dead. How could that be?

Holy shit.

Who the hell is Michael Tanner?

31

Will was suffused with dread, almost paralyzed with it. He kept staring at the text on the screen, his stomach queasy and tight and roiling with acid.

Michael Tanner—who else could it be?—had killed a man named Dennis Hurley, the thug known as the Problem Solver. And not just a thug, but a hard man, a tough guy, a Marine. How was it possible that Tanner had killed him?

He went through it all again in his mind, as if he were replaying the videotape.

First, Tanner had flatly denied that he had the senator's laptop, and then he'd *killed* the man Will had hired to retrieve it.

Which meant Tanner was not who he appeared to be, not just some businessman, some entrepreneur.

And that in turn raised the terrible question: Was it possible that Tanner had *deliberately* taken the laptop—that the switch was in fact no accident?

Will's head swam, trying to make sense of all the countervailing facts. No, it just didn't seem possible. Whoever Tanner was really, there was no way he could have deliberately ended up in line right behind the senator at the Los Angeles airport, or right in front of her . . . That theory just required too many coincidences. It strained credibility.

But what if . . . What if Tanner had come to realize that he'd ended up with the laptop belonging to a US senator, that on it were some of the nation's—the world's—most precious, most explosive secrets, and what if he had *done something with it*?

Say he'd recognized its value and he'd sold it to someone, to a ring. To any of a number of willing buyers. Spies from China or Russia or somewhere else, maybe even ISIS or al-Qaeda. Terrorists.

That would explain why all of his attempts, and the Russian's, had failed. He was in over his head.

And as much as he dreaded it, he had to tell the boss.

The senator was wearing her navy-blue suit, which concerned Will. The somber blue outfit meant she was in one of her all-business, no-breaks, work-late-hours moods. It meant she was grouchy, impatient, peevish. She would not welcome a private talk, especially one that threatened to derail everything in her carefully ordered life.

Will had to be careful in what he told her. She knew nothing about the Problem Solver, and that was how it had to stay. She knew nothing about his efforts to retrieve the laptop. She had to be kept innocent of the operational details.

Senator Susan Robbins gave him the death-ray stare over her reading glasses, and Will felt his guts churning. "I'm not sure I understand," she said, her voice quiet.

"I think there's more going on than we thought originally. Without going into details, we took some serious measures, and we keep coming up with nothing."

"What does that mean? You know what? No. Stop. Don't tell me any more." She put her hands up, palms out. "You have a job to do, and how you do it is up to you. What you have to do—I don't care. I don't want to know."

"I think it may be time to tell the Senate Security Office."

"Are you out of your *mind*?" she snapped. "We've talked about this. The moment they hear what I did, I'll be sanctioned, I'll be thrown off the intel committee, and the whole thing becomes public. And who knows where that leads? I could be forced to resign. Or worse . . ."

Will nodded, something bitter and metallic in his mouth. This was always the problem, the reason he'd told her it was ill-advised to slip classified documents out of the SCIF in the first place. If anyone found out, it could become a huge scandal. She was playing with matches in a gas plant.

But that was a fait accompli. It had been up to him to clean things up, and he'd failed at it. He was ashamed. Ashamed of having failed, ashamed to acknowledge his defeat. And—he might as well admit it—he was afraid of her anger.

"I don't know what you've done, what hasn't worked, but you have to do what's necessary to get that thing back. You understand?"

He nodded, looked into her eyes.

"I wonder if you do. This is something you need to take care of yourself. Personally. This isn't something you can . . . outsource. I think that's clear now. But if you're not comfortable with that—"

"No, I am—"

"If you don't want to get your hands dirty, let me know *now*. Will, do we have a problem?"

He shook his head. "Not at all."

"Sit down, Will."

He did.

"You ever wonder why I hired you in the first place?"

He narrowed his eyes a bit, unsure how to respond.

But Susan didn't wait for him. "The candidates I passed over for you. A Rhodes scholar from Yale, a lacrosse player, well-rounded. A summa from Middlebury with a graduate degree from the Woodrow Wilson School. An editor of the *Harvard Law Review*. That's the caliber of people I could have hired. But I chose you. William Abbott, an awkward kid from a decent state school. Why on earth do you think that was?"

Will's head was bowed, eyes downcast, a pensive pose. He shook his head.

"Because I saw something in you, Will."

Will raised his head, now looking directly at her, like a flower turning toward the sun. He gave a small smile. He noticed, not for the first time, the blue of her eyes, dazzling like some rare mineral. The whites were a pure porcelain white, with no trace of red. Every movement of her hands was precise and controlled. Like she belonged to a species more refined than his.

"I saw something in you," she repeated.

"Yeah?"

"You know what that was? Something *damaged*. Something not quite right. I'm damaged too, Will."

Will felt cold now, and the smile faded quickly from his face.

"You're damaged; I'm damaged. We don't play it safe. We don't always play by the rules. But it's people like us who *make shit happen*. Because there's a hole in us that can never be filled. Maybe it's a bottomless pit. But we're not like other people. We do whatever it takes. Can you do whatever it takes, Will?"

He swallowed hard, and at first his words were nearly inaudible. "Yes, I can, Susan," he said. He cleared his throat and said it again, louder. "I can and I will."

She leaned forward. "You know, for some people, being a United States senator would be the achievement of a lifetime. But for us, it's a stepping-stone. You know that, don't you, Will?" She leaned forward and gripped his forearm.

He nodded.

"If we get this right, and we catch a lucky break or

two, you and I will be aiming higher. We have bigger things in mind, the two of us. Don't we, Will?"

He felt tears leak into his eyes. He loved this woman like he loved no one else, not even Jen. But it was a different kind of love. Greater than the love of a man for his wife, a child for his mother. She was someone special, Will was certain; a person of historical importance. As she rose, so would he.

"Don't we, Will?" she said again.

"Yes," he said. "Yes, we do."

32

Will could hear baby Travis crying when he entered his apartment building, all the way down in the lobby. It was late, almost ten at night, and he was just returning from a fund-raiser. He wondered if everyone in the building could hear the cries throughout the day. They must. Which meant that his neighbors really were decent folks: no one had complained. Not yet, anyway. Maybe because the baby was just a newborn.

Well, so much for turning to his e-mail in the home office. As soon as he came in the front door Jen carried red-faced Travis over, waited for Will to put down his briefcase, and then handed him their baby.

"You try."

He held Travis tightly against his chest; the baby liked being swaddled close. But that didn't stop him from wailing. Sometimes that little creature broke his heart.

"He won't take a bottle. I tried again."

"How about you feeding him—you know . . . ?" Jen

had only breastfed him; they never used formula. They'd tried, but the baby had refused it.

She shook her head. "I saw the doctor today."

"What's wrong?"

"What do you mean, what's wrong? He won't stop crying. And you know what he told me? I'm not producing enough milk. Our baby is hungry!"

"Really?"

"We have to supplement with formula. No matter how much he fights it." She handed him a nursing bottle of white liquid. It was warm in his hand. He slipped the nipple end into Travis's mouth, mid-cry, and to his surprise Travis latched right on, sucking away greedily. The apartment was suddenly blissfully silent. He felt the little baby's warmth against his chest. He inhaled Travis's sweet milky smell and it melted something hard inside him, and he thought: *I can't lose this. This is life itself.*

I have so much to lose.

And he thought about what Susan had said. About him being damaged. She was probably right. He was damaged. He wondered whether Jen saw this in him. If she did, if she ever really saw inside of him, she wouldn't love him. He was sure of that.

"Well," she said. "Aren't you the expert." With no warning, she started crying. "I can't even do *this* right. Do you know what it's like spending all day with him? I'm going out of my mind."

"You need a break," he said. "You need to get out of the house." She was on maternity leave from her corporate law firm and didn't sound eager to get back to work.

"And how exactly am I going to do that? You know we can't afford a nanny or an au pair."

"I keep telling you, my mother would be delighted to help out."

"Your *mother*? You're kidding me."

"She can move right in upstairs. You've got too much to do. Mom's got too little. It's win-win. And she loves babies. Why don't I call her right now?"

"I do *not* want your mother living here."

He shrugged, smiled. "She'd be happy to do it. All we have to do is call."

"No way!"

She wouldn't complain again, not for a while. The threat of his mother moving in was, to her, too appalling. He felt a pulse of satisfaction: he'd successfully handled the problem. That was what he was good at. Sometimes he felt as if everything would fall apart if he wasn't there to hold it together. "I have to go out of town tomorrow," he said. "Just for the day."

"Chicago?"

He shook his head. "Boston."

"She giving a speech?"

He didn't like lying, but he also couldn't tell her the real reason he had to go to Boston. "Just a fund-raising thing. A donor-cultivation visit." He looked around. The apartment was a pigsty, but he knew better than to ask her to tidy up.

Will could never admit this to her, but he preferred being at work to being at home. That was the simple truth.

At work he was necessary and appreciated. He knew he was helping advance the interests of Senator Susan Robbins. He was sure she was destined for the White House, and he intended to be right there with her. Chief of staff to the first woman president sounded awfully good to him.

But this ongoing nightmare of the missing laptop—it was getting worse and worse, and he feared it might become uncontainable.

Because there were a few scenarios that now seemed likely. Like reading about CHRYSALIS in *The Washington Post* or *The New York Times.* And the Justice Department launching an investigation, which would surely lead to him. He could go to prison for what he'd done for Susan.

He didn't want to think about it, but he had to force himself to do so.

Retrieving that laptop was crucial. It would keep him from going to jail and keep the boss on the path to the White House.

But if he failed—if his trip to Boston was unsuccessful . . .

The possibility scared the hell out of him.

But he was equally scared of what he might have to do.

He flashed on what the Problem Solver had said. *I don't work on a leash, okay? I do what I do. You tell me what you need. You don't tell me how to get it. I do whatever I deem necessary.*

He had to do whatever was necessary.

But how far would he go? What would he do?

Maybe the better question was: What *wouldn't* he do? There was so much to lose.

33

Tanner woke at seven in the morning, his eyelids like sandpaper, his head throbbing. He'd barely slept.

Yesterday had been a blur. Early in the morning, rattled by his attacker's gruesome death, he had driven around aimlessly in the rain, in a state of near desperation. At one point he'd parked and got out and scanned the front end of the car, by the glare of a streetlamp, terrified he might find visible damage. But he didn't see any. If there had been blood, the rain had washed it away.

He'd killed a man. It had been in self-defense, but would that be enough to clear him if the police came around asking questions? Was that considered a hit-and-run? Not only had he killed someone, but he had left the scene of a crime. After running through dire scenario after dire scenario, he finally decided that he should just drive back to Carl's house and say nothing to anyone about what he'd done, what had happened. He could report what had happened to the police and spend the next year of his life dealing with a homicide inquest. On top of everything else. And that was impossible.

He was exhausted, but he had to go to the office early. A morning meeting had been scheduled at the last minute, some guy who represented a real-estate tycoon with major holdings in restaurants and hotels and who wanted to do business. A deal like that could represent salvation for Tanner Roast. So he had to get to the office and be alert and prepared.

When he was in good form, he was a top-notch salesman, sure. But he wasn't in good form now, far from it: he was tapped out and scared. He wasn't thinking clearly. He didn't trust his own judgment at a time like this.

Karen Wynant intercepted him at the coffee machine. He was pouring out a mug of whatever the coffee of the day was when she approached. She had her contacts in and had put on makeup, lipstick and eyeliner. She was dressed for a sales call.

"You okay?" she said, alarmed.

"How bad do I look?"

"Not so good. Are you sick? The guy's coming in fifteen minutes—I said I'd say hi, make him some coffee, show him around, and then you two can meet."

"That's fine. I can use a little more time to wake up."

"Seriously, everything okay?"

"I'm fine. What do we know about this guy?"

"His name is Thomas Berlin, and he works for Morton

Nathanson, on the hospitality side of his business empire."

"Any idea what he has in mind?"

She shook her head. "I wasn't going to turn him away. Egghead's definitely going with Cortado."

"Egghead—oh right." He could barely concentrate. He kept seeing that guy with a giant gun waving at him. He could hear the sound of the impact, of his car colliding with the killer, that *thump* when he ran the guy over, crushing him. The image and the sound played over and over in his head like a tape loop. He took a sip of coffee and could barely taste it. He was nauseated. His stomach felt filled with sloshing acid. "Any other cheery news to share?"

"Sorry. I wanted you to know when I knew." She paused. "Is the Four Seasons a done deal? Like, definitely not happening?"

"It's over. It's done. Why?"

"Because City Roast hasn't announced it."

He nodded. "Ah. I think I know why. Their IPO."

"What does that have to do with anything?"

"You know they're filing to go public, right? Well, they're in the quiet period before the IPO."

"So?"

"So they're not allowed to make any announcements material to the . . ." His mind had begun to wander. He heard the thump. "Whatever, whatever. That's all. After they go public, they'll announce their new customer."

"Okay. Do you want me to sit in on your meeting with Berlin?"

He smiled. The concern in her eyes was genuine, almost maternal. He must really look bad.

"Seriously, everything okay?"

"I'll be okay, I promise."

When he got to his office, he glanced at himself in the antique Maxwell House mirror on the wall and decided he needed to shave. He pulled an electric shaver out of the bottom drawer of his desk, plugged it in, and ran it around his face.

Now he was starting to feel spasms of anxiety. What if he'd been caught on camera yesterday morning? But the tattooed guy would have thought of this. He would have chosen a spot that wasn't surveilled. Still . . .

He sat down at his desk and opened his work e-mail, and a while later there was a knock on his open office door. It was Karen with an unprepossessing guy in his late thirties, prematurely balding.

"This is Tom," Karen said.

"Michael Tanner," he said, shaking the man's hand, looking him in the eye. Tom Berlin looked like someone who was used to being in the background, not the foreground. He seemed an odd type to be in sales; not a natural fit.

Karen left, and the man sat in the chair facing Tanner's desk.

"Can I get you some coffee, or are you all set?"

"I'm good," the visitor said. His eyes roamed the tight confines of Tanner's office. "Caffeinated to the gills."

"With the good stuff, I hope," Tanner said. "So you work for Mort Nathanson."

The man glanced around. "Actually, Michael, I don't work for Mort Nathanson, and my name is not Tom Berlin. I'm sorry for the ruse."

"Excuse me?"

"I'm here under false pretenses," said the man. "My name is Will Abbott, and I'm the chief of staff to Senator Susan Robbins. And I think you have something of hers."

34

Tanner Roast was a smaller operation than Will expected—just a modest warehouse space that connected to front offices. A couple of coffee roasters and maybe ten or twenty employees, located in a not-great part of Boston. He'd gone there straight from the airport, via taxi, and arrived twenty minutes early. He'd walked around the urban neighborhood, thinking, and the third time he went by the company's headquarters, he was buzzed in.

The sales director, a woman named Karen something, greeted him. She was short and sort of arty-looking, with an efficient pageboy hairstyle and a blue raw-silk dress. They'd spoken on the phone yesterday when he told her he worked for Mort Nathanson and was going to be in Boston for meetings and wanted to squeeze in one last-minute appointment, with the head of Tanner Roast. She'd quickly said yes.

He worried about how long he was going to have to keep up the pretense of being in the hospitality industry.

How long he *could* keep it up. He'd done his late-night homework, of course. He could pull off maybe five or ten minutes of coffee-related conversation with Tanner, but maybe that was all he needed.

But that anxiety was nothing compared to what he felt at the prospect of meeting a killer—the guy who must have killed the Problem Solver. Tanner was, had to be, a dangerous guy. To do what he did, to actually run a man over with a car.

And yet, to his surprise, Michael Tanner turned out to be an easygoing alpha male, the sort of guy to whom good things just seemed to happen, the sort of guy he'd always disliked. A guy who seemed to be comfortable in his own skin. Opportunities just threw themselves at him. He was a man who never had to struggle in life. Will didn't like the guy. He'd met people like that before, particularly in college. Tanner reminded him of Peter Green, the guy he got elected student president, whose campaign he'd managed.

But he didn't seem like the kind of person who could kill a man in cold blood.

He wondered what the deal was, why Tanner was holding on to the laptop. What he wanted. What his long game was. He didn't fit the profile of an activist, an agitator. Was he a mercenary? Did he plan to sell the classified documents? Was he in a ring with others?

Why was he refusing to give it back?

"Can I get you some coffee, or are you all set?" Tanner said.

"I'm good. Caffeinated to the gills."

"With the good stuff, I hope," Tanner said. "So you work for Mort Nathanson?"

And Will had a sudden realization. It was a clever piece of wisdom that Susan Robbins liked to repeat: Sometimes the best lie of all is the God's honest truth. Just carefully edited.

He would tell the truth.

He took a breath. "Actually, Michael, I don't work for Mort Nathanson, and my name is not Tom Berlin. I'm sorry for the ruse."

Tanner looked shocked, as Will expected he would. "Excuse me?"

"I'm here under false pretenses," he went on, his heart thumping. "My name is Will Abbott, and I'm the chief of staff to Senator Susan Robbins. And I think you have something of hers. Because we have something of yours."

He lifted his leather briefcase and unsnapped the latches. Then he pulled out Tanner's MacBook Air, with an air of ceremony, and placed it on the desk.

Tanner's eyes narrowed. "You called."

"I did, yes. That was me. And that was wrong. I made an error in judgment. I totally screwed up. I thought that if you knew the laptop belonged to a senator, you might look through it. And I'm sorry for that." He pointedly didn't ask whether Tanner had the laptop. He would assume it, take it for granted without requiring Tanner to confirm it overtly, not give him a chance to deny it, and in the process corner the guy.

Meanwhile he was waiting for the surge of righteous anger, and sure enough it came. "Was it an error in judgment to break into my house looking for it?" Tanner said, raising his voice.

"I don't know anything about that," Will said flatly. He'd been prepared for that too. "No one connected to Senator Robbins would authorize something like that."

"And was it an error in judgment to kill my friend Landon Roth?"

Landon who? "I have no idea what you're talking about!"

"A reporter for *The Boston Globe.* And a good man."

Will shrugged, spread his hands, shook his head. "I'm sorry; I don't know anything about that." What the hell was he talking about? Someone was killed, someone else? For an instant he thought of the Problem Solver—but no way the guy would have killed someone connected with Tanner without telling Will first, without demanding payment for it. Will had transferred ten thousand dollars from the Robbins Victory Fund to the Problem Solver's account and reported the expense as a campaign consulting fee. Oppo research, you could call it.

Tanner's face seemed frozen in an expression of anger mixed with hurt. Will went on: "Let me lay it all out for you, tell you why I'm here. I'm going to put myself entirely at your mercy. Your laptop got accidentally switched with my boss's, Senator Robbins's—and I need to get hers back. There's some sensitive information on it. Classified stuff."

Slowly, Tanner's expression began to soften. "Classified?" he said.

Will nodded. "And it would be a big black eye for me, and for the senator, if that got out. And so—I'm putting myself in your hands." He paused a beat. "Please."

Tanner now looked as if he was deep in thought. He put his hands together, tented his fingers.

It needed another note, Will thought, a touch more self-recriminatory. "I should have been straight with you from the beginning," he said. "And for that I apologize."

"How did you know it was mine? I didn't put my name on it."

Will took another breath, not wanting to divulge how nervous he felt. In his best manager's voice, he said, "We have IT specialists on our staff, and we asked one of them to get into your computer to find out whose it was. We had no choice. Given the circumstances."

He paused and looked Michael Tanner in the eye. "I have no idea how he did it. But he was able to pull up your name and the fact that you were based in Boston. We put two and two together and located you. I mean, you're not exactly in hiding."

Tanner nodded, compressed his lips. Then, without saying anything, he slowly got up, his eyes trained at some point in the distance.

Tanner's mind raced. This Abbott guy appeared to be telling the truth. Tanner was fairly good at reading people—as a salesman, he had to be—and Abbott seemed honest and straightforward. The man was pitching; that was obvious—but he was pitching with his heart. He meant it; he was speaking the truth.

Returning the laptop, with its classified documents, was the right move, he'd decided. The senator's chief of staff was no heavy. He was just an awkward DC staffer wearing a navy blazer that didn't quite sit right around the shoulders.

I won, Will realized.

He had done it. His sell job actually worked. The boss's old saw had turned out to be exactly right. The best lie of all is the God's honest truth.

He bit the inside of his lip but was unable to keep himself from breaking out in a big triumphant smile. He'd done it. *He'd manipulated by telling the truth.*

When Tanner had left his office, still slowly and deliberately, Will knew he was going to retrieve the boss's laptop. In a few minutes, Will would finally take possession of the thing.

And then—he'd thought this through a number of times, and there was no choice—Tanner would have to be involved in a traffic accident. As a fatality.

There was just no other way. Will had no choice. He would have to outsource the job to someone reliable. With the Problem Solver dead, that left the Russian guy who'd done the burglary. Arranging a car accident was probably in his skill set. People would say, *Oh, Boston drivers . . .*

It would work because it had to work.

Anything else was unthinkable.

As Tanner came around behind the desk, he happened to catch a glimpse of Abbott in the Maxwell House mirror.

Abbott, who thought Tanner couldn't see him.

Abbott was smiling.

It was more than just a smile; it was a smirk.

A triumphant smirk, the look of someone who's just gotten away with something big. Puzzled, Tanner left his office and walked into the adjoining warehouse. There, he stopped in front of the kitchen cabinet, behind which was the safe.

He stared at the cabinet for a moment.

And he realized that he was being bamboozled. He was being led on. Tanner, who could bullshit with the best of them, was being manipulated by a master bullshit artist.

That smile on Abbott's face—he'd seen that same smile on Blake Gifford. That fangy smile of triumph. The faint quiver of muscles trying to repress it. It was Bugs Bunny knowing that Elmer Fudd's lunch pail is filled with TNT.

Sal Persico, his genius roaster, was there. "I just brewed a fresh batch of the Colombian, the Villa Maria," Sal said. "It's awesome."

"Perfect," Tanner said. He'd bought the beans from a

finca in the Nariño region, in southeast Colombia, on the border with Ecuador.

He poured out two mugs of coffee and carried them back through the warehouse to his office. Abbott looked up expectantly as he returned. He no doubt expected Tanner to be carrying a laptop.

Tanner set the mug of coffee down on the desk in front of Abbott. "Tell me what you think," he said. "I'm pretty sure you'll like it."

35

Will arrived home in a taxi from National Airport in a funk. He was weary and defeated and angry, and he was in no mood to deal with a cranky Jennifer and a no-doubt squalling Travis.

But when he unlocked the front door, all he heard was quiet. Jen was sitting in her favorite chair reading *Entertainment Weekly* in a cone of light from the standing lamp. She put her finger to her lips. "*Shh!* He's actually sleeping!"

"Now that we're not starving him to death," Will said in a normal speaking voice.

"Shh!"

"I think Dr. Blum said you're not supposed to stay quiet while the baby's sleeping so he doesn't, I don't know, need to sleep in a cork-lined room for the rest of his life."

"I am finally getting a chance to read something that's not the label on a formula bottle. When you wake him up, *you're* taking him."

"Fair enough," Will said in a quiet voice. He didn't want to fight with her. He just wanted to be alone right now, figuring out his next move. He dreaded having to give the boss the bad news. He didn't know how she'd react, but he was pretty sure she'd be angry and not hold back.

He had thought he'd played things exactly right with Michael Tanner in Boston, that Tanner had gotten up to get the laptop, finally. But when he came back with a couple of mugs of coffee, he'd said, "I wish I could help you, Will. I really appreciate your coming to Boston to return my laptop. I feel like I should at the very least reimburse you for the train or the plane or whatever."

"What about the senator's . . . ?"

"I actually lost my laptop in LA," Tanner said. "I didn't take the wrong one. I just must have left it there—I was in a rush."

"You don't have the senator's laptop?"

"Sorry." Tanner shrugged.

He was lying, Will was certain. But how to get him to admit he had it? Will was stymied. He was near speechless. He'd almost had the guy, but somehow he'd lost him. He didn't know why. But he negotiated all the time, and he knew when the drawbridge had gone up.

Now Jen asked sweetly, "How was your trip?"

"Fine. No big deal." He set down his shoulder bag.

"Success?"

"Mm-hmm."

"You get a good contribution?"

Jen understood the money chase that politics had become.

"Not bad."

"God, wouldn't it be great if you got a cut of all the money you help raise? Like a commission or something?"

"Yeah, that would be illegal, I'm pretty sure."

His cell phone rang, and he saw who it was. His stomach twisted. He hit Answer as he moved toward the bedroom and a little privacy.

"Do you have it?" the senator asked without preface.

"No."

"What? But you—"

"I totally had him. Then the fish wriggled off the goddamned hook."

"I don't understand. What's going on? He won't give it back?"

"He denies he ever had it."

"He denies it? Is that— Is it possible he doesn't have it? Seriously?"

"He has to have it. I *know* he does."

"So how can we—"

"Maybe we shouldn't talk—" *on the phone,* he wanted to say.

"I want a plan to get it back."

"I'm on it," he said. "Not to worry."

"At this point," she said, "we both need to be worried. Very worried."

And she hung up.

36

After Will Abbott had left his office, Tanner sat at his desk and thought for a few minutes. He let the phone ring.

It had been a close call. He had almost opened the safe. Fortunately he'd been able to cover by pretending he'd gone off to get coffee, not to find the laptop. Abbott had left his MacBook Air with him.

He'd covered, too, in conversation with Abbott.

"You don't have the senator's laptop?" Will Abbott had said after Tanner had handed him a mug of black coffee.

"Sorry. But you're barking up the wrong tree. I was at the LA airport and I forgot my laptop. I mean, I left it there—I was in a hurry, I guess—in the security line."

"You don't have the senator's—"

He shook his head. "I wish I could help you. But I'm so glad you brought mine back. When I called TSA, they said they had loads of laptops but not mine."

Abbott had left, clearly disappointed, but also baffled.

Tanner had thought a lot. He could never tell anyone about how he had run over the tattooed guy, but he could talk about the break-in. Though the evidence was slim—a mouse put back wrong, a broken window, a disabled surveillance camera. It was Lanny's death, his murder. That's what tipped things.

He needed help. It was foolish to try to go it alone. It was, in fact, dangerous. Something could happen to him. Lanny had been targeted, and he could be next. He had to tell someone in law enforcement about the swapped laptop, the classified documents. He might need some kind of protection, something more serious than staying in a friend's house. And he wanted someone to investigate Lanny's death.

Carl knew people in the local police, but that wasn't the level of help he needed. He needed someone with a national reach, which meant Homeland Security or FBI. He didn't know anyone in Homeland Security, but he did know a guy who worked for the FBI. Not a friend, really, but an acquaintance, a friend of a friend, a guy he'd played poker with.

He called the Boston office of the FBI and asked for Brent Stover. He was connected to Stover's voice mail and left a message, asking him to call, telling him it was important.

By the time he left work, Tanner had returned calls and sat through three meetings, distractedly. He wondered about moving the laptop somewhere else. If they'd searched his house and found nothing, wasn't it only a matter of time before they searched the office? If they did, they might or might not locate the safe. It wasn't easy to find, but if someone opened every drawer and cabinet and so on, eventually he'd find it. But then they were dealing with a high-quality safe that was locked and presumably difficult to crack. Maybe not impossible. Not for the right people.

The problem with moving the laptop, though, was that he'd have to take it out with him, and he could easily be intercepted with it. It was still better not to move it, he decided.

At a little after six o'clock, he left the office—Sal was staying there, roasting, which he often did at night—and went to his car. The old Lexus was parked two blocks away, a Day-Glo orange ticket tucked under one of the windshield wipers. He'd parked in Brighton resident parking, though his sticker said South End. He took it off the windshield and tossed it into the car. It fluttered to the floor among the bottles and cans.

Was it paranoid to wonder whether he was being followed? Probably. But he was feeling a little jittery, and circumstances seemed to justify it. The guy with the tattoo had very likely been sent to kill him. The way Lanny Roth had been killed.

He had no idea how to evade surveillance. You see scenes on TV and in the movies of people losing a tail, but when it came right down to it, Tanner didn't remember how it was done. He drove in a circuitous route, took a few left turns, drove through a Stop & Shop parking lot, and didn't see any vehicle trailing him. He drove up Comm. Ave. to Newton and pulled into Carl's driveway. He walked around to the front of the Lexus and noticed some damage to the front right quarter panel that he hadn't seen before. That must have been caused by the collision with the tattooed guy. He wondered whether that meant there was some trace evidence on the tattooed guy's body. It seemed like an awfully remote possibility that the police might connect his car to the death of Tattoo Man. But it remained a possibility, and it weighed on his mind.

He unlocked the front door and found Carl in the kitchen making something in the blender that looked like a chocolate smoothie.

"Anything happen at work?" Carl said.

Tanner shook his head. He knew Carl meant anything resembling the break-in.

"Everything okay?" Carl said it in a fake-casual way, pretending not to care, when the opposite was true. His eyes revealed that the question wasn't casual to him. Tanner had seen this when Carl was training a woman with a stalker in self-defense techniques.

"Fine," Tanner said. "Thanks."

Carl tipped the contents of the blender into a tall glass. "Protein shake?"

Tanner shook his head. "I'm good."

"So I told you I know a guy in the Brookline police, right?"

"Yeah?"

"I got more on Lanny."

"Okay."

He held the glass aloft in his right hand, as if inspecting it. "They found some stuff in his medicine cabinet."

"Like what?"

"It sort of makes sense now."

"What does?"

"Him, you know, offing himself. They found a bunch of meds. Lithium—something called . . . Lithobid. And Lamictal. And Seroquel." He ticked them off on the fingers of his left hand. "I think I have the names right. Point is, know what those are for?"

Tanner shook his head.

Carl took a long swallow of the milk shake, a dramatic pause. "Manic-depressive. Or I think they call it bipolar now. Now his moods make sense."

"Moods?"

"He'd get really excited and then really down. Really depressed. Last time he talked to you, he was like crazy high, right? Manic, even?"

"I guess." Carl had a point.

"He said he'd found some big story—maybe a tip from you, do I have that right?"

"Yeah."

"And he was superexcited about it. Like, he's gonna win the Pulitzer Prize, that's how big the story was. He wouldn't tell me what it was."

It is *a big story*, Tanner thought. But Carl didn't know what it was. "That's right," he said. "Now that I think about it, he was really excited." And he thought about

Lanny and his moods, and it was true: the man did tend to extreme emotions, whether depressed or happy.

"Paranoia, elation, despair," said Carl. "It's textbook bipolar."

"Huh." It was not out of the question that Lanny had killed himself. He'd sounded almost paranoid when they last spoke. But that would be too coincidental. He'd been asking around about those classified documents, and he'd heard something alarming. People were after the senator's laptop. The guy with the tattoos had probably been sent to kill him, at least threaten him, and surely to get that damned computer.

Was it possible that Lanny had killed himself? Yes, sure it was. It was possible.

But what if he *hadn't* killed himself? What if he'd been somehow forced to swallow a bunch of pills, and the killers had taken pains to conceal the truth, make it look like suicide? Was that too paranoid a way to be thinking?

Perhaps.

The truth was, he didn't know what to think anymore about Lanny's death. Suicide was entirely possible, but he couldn't vanquish his suspicion.

"You know he didn't really have any family, from what I can tell," Carl said. "His parents are gone, and he didn't have a wife or kids, and . . . It's kind of heartbreaking. I'm his executor."

"No brothers or sisters?"

"No. He had a brother who died of leukemia in college."

"Huh." Tanner took off his jacket and hung it on the back of a chair.

His mobile phone rang.

"Yeah?"

"Mike Tanner?"

"Speaking."

"It's Brent Stover. From the FBI."

"Oh, Brent, right, thanks for calling. I, uh—" He hesitated. Was it even safe to talk on the phone, or was *that* excessive paranoia? "I have something interesting I wanted to talk over with you."

37

The chicken lobby was in town. He could tell because there were two people in yellow plush chicken suits sitting in the small waiting room of Senator Susan Robbins's office. They both—a man and a woman in their early twenties—had their red-beaked chicken heads in their laps. They were sheepish-looking chickens. They were waiting to meet with the senator to discuss tax breaks for commercial egg production in the new farm bill. The commercial poultry producers were constantly at war with small chicken farmers. But Will had too much on his mind to think about the plight of the small chicken farmer.

After a quick stop in his office to check his e-mail and landline voice mail, he popped his head into the boss's office. Twenty second graders were sitting in a circle being charmed by the senator. He gave a quick wave and made to duck away, but she announced to the children, "This is Mr. Abbott, my chief of staff. He's the real boss in this office."

They all turned to look. Will said, "Hi," and widened

his eyes, and they all said "hi" back in their adorable squeaky little-kid voices.

He smiled and left as quickly as he could.

He'd gotten a voice message from a staff member on the Senate intelligence committee named Gary Sapolsky. Gary was the boss's "designee," which meant he was a professional staff member assigned to work directly with the senator. Sapolsky used to be CIA. For some reason Sapolsky wanted to talk to him.

The offices of the Senate Select Committee on Intelligence were located on the second floor of the Hart building, one floor down from Senator Robbins's office. From the outside there wasn't much to see: a door and, next to it, what looked like a bank teller window, behind which sat a police officer.

This was a Sensitive Compartmentalized Information Facility, called a SCIF, partly because no one could remember what the letters stood for. It was a secure facility, a generic-looking office that was physically hardened, encased in two layers of sheet metal, a box within a box. Breaking in would require a blowtorch.

You couldn't bring in your cell phone or BlackBerry. When you were inside the SCIF you were out of touch with the rest of the world. Some senators enjoyed that. Will did too. He had a security clearance, mostly because the boss had asked him to get one so he could read through the intelligence documents along with her. Which was flattering. Most chiefs of staff didn't get security clearances.

He left his phone in the tray and pulled open the heavy door.

As soon as he entered, he saw Gary Sapolsky coming toward him as if he had something on his mind.

That wasn't good. Will felt a spasm of unease.

Gary was around ten years older than Will, a weedy, frail-looking man in his late forties with a face that always looked scrubbed raw and a head of sparse gray hair. He had once been a CIA officer on the fast track to senior management. But then his wife had twins, and he had to take care of his aging parents, and the CIA wanted to send him overseas, and he couldn't do it. So he took an intelligence-related job on the staff of the Senate intelligence committee.

The work was interesting but hardly glamorous. He'd been given the choice between being a good intelligence officer and being a good father. And he chose being a dad. Which was no doubt something his daughters would know nothing about and therefore not appreciate him for.

By Capitol Hill standards, Will was no kid—he was thirty-seven, when most staffers seemed to be ten years younger. But Gary, in his late forties, was, relatively speaking, a grizzled old man.

"There you are," Gary said. "I went by looking for you yesterday, a couple of times."

"Sorry, I was out of town for the day."

"Okay, um. Do you have a few minutes? Maybe we could grab some coffee off campus?"

"Sure," Will said, and that paranoia came surging back,

prickling the hair on the back of his neck. *Off campus.* That meant he had something serious to talk about. Something he wouldn't put in an e-mail or discuss over the phone. "Right now?"

"If you can."

"Regular place?"

The two walked out of the Hart office building together, talking about politics and legislation and then lapsing, inevitably, into gossip, which was what most people on the Hill talked anyway. Will could barely concentrate, though. What the hell did Gary want to talk about in a private setting?

Dear God, it couldn't be.

"So what's on your mind?" Will asked.

"Not until we're at the place."

They went to the Corner Bakery on North Capitol Street, a few blocks away. When Will had bought his coffee and sweet roll and Gary had gotten a cup of decaf, they settled on a table by the window, far away from everyone else. Who were surely Capitol Hill types also having talks they didn't want to have in the office.

"All right," Gary said. "Bad news."

"Okay." His stomach tightened.

"There's some kind of security investigation going on. Everyone's on high alert."

"What are you talking about?"

He shrugged and let out a breath slowly. "Have they talked to you? They're talking to everyone."

"Who's 'they'?"

"Office of Senate Security."

Will nodded. The OSS was an obscure Senate office that granted security clearances and was in charge of the security of the SSCI offices. They probably did other things too; Will didn't know.

Gary went on. "Along with the NSA."

"NSA?"

"Everyone's being pretty closemouthed, but there was apparently a leak of NSA documents. This reporter from *The Boston Globe* called a couple of retired NSA types and asked about some program, and the place went into code red."

"What documents?"

He shrugged again.

"Why are they interviewing intel committee people?"

"Must have to do with stuff we have. So they're interviewing everyone."

"Huh." All of a sudden he felt cold.

If it got out what he'd done, it would harm the boss irreparably. She'd be the senator who stole classified information and put it on a laptop and *lost it*. She would be accused of mishandling classified information—what if the Russians got it? or the Chinese?—but worse, she'd be ridiculed. Her career would be over. Meanwhile, Will Abbott would be charged with a felony for illegally facilitating the transfer of classified documents, for copying the documents, and he'd go to prison. Maybe for a long time. Not only ruining his own life, but ruining his family too.

For one brief moment Will felt overcome with panic. What if Gary had seen what he'd done? Did Gary know? Was it possible?

But just as quickly he came to his senses. Gary hadn't been anywhere near the computer that Will had used within the SCIF. He hadn't seen. If he somehow knew—if there was some computer record of Will's theft—Gary would have said something.

All he had done was copy documents onto a flash drive and then put them on Susan Robbins's laptop. It had taken two minutes, and no one had paid any attention to what he was doing.

He knew it was against the rules, but Susan had wanted a copy to peruse on her computer when she flew to LA, and Will would do anything for her. She was more energetic than anyone else he'd ever met. She was also smarter—she just seemed to process everything faster—than anyone else he knew. And she was a serious person. She truly cared about her job. It was the biggest thing in her life, to the detriment of her personal life. She was a genuine patriot, believed in America, and had a sense of mission.

If she wanted to read through documents on the flight to LA, she had the right to do that.

He had broken a rule, yes, though it hadn't been a big deal at the time.

Now he realized it was only the biggest mistake he had ever made.

He suddenly had a thought. "Gary, you ever hear from Arthur Collins?"

"Artie? Once in a while."

Arthur Collins was a sort of private investigator who lived and worked in Virginia. He used to be a "technical operations officer" within the CIA's clandestine service. That meant he used to do black-bag jobs for the CIA. He'd travel around the world undercover, break into people's offices and homes, and steal computer backups or disks, copy files, plant taps or software.

A few years ago, Arthur had done some investigating for the committee. Will had met him a few times, thought he had something of an attitude, but was nonetheless impressed by him. The word on Arthur was that he was "underutilized" by the committee—he could do more than background checks.

"He still working as a . . ."

"Private spy, he calls it. An investigator. Yeah, he does, why?"

Will paused. "I can't really say."

"Got it." Gary would assume it was for Susan, something confidential, and he knew not to ask. "I'll get you his e-mail."

When Will got back to his office his phone's message light was blinking. He listened to his voice messages, taking notes on the computer.

One of the messages was from the Office of Senate Security. They wanted to speak with him.

38

The next morning at eight, Tanner was sitting in a sandwich place in Boston, across Cambridge Street from the nine-story curved building in which the FBI had its Boston office. It was one of those places that pretends to be a café but offers a long list of smoothies and sandwiches. There were six stools and a bowl of bananas next to the cash register.

"Michael?"

Tanner looked up. Brent Stover was a handsome, healthy-looking guy in his early forties. He had the innocent, open face of an altar boy, the trusting face of a kid on Christmas morning. He had small brown eyes and a graying buzz cut, and he looked like former military. He had to be.

"Brent."

Stover offered his hand and shook extra-firmly. He was wearing an ill-fitting gray pinstriped suit that puckered at the shoulder lines, a blue button-down shirt, a nondescript navy repp tie.

Tanner remembered that they'd talked football, and that Stover had four kids, two sets of twins. They played in a monthly poker game at the Plympton Club, a very old-line Boston Brahmin social club. Usually seven guys—an eclectic mix of interesting people, playing dealer's choice, a bunch of anaconda variations. They'd play for an hour, then have dinner (and plenty of lubrication), and then play afterward. Stover didn't drink, which meant he tended to make a lot of money after dinner.

"So how'd you make out last time?" Tanner asked.

"Not like you did. Actually, I was down a little, but not too bad. I wound up almost breaking even."

"Marshall got lucky."

"Yeah, he kept catching that inside straight. I can't wait to get back to the table with him. His luck is going to turn."

They talked for a couple of minutes about their work. Stover said he'd taken a management job at the FBI, which at least had regular hours. He got in every day at eight thirty and left at six, and he took the T, and he got home in time to help put the younger twins down.

"Listen," Tanner said, "something really odd has happened to me, something disturbing, and I'm sort of at wit's end. I don't know what to do. I just know I need to do something. And I think the FBI is the right place to go with this."

Stover knitted his brow. "Tell me."

Tanner narrated, flatly and matter-of-factly, the whole

story, from the switched laptop at LAX to the classified documents to the break-in at his house to Lanny's murder, or possible murder. He leveled. Not all of it made him look good, he realized. After all, he was holding on to a computer he knew belonged to a United States senator, hadn't given it back. He left out any mention of running over the tattooed guy. If he had to talk about that, he would, but to raise it now would complicate matters unnecessarily.

"Oh jeez," Stover said when Tanner was finished. He shook his head. "Do you have it with you? The laptop, I mean."

"It's in a safe." For some reason he didn't want to say where. He had his own laptop in a black nylon case on the floor. Stover must have noticed it.

"Do you have a copy of the documents? A thumb drive, whatever?"

"No."

"Did you get a look at them?"

"I looked at them. I frankly didn't understand what I read. A lot of jargon and abbreviations and acronyms." Tanner recalled what he could.

Then Brent Stover looked at his watch and asked Tanner to walk with him to Center Plaza. He had a morning meeting to get to. They crossed the street and followed the curved building around to One Center Plaza.

Standing outside the doors to the elevator bank, Stover said, "All right. I'm going to make some inquiries and get back to you. In fact, here's my cell number. Call me if anything else develops."

"Okay."

"You absolutely did the right thing in coming to me. And, Michael—"

"Yeah?"

"Thank you."

39

After Brent Stover had left, Tanner looked at his phone and saw he'd gotten two calls. One from Karen Wynant and the other from Lucy Turton, the office manager. He knew Karen was just going to agonize about another lost deal, and he wasn't up for it just now. He was about to listen to Lucy's voice message when she called back and he picked up.

Tanner was by now late for work, and Lucy had to go over a few administrative things with him, mostly payroll related. When they were finished, he said, "For the next few days I'm not going to be in the office much. I've got some personal business."

"Yeah?"

"Boring, nothing serious. Call it family business. The office can run just fine without me. I'll be checking e-mails and such, and people know how to reach me if a problem comes up."

"Will you be out of town?"

"I might be," he said.

* * *

He left the café and stood outside it, facing One Center Plaza. He needed a place that had Wi-Fi he could use. Someplace that wasn't this place, where he'd just met with an FBI agent. Then he remembered a good café in the Godfrey Hotel, on Washington Street, a few blocks away. He'd been there, mostly to check out the competition, and was impressed.

There were only a few people in the café. He found a table in a nook in the back of the sprawling customer space. Carrying his laptop in a black shoulder bag, he ordered a large pour over.

When he returned to the empty table, he set up his laptop and took out a thumb drive, on which he'd made a copy of the classified documents. He copied the large, multi-gig file onto his laptop.

He opened the top folder.

He'd looked it over before with gawking incomprehension. The documents were impenetrable, filled with acronyms and abbreviations and jargon, written in a language he couldn't begin to understand.

"TOP SECRET//COMINT//NOFORN" and "TOP SECRET//SI//REL USA, FVEY" and "TS//SI//NF." Phrases like "data flow" and "protocol exploitation" and "CHRYSALIS."

He started typing in a blank Google window and then paused, deleted the words. Lanny had told him that Google gave the government access to all your searches, and he wanted to avoid that. Lanny had recommended a search engine Tanner had never heard of, DuckDuckGo, which called itself "the search engine that doesn't track you." He opened DuckDuckGo.com and entered the first phrase. He did this over and over, slowly and carefully, with each opaque phrase, each obscure string of jargon, and gradually he began to put together a shaky understanding. It was like glimpsing a castle distantly and through fog. He could see some contours, could see some turrets and a parapet and maybe a moat.

It talked about collection of electronic communications and remote access, and Tanner wasn't sure what this was. He remembered a few years ago the big headlines about how the US government could and did monitor your e-mail and texts. The revelations somehow didn't shock him, but they sort of creeped him out. Wasn't this how George Orwell's *1984* would eventually come about? But it wasn't long before everything moved on and no one talked about it anymore except in magazines he didn't read and websites he didn't see.

Now he noticed movement, in the corner of his eye. He turned and saw a guy enter the café, bypass the counter, and walk slowly along the aisle of tables, clearly looking for someone. He was midthirties, tall, bullet headed, dressed in a conservative suit. He looked to his right, scanning the area where Tanner was sitting, his eyes raking over the tables, the handful of patrons, until his eyes met Tanner's for just a fraction of a second, and then he quickly glanced away.

Something about that averted glance gave Tanner a chill. As if he was deliberately shifting his gaze, not wanting to be obvious. As if he'd spotted his target but didn't want to let on.

The bullet-headed guy continued looking around the café, then turned and left, pushing through the glass doors. But he remained standing just outside the glass doors, and in a moment he was met by another guy with short hair, also in a suit. The two looked like Secret Service agents: fit, confident, generic. But they could also be just a couple of businessmen meeting in a café: an investment manager and his client. Two executives at John Hancock. They talked briefly and then entered the coffee shop, one right after the other.

They were heading in his direction.

But Tanner was not going to wait around to find out if they were looking for him and what they intended to do.

He stood up, flapped his computer closed, jammed it into its case, and peered swiftly around. The café occupied part of the Godfrey Hotel's lobby, and its rear service exits opened into the hotel. The only marked exits in the café were the front glass doors. But there was, he remembered—he'd been here just once before but he remembered its basic layout—a kitchen exit that led to a service corridor within the hotel.

He slipped behind the long front counter, then veered left into the kitchen, where he nearly collided with a guy carrying a tall metal coffee urn. Had the two guys—pursuers?—seen him disappear into the kitchen? He didn't think so, but he kept moving in any case, through the kitchen's back door, into the hotel, and then he meandered through the halls until he found an emergency door. DOOR IS ALARMED, the sign said.

Actually, they rarely were, he knew.

He pushed the crash bar and the door opened out onto the street and a tall Dumpster, and he was gone.

No alarm sounded.

40

Mr. Abbott, please."

He sat in the waiting room of the Office of Senate Security, on a hard antique-knockoff chair, and looked up at the young woman who'd just opened the heavy wooden door. She was a pretty young intern with a mannish haircut and superblocky librarian glasses, one of those women who dress against their beauty.

Mr. Abbott, please.

His stomach clenched as he remembered being fourteen years old and sitting in social studies class when the classroom door opened and Mrs. Knorr from the principal's office said, "Mr. Abbott, please."

Something in her voice had told him that this was bad news.

Worse, Mrs. Knorr had given him a compassionate look as he left the classroom, which had struck terror into him.

She walked him to the office, calling him "dear," in her exotic New York accent, which made it sound like "dee-uh."

He had never met Dr. Hookstra, the school principal,

a legendary and much-feared character in Millwood Junior High School, a tall, glowering man. He only knew his voice from the school's public-address system. Dr. Hookstra gave him a dry, papery handshake and a pitying look, and tears sprang to Will's eyes because he had an idea that bad news was coming and that it might involve his younger brother, Clay, or even, God forbid, his parents.

Dr. Hookstra spoke to him softly. This surprised Will, who didn't know the principal had any voice other than his stentorian PA voice. "I'm sorry to tell you, Will, that your father has died."

"What?" Will said stupidly, as if he didn't understand the words. Why was the principal telling him something so personal?

"Your mother is coming to pick you up soon. You're excused for the rest of the day and for however long you need. You're the man in the family now, Will. There's a lot on your shoulders." Will could still remember the smell of Dr. Hookstra's Aqua Velva aftershave. He forever after associated it with death.

He thought of all of those political leaders, the best and the brightest, who had lost a parent young, usually a father. Like Barack Obama, whose dad left him when he was two. Supreme Court Justice Sonia Sotomayor lost her alcoholic father when she was nine. Alexander Hamilton was orphaned at the age of thirteen. And Bill Clinton's dad was killed before he was even born. The loss or absence of a father somehow spurs you to strive and achieve, overachieve, accomplish great things. You become an eminent orphan.

For a moment he thought about Gary Sapolsky and how good of a father he was, how he'd chosen dadhood over being a superspy in the CIA. That made him think about baby Travis and what kind of dad he'd be and whether he was even cut out to be a father. The little kid could turn Will into a bowl of mush, just besotted with love. But Travis would one day turn into a surly teenager who resented his presence, then an adult who wouldn't have time to call and say hello. And he wasn't sure how he'd deal with that. If he was given the choice between becoming, someday, White House chief of staff or the best dad in the whole second grade, he'd choose the White House any day.

But he could never tell anyone that. And he also knew that what happened in this room would determine if he even had a choice.

Now he followed the intern into a small, formal room, where a middle-aged man and a young woman sat in two chairs on one side of a mahogany conference table. There was an oriental carpet on the floor and, on the walls, paintings of ships at sea. All of the ships in the paintings, he noticed quickly, were caught in storms. He wondered if the choice of art was deliberate.

"Mr. Abbott," the woman said. She was around Will's age—therefore young, in his estimation—large framed, broad shouldered, with light-brown hair loosely knotted at the back of her neck in a complicated arrangement.

"Will."

"Will. I'm Nicole Erdman, from the Office of Senate Security, and this is John Hathaway from the National Security Agency." Curious, Will thought, that she felt the need to say the whole name of the three-letter agency. As if they didn't all know what it was. "We want you to know this interview is being recorded."

There was no tape recorder on the table, no iPhone. Obviously they didn't need one. The room was wired.

"Why am I here?" Will asked. He looked at the woman and then turned to the NSA guy, an odd-looking man with pale freckled skin, brown eyes, short black hair, and overlarge ears. The man looked right back, defiantly, and Will couldn't help but glance away.

"Mr. Abbott, we have reason to believe that some classified information, classified at the highest level by the NSA, was stolen or mishandled. This investigation is tasked with determining the source of that leak—"

"Okay, but why—"

"We have reason to believe classified information was stolen or mishandled within the Senate, uh, intelligence committee offices, about a week ago," John said in a reasonable baritone. "Within the SCIF." He sounded like an accountant explaining some complexity of tax law to an inattentive client.

Will felt acid wash up into his throat. He wanted to ask what made them say this and he thought, *My God, there are cameras in the SCIF! There have to be concealed closed-circuit TV cameras. What if what I did was recorded on video?*

But instead of giving in to the panic, he tipped his head to one side and cocked a brow inquisitively and said, "My God, really?"

Nicole said, "As I'm sure you know, according to the Rules of Procedure of the Select Committee on Intelligence, copying, duplicating, or removing from the committee offices classified materials is prohibited—"

"—'except as is necessary for the conduct of committee business,' " Will said. "Yes, I'm familiar with the rules. What is your question: Did I break any rules? The answer is no."

Nicole flushed and said, looking down at a sheet of paper on the table in front of her, "Did you at any point last week bring in a portable electronic device?"

"You mean, like a phone?"

"Right."

"No, I did not."

"Um, writing to removable media such as USB or DVD/CD drives is prohibited without express authorization—"

"I said, I didn't break any rules. Is that not clear enough?"

John Hathaway spoke up now, loudly and firmly: "Did you copy any files to a USB drive, a flash drive, a thumb drive, a memory stick, a disk or any other form of removable media?"

"No."

"Well, someone did last Wednesday. That limits the pool of suspects to SSCI staff members, any of the senators on the committee, and any members of any senator's staff who might have access."

Will felt as if one of the lobes of his brain had just lit up. He realized then: *They don't know who did it!*

They probably knew that somebody plugged in a thumb drive. There was probably some sort of intrusion detector in the computer network. He should have thought of that. He would never have taken the risk. But that meant that there was no hidden video recording activity inside the room.

They knew someone had copied top secret documents. How many suspects were there, then? Thirteen senators plus their staffers who had security clearance plus the professional staff. He did the math in his head. That meant a pool of seventy-six people who could have done it.

But *they didn't know it was him.*

"Hold on a second," Will said, holding up his hand. "You're telling me there's been *another* NSA leak?"

John looked sidelong at Nicole.

"How many does this even make since Snowden?"

"Um," John said.

But Will didn't wait for his answer. "What the hell is going on with you people? Another NSA screwup? My God, you guys leak like a, a salad spinner." He considered saying something about Huggies diapers and how *they* didn't leak, but he decided that not everybody had baby on the brain. "You sure as hell are better at collecting secrets than keeping them. And let's not even talk about 9/11." Will knew that the NSA shouldered the primary blame for not catching the September 11 terrorists, and that this was more than a sore point for the agency. "As you well know, my boss pretty much controls the purse strings for you guys. Every intel budget, every program—she decides thumbs-up or thumbs-down. She can yank those purse strings or she can just snip them off. So what I want to know is: This new leak—do we have something to worry about?"

"Not at all, sir. Nothing at all to worry about. We don't need to take any more of your time."

41

Tanner drove to the office, making a few extra turns, taking a circuitous route. Just in case he was being followed. Though in truth he was as sure as he could be that he wasn't.

In the afternoon, when it had been five hours since his meeting with Brent Stover, he gave in to his anxiety and called the guy, on his work number. Calling his mobile phone seemed a little too aggressive. He reached a woman named Linda who seemed to be his assistant, or maybe an assistant for a group of FBI officers. She said he was out of the office and that she'd take a message for him. A couple of hours later he tried Stover's mobile. He got a recording of Stover saying, "Please leave a message." He did.

At seven he left another message on Stover's cell phone.

The next morning, Tanner was up early. He checked his e-mail and wondered for the first time whether anyone—

"they"—might have tapped his Internet connection. He didn't even know if that was possible.

He decided to go into work early. Sal the roaster might be at work—he kept long hours, by his own choice—or he might have to open the place, which he rarely had to do.

At seven thirty, before getting into his car, he called Brent Stover's mobile phone. This was the third time. He got voice mail again. And he wondered: Was it possible Stover was just too busy to get back to him? If that was the case, leaving another message would be obnoxious. He ended the call before the beep. Then he called Stover's office number and got a voice mail message. It was too early for the office there to open. He didn't leave a message.

He wondered whether Stover was avoiding him for some reason. Maybe he was too busy with FBI casework and meetings and paperwork to have checked into the classified documents Tanner had told him about.

Sure . . . but Stover had sounded alarmed at what Tanner had told him. He had sounded intensely interested, and it wasn't an act. It didn't seem plausible that he'd drop it when he got into work.

There must be a good reason he was avoiding Tanner's call.

At eight thirty he called Stover's work number from his office landline. Linda answered.

"Yes, Mr. Tanner, good morning. He's in a meeting, but I can take a message."

Tanner left Stover a second message and told her it was important. "How long does that meeting go on for?" he asked.

"Usually no more than an hour. Half an hour to forty-five minutes, max."

"Okay. Well, he'll know what this is about, but please tell him I need to talk with him soon."

"I will," she said, pleasantly.

At ten thirty, he called Stover's FBI line and got Linda again. "Is there a good time to reach him? I don't want to keep bothering you."

"I'm giving him the messages, sir," she said testily.

"I appreciate that. It's a matter of some urgency."

"I understand," she said. "He's a very busy man."

"Is there a good time to reach him, do you think?"

"I'm sorry, sir, all I can do is give him your message."

"So he knows I've been calling."

"I don't know whether he's seen the messages, sir. I'll tell him you called again."

Tanner had his own meeting to get through, with Karen. At the end of it he asked if he could borrow her cell phone. She looked surprised—she could see his on his desk—but said sure.

She unlocked her home screen and handed it to him. As soon as she'd left the office, he called Brent Stover's cell phone.

Stover answered right away. "Yeah?"

"Brent, it's Michael Tanner, and I want to apologize for hounding you."

"Yeah, uh, Michael, I'm afraid I can't help you. I'm really awfully busy, I'm sorry, best of luck."

There was a click. He had hung up.

Tanner was stunned. The FBI guy was avoiding him, that was clear, but why?

I'm afraid I can't help you.

What did that mean?

Brent Stover left work at six, Tanner remembered him saying.

At quarter of six, Tanner was standing outside the glass doors to a small lobby area and a bank of elevators in One Center Plaza. There was a constant surge of people, mostly government workers, leaving work for the day. Some looked bedraggled and unhappy; some were voluble and boisterous.

At five minutes after six, Brent Stover came out of a crowded elevator.

This was sort of like stalking, Tanner knew. But it was justified.

He waited for Stover to emerge from the glass doors, saw he wasn't talking to anyone, and approached him.

Stover saw him. A flash of panic on his face. Subtly, he shook his head.

Tanner came closer, and Stover said, quietly, "Not here." His eyes darted upward and to his right. Tanner saw a surveillance camera mounted on the building face high above, and his stomach twisted.

Stover kept walking, Tanner following at a distance.

Stover crossed the street in the direction of the sandwich shop where they'd met the day before. Tanner waited a few seconds and then crossed. Stover was still within view, walking past the Starbucks and down the street. He seemed to be leading Tanner. He certainly wasn't trying to lose him.

Stover rounded the next corner and then turned into an alley. He stopped beside a Dumpster. As soon as Tanner came up to him, Stover spoke to him quietly and quickly. "Do me a favor, Tanner, and turn off your phone."

"What the hell is going on?" Tanner said.

"Here's what's going on. I got a wife and four kids who depend on my salary. I got a pension. I got a career. I got a life. And they're shutting me down."

"Who's shutting you—"

"I cannot touch this. Please, just forget my name and never call me again."

"Will you explain to me what you—"

"I don't know what you did, but please—just stay away from me. This conversation never happened. Don't contact me again. Please."

42

There was something deeply unnerving about seeing a man like the normally stolid Brent Stover so visibly frightened.

This conversation never happened. Don't contact me again. Please.

What the hell had the FBI agent discovered? What had he been told?

And what was this about turning off his phone? Tanner wondered whether it was true that you could be tracked via your mobile phone. He'd heard that somewhere but had never given it much thought.

But he kept his phone turned off just in case.

He stopped at a convenience store and bought three prepaid cell phones. He had to be reachable, had to stay in touch with the office, yet he couldn't use his iPhone any longer. He returned to Carl's house in Newton, warily—parking down the street and around a corner and walking back to the house. Was he being followed? He didn't think so. Not that he could tell, anyway.

He unlocked the front door, couldn't help noting the house smell. Every house had a different one. Carl's was a blend of faint mildew, mothballs, old vacuum cleaner bag, and coffee. Tanner was like a bloodhound with a highly specialized skill, or maybe more like a truffle hound: he could detect the odor of coffee anywhere.

Carl wasn't home—Tanner called out—so he switched on the lights in the living room and opened one of the disposable cell phone's blister packs using a pair of scissors, though a hacksaw would have been a lot easier. The phone's battery came with a minimum amount of charge, but enough to call Lucy Turton, Tanner Roast's office manager. While they talked, he plugged the phone in to charge, then set up and plugged in the other two phones in the outlet on the kitchen wall.

"I'll be away from the office a few more days," he said.

"Okay . . ." Lucy sounded like she wanted to ask why but it wasn't her place.

"And I'll have a different phone number for a while. My iPhone died."

"I see the number . . . Okay. Hey, a couple of guys came by here looking for you."

"When was this?"

"Just a couple of hours ago. Serious-looking dudes. They said they were from Homeland Security."

"What'd they want?"

"They wouldn't tell me what it was about. They said they'd only talk to you, and they said they'll be back."

"Thanks." Tanner ended the call. They'd probably

tried his house, too. And it wouldn't take them long to determine the names of his employees and friends, and soon enough they'd find him here, at Carl's house.

Which meant he had to leave here as soon as possible.

At the same time, Tanner couldn't help but think: *Is this all about the goddamned senator's laptop? What if I just give it back?* What would happen if he simply handed it back to the senator's office? If he called that guy, Will Abbott, and said, *You know what, you're right, I have it, and here it is, and let's end this.*

Lanny had insisted that the laptop was his life insurance policy, that once he surrendered it, he was disposable; he could be killed. Because the real issue was what was on that laptop: the top secret documents. Lanny had them, on a thumb drive; he let people know he had them, and he was killed. Before he had the chance to publish a story. Maybe Lanny was killed because he knew about these documents—to stop him from making them public.

Whereas Tanner was still alive. Maybe that was because someone wanted to get that computer back. And once they'd gotten it, they'd surely kill him too.

So: no. The computer had to stay hidden, held as a hostage.

But it occurred to him, with a spasm of terror, that maybe things had changed. Maybe things weren't so simple anymore. Maybe having the laptop hidden away wasn't enough to keep him safe.

After all, he had killed a man.

Maybe that had marked him. Maybe he was in a different category now. Maybe they knew he'd done it. They—whoever sent the tattooed guy after Tanner—would have a pretty good idea of who must have done it, a couple of blocks from the Tanner Roast office and roastery.

He heard a key turning in the front-door lock and for a moment he froze. He looked around for a weapon, something he could use if it came to that. A lamp? Then his eyes lit upon the fireplace and the metal tools next to it, including a fireplace poker. That would do nicely. He grabbed it and took a few steps toward the entry hall, poker up in the air, ready to swing, in case—

"Whoa there, dude," Carl said.

"Sorry." As he lowered the poker, he realized his hand was shaking.

Carl frowned. "Did something happen?"

Tanner shook his head.

"Someone try to get in?" Carl was maybe twenty feet away, but Tanner could smell the funk of his sweat. He was just back from a day of lessons and classes and he hadn't taken a shower.

"No. But it's only a matter of time. They've already been looking for me at work. I'm sure they looked at my house. Now I've gotta move."

"But *who's* been looking for you?"

"I have no idea who. They say Homeland Security. But I don't know."

Carl crinkled his brow. "FBI, maybe?"

"I don't think so."

"CIA? Some other three-letter agency?"

Tanner shrugged.

"Where are you gonna move to? Come on, man, I'm worried."

"I don't know, but I have an idea. I need to see my wife."

"Can we talk?" Tanner said.

"Uh-oh. Now it's your turn," Sarah said.

"This is really important."

Her tone changed suddenly. "What is it?"

"I can't talk on the phone." Maybe he was being unduly paranoid, but he assumed that they had the ability to listen in on Sarah Tanner's mobile phone and that they might in fact be doing it. He didn't want to take the chance.

Tanner and Sarah arranged to meet on Huron Avenue in Cambridge, in front of her real estate company's offices. It was cold and windy, a fall nip in the air, the threat of a Boston winter on the way. He saw her from a distance, illuminated by a streetlamp. She looked small and vulnerable.

"Tanner, what's going on?" She was dressed in one of her business suits, a loden green jacket over a matching skirt. She'd obviously just come from a showing. No coat. Wind was whipping her hair.

Her arms were folded. He gave her a quick kiss. "Aren't you cold out here?"

"Yeah, freezing." He took off his jacket and held it up

for her. Gratefully, she slipped her arms in. He looked around, saw a pizza place across the street that was open.

She saw him spot it and said, "Good idea."

Inside the pizza place they found an open table. "How come you can't talk on the phone?"

"It's a long story."

"Tell me. Is—everything okay?" She covered Tanner's hand with hers, a protective reflex. "You seem totally stressed." He was touched by her gesture. It was like a glimpse of the old Sarah, pre-separation.

"Yeah, you could say that."

Dread in her face, she said, "What is it?"

When he was finished, she looked shaken. "Give the goddamned laptop back."

"It's the only leverage I have."

"Which you're not going to be alive to use, Tanner!" she whispered.

"I think it's too late to just give it back. If I could do it and survive, I would."

"Then you need to make this public. It's like Lanny told you—they can blow out a candle but not a fire. If you tell, like, *The New York Times* and they run with it, you're protected. The world knows, not just you. They'll no longer have a motivation to . . . you know, do anything to you."

"Yeah, but I don't know anybody at *The New York Times*."

"What about the *Globe*? Remember that nice piece they did about Tanner Roast when we were just getting started?"

"Lanny's editor," Tanner said abruptly.

"You know him?"

"No, but that should be easy to find. I'll just call. That's the guy to talk to."

"They'll want to see the documents. Do you have a copy?"

"I made a copy on a thumb drive. Also uploaded to the cloud, whatever that means."

"Great. If they see the documents, they'll know you're serious. They'll get it. It could be a huge story."

"Maybe this is the only way," Tanner said, more to himself than to Sarah.

"You said you wanted to ask me a favor."

"Yes. Two things. Both are big asks."

"Whatever you want."

"Can I borrow your car?"

A shrug. "Sure. What else?"

He told her, and handed her one of his burner phones.

She bit her lower lip. "I could get in serious trouble, Tanner."

He nodded, solemn. "That won't happen. I'll be careful."

43

Tanner returned to Carl's house. Carl was watching a football game, the Patriots. Tanner asked to borrow Carl's home computer for a little while. Carl kept it in the kitchen, in a little nook. Tanner pulled up a chair and went online, found a list of phone numbers for departments at *The Boston Globe*. After poking around some more he discovered that the newspaper had a secure drop box for whistle-blowers called Safebox. He read the instructions. He found where you could upload a file, which was like dropping it into a strongbox.

He had decided he was going to send the top secret documents to *The Boston Globe*. But he wanted to do it right. He didn't want to send the file by regular e-mail, because that was insecure. The Russians might well have access to the *Globe*'s server. Hell, they were everywhere in cyberspace these days. It was a huge step, what he was doing. He was revealing a whole bunch of highly classified documents. He wanted to do it responsibly every step of the way. Not just some random dump of secrets from an anonymous source. Plus he didn't want to get Carl in trouble, just because he was kind enough to let him use his computer.

So he went through the elaborate process, step by step, and uploaded the file from Apple's iCloud, where he'd left a copy. The *Globe*'s Safebox allowed you to upload anonymously. It didn't record your IP address or anything like that. It was safe. It was also so ridiculously complex that he wondered who would go through the process. You'd have to be desperate.

When he'd finished uploading the file—it was a large file and took several minutes—he sat back, heart pounding as he realized what he'd just done, and realized his palms were sweaty.

In the late morning, Tanner took a cab to the South Boston headquarters of *The Boston Globe*. At the security desk at the entrance, he picked up a phone and asked for Hank Brennan in the Metro department.

"Brennan."

"My name's Michael Tanner. I'm a friend of Lanny Roth's. You were his editor, right?"

"Who's this, again?"

"Michael Tanner. I'm down at Reception."

"What can I do for you, Mr. Tanner?"

"I have some documents for you. Documents I gave to Lanny. He might have mentioned."

"Ask them to send you up to the newsroom."

* * *

Hank Brennan's cubicle was stacked high with old newspapers and books and piles and piles of paper. He apologized for the mess and indicated a folding chair next to his desk where Tanner could sit. Brennan was a black man of around forty wearing a crisp white button-down shirt and heavy-framed black glasses. He smelled of a vaguely familiar men's cologne.

"Hey, so you're a friend of Lanny's," Brennan said gently. "What a loss. What a goddamned loss. It's tragic."

"I know."

"I mean, I know he was troubled. But, man—suicide? How heartbreaking."

"If it *was* suicide."

"Excuse me?"

"I have reason to believe it wasn't."

Brennan paused. "I see. Okay, then. So, those documents. Lanny never said anything about any documents, but he usually didn't clue me in until he was fairly sure he had something. Let's take a look, see what we got." He put out his hands, pantomimed grabbing something.

"I uploaded them to the *Globe*'s Safebox."

"Okay. Got it. Great. So, that damned Safebox thing—I mean, it's such a pain to download, a million steps you gotta go through. Let me ask—" He sighed, frustrated. Shook his head. "We've just been through another round of layoffs. Man, this business—I mean, it was one thing when our chief competition was the *Herald,* but when your competition is Twitter and Facebook and Snapchat? I mean, seriously, *Snapchat*? Jeez Louise. Anyway, I'll ask one of the interns to do it." He typed something quickly, clicked a key with a finger. "The last time someone sent me something in the Safebox, it turned out to be Hillary Clinton's secret chocolate-chip-cookie recipe. She puts in oats. My wife tried it. Wasn't half-bad."

"These are top secret documents," Tanner said, "from the National Security Agency. About a secret program. And I should tell you, the FBI didn't want to hear about it. Which I thought was interesting."

"Gotcha." He nodded slowly. "And how did you come across these documents? Do you . . . work for them?"

"No."

"Are you a government contractor?"

"No."

"What do you do, Mr. Tanner?"

"I'm in the coffee business. I own a company, Tanner Roast."

"I've heard of it, sure. Okay. So . . . did someone give them to you?"

"I picked up the wrong laptop at an airport."

He bounced a pencil on his desk. "Okay. And did Lanny actually get a chance to review these documents?"

Tanner nodded. He could hear the guy's skepticism and found it annoying. "He thought they were a really big deal."

Brennan blinked a few times, then nodded.

"It's apparently some top secret program called CHRYSALIS. It's, like—the government now has the ability to look at us through our webcams. Without us knowing. If I'm understanding this right, we're talking about the little camera on your cell phone and on your laptop and—I mean, it's totally terrifying. Lanny said it was the biggest story of his career."

"Lanny—" Brennan gave a quick smile. "He was terrific, and not only a great guy but a great investigative reporter. And one thing I've learned about the job is that, well, the best investigative reporters are a little crazy. You gotta be, I think. Lanny always had his pet conspiracy theory. George H. W. Bush's alleged mistress. Webb Hubbell was Chelsea Clinton's father. And why did Clinton's commerce secretary's plane really crash? I remember for a long time he was convinced that Osama bin Laden was never killed, that there was no 'burial at sea,' and that's why no one's seen the body, right?"

"Right, but—"

"So my job as editor is filtering. Because Lanny went down a lot of rabbit holes. I just had to stop him before he dug too far into Crazy Land. Did he discover a gold mine or was it a rabbit hole? At first glance they look the same, right? They're both just holes in the ground. Lanny would dig when there was a bone, and he would dig when there wasn't. So my question is, which one are you? Rabbit hole or gold mine? I'm just being really frank with you."

"I understand," Tanner said. "You can review the documents and tell me what you think. If they're all just a rabbit hole. But I think he was killed because of them."

"Oh yeah?"

"In fact, someone tried to kill me." Tanner could hear himself speak, his panicked-sounding staccato. He sounded like a crazy man. And he could hear Brennan's tone slide from warmth to wariness.

Brennan nodded slowly. "I imagine the coffee business can get pretty damned competitive."

Exasperated, Tanner sighed. "You're making light of this, but it's no joke, I can assure you. I can prove it to you."

"No offense," Brennan said, "but I get people calling me all the time. And sending me e-mails about 9/11 was an inside job and is there an Islamic terrorist training compound in rural Texas?"

"What I'm trying to tell you—"

"And these people—they're hurting. I always treat everyone with respect. I have this one guy from Malden who calls me once in a while. He always starts off pretty normal, and then he just goes off the rails. Everybody's in on this conspiracy against him, the governor and the attorney general, and they all came to his house, and—"

His computer chimed. Brennan said, "There it is already. Didn't take long at all."

"You have the file there?"

"I do," Brennan said. "Okay." He looked at the screen, his eyebrows rising in surprise and then lowering in puzzlement. After a minute or so, he looked at Tanner and said softly, "Okay, I see. So, well, Mr. Tanner, is there a reason you sent this to me? It just seems very personal."

"Personal?"

Brennan turned his monitor so Tanner could see what was on the screen. "I'm not sure I should be reading this."

On the monitor was a document headed: "McLean Hospital—Harvard Medical School." Centered at the top of the page it said, "Psychiatric Evaluation of Michael E. Tanner." It was signed "Dr. Raymond Osment, MD, Clinical Professor of Psychiatry." Shocked, Tanner skimmed the document, his glance snagging on phrases like "florid paranoid psychosis" and "delusional thinking" and "psychotic break" and "schizoid personality disorder." He read things like "convinced his phone was being tapped" and "same people day after day" and "his computer being remotely controlled by unknown persons" and "DSM IV 295.30."

"This is bullshit!" Tanner whispered. He looked at Brennan, who averted his eyes. "I don't know where the hell this came from, but it's a fraud. It's a plant. This is just an attempt to discredit me—to make me seem crazy."

"I know," Brennan said gently. He stood up. "I also know how stressful the death of a close friend can be. Can I—let me walk you to the elevator."

"I can show myself out," Tanner snapped and stood as well.

"No, I'll walk you there," Brennan said.

But Tanner had already turned to leave. Now the editor had reason to believe he was out of his mind, and trying to convince him otherwise was a waste of time.

"I'll accompany you, Mr. Tanner," Brennan said, following him close behind. "Please don't make me call Security."

44

The house was in a wealthy part of Boston called Chestnut Hill, an area of leafy streets and large houses and private schools. It was a redbrick Georgian mansion with ten bedrooms (or so Sarah had said; he wasn't going to double-check).

Looped around the front door handle was a device that looked like an oversized padlock. Tanner entered the four-digit code on the lockbox's keypad, and it unlocked. He pulled it open and removed the front door key.

Inside, it smelled like apple cider and fresh paint. He'd heard that mulling apple cider in the kitchen produced a smell that most people found welcoming; maybe that was a trick Sarah had employed.

Because the owners of the house didn't live here anymore, but you couldn't tell that at first glance. Potential buyers would see the Persian carpets and the elegant furniture and admire the spare but perfect décor. They wouldn't know that all the furnishings were on loan, put there by someone who specialized in staging houses for sale. In the entry hall there were fresh flowers in a glass vase on a demilune card table in a nook by the landing of a swooping staircase. The flowers were probably changed daily by the stager. In the front sitting room, on a coffee table, was a neat stack of oversized art and photography books, expertly askew, probably borrowed from the stager's warehouse. In the kitchen, besides the pot of apple cider that he'd smelled, there were a few, mostly very expensive, appliances on the counters. A bowl of perfect fresh fruit, fresh flowers on the marble-topped island, and nothing in the Sub-Zero. The dining room table was set for a dinner party, with blue hydrangeas in low vases at the center of the table. No family photos anywhere, but that was deliberate too. They wanted buyers to imagine the house as their own.

Tanner turned on lights as he entered. He went to the kitchen, looked for a drinking glass for some water, which was when he discovered the cabinets were empty. He drank from the tap in the soapstone sink. Then he went upstairs to the master bedroom and saw, at the center of the room, a king-size-plus bed with a magnificent silk duvet cover. Not a bad place to crash.

He set the alarm on his phone to two A.M., figuring he could at least get a couple of hours of sleep.

As he tried to fall asleep, he found himself thinking about the Box again.

A few years after Tanner's father died, he was sitting

with his mother at the old kitchen table, drinking coffee from beans he'd bought in Guatemala and his company had roasted. She complimented him on the coffee and then said, "You did it, didn't you?"

"What do you mean?"

"This." She held up her coffee mug. "Your dream."

"Tanner Roast?"

"Yes. Tanner Roast. You've wanted to start your own company since you were a boy."

"I guess."

"I'm so proud of you. Your dad would have been proud of you."

"Yeah, yeah, yeah," Tanner said dismissively, pleased but embarrassed.

"Do you know how old I was when I had you?"

"Twenty-one, twenty-two, right? Young."

"Daddy was twenty-six. We—" She hesitated a moment, then proceeded. "We weren't planning on having kids just yet."

"I was an accident?"

"Pretty much, yeah. A blessed accident."

"You're kidding! Is that why you guys got married then?"

"We were going to get married anyway. But that sort of sped things up. In our world, in our families, that was what you did. So Daddy knew he had to get serious. Make a living. And you know something, we wouldn't have it otherwise for the world."

"So the barbecue place, Tanner Q—"

"He was really thinking about a chain of barbecue restaurants, like the places he used to go when he was a kid in Kansas City."

"So he gave up on the barbecue place and got a job in insurance because he was having a baby."

"He had to make sacrifices. That's what you do when you have kids. You do what you have to do. You make a choice. And you do it out of love."

"And you put it away in the attic," Tanner said, moved. His father had talked about throwing "that crap" away, but he couldn't bring himself to do it. He'd kept the Box.

The Box was where you put your dreams.

The iPhone's alarm pierced a disturbing dream. He bolted upright.

Ten minutes later he was driving in Sarah's little green Fiat 500, which he'd parked a few blocks away. His Lexus remained parked on Huron Avenue, no doubt collecting parking tickets.

The streets were empty, and he got to Brighton in fifteen minutes. Spotting a residential-looking street, he pulled over and parked. The street was dim, lit by a distant streetlamp, the asphalt pitted and broken. A few lights were on in windows, probably night owls, but all was still.

He waited ten minutes, the radio playing quietly, and constantly checked his rearview and side mirrors. When he was sure no car was following him—as sure as he could be, anyway—he made a U-turn and drove over to Mayfield Street, three blocks from Tanner Roast, and pulled over again and waited.

After five minutes he was satisfied, again, that no one was lurking nearby.

He parked and walked, instead of directly to the office, around three sides of the block, looking for loiterers, or people sitting in dark cars, until he came to the seldom-used side door. He inserted his key card, which buzzed it open. The inner door was locked with a funky-looking narrow key. An Abloy lock, made by a Swedish company, supposedly unpickable. After a rash of break-ins in the neighborhood, Tanner had had the warehouse and office rekeyed. Only he and Lucy and Sal had keys to the exterior doors.

Of course, that didn't mean that government agents couldn't break in. Surely they had ways.

Once inside, he heard the constant low tone from the burglar alarm and he flipped on a light, found the keypad, and immediately punched in the code to shut it off. Then he turned off the light. There were a few high windows, visible from the street, and he didn't want to give away so easily that someone was here. The truth was, he didn't know what to look for. He sold *coffee,* for God's sake. He wasn't a spy. Apparently they weren't staking out the office, or at least not in the middle of the night. That told him something. They were expecting him to keep traditional hours.

Or maybe they weren't looking for him, not in that

way. The guys from Homeland Security who came by the office earlier in the day: maybe that's all they were, agents from Homeland Security. Glorified cops. Not from some deep-secret agency of the government. Maybe he was overreacting to Lanny's death. He refused to believe it was a suicide, no matter what the evidence said.

Problem was, he couldn't be *certain*.

He decided he would act as if they were looking for him; he'd take measures, be careful.

He had an urgent, simple task now.

Faint blue-gray light filtered in through the windows, barely enough for him to navigate his way to his own office, his desk. There he stood, thinking, for a beat, his finger on the switch to his desk lamp. His office (smaller than his sales director's) wasn't near a window, but the light would still be visible through the windows that faced Mayfield Street. Better not to put it on.

He sat in his desk chair, closed his eyes briefly, then opened them, his eyes slowly acclimating to the dark. There was enough available light to see the keyboard on his computer. He logged in, moved some files onto his Dropbox, then sat still for a minute, wondering if it was safe.

At the far end of the warehouse there was a rustle.

He waited, still, listening. Nothing for fifteen seconds or so and then, again, an unmistakable rustling sound. Like paper rustling. Maybe it was nothing.

Or maybe it was someone, or something, moving at the far end of the warehouse.

That was also possible.

He got up noiselessly from his desk chair, walked slowly and quietly out of his office, and began advancing along the carpet. Underneath, the old floorboards squeaked intermittently, but not loudly. He stopped, listened for twenty seconds or so, heard nothing. Still, he advanced farther along the carpet to the entrance to the adjoining warehouse.

He stood in the entrance, at one end of the warehouse, and listened again. He felt his heart rate accelerate.

This time he heard it again, that furtive rustle. He looked around the warehouse, the shadows, the hulking shapes, the rows of shelving that held bags of green coffee, the big old roaster, the worktables. He could probably traverse the floor blindfolded.

The floors in here were poured concrete. They were quieter. They didn't squeak when he walked. But now he realized he was a moving shadow in this vast space, immediately identifiable as a person to anyone whose eyes had adjusted to the light the way his had.

Was it paranoid to wonder, or maybe half wonder, whether someone was waiting in the warehouse with a handgun? Maybe so; maybe he was being crazy. They came to get Lanny because he was about to report a story they didn't want made public. But why go after Tanner? Maybe to grab him and somehow compel him to turn over the laptop. That wasn't beyond the realm of plausibility. Not at all.

He walked farther along the floor, heard the rustling,

stopped. Turned his head and cocked his ear. Heard it again. Turned his head toward the sound.

A rat scurried along the packing table.

He made a mental note to have that table cleaned first thing tomorrow and bring in the exterminator again.

He went to the kitchen and opened the cabinet drawer, then dialed the combination of the safe.

The laptop was there. He slipped it into his gym bag.

Returning to his office, he put his iPhone in the top drawer of his desk. Then he spent another ten minutes or so gathering things and then slipped carefully out the building's side door.

45

Sarah's Fiat was parked a few blocks away, near a playground. The street was dim and narrow, and no one was around. It was residential—wooden three-deckers, tiny yards, their cars parked on thin slices of driveway.

He knew he was being overcautious. There was no reason to believe he was being followed or watched. But there was no downside to being extremely careful, taking extra measures. If they made for a longer return "home"—to the house for sale in Chestnut Hill—so what?

He started the car. At a slow and steady pace, he drove down the street and took a right onto the main drag here, Western Avenue, a broad two-way street. Cars were parked along one side. He passed a car wash, a couple of half-empty lots, a few auto-body places ("Collision Specialists!"), a used-car dealer. A lot of auto-related enterprises on this stretch, he noticed. On the right, a bank. Then a gas station. A couple of freestanding, modest wooden houses in disrepair.

No one behind him.

He turned into the no-name gas station, which was on a corner, cut through the lot, and turned onto the side street. A detour, probably unnecessary. He circled around the block, took a right and then another right onto Market Street. He went straight for several blocks, at moderate speed, down the nearly abandoned street. He stopped at a red light, even though the intersection was empty in all directions. In his rearview mirror he saw a car approaching behind him, a black Suburban. Behind the wheel was a blank-faced young crew-cut man, probably just returned from a late-night shift. Probably a limo driver just returned from dropping off a wealthy customer on Cape Cod. Tanner was glad he didn't have to work at night, even though some people didn't mind it, maybe even preferred the night shift. As the CEO of Tanner Roast, his hours were his own. No doubt he worked longer hours than most people had to. But he owned his own business; that was the key part.

And then he remembered that everything was on the bubble, in flux, and he felt tense.

He'd driven through three intersections and made a couple of turns, and he checked his rearview and saw that the crew-cut guy driving the Suburban was still behind him. Then he noticed that there was another crew-cut guy in the Suburban, in the passenger's seat. These weren't limo drivers.

He felt the paranoia start to creep over him with an

almost physical sensation, coming up his neck from his shoulders.

He hadn't made any extra turns, nothing designed to flush out a follower. He'd allowed himself to drift a bit mentally and so had let down his guard. He saw a sign for a Dunkin' Donuts and took a sudden right immediately after it, without putting on his turn signal.

The Suburban did too, swerving wildly with a loud metallic squeal, staying right behind him, and there was no question now the driver was following him.

For a moment he panicked, thinking he might have turned into a dead end, but then he came to a small intersection, where he turned left, accelerating as he did, scraping into the side of a parked car.

He'd damaged Sarah's car. "Shit."

He stepped on the gas, and the Fiat responded immediately, the car bucking as it shot forward. He turned left again, the Suburban just behind. Then he accelerated some more, cutting the wheel to the right, up and over the curb, the car jolting as it dropped to the pavement of Market Street again. For at least a block ahead he could see no cars.

So he floored it. The Suburban was a lumbering truck, more powerful than the Fiat for sure, a great American-made beast.

Only at the last minute did he see, on his right, a car door suddenly open, right into his path. He reacted at once, spinning the wheel to the left, but it was an instant too late.

The Fiat crashed into the door, steel crunching loudly against steel, shearing the door right off, wrenching it off its hinges, the door flying into the air and then—he glanced at his rearview—slamming into the windscreen of the Suburban. The glass spider-webbed. Thank God no one was hurt.

But it didn't seem to slow his pursuer down. The Suburban was right on his tail, actually chasing him. A goddamned car chase! At three thirty in the morning. Adrenaline coursed throughout his body. He felt the tremor in his veins.

The Fiat was nowhere near as powerful, but it was smaller, peppier, and nimbler, capable of going places the Suburban could not, of accelerating much more quickly. That had to be an advantage. He barreled ahead down the street, swerving wildly to the right and then back around, across the empty oncoming lanes, a U-turn, then turning into a side street. The maneuver had put some distance between him and the Suburban. He was almost an entire block ahead of the Suburban, which enabled him to abruptly swing the car to the right, into an alley. Mentally he ran through several possible scenarios, rejecting each one as foolish and dangerous.

But apparently he'd lost the Suburban. He raced down the alley and out the far end. Up ahead loomed Harvard Stadium, illuminated by the moonlight, like some Roman ruin. As he approached, he noticed the black iron fencing around the athletic complex, making a large island, the fence broken by several pedestrian entrances.

In his peripheral vision, the Suburban lumbered into view.

A block away.

But the Fiat and the Suburban were, at the moment, the only moving cars on the street. The Suburban sped up, coming toward the Fiat from behind.

Tanner floored the accelerator, and the Fiat nearly vaulted ahead. He had a one-block head start. Now he faced a choice. Three possible routes. Barrel ahead to the next intersection and right up the boulevard to Harvard Square. Or up to the intersection and right on Soldier's Field Road, the sunken highway that ran by, heading toward Boston.

Or just pull over, park, and surrender. Give up. Instead of running, and continuing to run for some indefinite period of time, maybe forever. Giving up made a certain kind of sense. He'd done nothing wrong. He had a United States senator's laptop computer, true. He'd be happy to turn it over to its rightful owner as long as he could be assured that he and his wife would be safe.

But in truth, he didn't know what to expect. Lanny's bogus suicide was a warning, all the warning he needed, of the possible consequences of being caught up in . . . whatever this was. Some kind of secret government program, it had to be. Knowledge of which was clearly a dangerous thing.

Giving up was not an option. Tanner processed and decided this in a split second. Then he saw, on his left, the main gate to the athletic complex, which was really three gates—one, in the center, for autos, and two smaller ones on either side for pedestrians.

The automobile gates were closed, but the left-hand pedestrian gate was open.

And then he did a quick calculation. The Fiat was probably just over five feet wide. The gate looked to be six feet wide, maybe a bit more. Or maybe the gate was exactly six feet wide and the Fiat was a few inches less.

Or so he hoped.

Was it worth taking the chance?

The longer he kept driving, the greater the odds of getting caught. They would have other vehicles; the government always did. They could call for backup. Maybe they already had.

He had to take the chance.

He jacked the wheel to the left, aiming as carefully as he could at the dead center of the open gate.

And he floored the gas again, and time slowed down. He stared at the opening, his eyes shifting from side to side. He could eyeball the dimensions of a shipping container without error. But to estimate the size of an opening in a fence from a moving car? He could be off by two feet.

If the span between the brick-ornamented stone gateposts was much less than six feet, he would crash into the wrought-iron fence and brick and stone and quite possibly be killed at this speed.

But if his estimate was accurate, he'd have maybe two inches of clearance on either side of the car. Which would be enough to pass through. Leaving the Suburban behind.

And then came a loud, ear-splitting screech of metal against metal as the car scraped against wrought iron, both sides of it, and then slammed to a halt. It was lodged halfway through the gate. From behind came the squeal of brakes, and the Suburban stopped just short of crashing into the Fiat.

He realized with surprise that the airbags hadn't deployed.

He yanked at the handle of the car door to open it and then pushed it outward. It opened maybe half an inch. The door was stuck against the gate. He could not get out.

He could see, in his peripheral vision, movement on the other side of the fence, heard a door open and then close. One of the guys was out of the vehicle, and maybe he had a gun—a safe guess.

But somehow Tanner had to move.

Again he tried to shove the door open, but it was wedged tightly.

He hit the button to roll down the window, and as soon as it was all the way down, he maneuvered his legs out of the well of the driver's seat, flipped himself around, and thrust his legs out the open window. He scrabbled his legs over and out and down, then wriggled his body along the windowsill until he was able to grab onto the steering wheel and shove himself all the way out. He dropped, almost tumbled, out of the car. He stumbled against the pavement, jumped to his feet, and reached back into the car, the passenger side, and grabbed his gym bag.

He glanced at the fence behind him and saw that the driver of the Suburban had abandoned the vehicle on the shoulder of the road and had taken off, by foot, no doubt in search of another open gate. And he saw that the metal skin of the Fiat had buckled and warped at the sides.

He turned. Directly ahead of him was Harvard Stadium, the big old concrete coliseum, built a hundred years ago. He raced toward it, toward the nearest gate, a tall arched portal. More wrought-iron fencing here, the gate closed. He pushed at it, and it came open. He ran into the darkness.

He had a rough idea of what was located where in the stadium, because some years ago, in a short-lived fit of self-improvement, he used to "run stadiums," which meant running up and down the concrete steps until he couldn't take it anymore, when his legs had turned into spaghetti. A brutal workout. The Steps of Death, people called it.

He paused for a moment. Up the stairs to the stadium, then down to the football field, and out?

He wondered how much time he had before the Suburban driver came after him. Because he had a feeling the driver was more than a driver. The Suburban was stuck outside the wrought-iron fence. Even if the driver jumped out of the vehicle to pursue Tanner on foot, he might not find another open pedestrian gate. Not close by. Though maybe, down the block, another gate would be open.

Either way, he had about a minute on his pursuer. Maybe two. He kept in decent shape, worked out almost every day, though he hadn't in the chaotic last several days. And he was a natural athlete.

But he was an amateur, and his adversary was probably a pro. Even if Tanner could outrun his pursuers, which seemed probable, backup was likely to show soon.

He had an idea.

He turned to the right. He could hear loud buzzing from high-voltage power lines and could just make out a sign: STADIUM HIGH-VOLTAGE ROOM. He had a vague memory of once turning the wrong way, looking for a restroom here, and coming upon a dark area under the concrete steps where the floor was earthen.

He passed through a narrow space between the high-voltage room and an array of wall-mounted fuse boxes, and then the pavement gave way to gravel and dirt. He could feel the ground yield underfoot. His shoes crunched on the gravel. There was enough clearance between the ground and the underside of the concrete steps for him to stand up.

Moonlight filtered in through the gaps in the stadium overhead, so that he could make his way over to a large sheet of plywood leaning against a concrete support beam. It was wide enough to stand behind. To hide. He set down the gym bag quietly.

His pursuer would run into the stadium, because he'd seen Tanner enter. But then he'd face the same choices as his quarry. He would surely assume that Tanner would race through the stadium and immediately out. Because no one would be stupid enough to stay here.

Which is exactly what he would do: stay here, concealed behind the four-by-eight sheet of plywood, in the shadows in a hidden area beneath the stadium steps.

And wait.

46

He waited and listened.

The buzz of the high-voltage room. The whoosh of a car passing by. He listened for footsteps, running.

But he heard nothing else.

Then a distant voice, a shout coming from far off.

The driver and the backup?

He stood still, controlled his breathing, kept it as quiet as possible. And listened.

After two or three minutes, he heard rapid footsteps: someone running nearby. Whether passing by or approaching, he couldn't tell. He could smell freshly cut lumber from the plywood.

The sound of footsteps ceased. He breathed in and out slowly, steadily, quietly. Still no more footsteps. He knew that if someone thought to check underneath the steps where he was, he would hear them enter, hear the crunch of gravel.

What he would do then, though—he had no idea. Probably surrender. Or maybe try to run. He didn't know, actually, what he'd do. He'd decide if and when it came to that.

For now he just listened.

A minute went by without the sound of footsteps. He heard that distant shout again.

The snarl of the high-voltage room. That was all.

Somehow he managed to stand there for close to an hour. He thought. He kept his guard up. He didn't cough. His thoughts raced, about Tanner Roast and all that was going on with that, and about the damned laptop and how it had turned his life into some sort of hell.

Finally, he picked up the gym bag. He peered around the plywood panel and saw no shapes, no shadows moving. He sidled out from behind it, walked slowly across the gravel, trying to keep the crunch underfoot to a minimum.

And still he heard no footsteps.

He walked up the gravel slope, returning to the pavement of the public area of the stadium. When he reached the high-voltage room, he stood still, the buzzing loud in his ears. He realized that the sound, this close, made it impossible to hear most other sounds. So he was at a disadvantage.

He peered around the high-voltage room and saw nobody. Slowly, quietly, he walked through the shadows of the stadium, parallel to the street. When he came to the next arched gateway, he was able to see out to the street. The Suburban was gone.

What did that mean?

Would it be waiting for him at the next street exit out of the athletic complex?

Or was it gone—and the driver had given up?

Tanner was hyperaware of how visible he now was, walking past the stadium, past the parking lot turnstile. He passed a couple of empty side lots.

No Suburban passing by.

He kept walking. A car shooshed by and kept going.

He came to a low chain-link fence, maybe three or four feet high, protecting a running track that surrounded a soccer field. Try to vault it? He scrambled over the fence, lifted himself, swung his feet. Crossed the track and field. Scrambled over the next fence, and walked, didn't run, to the outside fence, also chain-link, around the whole complex. On the other side was Western Avenue, a few cars passing by in either direction.

Slinging the gym bag over his shoulder onto his back, he climbed the chain-link fence, maybe seven feet high here, went up and over, and landed softly on the sidewalk.

After walking for about twenty minutes, Tanner was able to hail a cab, which took him the rest of the way there. Pale sunlight glimmered on the horizon by the time he reached Brimmer Street in Chestnut Hill and the Georgian mansion where he was going to sleep for a night or two. He began to follow the same procedure as before, punching in the code to release the padlock on the front door, when he realized that the padlock was already unlocked, its hasp open.

Strange, he thought. *Maybe a real estate agent forgot to lock it.*

Was that possible?

Possible.

The other possibility was that someone was inside, waiting for him.

But he was overreacting, he told himself, letting the fear sink its hooks into him. He slowly opened the door, the foyer pitch-dark.

It smelled different here. He couldn't explain it to himself, couldn't say for sure what was different, but it was. Something besides the fresh paint and the apple cider.

He wondered if that meant that someone was inside the house. Or that someone had been in the house since he'd last been here. But it was too early for a showing, right? Or whether he was just picking up on a scent he hadn't noticed earlier. Because he felt the prickle of fear, of paranoia, and maybe that was distorting his perception.

He stood still a moment and listened, and he heard nothing.

Leaving the lights off, he climbed the staircase. The master bedroom was at the end of the dark hall, after a series of smaller rooms and a bathroom. He knew this from his prior exploration.

As he rounded a turn, he saw light spilling out of the master bedroom, its door open. He approached slowly, quietly, his tread silent on the wall-to-wall carpeting. All he could hear was his heart pounding. He could smell that familiar note more strongly here.

He entered the bedroom.

And at the same moment he remembered what that smell was, he saw a pair of familiar jeans-clad legs and stockinged feet sticking out of the side of an overstuffed chair.

She turned, and now Tanner could see she'd been reading a book—*Ragtime,* by E. L. Doctorow.

"What happened to your face?" Sarah said.

47

My face?"

Tanner set down his bag and felt the left side of his face, which in fact felt a little warm. His fingers came away sticky. Blood. It must have happened when he crashed the Fiat through the gates of Harvard Stadium, when he was thrown forward.

"Did you get attacked or something?" Sarah said.

He shook his head. "I went back to the office to get some stuff."

"You risked that?"

"Not a good decision, as it turned out."

"Why? What happened?"

"Some guys followed me when I was driving. Damage to your car might have resulted."

"They hit the car?"

"No. I hit a fixed object and got kicked around a very little bit. I'm fine."

"Do I dare ask about my car?"

"That's a complicated story. But I think it may be time for a new one."

"Tanner! You know I don't have any money."

"I'll take care of everything." Not that he had any money either. But he was going to have to buy her a brand-new Fiat somehow.

She shook her head disapprovingly, but a tiny smile crawled across her face. "That's so you. You'll take care of everything."

"Why are you here? I mean, don't get me wrong, I'm glad to see you, but—"

"One of the brokers had a late showing, and they changed the code on the padlock. So I came here to meet you last night, and it was cold, and I decided to come inside and wait. And then I thought I'd just take a nap, and— Tanner, I need to talk to you."

"Is it about my face?"

They went down to the kitchen to make coffee. Sarah fired up the Nespresso machine on the kitchen counter.

Tanner grimaced. "Fancy instant coffee."

"It's pretty good, actually, Tanner. Give it a chance."

Tanner agreed to a demitasse of Dharkan—not bad at all—and Sarah had one too, and she said, "Look, I haven't been sleeping at night. I'm basically scared shitless about what's happening to you."

"It's going to be okay," Tanner said. "Don't worry about it."

Sarah looked at him. Their eyes met. She took a sip of espresso. "I always know when you're lying to me."

"It's nothing to worry about."

"Except you can't go home, you can't go to work, and you were just almost killed."

"Not even close to being killed. Please stop worrying."

Sarah took another sip. "Do you remember that time when we were driving in the Adirondacks, going to Uncle Johnny's cabin, and we got stuck in that blizzard?"

"Sure do."

"And we were driving that crappy old Jetta, the Rustmobile as you called it, and we got stuck in the snowdrift?"

Tanner chuckled. He remembered a near-death experience and Sarah close to freaking out, and only now could he laugh. They'd been together for a couple of years by then, and he was learning to navigate the complex topography of this beautiful woman's personality.

"And the tires are spinning in place and we're getting spattered through the rust holes in the floor, and the car's not moving, and all of a sudden this huge tractor-trailer in the other lane loses control, it's *jackknifing* on the black ice, and it's coming at us, this eighty-thousand-pound truck?"

He nodded. He remembered wondering if this was their last few seconds on earth. Wondering whether they should scramble out of the car into the snow, whether they had time to do that, deciding to stay put. He remembered her screaming, terrified, and him not wanting her to see he was just as frightened.

"And I'm basically losing it, and you just grab my hands—you're perfectly calm—and you say, 'We're going to be okay, don't worry about it, we'll be fine.' "

"Yeah?"

"You must have been just as terrified as I was; we're just trapped in that tin can and this gigantic truck is about to squish us like bugs. But you stayed calm; you had to stay strong for me. All you cared about was how scared I was."

"I told you we'd be fine." He remembered going into that calm place, a peaceful acceptance of the fact that they had no control over what was about to happen to them. And that weird calmness somehow looked like bravery.

"You're doing it again now. Only this time the tractor-trailer's not going to miss us."

"This is not about us. This is just about me. And I'll be okay."

"How long do you think you can hide from—from whoever these people are? You, one person, against who knows how many, the whole goddamned government!"

"First of all, the US government doesn't kill American citizens—"

"Oh, that is so not true. The president has the right to kill Americans on American soil."

"Honey, this is all going to blow over soon. I'm sure of it." He put down his espresso cup.

"You know this because you have a plan?"

"Yes. I mean, not yet. But I will."

"Tanner!" she said. She was crying, tears pooling in her eyes, her face red. "I can't lose you."

"Hey," he said very softly, and he put his arms around her. She drew herself into him. The room was cold, and he could feel the warmth of her body.

"I can't lose you," she said again, and she put her mouth on his. He could feel the hot tears on her face.

48

A minute?" Will said.

Senator Susan Robbins was sitting in her office, meeting with their legislative director. Her office door was open, which meant she was doing routine work she didn't care if everyone knew about.

Today's suit color was amethyst, which he'd learned was not the same thing as purple. It also meant she was trying to cheer herself up on Dull Committee Work Day. All of her suits were Elie Tahari, or Tahari-style, but this was one of the older ones in the rotation, a few frays here and there.

She looked up from a sheaf of papers she was holding in both hands. Her death stare over her Benjamin Franklin reading glasses. "Urgent?"

He thought: *Do you really think I'd interrupt you if it wasn't something urgent*? He nodded. "I'd say, yeah."

"Samantha," Susan said, "can we pick this up a little later on? All right, Will, come on in. Sam, could you close the door behind you?"

On the left of her desk was the big American flag, furled, and on the right was the Illinois flag, also furled. Between the two flags was a painting of the Chicago skyline by some renowned Chicago painter, done in a sort of pointillist, Georges Seurat manner. No family photos on display—which was a subject of disagreement between the two. She insisted that women politicians should always downplay the family thing.

As soon as the door closed, Will said, "Have they interviewed you yet?"

"Who?"

"OSS."

"The . . . OSS? The old spy agency?"

"Office of Senate Security."

"What's this . . . ?"

"They haven't yet. Good." He didn't think she'd been interviewed yet. She'd have come to him first.

"Interview? What's this about?"

He inhaled slowly. "The documents."

"The laptop? This is about the goddamned *laptop*? They *know*?"

"No, they don't know about the laptop. Not as far as I know, anyway."

"Then what the hell are they interviewing for?"

"They believe that classified information was downloaded."

He could see the tension, the worry, crease her face. She shook her head, which seemed to mean *I don't understand*.

"A reporter called around asking about some NSA program."

"CHRYSALIS?"

"Probably."

"How is this going to lead to me?"

"It won't."

"But what happens when the guy in Boston gives my laptop to WikiLeaks or one of those websites, you know—"

"That won't happen."

She lowered her voice to an urgent whisper. "But you don't have the laptop! Where is it?"

"I'm working on something that you don't need to know about."

"And what's my strategy when they interview me? Just deny, deny, deny?"

"You don't know what they're talking about."

"But don't they have some computer way of finding out who used the computer at a certain time? A log or whatever?"

"I'm not sure what they know. But here's the thing: if they knew it was me, they wouldn't have let me off as easily as they did. They wouldn't have let me go."

"So you think they have no idea who did it?"

"Someone on the committee; that's all they know."

"But Gary doesn't know, does he?"

"I would never tell him."

"You . . . trust him?"

And then Will had an idea. "I'm not sure, actually.

Maybe . . . it might be worth mentioning his name in your interview."

"Gary's?"

He nodded. "It's not far-fetched that he might have done it."

"But there's no grounds for the accusation—"

"You're just wondering. That's all. Vague speculation. Coming from you, they'll take it seriously."

"Hmm," she said. "Interesting."

"It might deflect suspicion. Send them barking up the wrong tree. While I get the laptop back."

There was a long moment of silence. Will didn't want to break the silence. He knew she was thinking, considering the idea. Let her mull it over.

"That's an interesting idea," she said.

He smiled and nodded. He knew what that meant. He didn't want to push too hard. She was on board.

It was, Will knew, a game of chess. You sacrificed pieces to avoid checkmate. You always had to take the long view. That was a lesson Will had learned the year he first became Senator Robbins's chief of staff.

He'd made a trip back home to Greenville to visit his ailing mom. While he was there he got a call from an old friend of his mother's, Mrs. Karabell. She wanted his help.

She told him that the town was using its powers of eminent domain to take away her flower farm and transfer the property to the Carmichael Corporation, the chemical giant.

Will was outraged and told Mrs. Karabell he'd take care of it.

When he was in grade school, he was a sort of latchkey child—both his parents worked, and his mom sold houses on the side—and he used to hang out a lot at Mrs. Karabell's house. He didn't have a lot of friends. Mrs. Karabell was like his second mom. He always did his homework on her kitchen table. There was always a slice of chocolate cake waiting for him, with a glass of cold milk, when he got there. In the winter she made the best hot chocolate Will had ever tasted. He loved Mrs. Karabell.

So when he got back to Washington, he walked into the boss's office and told her he needed a favor. He needed her to help out Mrs. Karabell's flower farm.

He would never forget her reply.

Susan Robbins said, "You're right. I could make a call and save those four acres of petunias. But let me give you the bigger picture. Everything is connected, Will. When I make that call to your town, I'll save the flowers and earn Mrs. Karabell's vote—and also the everlasting enmity of the Carmichael Corporation. And you know what's going to happen?"

Will shook his head, nearly hypnotized by the senator's direct gaze, her deep blue eyes.

"My next primary, I'm suddenly going to discover that I have a surprisingly impressive, well-funded opponent.

Now, I'll probably defeat him, or her, but then another well-funded opponent will pop up in the general. And who knows if I keep my seat. Maybe I do. My coffers will be depleted, and I'll be like a bird with a broken wing. A target for all sorts of political opportunists."

"Okay," Will said, but the boss was not yet done.

"In two years I'm up for reelection. And I want you to think about all the great things we want to get done, every legislative achievement that we could realize that's never going to happen because I did a good deed—and then I want you to think about Mrs. Karabell's four acres of petunias. Do you really want me to make that call, Will?"

The next time Will went back to Greenville, he went to see Mrs. Karabell. Wonderful Mrs. Karabell, with her walker and her breast cancer, who was now ruined. She said, "I don't understand."

And Will looked straight at her, unconsciously aping Senator Robbins's direct gaze. And he lied. He spun some fable. And he felt like crap.

He knew he'd done the right thing. But that didn't make the shitty feeling go away.

That was the stink of power. Sometimes doing the right thing could make you feel lousy.

49

Sarah woke him, shaking him by the shoulder.

"Sorry, Tanner, but you have to get up." He must have dozed off, caffeine notwithstanding. She was naked and had something in her other hand. He could smell coffee.

"What time is it?" He glanced at his watch but his eyes were too unfocused to make out the watch face.

"Six thirty. There's a seven-thirty showing."

"Who looks at houses at seven thirty?"

"Extremely serious buyers, I bet." She handed him an espresso. Her breasts were small and shapely, with light pink areolas, small raised mounds. He remembered a novelist once describing a woman's breasts as two scoops of the smoothest vanilla and thought that aptly described Sarah's. "Most of my showings are on weekends."

"Instant coffee," he said. "Yum."

"You didn't spit it out last time. That's how I know you like it."

"Busted." He grinned, took a sip. His clothes were strewn across the carpet. "Thank you."

"For what?"

"For the coffee." And he grinned again.

Her clothes, too, were arrayed on the floor. She picked up her panties and slipped them on. Then she picked up her bra, black and lacy, clasped it in front of her, and spun it around and into place. "Tanner," she said, "I'm not going to cash out."

"Why not?" She was coming back home, he now knew for sure, almost.

She looked at him mischievously, leaned over, and gave him a peck on the lips. "Because I don't want to lose money," she said.

"Thanks," Tanner said with a faux scowl.

"No," she said. "Because I don't want to lose you."

Sarah was out of the house before Tanner, leaving him to straighten the bedclothes on the big inflatable bed and making sure he didn't have anything in the master bathroom. She'd given him a printout of houses for sale, and next to the first three on the list were scrawled numbers. Codes to their padlocks.

Before he left the house, he peered out the front sitting room window and satisfied himself that there was no one out there waiting for him. There didn't seem to be.

Then he left through the front door and padlocked the

house, looking around as he descended the steps, his gym bag slung over one shoulder. He hadn't been aware of anyone following him after his escape in Harvard Stadium. No one knew he was here.

He had no car, and without his iPhone—it took him a moment to remember he'd left it in his desk at work—he couldn't call an Uber. So he walked a few blocks to Beacon Street, where he could flag down a passing cab. But first he got a fried egg sandwich at a deli and a coffee, which tasted burnt. He called Lucy Turton, got her at home, and talked a few minutes, Tanner Roast business. He called Karen, got her in her car on the way to work. He let her vent for a minute or so, then went through a list of potential deals and ones that fell apart and she couldn't get back together. He thanked her and reassured her, told her everything was going just great.

Then he grabbed a cab.

On the way in to his gym, he bought a bottle of water from the plump Nepalese guy's fruit stand on Tremont Street.

"Good morning, Ganesh," he said. "How's your sister?"

"A gallstone is all it was," Ganesh replied. "She's much better."

"Good."

He got on the elliptical trainer for an hour. He needed to work out badly, he hadn't in days, and he thought that maybe a good solid hour of cardio would calm him, make him less jittery.

That it did. When he'd dressed in his street clothes, he put everything back into the locker, including the used workout stuff, and took the gym bag. He clicked the brass combination lock closed and spun the dial.

He came up the steps and pushed open the glass door and came out on Tremont Street.

He felt a little prickle at the back of his head. He was immediately on alert. He didn't see anyone suspicious, but his subconscious must have picked up something. It was morning rush hour, the street busy with people walking past in either direction. He smelled a passing woman's perfume.

Then something grabbed his right wrist, and when he whipped around to look, something, or someone, grabbed his left arm too.

Tanner wrenched his left arm free and swung a fist around at whoever had grabbed him. His fist connected hard with a man's face. He could feel something give way. His knuckles instantly began to throb, but he was sure the other guy's nose must have hurt a lot more.

Then something stung the back of his neck, like a wasp or a hornet. He winced as he torqued his body around, slammed his right elbow back into whoever had just stung him, and kneed one of his assailants in the groin. But he felt as if he were melting like a stick of butter in the microwave. He could barely summon the strength to fight. He jabbed his fists into his attacker's abdomen, but he knew it was pointless; he didn't have the power.

He was trundled to the curb, where an SUV sat parked, rear door open. He yelled, jerked both his arms and his legs, not that he expected to free himself but to signal to passersby that he was being forcibly taken, against his will. He stumbled, feeling molten, and the two men who'd grabbed him lifted him and glided him along without his feet touching the ground again.

Several people stared as they went by, surprise on their faces, but no one shouted out or did anything to rescue him. He probably looked like a drunkard, stumbling around. A mental patient.

He was pulled into the back of that black Suburban, the two guys on either side of him in the row behind the driver. His wrists were zip-cuffed by the first guy, while the guy on his right pulled a set of goggles over Tanner's head. They were blacked out, like opaque sunglasses. Then he put a pair of acoustic headphones on him, instantly deadening the sound. He could see and hear almost nothing, and he was powerless to do anything about it.

There was a faint high-pitched electronic hum in his ears. Then a man's voice spoke crisply in his ears.

"*Mis*-ter Tanner," said the voice, which seemed to be coming from inside his head. "Michael Evan Tanner." A southern accent. The words spoken with a formal intonation, as if announcing a dignitary's arrival at a royal ball. "You are not an easy man to find."

"But you did," Tanner said, and he was unsure whether he had actually said it aloud. He tried to locate a calmness inside but was unable to slow the walloping of his heart.

"Oh, we always do," said the voice.

In a minute or so, the warmth overtook him, and then he felt and saw nothing.

50

The senator was eating a salad at her desk. She'd just come back from two fund-raising lunches, but she didn't like eating in front of other people. Except Will, which was something he was secretly proud of. She waved hello with her plastic fork and finished chewing her mouthful. Will closed the office door.

"I don't have any news," Will said, sitting in her visitor chair. "Any good news, anyway. But we've got to talk about the possibility that this thing might get out. That the cat might get out of the bag. Because this is a very, *very* big cat."

She looked at him for a long time before she said, "CHRYSALIS."

He hesitated. "And the fact that you signed off on it."

"Reluctantly. Along with a majority of the committee."

"I've given this a lot of thought. You know, they'll call you an 'NSA stooge.'" She was known to be a supporter of the intelligence community but of the "tough love" variety. Agency budget requests always got a haircut.

She'd been quoted as saying, "We all need to do more with less, including our vital intelligence community." But in public she was rarely critical of the intelligence agencies.

"Oh, it'll be a shit storm, all right."

"A shit storm? Boss, it'll be more like a vast *asteroid* of shit slamming into the continent. I mean, politically speaking, this is an *extinction-level event,* okay?"

She looked surprised at his intensity. Tonelessly, she said, "Go on."

He thought about CHRYSALIS. Goddamned CHRYSALIS. The product of the NSA's finest minds. The most advanced example of its technical wizardry. CHRYSALIS would enable the agency to invisibly access any of the cameras in every phone, every laptop, every desktop, every personal digital assistant. Without the user being aware of it. Turning hundreds of millions of cameras into always-on nanny cams. Naturally, there were assurances made that the teraflops of data would be algorithmically gathered and stored away, never to be seen by any human observer, blah blah blah—unless a secret court deemed it relevant in the course of an investigation.

He stood up and came around to her side of the desk, his voice quiet, urgent. "You know how this is going to play out, right? Once it goes public? This is what they'll say about it. This is the portrait they'll paint. Millions of people, American citizens, recorded against their will in their most intimate, most private moments. Farting, picking their noses, getting off to porn, taking a dump. Every goddamned laptop and cell phone and anything with a camera turned into a staring, always-open eye."

She closed her eyes, shook her head. "That's not how it sounded when they presented it, with all that hoo-ha about optical signal feeds and getting full feeds on the bad guys. And how it's only inspected by machines, not human beings. It sounded safe—and necessary."

"It's mass surveillance, and the American public's going to freak out."

The senator stared at him for a long while. "Will, do you think we made a mistake?"

We? he thought. He'd argued *against* it! But no, there was ISIS and al-Qaeda, and the tragic terrorist attacks last year, and her constituents wanted scalps. "I think that's irrelevant at this point," he said. "There's already rumors about how the government has ways of turning on the camera on your computer. People are going to feel humiliated—they'll feel *violated*—and they will come for us with pitchforks and torches and there will be no forgiveness and no bargaining."

"Will, the data won't actually be accessed unless there is—"

"Unless some secret court makes a secret authorization with no real oversight? That's how they're going to play it. We are turning the sanctity of the home into a . . . a movie set. Every house a glass house. Big Brother stuff. I'm not arguing the rights and wrongs of this. I'm talking about the *optics.* That's how it's gonna play. On CNN, the volume dialed up to eleven. *These US senators just abolished privacy.*"

"With the proper explanation—"

"Susan, it's that rule of politics you taught me on day one: when you're explaining, you're losing."

He wondered if he'd gone too far with her, been too candid, too blunt. He expected her exasperated gaze, but to his surprise she looked pained.

"Then there's the question of what happens if the NSA gets it before we do."

"That can't happen. They'd hold it over me, use it as blackmail—use it to *control* me. They'd turn me into a marionette, with its strings in their slimy hands. You realize that cannot happen. You *cannot* let that happen."

"I won't," he said. "I have a plan. I may need to be out of the office for a couple of days, but Jodie can take over."

"Fine."

"I'm on it," he said.

51

Tanner became aware that he was talking, or maybe mumbling, to someone in front of him, in a very white room. His vision was blurry, and everything seemed strangely bright. He felt hungover. He was able to make out a woman with short blond hair sitting across a table from him.

"A brother and a sister," Tanner was saying, his words slurred. He must have been asked if he had any siblings. Who was this woman asking him questions, and where the hell was he? His feet felt cold, and he realized he was wearing socks and no shoes.

"Hey, where the hell are my shoes?" he said, his voice hoarse.

He was in a white room that seemed to have nothing in it except the long table he was sitting at across from the blond woman. On the wall behind her was a large mirror. He was still dressed in his clothes, but they'd taken away his shoes and his belt.

He hurt in a number of places. The knuckles on his left

hand. His right side. A painful spot at the back of his neck, at the base, where the wasp had stung him. No, he remembered, it wasn't a wasp, more like a needle, a hypodermic syringe. A large area on the back of his right arm felt bruised and tender. His lower back, around his right kidney, was painful and covered with a bandage.

He remembered now: he'd been grabbed outside the sports club, he'd fought with a couple of guys, and he must have been injected with something, and then he was hustled into the back of an SUV. They'd put opaque goggles over his eyes and earphones over his ears, and then he couldn't see or hear anything.

"And where were you born?" the woman went on.

"No," he said slowly. "I'm done here. Where the hell am I?"

"This shouldn't take much longer."

"Not gonna take any longer. Because I'm not answering any more questions. I want to know where am I, and am I under arrest or not? What's the deal?"

The door came open and a man stepped in. He said, "Excuse me, Deborah. I'll take over now, thank you."

He was middle-aged and stoop shouldered and wore an ill-fitting navy-blue suit with a dress shirt and no tie. He had dark hair, which looked colored, cut short, cut into short bangs atop a high forehead.

He gave a lopsided smile. The man had a craggy, pitted face. A homely face, but somehow a friendly one.

Deborah got up with her clipboard and exited the room.

"Who are you?" Tanner said.

"Earle." He put out his hand as if to shake.

Tanner ignored his proffered hand. The guy smelled like Irish Spring soap.

"You're Michael," the man said. "Mike?"

"Tanner."

"All right, Mr. Tanner." He spoke with a deep-southern accent. His voice had an abrasive edge, like a buzz saw. It sounded familiar. It had been the voice over the headphones earlier, when he'd just been taken.

"You have a last name, Earle?"

"I think my Christian name is good enough for now. You certainly did a number on my friend Joshua."

"I don't know what you're talking about."

"Pretty sure you broke his nose."

"Oh, right. It got in the way of my fist."

"The reason we brought you here is that you are in possession of a laptop computer that doesn't belong to you, on which there are numerous top secret classified documents. Are we in agreement on at least this much, Mr. Tanner?"

"Who are you?"

"National Security Agency. You've probably heard of it." When Tanner didn't reply, the craggy-faced man went on: "Let's just make this simple. You need to hand over that laptop forthwith."

"You want to tell me what laptop you're talking about?"

Earle sighed, like the disappointed father of a wayward son. "Mr. Tanner, please don't waste your time and mine.

My agency has the legally established right to read your e-mails and your texts and much else besides. And not just you but anyone and everyone you're in touch with. Which includes your wife, from whom you appear to be separated, your friends, and your employees at Tanner Roast."

"You've been reading my e-mails and listening to my goddamned *phone* calls?"

He smiled, displaying a spread of crooked teeth. "I didn't say we did anything. I merely said we have the *right* under United States law. It's perfectly legal."

"So was slavery."

"Fair enough."

"And so much for my constitutional right to privacy."

"Privacy? Really?" He shook his head. "Get over it. No such thing anymore."

"Says who?"

"Last time you upgraded software on your computer, I'll bet you clicked that little Agree box, right? But did you actually read what you were agreeing to? Who the hell's gonna read twelve thousand words in seven-point type, right? You don't know what it says. What if it requires your first-born child? A pound of flesh? Welcome to America, land of *Click Agree!* You didn't read the privacy policy, and you wouldn't understand it if you did."

"That's got nothing to do with—"

"Fitbit knows how much you exercise and how long you sleep, and Netflix knows when you stopped watching *Legends of the Fall* and when you're binge watching *Ar-*

rested Development. You'll give away data on all your purchasing habits in order to save a quarter on Honey Nut Cheerios."

Earle scratched the top of his head, mussing his hair. "Forget privacy; what we all really want is *convenience*. We write private e-mails that our employer has the legal right to read, am I right? Every time you use your SpeedPass on the turnpike or swipe your debit card at Walmart or buy your meds at CVS, you're being tracked. You got OnStar in your car, Waze on your phone? You know they track where you went and how fast you got there, and they can sell your data to anyone they want? And if you don't know all this, you're not as smart as I thought. You really think you got privacy anymore?

"Every time you walk down the streets of the city your picture's being taken by a surveillance camera. There's automatic license-plate readers all over the place. Google knows everything you've ever searched online. We live our lives in public all the time, like it or not. We're on Facebook for hours posting pictures of our dinner or Emma's pie, and noting Important Moments in our lives, like Matt's graduation and Kelly's confirmation and the baby's christening. We're posting our political opinions and our musical tastes and what we think about Donald J. Trump. But the kids, they're the ones who really get it. They *know* we live our lives in public now. They're always on Twitter or Instagram or Snapchat—that is, when they're not texting. They tell each other everything; they put everything online; they don't think twice. They know there's no such thing as privacy anymore. We all love our social networks and we love convenience and we *really* love exposure. It's the *transparent society,* and you know what? It's not half bad. You wanna guess why crime's been going down in New York City? You think everyone's gotten nicer? The cops are better? Hell no—it's cameras! They're everywhere, and we behave better on camera; we just do. Surveillance is civility, my friend, always has been. Surveillance is civility. You got nothin' to hide, you got nothin' to fear."

Tanner stared at Earle, who had finally fallen silent. "That laptop doesn't belong to you.

"In point of fact, those classified documents are the rightful property of the National Security Agency. They concern matters of national security, and under the law, once we demand them back, you are required to give them to us. No matter whose computer it is. It's the law. It's really that simple."

"You drugged me."

Earle shrugged, said nothing.

"I'm a legal US citizen, and you—"

"Mr. Tanner, let me be clear what your situation is. By receiving and holding top secret documents pertinent to our national security, you are in violation of 18 USC section 793. Which basically says, anyone who 'receives or obtains' a document relating to the national defense has committed a felony and shall be sentenced to a term of not more than ten years in prison."

"I have no idea what's on that laptop. If you tell me

there are classified documents on there, okay, sure, maybe there are, but how the hell would I know that?"

"Actually, Mr. Tanner, you passed on classified national defense information to a journalist, *knowing* it was classified, presumably with the intent to publish. And then a few days later you leave your home and go totally off the grid. You want to tell me that's not suspicious behavior?"

Tanner didn't reply. After a few seconds, Earle went on. "Look at it this way. You have a business that requires you to spend time in Guatemala, Honduras, Ecuador, and Nicaragua, countries where the CIA has historically had extensive involvement."

"Right. Where I was buying coffee."

"A perfect cover. Precisely the sort of legend we'd set up. Michael Tanner, coffee guy. The perfect part to play if you're an operative who needs to travel a lot. To countries with active insurgencies, death squads, people with long memories and deep pockets."

"Oh, bullshit."

"It would certainly explain how you managed to take out a highly trained ex-military specialist." He shrugged. "Personally, I'm agnostic as to whether you're a spy or a traitor. But certain colleagues of mine, including most notably my supervisor, have looked at your bio and have serious concerns. Give you an example. When Deborah asked if you've ever lived abroad, you conveniently left out the part about your junior year abroad. In Moscow. I find that interesting. It makes me wonder whether there's a part of your life we haven't been aware of."

Of course: Earle had been watching through the one-way mirror on the wall. "I have no idea what I might have said on drugs."

"I'm not making any accusations, Mr. Tanner. I'm just telling you what it looks like. I've been trying to assure my colleagues that you're simply a good man who made a bad mistake. I think you're just a guy who got lucky. Or should I say, unlucky. You somehow ended up with someone else's laptop. You saw that it had some interesting stuff on it, maybe newsworthy, so you make a copy of the files and hand a USB drive containing the documents in question to a friend of yours you drink beers with every week, who also happens to write for *The Boston Globe*."

"Oh yeah?" Tanner said, sarcastic.

"Maybe you weren't familiar with the laws on the mishandling of classified information. And maybe, in a more innocent time, the courts would have given that a pass. Dismissed all charges. But not these days, my friend. Not given the terrorist threat we live under. All right, look, Mr. Tanner. If I wanted to, I could have you arrested in about half an hour, and you would be prosecuted to the fullest, I *promise* you. But today you've won the lottery. Because I'm choosing to believe in your basic goodness. And I'm giving you twenty-four hours to save your life."

Tanner just looked at him.

"I don't care what Psych Analytics says. I think you're exactly who you seem to be. And I think you're in over your head. Doggy-paddling in deep waters. And I'm here to throw you a lifesaver. You only have to do one thing.

Come back tomorrow with that laptop computer. And any copies you might have made, flash drives, hard drives, everything." He handed Tanner a white business card. It was blank except for the name "Earle Laffoon," in small type, and underneath it, a phone number with a 410 area code. "Call me or text me at this number no later than ten A.M. tomorrow, and we'll meet you, wherever you are. You'll have the laptop with you."

"And in return?"

"In return you no longer have to worry about your friends from Fort Meade."

"I want this deal in writing."

"I'd be happy to shake your hand."

"Handshake deals are worthless."

"You have my word."

"I don't know you. I want it in writing."

"Not going to happen. That's not in the offing, and let's be honest, Michael, you're not exactly negotiating from a position of strength, now, are you?"

Tanner said nothing.

"Understand something, Mr. Tanner. By letting you go, I am putting my own career in jeopardy. You are, after all, a security risk. So I will be taking this extremely seriously. And if we don't see you again within twenty-four hours, I will be forced to escalate. You really don't want me to escalate. And we'll find you anyway—we always do."

52

Will waited for the scheduler, Rachel, to finish with the senator. He caught the senator's eye, nodded to let her know he was okay with waiting. Rachel got up two minutes later and blurted out, "Sorry!" when she saw that Will had been waiting.

"No problem," he said.

He closed the office door, turned, and folded his arms. "They've just released Tanner in Boston."

"Who, NSA?"

He nodded.

"What do you mean, 'released' him? I didn't even know they'd found him. Didn't you say they're looping you in?"

"They agreed to keep me apprised of their efforts to locate the guy, yes. But they didn't say they'd do it in a timely fashion."

"Damn them. I don't understand—what's the point of releasing him?"

"It's a deal they made with him. He's agreed to retrieve the laptop and bring it to them."

"That can*not* be allowed to happen."

"I know."

"Will, when someone tells me something is handled, I expect it to be handled."

Will didn't answer. He just waited for her to speak again, as he knew she would.

"Did he *talk* to them?" Robbins said. "Do they know whose laptop it is? They've *got* to know."

Will closed his eyes, shook his head. "If they knew, we'd know."

"What are you—?"

"One of their legal folks would have been in touch with you already."

"All right, then, can we—can you—?"

"Susan, this guy isn't going to cooperate. I don't know what he's up to, but he refuses to admit he even has it."

"Is it possible he doesn't?"

"No. He has it, and NSA knows that too. Problem is, he's got it hidden somewhere. I tried the sneaky approach; I tried the direct approach; nothing works. When—"

"Olshak," she said abruptly.

"Bruce Olshak? The—"

"He owes me a favor."

"Bruce Olshak does?" That was one of those names you didn't let pass your lips casually, Will reflected. Not, at least, in this town. Bruce Olshak was a notorious, near-legendary lawyer and fixer for the New England crime family. He was involved, in some way, with the Teamsters'

East Coast operations. He was known for paying off judges. It had been said of him that he lost his moral compass when Roy Cohn died. Olshak was basically Lord Voldemort with a collar bar. What was remarkable about him was that he'd never been caught doing any of the things he was famous for doing. He had never once been indicted for anything. "I don't think it's a good idea for you to be calling a guy like that."

"We're friends."

"It doesn't look good."

"Get me his phone number," she said.

"But you're not talking about—"

"Desperate times," she said. "Desperate measures."

53

They gave Tanner his shoes and belt back. Then the contents of his pockets: his phone, his wallet, his keys. Then his gym bag, which he hiked over one shoulder.

They put the headphones and the blacked-out goggles on him and ushered him out of the room. Someone held each of his elbows. They'd obviously done this many times before. They had their choreography down, sidling Tanner through what he guessed was a doorway, and then straight ahead for a long time.

In a while he was brought to a stop. Walked some more. Pulled to one side and then the other. Up a flight of stairs, then straight ahead again.

It was the strangest sensation: he saw only darkness and heard just the faintest electronic buzz, feeling dislocated and disengaged, yet he was able to walk, to propel himself just fine. He remembered reading that they did this to the prisoners in Guantanamo. No more black hoods.

He said, "Now, is this really necessary, gentlemen?"

He didn't know how loudly he'd just spoken. Could anyone hear him? He kept walking. Soon he felt cold air and smelled gasoline, the odors of a parking garage.

He was juked first one way, then another. Then he was stopped again.

With considerable difficulty, he was pulled and pushed and tugged until he was seated. On a car seat, it felt like. He could smell the kind of air freshener that comes in the shape of a pine tree that people dangle from their rear-view mirrors. Pretty soon he felt a rumble and a vibration and he knew the vehicle was moving.

He was driven somewhere for about ten minutes. The vehicle came to a stop.

Suddenly his goggles came off and everything around him was blindingly bright. His eyes ached at the dazzling light as shapes began to emerge. He was sitting in the same Suburban he'd been taken away in. They were parked on the side of a street at a busy city intersection. He could hear the metronomic ticking of the emergency flashers.

He knew right away where he was: at the corner of Washington and Milk Streets. They were double-parked in front of a Chipotle. All around him were the skyscrapers of Boston's financial district. Up ahead on the left was the Georgian steeple of the Old South Meeting House.

The guy on his left, who had a shaved head, was working with a strange metal tool, snipping the flex-cuffs off of him. When he had finished, the guy on his right, with a blond buzz cut, got out and opened the car door and held it open for Tanner.

"See you in twenty-four hours," said the guy on the right.

Tanner got out, and the blond guy got back in and swung the door closed and the Suburban gunned its engine and took off.

Standing unsteadily in front of Chipotle, he looked around, disoriented, at the lunchtime throngs. Someone jostled him out of the way. The wound on his lower back throbbed.

Now where?

He pulled a phone from his pocket. It was one of the disposable phones he'd bought. They'd taken it away from him and handed it back at the end. It indicated he had three voice messages. He listened to them. They were all from Lucy, mostly about small issues, nothing urgent.

He looked at the phone, wondered if they'd done something to it. He assumed they did, put in a bug or a tracker or something. Maybe that was why they had let him go. Because they could always find him. They were probably still surveilling him, watching where he went.

And they wanted the laptop.

He was fairly certain they didn't know whose it was. If they did, they probably would have focused on that. Talked about it, brought it up, threatened him some more. A senator's computer. A government big shot.

So the first order of business was to get some new disposable phones. He passed a Falafel King and Vitamin Shoppe and Subway and eventually found a CVS, where he bought an assortment of phones. Maybe the cashier figured him for a drug dealer. At the front of the store he was surprised to find a pay phone. They were getting more and more rare, used mostly by the few who didn't have either landlines or cell phones.

This gave him an idea. He wrote down the pay phone's number.

Since he was no longer on the run, he could now safely return home, for the first time in days. He walked—it was a crisp, clear day, Boston postcard weather—and arrived on Pembroke Street half an hour later. The alarm was still on. He entered the house carefully, looking around, sniffing like a dog. Nothing seemed, or smelled, different or unexpected, as far as he could tell.

But how did he know the place hadn't been wired for sound and video, implanted throughout with bugs?

In his bedroom he stripped and showered and dressed in a fresh set of clothes. He examined himself in the full-length mirror on the back of the bathroom door. Bruises were starting to emerge on his chest and his upper arm. There was a small bandage on his lower back, and a bruise on the back of his arm that was really starting to hurt. Interesting that they'd bandaged up his wounds. Because they hadn't avoided hurting him in the apprehension.

He finished dressing. Just as he was about to put on his usual leather belt, he stopped and looked at it. They'd taken this away from him, this and his shoes. He held it up and examined it. Nothing was attached to it. The buckle was brass and solid. He inspected the buckle end, where the leather strap was looped around the middle post. They might have inserted a miniature tracker or something like that in here. Possibly. He hadn't seen anything, but it was best to assume they did. He hung the belt up in the closet, selected another one just in case, and put it on. He picked out another pair of shoes.

He assumed they intended to tail him everywhere he went in the twenty-four hours until they met him again. He didn't intend to evade the watchers, not yet.

But the time would come.

In a closet in the basement where he stored luggage, he found an old backpack. In it he put the belt and shoes he'd been wearing when he was grabbed, along with a change of clothing and a pair of sneakers. When he left the house, he set the alarm.

Had he been followed? He wasn't sure. But it made no difference: he was going to his office. Maybe they had watchers on the streets around Tanner Roast. He didn't care. He'd assume they did.

By instinct he looked for his car in the alley behind the town house, then remembered that he'd left the Lexus parked on Huron Avenue in Cambridge. Definitely out of the way. So he hailed a cab and took it to his office.

On the way he called Sarah, on the burner he'd given her.

"Do you know any lawyers who do national security law?" he asked.

"National . . . is that a special practice? I can't think of any—"

"You think Jamie might know someone?"

Jamie North was an ex-boyfriend of hers, even, for a time, an ex-fiancé, until she'd come to her senses and decided she didn't want to spend the rest of her life with an uptight humorless lawyer. At which point she got back together with her college boyfriend, Michael Tanner, and realized she'd found a life raft. Still, the subject of Jamie would come up from time to time. He was a partner at one of Boston's biggest firms, Batten Schechter, who was often in the paper for some pro bono case or another. He was one of the few people Tanner had met who didn't like him, through no fault of Tanner's, of course.

"Wait," she said, "I think that's what Jamie does."

"I thought it was First Amendment stuff."

"Yeah, and—hold on, I'm Googling him—yeah, I was right, national security is one of his specialties."

"Let me take his phone number."

54

Arthur Collins was an unimpressive-looking man. He didn't appear to be someone who could kill you noiselessly, though apparently he was, or had been. At least, that was the rumor. He had a short, squat build and looked at least ten years older than his sixty years. He had a sun-reddened face, a deeply creased forehead, and large doughy ears that stuck out like a monkey's. His hooded eyes could sometimes look sad, sometimes look dead, menacing. Underneath them was a grid of crosshatched lines. He'd grown a gray-white goatee since they'd last seen each other.

He welcomed Will unsmilingly to his neat, small brick house overlooking the Chesapeake Bay.

"Directions okay?" He was not a talkative guy.

"Perfect."

"Okay, then," Artie said and turned and led the way to a wood-paneled room that was probably called a "den" but was his office.

There was a burnt-orange shag carpet on the floor that

looked a lot like the carpet in the den in the house Will grew up in, a small desk, its surface bare, and a couple of chairs. A window looked out on the water, the view gridded by venetian blinds.

Artie sank into a brown plaid BarcaLounger, which was clearly his usual spot, his throne, facing a large flatscreen. Tented on a side table next to his lounger was a paperback. Will sat in a swivel chair next to the BarcaLounger, turned to face Artie.

Artie wasn't a friend, really, but they were friendly, and a few years ago Artie had taken him shooting at his local gun range. Artie gave him a lesson, using his own guns—a whole slew of them, from a Smith & Wesson .38 revolver to a nine-millimeter Glock, from a little .22 to a massive assault rifle. Artie seemed to be something of a gun nut. He was also a good teacher, though Will wasn't necessarily a good student. He'd forgotten most of what he'd learned about guns. Guns were not a necessary part of his world.

Not long after that, Will did him a favor. When the staff director of the intelligence committee had gone on a cost-cutting jag and had decided to get rid of most outside contractors like Arthur Collins, Will had put in a word for Artie. He let the director know that his boss specifically wanted Artie kept on retainer, and so he was.

"You're still the majordomo for Senator Robbins, right?"

Will smiled, nodded. He glanced at the book open on the side table next to where Artie sat. It was called *The Power of Now,* by Eckhart Tolle.

"She's not up for reelection this cycle, is she?"

"Not this year, no."

"So you're not here to pitch me oppo work."

"Not at all."

"Good. Because I don't really do that kind of work anymore."

"Nothing like that."

Will was circumspect in what he told Artie. He certainly didn't mention the classified documents pilfered from the committee's computers. (Who knew if Artie maintained contact with any committee staff members?) He just told Artie about the missing laptop and the furtive guy in Boston who he was sure had it, Michael Tanner. "I need to get it back, one way or another. However you have to do it."

In reply, Artie just gave him a blank look.

"You asked him to give it back?" He spoke slowly, as if to a child.

"Of course."

"This would seem to be a matter for law enforcement."

"Absolutely out of the question. We can't risk the exposure."

"Of the senator's personal information on the laptop, is that it?"

Will nodded.

"Must be some pretty explosive personal information."

Will shrugged.

"You want me to get it back however I have to.

Whether it's dealing with him directly or breaking into his workplace or his residence."

"I mean whatever it takes to get it back," Will said with an arched brow. "*Whatever* it takes."

There was a long pause. "Why is this so important to you?"

"Because it could do real harm to my boss."

"And to you."

"For sure. That too."

Another long pause. Then Artie said, "Not interested. Sorry."

"Is it about the money? Because I'm not asking you to do this for nothing. I'd pay your normal rates, of course." He'd wire the funds from the Susan Robbins Victory Fund again. Easily done. Artie was a consultant.

"That's not what it's about," Artie said. He exhaled. "Look, anyone who tells you that nothing can go wrong is lying to himself and you. Believe me, I've been a field operator. I've had my adrenaline fix. At this point in my life, this sort of risk, I don't need it. That's not where I am right now. I like my life."

"How about, if it gets risky, you just pull out? You don't need to let it get to that point."

Artie shook his head slowly. "You want this so much, and you don't even realize that the wanting of it, that's not the only way to live."

"I don't understand."

"When I was a kid, my daddy used to take me to the dog track, in Tucson. Watch the greyhounds race, right? And I used to wonder, what must it be like to always be chasing that flannel rabbit doll and never ever catch the thing? But that's just how the track works. Right? And years later, I had this realization—I'd become one of those greyhounds. Always chasing the fake rabbit and never catching it."

Will didn't know what to say. He was uncomfortable with self-examination anyway, and certainly wasn't going to share with Artie. "Oh yeah?"

"You, my friend, are primed to chase after rabbits. But so's nearly everybody. The assistant vice president wants to be the vice president, and the vice president wants to be the executive vice president. And he and all the other executive vice presidents want the corner office. Meanwhile, the CEO wants to acquire another company. We all want more, bigger, harder, higher, stronger. I know a hedge fund manager who has more money than God, and he still works Saturdays and Sundays. He misses his kids' football games, often doesn't eat dinner with his family, barely sees his wife and kids. It's all frantic movement toward something we can never attain. All the while, we're missing out on something. You know what that is, Will?"

"What?"

"It's life. Being driven by ambition is just as bad as being driven by anger or fear or jealousy. It's an insatiable drive. You need to know about mindfulness. Thich Nhat Hanh has some excellent books. Or this one." He picked up the book on the table next to him.

"I see."

"See, the thing is, Will, you already are what you want

to be. Be who you are now. Realize how perishable our existence is. Understand?"

Will didn't, but he nodded.

"I'm not sure you do," Artie said. "See that dock out there?" He pointed at the window. Will stood, tugged down a slat of the venetian blinds, and saw the brown wooden dock off to the right.

"Yeah?"

"I have an oyster garden out there."

"An oyster *garden*?"

"Not an oyster bed. I raise eastern oysters in a cage under the dock."

"Huh. Do you sell them or eat them?"

He shook his head. "When they're grown, I give them to the Chesapeake Bay Foundation. They plant them on sanctuary reefs. They filter the water. Helps save the bay."

"Huh."

"The baby oysters, the spats, they affix themselves to an old oyster shell and then they don't move. They're never running away or running toward; they're just *being*."

Curiosity got the better of him, and Will had to say, "With your job—I guess I never would have expected, you know—"

"I wasn't always where I am now. In the late nineties I was tasked to do a black op against the Maoist insurgency in Nepal. My assignment was to eliminate one of their leaders. Which I did."

"Really?" Will was shocked to hear him speak about his prior work so openly.

"Couple years ago I took a trip back to Nepal. And while I was there I tracked down the brother of the man I killed. In Kathmandu." Artie was looking off into some vague middle distance. "And I tried to make amends to the guy. I came clean—'I killed your brother.' And this guy—his name was Manish—he didn't look at me with hatred. He'd become a Buddhist monk; he wore one of those saffron robes. The look he gave me. I was expecting—I don't know what I was expecting. Fury, I guess, or anguish. I thought he'd break down weeping, or lash out at me, maybe even lunge at me. That's what I was prepared for. But the one thing I wasn't prepared for? Was how he actually responded. The gentleness in his eyes. The look he gave me. So much . . . love. I don't know how to put this in words, but Will? *I* was the one who broke down. I spent the next month there. Way up on top of a mountain north of Kathmandu. And it's like I took myself apart, and then I put myself back together."

"Wow," Will said. "That's incredible." He thought that a lot of what Artie said made sense, but he didn't want to think about that kind of stuff now. Maybe later, someday.

Artie smiled, kind of a sad smile, his eyes serene. He spread his palms. "Anything else I can do for you?"

"Yes," Will said. "One more thing."

55

Tanner Roast had survived without him. He spent half an hour going over administrative things with Lucy, signing some paychecks for the few employees who for some reason didn't do direct deposit. Karen wanted to talk sales, which really meant agonizing over deals that should have been and still might be. Like the Four Seasons account.

"We can't submit a new bid? It's definitely lost?"

"The deal's done," Tanner said.

"That's so totally not fair."

"I have an idea."

"What is it?"

"I'm getting into a sort of scorched-earth frame of mind," Tanner said. "Do me a favor. Get hold of City Roast's S-1."

"Which is what?"

"It's a form you have to submit to the government when you're planning to take your company public. It's online."

"When is City Roast going public?"

"In a couple of months, I think. Who's this new kid hanging around with Sal?"

"The intern or whatever? From Northeastern, remember?"

"I forgot. Do I have to explain stuff to him? I'm a little preoccupied." He remembered that he'd agreed to let a college sophomore intern at Tanner Roast learn the business of running a coffee company for a semester or two. But that was months ago. Before all this.

And then he thought of something. "Actually, tell that kid to get in here. Meet the boss. I want to teach him about delegating."

Tanner sent the Northeastern student on a run to a sporting goods store and the Computer Loft. Meanwhile he called Carl Unsworth. "Do you have any downtime between lessons or classes or whatever? I need to talk to you."

"Some. But I got a pretty full day today."

"You don't have to go anywhere. I'll drop by."

He left the office a few minutes later and took the turnpike to Newton Centre. Carl's martial arts studio was in an office building that had a good deli on the ground floor.

Tanner had imagined that Carl's martial arts courses were full of state troopers and FBI agents. Instead, it turned out that most of his students seemed to be suburban women. At least, the daytime classes. Carl wore workout pants and a T-shirt with his studio name emblazoned on it.

"Do you know anyone who knows wiring?" Tanner asked.

"Like an electrician?"

"Could be, sure—wait. Scott!"

"Who?"

"A buddy of mine who installs home theaters and TVs and sound systems and all that. I play squash with him."

Toward the end of the day, Tanner met Jamie North for a drink in the Back Bay, at a loud after-work bar on Boylston Street. Tanner ordered a bourbon on the rocks. Jamie ordered a Diet Pepsi, because he had to return to the office. There was no small talk. Tanner tried, but Jamie was not a small-talk kind of guy. He didn't even ask about Sarah, though he had to be thinking about her.

After ending his engagement with Sarah, Jamie quickly met another woman and was engaged within a few months. Clearly he'd decided he was on the marriage track and was going to get there one way or another. His male biological clock—there is such a thing—was ticking loudly. They had two kids and then quickly got divorced. So Jamie felt that he'd gotten the shitty end of the stick, that Tanner had won. He was a rival who had been defeated, and that made him foul-tempered.

Jamie listened to Tanner impatiently, drumming his fingertips on the table, playing with a straw's paper wrapper. "What does that mean, you're in trouble with the NSA?"

"They're demanding the senator's laptop. They claim there's classified information on there."

"Is there?"

"Yes."

"Dude, you don't mess with the NSA. Give it to 'em."

"Let's say, for the sake of argument, that I don't want to hand it over."

"Why not?"

"Let's just say. Do they have legal grounds to arrest me? This is what the NSA guy was threatening me with."

"Well, did you come into possession of this laptop legally?"

"Like I said, accidentally. At the LA airport."

"All right, so you have someone else's computer, which is not theft. I mean, it's mushy. Anyway, that's not the point, and that's not my expertise. You are in possession of national-security-classified, top secret documents. And you have given them to a reporter who intended to publish. You leaked it to a journalist. Right?"

"Right. But is it still a leak if the journalist I leaked them to is dead?"

Jamie shrugged a couple of times. "Everything gets complicated when it involves a journalist. And how do you know your buddy Lanford or Landon, or whatever, didn't give it to a couple of his reporter buddies? Or his editor?"

"I don't."

"Exactly. Look, the pertinent law here is the Espionage Act, which dates back to World War I, and the Patriot Act. Then there's Executive Order 12333. But this stuff hasn't really been litigated in modern times. It's all about how far the Justice Department prosecutors feel like going. And, you know, there's more enforcement when you're at war."

"Are we at war?"

"Against terror, sure."

"Still?"

"It's the forever war. Anyway, that's the crux of it. Have you actually taken a peek at the documents?"

Tanner looked away. He took out his wallet and pulled out a twenty, which he handed to Jamie.

"What's this for?"

"I'm hiring you as my lawyer."

"And how much of my time do you think twenty bucks buys? I'm fifteen hundred bucks an hour."

Touché, he thought. "This conversation. Beverages included. Your Diet Pepsi is on me. That makes this a privileged conversation between attorney and client."

"Okay, okay. As a favor to Sarah. But let me be clear: I'm *not* representing you."

"Got it. Yes, I looked at the documents. Most of it went over my head. It's about some top secret NSA program. Something involving mass surveillance."

"How? In what way?"

"I think it's this secret program where the government can switch on cameras on our computers and phones and watch us without us knowing."

"Jesus." Jamie shook his head slowly. "Thing is, once

you get into legal matters involving the National Security Agency, it's like we're on a different planet, where the law of gravity no longer applies. Everything's backward and upside down. There are secret executive orders; there's a secret court. And your situation looks bad. The fact is, you knowingly passed on classified information to a journalist who fully intended to publish it. That's what they're going to say."

"How did I know what Lanny planned to do with it? He's a friend. Maybe I wanted his advice on what to do."

"Okay, good. But you gained access to classified information. Then you passed it on to someone. If they want to, they can go after you for that. That's all there is to it."

"And what would you do? As my lawyer. Theoretically speaking."

"I wouldn't take the case."

"But if you did."

"Let me say it again: I am not representing you."

"Got it."

"Your case would be not only extremely time-consuming but probably unwinnable."

"I see."

"If they want to put you on trial for mishandling classified information, you might even be tried in a secret courtroom, represented by a civilian lawyer who basically has his hands tied behind his back. You'll likely be sentenced to at least ten years in prison, and that means a federal prison. Very few lawyers will want to represent you."

"Why not?"

"Because the case would take five years and you're guaranteed to lose. The courts almost always side with the government."

"Since when?"

"Since 9/11. The world changed. I don't think most people get how much things changed. Unless you use serious encryption, assume that all of your e-mails are being read. Assume your phone calls are being recorded or monitored somewhere. Just assume the worst and you'll probably be right."

"You mean we're in a surveillance state."

He shrugged.

"How long has this been going on?"

"In practical terms, it started with W., with the George W. Bush administration after 9/11. But things got worse in the Obama administration. And then the new president took it to a whole new level."

"News to me."

"And to most people. Most people have no idea, and that's how the government wants it. Keep people in the dark and confused. No one's going to protest."

"You think I could just be . . . *disappeared* . . . I mean, arrested and locked up somewhere like Guantanamo?"

"It's possible."

"It *is*?"

"I can't tell you for certain. Just . . . things I've heard."

"US citizens, imprisoned without a trial. In America."

"Yep. Don't tell me you're disillusioned now. This is the way it is. This is the way the world works now."

"Like *1984.*"

"Orwell was off by about three decades."

"And what if I just disappear, just go off the grid?"

"What about it?"

"Do you think I can do that and get away with it?"

He shrugged. "I can only give you legal advice. Survival—that's something totally different. That I can't help you with at all. I'm sorry. Wish I could help you."

He didn't sound like it.

"Why do you think they didn't arrest me in the first place?"

"That's easy. They didn't want you to lawyer up. They want the computer back really badly, and it's a lot easier if you don't have a lawyer. And speaking of which, let me say it one more time—"

"I know," Tanner said. "I got it. You're not my lawyer."

56

Tanner walked home from the bar, along Boylston Street, which was noisy and crowded with frat bros and college kids and assorted barhoppers. He sneaked glances at some of the scantily dressed college girls and tried not to be creepy about it. And he thought.

He had come to some clarity, finally. For some reason he trusted this guy Earle. Even if he wouldn't put a guarantee in writing, Earle gave off a trustworthy vibe, and Tanner relied on his own instincts. It was time to just give the damned laptop to the NSA. They wanted the files; they didn't want him. And obviously they demanded secrecy about CHRYSALIS. If he never heard the word "chrysalis" again, he wouldn't mind.

As he sidestepped a couple kissing right in the middle of Boylston Street, he noticed a car pull up alongside him, a black Lincoln Town Car. The rear passenger's door flew open and someone got out.

"Michael Tanner!" said a short, powerfully built man in his late sixties.

"Do I know you?"

Tanner looked, didn't recognize the guy getting out of the limo. He took a quick inventory of what this guy was wearing: a black dress coat that flapped open over an elegant gray three-piece suit. Blue shirt with contrasting white collar, red tie. A collar pin and heavy cuff links. He was like a bull that had wandered into Turnbull & Asser. He had the sleek look of someone used to being in charge, maybe a senior partner at a law firm or a CEO.

In a feline purr, the man said, "Oh, I know everybody. I'm Bruce Olshak. Come on, let's have a little chin-wag. Walk with me, my friend." He sidled up to Tanner.

Tanner had heard the name Olshak before. He was some sort of major player in legal circles. He remembered hearing the phrase "Mob lawyer" affixed to Olshak's name.

"I'm afraid I'm in a hurry," Tanner said and continued walking. Olshak walked alongside.

"Make haste now," Olshak said, "and repent at leisure. I understand you're lawyer shopping."

"Says who?"

Olshak shrugged. "The Ethernet of whispers. I know people. Lucky for you, I'm a counselor."

The Ethernet of whispers. Olshak probably had some connection to Batten Schechter. The kind that didn't show up on any letterhead. Up close, Tanner caught a faint whiff of cigar, probably Romeo y Julietas.

"So?" Tanner said warily.

"Way I see it? You're about to make the biggest mistake of your life."

"What are you saying? What do you— What do you know?"

"I know everything I need to know. Question is whether you do. You've heard the old joke: NSA stands for No Such Agency, right? And our friends at the NSA— they're trying to bully you. To panic you. To get you to turn something over to them—something that doesn't belong to you and doesn't belong to them."

Tanner, alert, said, "I'm listening."

"That would be the wrong thing to do. And when we do wrong things, Michael, there's always a penalty. Have you noticed that?"

"A penalty."

"Some kinda penalty. You pass a note in class, you get after-school detention. Drive through a stop sign, you get a traffic ticket. Penalties, right? So you do something stupid like hand this article over to the—the men in black? What do you think is going to happen?"

"Let me guess. Something bad."

He lowered his voice. He was almost muttering to himself. Tanner had to listen closely as they walked along, ignoring the competing noise, the shouts and the babble. "Something bad? Nah, worse than that. Something *sad*. Bad is: someone chops off your finger. Sad is: something happens to your wife. To Sarah."

"What the hell are you trying to threaten me with?"

"Girl like that, she could have decades of life ahead of her. She loses that, it's *sad*. Sad for everyone."

Tanner came to a stop in front of a bank where the

inset sidewalk made a kind of plaza. He drew close to Olshak.

"You're insane if you think—"

"Oh, we're subtle people. Nothing's gonna happen real soon. That would seem *suspicious*. That would invite questions. Nah, we let time pass. Months and months. Maybe it's the end of the year. Christmas, New Year's. Hell, maybe we wait longer. But one day the penalty will come due. The *sad* thing. A car that went too fast and jumped a curb. Who knows? And nobody's gonna take any pleasure in this, I promise you. But, you see, this is the real decision that's in front of you. That's why we don't want you to hurry and make a mistake. Because life is precious, Michael. So very precious."

Tanner tried to control his breathing. "Who are you working for?"

"Don't get distracted. You can't afford it. Focus on the takeaway."

"Meaning that if I don't give the NSA this thing—"

"You give it to *me*, I'll take care of it. *Capisce?* It's really your best move. Life, you know, doesn't always give you the best options. You just gotta make the best choices you can. And in this case, well, there's really no choice at all."

"Because if I give it to the NSA, my wife—"

"Sarah. A lovely girl. And smart as a whip."

Tanner suddenly grabbed the man by the tie, yanked him close. "Listen to me," he began.

Olshak, red in the face, said, "You don't want to do this, Michael. You really don't want to do this."

"You want to go after someone, go after me. Just don't even think of going after my wife." Tanner let go of the tie and Olshak fell back, stumbling a bit.

He looked at Olshak, at the Town Car that was still keeping pace, inching along the street as they'd walked.

Then he cut down Clarendon Street in the direction of home.

57

Tanner spent a second night in the mansion on Chestnut Hill. This time he decided to sleep on the floor, on the thick carpeting of a guest bedroom. He was tired, and sleep came quickly. But it was a troubled sleep, and he woke at dawn, anxious about what he was about to do.

He relocked the house and went for a walk and found a diner on Comm. Ave., where he had a good breakfast of eggs and toast, fortified with a lot of bad coffee.

He wondered whether the NSA knew where he was right now. He thought not; he hoped not. Though he couldn't be sure.

He was only one person against innumerable others; he was vastly outnumbered. But he would not be out-thought.

Maybe they did know where he was but had no need to follow him. After all, they had him on a digital leash.

At the very least, they must have put something in the burner phone he'd had with him. Or cloned it. Or maybe they had some other way to listen in to a phone; he didn't know. In any case, he'd turned it off, because somewhere he'd read that a phone had to be on—transmitting to cell towers—to be trackable.

No one seemed to be physically following him. Not as far as he could tell.

Sitting at the diner's counter, he took out the GPS unit, a low-end Garmin, that the intern at work had bought. After struggling for a bit with the owner's manual, he managed to enter the decimal coordinates Carl had given him. He put the location in the unit and marked it with a little icon of a treasure chest. He drank more coffee and lost track of how many cups. Too many. He was awake now, but the caffeine just amped up his anxiety.

He made a few calls. He needed to drive about twenty miles west of Boston, to the town of Lincoln. Which meant he needed a car. His Lexus, on Huron Avenue? They'd probably put a tracker in it. So that wasn't usable. He'd have to rent one.

But he found out after a few calls that none of the auto rental agencies in Boston would do business in cash. They all required a credit or debit card. And every time he used one of his cards, he was pretty sure the NSA would be alerted. He didn't know for certain, but he'd read enough spy novels and watched enough TV to suspect this. And taking an Uber was out, since he didn't have his iPhone with him.

So he had no choice: he would rent a car. They'd get

an alert telling them he'd done so. And then he'd watch to see whether they followed the car, whether they knew where he was.

Down the block he found a car rental place that was open early, and he wondered whether this would be the last time he'd be able to use a credit card for a long while.

58

On the front passenger's seat of the rented Nissan was the backpack stuffed with the possibly bugged shoes and belt, along with the burner he assumed had been tampered with, and the GPS unit, and a pair of hunting binoculars.

He took 93 North out of the city, the lower deck of the Tobin Bridge over the Mystic River, steel girders crisscrossing all around.

By the time he got to Route 16 West, he still hadn't seen any vehicle appearing to follow him. But that didn't mean it wasn't happening. Between the burner phone, the shoes, and the belt, all of which the NSA had taken away for a while, there had to be a GPS tracker in *something*. He was just guessing, of course, but he felt reasonably sure about it. They were probably following him in some government building somewhere by watching a pulsing, moving dot on a computer screen.

Then he took Route 2, west through the Boston suburbs, then a smaller road south for a few miles, and another, until he came to the town of Lincoln. He drove down a narrow road for a little over a mile until he reached an old cemetery. The headstones here, which dated to the eighteenth century, were thin and worn and close together. Around the graveyard was a low split-rail fence. He parked at the side of the road and waited for a couple of cars to pass. None of them slowed or stopped or did anything remotely suspicious.

If he was being followed, he'd scrap his planned getaway, as simple as that. He'd figure something else out. But there didn't *seem* to be anyone in the vicinity watching him, or driving past repeatedly, or staying too close behind him on the road.

That just confirmed his theory. They didn't need to be close by. They didn't *need* to tail him.

He took out the possibly compromised burner phone, switched it on, and while it came to life and played its little start-up ditty, he searched his pockets for a scrap of paper until he found it. On it was the phone number of the burner he'd given Carl.

Somewhere, in a top secret government office, on a map display on some impossibly powerful computer, a flashing dot would wink on. He was sure of it.

"Ted," he said. "It's Tanner."

"It's okay to use our real names?"

"As long as we're talking on burner phones, yes," Tanner said. "Don't call me on your regular mobile phone or your landline. Don't e-mail me. Any of these ways, they could be listening in."

"*My* phones?"

"They probably have you under surveillance because you're someone I e-mail often. Because you're a friend. And you really are, by the way."

"Thanks, Tanner," Carl said. "I guess."

He knew he was to answer to the name Ted. It didn't require any acting talent, fortunately. Carl Unsworth wasn't much of an actor. This way, Carl wouldn't be implicated, dragged into this trouble.

"Ted, I'm in Lincoln, on my way to the woods to dig up the laptop. I need you to meet me out here so I can hand it over to you. You know how to get to the spot, right?"

"I got it, I got it."

"See you soon."

He slipped the car key under the front seat, grabbed the backpack, and got out. He hefted it over one shoulder and started off. A narrow dirt path alongside the graveyard fence led straight into a forest.

He looked around and then strode quickly along the dirt path into the dense pine woods. After a few minutes he took out the GPS unit and located himself, a little blue arrow on the map display.

The GPS had been Carl's idea. He was a geocacher, which was apparently a hobby involving a search for hidden things using GPS. Something like that.

Then he set off again. Once, he heard the snap of a twig and turned swiftly, alarmed, only to realize it was his own doing. He was still not being physically followed, as far as he knew.

Whose woods these were, Tanner had no idea. But as a kid he and his friends had hiked here often. He knew where he was going. Once, on a break from college, he and his best friend, whose parents both taught at Harvard, had gotten lost in this forest. Not far from here, his friend's dad had told them, Henry David Thoreau used to hike and then write about it in his journals.

The way was twisty at first, but soon it yielded to a clearing. A few of the trees were marked on their tall bald trunks with yellow blazes that had been painted and repainted over the years. This was the trailhead.

Consulting the GPS occasionally, he followed the trail for a while; in places it became narrow and choked. From time to time he peered back the way he'd come. After about ten minutes, the light gradually changed, as the trees turned from mostly pine to hemlock. For more than an acre, the hemlock trees had crowded out all competing species, creating a tight, dim forest. Soft mottled light filtered through the dense canopy.

He was close. The location dot was just about an inch away from the destination dot.

He proceeded west a few hundred feet, out of the hemlock canopy and back into the sparser pine forest, until he came upon an area that just looked right. The GPS unit confirmed he was in the right place. A stand of pine trees ringed a bare spot about ten feet in diameter. Here there was the stump of a dead tree, vibrant with green moss. Next to it the earth looked disturbed, as if someone had been digging.

He looked up and saw the tree directly north of the stump. His friend Scott had chosen well. It was a cedar, tall and conical, dense with needles.

He looked around and then came closer until he was standing just a few feet from the cedar, and then he saw the tiny red light of the small video camera nestled in a crook of the tree. The camera was barely visible. But its red light might attract scrutiny. He'd asked Scott to cover the light with a piece of electrician's tape, but he'd clearly forgotten.

Well, by the time it was noticed, it would be too late.

The camera would record the faces of the NSA team as they approached and attempted to dig up the laptop. It would simultaneously stream the video, and Scott would record it. Was it a violation of the NSA's charter for a clandestine operations team to be operating within the country? Tanner wasn't sure, but he knew negotiating, and he knew he'd have something that Earle would respect. It was blackmail, plain and simple. But what was the expression the Ukrainian financier used? *You kill my dog, I kill your cat*? That video was the sort of thing that could prompt Senate hearings. It would be a damaging revelation. The NSA would not want that video out.

Now he dropped the backpack and the phone on the ground, against the tree stump. He hung the binoculars around his neck.

The flashing dot on that computer map on a monitor in a government office—as he imagined it—would stop moving. Which would be as expected: Tanner was digging, they'd think.

But by placing a call on the probably cloned or bugged cell phone, Tanner had just given them a reason to come out and grab him again.

They would want to intercept him before he handed off the laptop to his friend.

Now he had to move.

The NSA would be scrambling to send a capture team out to where he was.

He had no idea how quickly they could move, but now that he'd turned on the phone, he had to get as far away as he could. The rental car was out: they'd know, the moment his credit card was charged, the make and model and license plate number. They'd be on the lookout for it.

No, he had to move, at first on foot, and then—what?—maybe he could hop on the commuter rail, the train that stopped in Lincoln town center. You could pay in cash once you boarded.

He had enough cash on him.

He kept going through the woods, dead leaves rustling underfoot. He thought he heard something, a distant noise, and he looked behind.

For a moment he thought that he'd seen something moving far off, a shape, maybe a human figure. Then he decided it had been only a trick of the light.

After all, they could not possibly have located him that quickly. Since they didn't seem to be following him in person, it would take them some decent amount of time—whether that meant fifteen minutes or an hour—to get out to where he was from wherever they were monitoring him.

He put the binoculars up to his eyes and focused. There was something moving in the woods, though all he could see was moving shadows. It was too far away, through too much underbrush.

Surely it had nothing to do with him.

But if it did.

He walked west, juking left and right. He could not get up any speed here; the obstacles in his way were too many. So he zigzagged for a few hundred feet.

Not too far away was a farm, he recalled, neighboring the forest. He remembered a cornfield. That offered possibilities. You could hide in a cornfield.

But where was it?

He passed a small, dank pond scabbed over with lily pads, and he remembered vaguely that they'd once tried to swim in it, one summer, and were put off by the sludgy bottom and the thick tangle of plant growth beneath the surface. Now he was relying on distant memory. Where was the cornfield?

Just up ahead he noticed some two-by-fours nailed to the trunk of an old oak. He recognized it at once as a deer stand, used by deer hunters. The two-by-fours were actually nailed between the oak and a neighboring pine tree in a ladder formation. The boards went up easily forty or fifty feet. Hunters climbed up the tree and put something like a milk crate high up in the tree to use as a seat. Up there they could see deer coming from far away.

He climbed the makeshift ladder. The nails had been sunk in deep; the boards held fast. He ached all over, especially his lower back, where he'd been hurt in the struggle with Earle's men. In a minute he was probably fifty feet off the ground and could see the full swath of forest spread out before him. Nestled in the tree, behind foliage, he wasn't visible.

He saw shadows moving through the woods. Several human figures, he was now certain. This wasn't a group of friends enjoying a hike. They were swarming in a rhythmic, coordinated cadence. Only a few minutes away, he calculated, at the rate they were going. Ahead of schedule.

It was them. It had to be.

His heart began to thud. Off to the west he saw the forest give way to lawns and houses. That was where the old cornfield used to be, now a suburban neighborhood.

He hustled down the ladder, scraping his arm against a nail that was sticking out of the tree, and raced through the woods due west, toward the neighborhood.

He plunged into a tight cluster of trees and immediately tripped on a dead log.

Scrambling to his feet—chagrined at losing a precious few seconds—he bounded through the woods as fast as he could, weaving among the trees, zigzagging back and forth.

Soon he reached an open field, a lawn he'd seen from the deer stand, and he raced across it to a paved road and then out to a heavily trafficked street, and there, standing on the narrow shoulder of the road, he stuck out his thumb to hitch a ride.

59

Will wanted chili con carne but decided he would get a salad.

He could smell the chili as soon as he got down to the ground floor beneath the Hart and Dirksen buildings. As he walked into the cafeteria he saw several people walking by with chili and corn bread on their trays, and it looked tremendously appetizing.

But he would get a salad. Just as he'd done every day this entire week. He wasn't just getting tired of salads; he was beginning to actively resent them.

He was hungry and the line was moving slowly.

He was mulling over what Arthur Collins had said to him. About ambition being as bad as anger or jealousy. Being an *insatiable drive*. And: *Be who you are now.*

He didn't really understand, in any depth, what Artie Collins meant. But he wondered what could have turned a CIA killer into a pacifist philosopher. He wondered if you could go the other way just as well.

Someone he knew walked by, the chief of staff to the

Democratic senator from California. Will nodded, and the guy nodded back. He was sort of a tool.

Then someone else familiar came by, and it took him a second to recognize Gary Sapolsky. And when he did, his stomach clenched, and he felt a splash of acid in his throat.

Gary was holding an overstuffed bankers box. On top of it were several desk picture frames. His normally chafed face was a surprisingly dark crimson, and his thinning hair was mussed. His eyes were bloodshot.

"Gary, you okay?"

"I just got fired." Gary said it in a small, tight voice, as if he didn't believe his own words.

"What do you mean, 'fired'?"

"Krauss put me on indefinite leave without pay, but we know what that means." Don Krauss was Gary's boss and the staff director of the Senate intelligence committee.

"What?" Will now realized what had happened. The boss had casually mentioned Gary's name at her security interview as someone she *wondered about*. That was all it had taken.

"Do you know my salary is supposed to support my wife and two kids and both of my elderly parents too?"

Gary sounded angry, and it took Will a beat to realize the guy wasn't being accusatory. Just angry at how unfair the world is. "That's terrible." Will did indeed know that but had forgotten. He felt bad about what had happened to Gary but tried to put it out of his head.

"Krauss thinks I was the one who took classified materials out of the SCIF! I told him no goddamned way I did that. But he just sort of weaseled around and said he was acting on 'guidance' from the NSA. That goddamned toad."

"Sorry about that, man," Will said, putting a consoling hand on Gary's sloped left shoulder. "That really sucks."

"Can you put in a word for me?"

"Uh, sure. You mean, with—"

"Krauss, right. That would be great."

"How long is this for?"

Gary shook his head. "Indefinite. But I'm not coming back. I know how the system works."

"They think it was you who"—the line moved forward, and Will lowered his voice so as not to be overheard—"took the documents?"

"Insane, right?"

This could be a very good thing, he realized. If the NSA fingered Gary Sapolsky for the leak, that took the boss off the list.

"They have any evidence for this?"

"Of course there isn't any evidence. I didn't do it."

"But I mean, did they say they had something?"

Gary shook his head. "I didn't talk to them. I wasn't allowed to. Krauss called me in and told me to pack and get out, and they brought in an extra security guard to stand by my desk and make sure I didn't take anything or copy anything I'm not supposed to."

The line had started moving quickly, and Will had reached the salad bar. He stuck out his hand and only then realized that Gary's hands were both gripping the file box. He withdrew it. "That totally sucks, Gary," Will said. "I'll see what I can do."

A strange memory floated into his brain. He was sixteen and his brother, Clay, was thirteen. This was just two or three years after their father had died.

Will was watching TV in the family room while Clay was doing something in the garage, probably putting together one of his model cars using that chemical-smelly glue he wasn't allowed to use in the house. It was just the two of them at home, while their mom was at work, probably showing a house. Technically, Will, as the eldest, was in charge.

He heard a sudden shriek, and he got up and ran over to the door that led into the garage, where the sound was coming from.

He flung the door open and saw Clay cowering in the far corner of the garage. Around twenty feet away from him was some kind of a big animal, hissing and growling at Clay, trapping him in the corner. A cat? No. He saw a striped tail flicking, saw the black bandit-mask fur around the eyes, realized it was a raccoon.

His heart began to wallop. While Mom was away, he was supposed to take care of his younger brother, who stood there red-faced and gasping, his hands out, trying to protect himself against what Will only later learned was a rabid raccoon.

Frantically, Will scrambled over to the wall of tools and yanked down the longest one he could find, a sharp-bladed shovel. He took a few steps toward the raccoon, which continued to menace Clay, hiss-growling. Will tinged the shovel's steel blade against the concrete floor.

The raccoon spun around, facing Will, fangs bared, hissing, tail whipping around. It was mangy-looking and matted. Its bandit-masked face looked crazed. Then it reared up, rounded its back—and suddenly sprang at him, making its horrible hissing growl as it flew through the air.

Terrified, Will stepped back, a reflex.

But then, in the next second, he felt something he'd never felt before. His fright, his fear of the maddened raccoon, abruptly turned into outrage, a kind of *indignation,* an anger that this beast had dared to launch at him.

And Will leapt forward and swung the shovel with a strength he didn't know he had. It clanged against the oil-stained concrete of the garage floor. Then he swung again, with a force even greater, and it hit the raccoon in the head.

The raccoon screamed, and a spray of blood spurted into the air. The blade of the shovel, Will saw, had sliced into the creature's head or neck.

Yet it was still alive, and it kept screeching and hissing, its claws flailing around, gouging the air.

Will lifted the shovel to take another whack, but the raccoon's body lifted along with it, as if it had attached itself. He was disgusted and horrified, but his heart was still skittering along and he had *superpowers.* He slammed the shovel's blade against the floor, and then something repulsive happened: the creature's head came off its body, rolling a few inches away, into a little greenish puddle of transmission fluid.

He had beheaded the animal. Gagging, he dropped the handle. It clattered on the concrete.

Clay took a few tentative steps and said, "Cool!"

At supper, Clay told the story of Will's heroism, and Will kept himself from making fun of the way Clay screamed like a silly little kid. Will shrugged modestly, said it was no big deal, even though it had been the most intense thing he had ever been through.

And he never forgot what he'd learned that day, about the way his deep terror of the raccoon had transmuted into outrage and bravery and a wild, intoxicating fury.

And about how a frightened person could become a brave one.

60

The man Will Abbott hired to give him a gun lesson was a mountain of a man, a retired DC cop with a deep, rumbling voice that seemed to vibrate the card table they were sitting at.

"You ever shoot a gun before?" the man asked. He was a black man in his sixties with a large domed head and close-cropped white hair.

Will nodded. "One lesson, once. A while ago. So let's start from the beginning."

"First thing is, treat all guns as if they're loaded."

The cop, named Joe Randall, shoved a revolver across the table at Will. Joe Randall was an employee of this gun range, an indoor range in northeast, close to the National Arboretum.

"Go ahead, pick it up."

Will considered interrupting his rap and telling the guy to speed it up. He didn't want to learn safety and handling and all that crap; he wanted to learn how to shoot to kill someone.

He knew that if he focused on logistics, the how-to, he could distract himself from his terror of getting caught. And getting caught was unthinkable. There would be no explaining himself without dragging in the boss.

Will picked up the gun as if it was loaded and he planned to kill Joe Randall: he gripped it in his right hand and poked a finger into the trigger.

"No!" Randall said. "Jesus, no. Keep your finger off the trigger until you're ready to shoot. You have no idea if that thing's loaded or not!"

"You're right," Will said meekly, and set it back down on the table. "But can you teach me on a semiautomatic pistol instead of a revolver?"

"You start with the alphabet. The basics. A revolver is more basic."

"Okay, sure. You're the boss." Will said it lightly, but it sounded off, condescending. He knew he had that tendency, which he'd have to moderate if he was going to make it to the big white house at 1600 Pennsylvania Avenue, the center of the universe, as far as he was concerned.

"You want to learn on a pistol, I'll teach you on a pistol. But for the license you got to know both."

"I understand."

Randall slid another gun over to Will, a Smith & Wesson nine millimeter. He taught Will to load bullets, which he called "shells," into the magazine. Will paid close attention. He figured he'd have to do this just once, anyway. He'd figure it out when he had to. He wanted only to make the shot, make it once, kill the guy, and get out. Without being connected to it.

Will learned how to load the magazine into the magazine well, which was in the handle of the pistol. How to grip the slide overhand and pull it back and let it go. That was how you inserted the first cartridge. Will was unclear about the difference between a shell and a cartridge and a bullet and a round; Joe Randall seemed to use them interchangeably.

Will started paying closer attention now, even though his mind was, at the same time, thinking about a couple of e-mails he had to write. Work stuff. He felt bad leaving work as early as he had, at five, and he knew he'd have to spend at least an hour at the computer at home before he went to bed. And he knew that Jen would want him to take over with Travis the second his feet touched home. Sometimes she'd almost shove the baby at him, a live grenade.

"You got me?" Randall said. "You just inserted the first cartridge into the chamber. Your gun is now loaded, right? It's loaded. You are packing heat. Keep that thing pointed in a safe direction, and do not point this at anything you don't want to blow clean away. Right?"

"Right."

"Point that thing downrange."

Will fumbled for a moment.

"That way." Randall pushed the muzzle of the gun away. "Every time you fire, this pistol ejects the old round and loads a new one until your magazine is empty."

"Okay."

Will sat up straighter. He was excited. His phone, in his coat pocket, rang. He let it go, even though he suspected it might be Susan. He wasn't all that far from Capitol Hill; he could return to the office quickly if he had to.

Randall put out both hands, palms up. "May I have your weapon, please?"

Will handed the gun back, carefully pointing it off to the side.

Randall did something complicated and quick to the gun, and suddenly he'd taken it apart, or at least separated the business part of the pistol from the magazine full of bullets, or cartridges, or whatever.

"I want you to load the next magazine," Randall said.

"Okay," Will said. "But really I need to learn how to aim halfway accurately and, you know, shoot. Actually shoot."

Will felt sick to his stomach all of a sudden. *Joe Randall was a retired policeman,* for God's sake. Which he hadn't known until he arrived at the gun range this afternoon. He would never have knowingly taken shooting lessons from an ex-cop. That was just asking to get arrested. "I'm going hunting with my brother-in-law," he said. "I just need to not make a total fool of myself." He chuckled.

"Then you want to learn on long guns! I can teach you that, but not here, it's gotta be outside, and—"

"I just need to learn how to shoot. You know, hit the target." He pointed to a battered old paper target pinned to the wall, a black silhouette of a man with arms at his sides. In the middle of the man's chest was a neat round hole, and around it were decreasing numbers in concentric oval rings. The hole was probably where ten bullets had punched through, one right on top of the other. A bull's-eye.

"How far you gonna be from the target?" Randall asked.

"I don't know. Maybe five or ten feet?"

"That close? What are you hunting?"

"I—I have no idea. Game, probably." He didn't know if game meant birds or all animals. "Just need to learn how to shoot."

Will's mind wandered briefly. He thought about Gary Sapolsky's flushed face, the way he carried that sad little box of his earthly possessions. How bad he felt about it, but how, at the same time, proud. He had set this in motion skillfully. Gary had to go. The FBI and the NSA were probably already combing through Gary's articles for his college student newspaper, whatever the Wesleyan paper was called, looking for a radical anti-American bias. That was the thing about federal investigations: they went on forever, moved lumberingly, and never seemed to end.

Michael Tanner, by holding on to the senator's laptop, was extorting him. He probably wanted some giant payday. But he had also done the one thing Will had feared most: he had handed it to the press. These days, the news media were on the lookout for violations of civil liberties they could blast the White House on. And CHRYSALIS was surveillance taken to a new extreme. The press would be all over it.

And the NSA and the entire security apparatus of the US government would not give up until they'd found out how the plan had leaked.

The public, the rest of the Senate—in fact, everyone—would assume that Susan Robbins had deliberately leaked it for political reasons, because she wanted the program killed. But whatever Susan actually felt on the subject, and Will didn't know for sure, she was savvy enough to know that extremists don't make it to the White House. No one must ever know that the leak had come from her, because no one would believe that it was accidental.

But if what actually happened came out, Susan would be damaged far more. She had directed her chief of staff to copy documents and take them, in violation of all procedure, out of a secure environment. So that Senator Robbins, who couldn't be bothered with sitting in a locked SCIF, reading documents, could have the luxury of reading it on her flight to LA.

The outrage would be swift and severe. No politician who had deliberately mishandled classified information would ever make it to the White House.

He'd lose his job, of course. She would have to fire him; he'd insist on it. He'd hate it if this ever happened. He daydreamed about walking into the Oval Office unannounced and advising Susan on how to handle the latest crisis with, say, China.

But if all that stood between him and unscheduled

visits to the Oval Office was this one arrogant coffee merchant, this rich guy with his own name on his company, then he knew what he would do.

It would be like when he decapitated that rabid raccoon all those years ago. There was a part of him, that dark place, that could not only commit an act of violence but thrill to it.

As long as he wasn't caught.

He just had to get to Tanner before the NSA did.

"Isosceles," Randall was saying. "Can you do that? If you can't, we'll learn the Weaver."

Learning the proper stance was easy. When he finally pulled the trigger he heard only a disappointing little click, because the gun wasn't actually loaded. He put on a pair of safety glasses, like he used to wear in shop class in high school, and a pair of headphone-type things, which Randall called "ear protection."

Randall took a fresh target paper and clipped it to a bracket in the lane in front of them, then flicked a switch, and the paper zipped forward twenty feet. Then he loaded a full magazine into the gun and handed it back to Will.

"Okay," he said. "Fighting stance, knees shoulder width apart, one leg slightly back. That's it."

This time when he pulled the trigger—*line up the front sight with the top of the notch on the rear sight, start to exhale, pull the trigger slowly, equal pressure all the way back, keep it steady, no movement*—it made an explosion that, even with the ear protection, jolted him.

"Nice job!" Randall said. Will hadn't seen the man smile before. He had a big gap in his front teeth. "You're a natural."

Will *was* a natural. Randall was right. Never again did he hit the target dead center, on the bull's-eye, but most of his shots stayed within the concentric ovals. A good "grouping," Randall said.

He seemed to have an aptitude for it. At least at twenty feet. When Randall moved the target back to fifty feet, it was more challenging. Plenty of his "rounds" hit the paper outside the black silhouette or missed the target entirely. Then again, some came pretty close to the center. Randall seemed to be impressed with him.

Anyway, he didn't expect to be aiming at Tanner from fifty feet away. That was a chance he wasn't going to take.

Even though gunfire kept startling him—he might not ever get over that—he felt an excitement that emanated from his groin, where he actually stiffened. He hoped Randall didn't notice.

As long as he thought of Tanner as that rabid raccoon in the garage, rather than a human being, he would hit the target. Even with his adrenaline pumping away, and maybe even running, if he had to.

"Your brother-in-law is going to be impressed," Joe Randall said.

"My— Oh right, yeah, he will."

"Where do you live?"

Why was the guy asking that? Will wondered, suddenly alert. "Stanton Park," Will said. "Why?"

"Living in the district, it's not so easy. It's going to take you four trips to the police department, two background checks, fingerprints, a five-hour class, and almost a thousand bucks in fees."

"What's not so easy?"

"Getting a license to carry. You're trying for that, right?"

"I told you, it's just for this hunting trip I'm going on—"

"You should. You got a gift."

Randall flicked a switch again, and the target zipped toward them. He unclipped the paper from the bracket and handed it to Will. "Souvenir."

"Oh." Will laughed. "No, thanks."

"You don't want a souvenir? You hit the bull's-eye, pal. Your wife is going to be impressed."

"All right, sure," Will said, taking it. He figured he'd toss it on the way home.

"So when's our next session, cowboy?" Randall had taken out a little black book and a ballpoint pen.

"I think one's probably enough," Will said.

"Lots more to learn."

"I'll see how it goes," Will said. "I might not need another lesson."

61

No one stopped for him.

This was the part of his plan that had most concerned Tanner. He had to move quickly but without a car or any public transportation. He held out his thumb and tried to look friendly and unthreatening. Not like the serial-killer hitchhiker you shouldn't have picked up. After the tenth car had passed him by, he looked down at himself and realized his shirt was torn; his khaki pants were soiled with mud. His face was probably scraped and muddied too. He must have looked like a swamp creature.

So he sprinted along the side of the road, on its narrow shoulder, in the direction of the town center. His pursuers—NSA guys, they had to be—had lost him. But they would soon conclude he'd left the woods, broaden their search, and it was only a matter of time before they found him. Any car that came up on him from behind could be the NSA team. He had to get a car of his own and get the hell out of here.

In a number of thriller movies he'd watched, when the

bad guys used their stolen credit cards, an alert went off at the police department. Or somewhere. He couldn't use a credit card. The NSA would locate him immediately.

And as he'd already found out, he therefore couldn't rent a car. He had a little over a hundred bucks in his wallet, which was normally plenty for him. But he sure didn't have enough to buy a used car.

He would have to steal one.

He'd never done anything like that before—he didn't even cheat on his taxes—but he had an idea of how he might do it. Years ago he'd learned from his father how to hot-wire a car. They had an ancient Chrysler LeBaron whose starter relay had gone bad. The car conked out at the worst moments, and starting it up was tricky.

But knowing how to hot-wire a big old rust-bucket late-seventies automobile didn't mean he knew how to hot-wire a more recent one. A lot had changed.

Simply finding a car to steal was hard. Along this road lived people in modest wood-frame houses; here and there, new developments were cut in. It would be insanity for him to try to steal a car in a suburban neighborhood where the car was in the driveway in full view of the house and its neighbors. Or try for a car in a driveway off the street, where people were driving by constantly.

For almost two miles he ran, past a church, a gas station, a bank. All were open and doing business. He ruled them out. Also, stealing a car from a church parking lot seemed somehow wrong. He'd have to find a car that was old enough, and deserted enough—out of view—to try to hot-wire. And it would have to be at night. He got to the town center without seeing any cabs, but he knew they'd be scarce out here.

He didn't recognize the stores, knew he had to be in one of the adjoining towns, probably Concord. He was looking for something else as well, any kind of discount retailer, like a Marshalls or a Kohl's. He found nothing like that. He did find a men's clothing store that seemed to specialize in preppy clothing. Avoiding the pink pants and the lime-green sweaters, he found a pair of pants, ready to wear, and a sport shirt. He changed in one of their fitting rooms and threw away his muddied clothing.

What he needed was a place to sit that had Wi-Fi and a computer he could use. There used to be places, he remembered, called Internet cafés, where you could pay for Internet access by the hour or the minute. Maybe there still were. But there was nothing like that here. He saw a few restaurants, another gas station, a Dunkin' Donuts.

Entering the doughnut shop, he bought a coffee and sat at a table in the back. He took out one of the burner phones and turned it on. It was still mostly charged. That was the good thing about cheap phones: they held their charge.

He took a sip of coffee. Then he called work and asked for Lucy.

It was a safe call to make, he'd decided. They didn't know the number of any of the burner phones he'd bought. Without that, and without physical access to the phone, he didn't think they could trace a call. Everything was guesswork and instinct. But he was beginning to trust his instincts in ways he never had before.

"We haven't gone out of business yet," Lucy said brightly when she picked up the phone.

"Good morning."

"You mean, good afternoon."

"Right. Anything I need to know?"

"Other than Connie Hunt really needs to be fired?"

The bookkeeper was the least of his worries. "Do me a favor and check my iPhone for messages again."

"If you want, I can drop your phone off at your house."

"No, that's okay. Just let me know if there's any messages on there."

She put him on hold.

A minute later she was back on the line. "This is weird. Your phone just says 'Hello.'"

"Excuse me?"

"The screen just says 'Hello' in big letters. It doesn't have your normal start-up screen. The picture of you and Sarah." That was his favorite picture of the two of them, on a Cape Cod beach.

"Can you enter the passcode?"

"No, it's like, it doesn't ask for your password; it just has the word 'Hello' on the screen. Like it's a brand-new phone you haven't set up yet."

"Huh? I don't get it."

"It's like your phone got erased or something. Like maybe there was a power surge?"

"Weird." That didn't make sense. Unless, of course, the NSA had done something. But that seemed a stretch. They didn't have the power, surely, to wipe a phone remotely. And even if they did have this ability, why would they do it to him? What could they possibly gain? "I'll check in later," he said.

He called Sarah on the burner he'd given her. "I'm out in—" He stopped before he could say "Concord." Then he remembered that she was talking on a burner as well. They could speak openly. He told her where he was. "I need a house to crash in out here."

"I don't sell a lot of properties out in MetroWest. But Katya does. Let me get back to you."

She called back a couple of minutes later. He drank some more coffee. In fact, he began to realize, he didn't mind it. It was bland and undistinguished, but not bad at all, really, as a caffeine-delivery system.

"Tanner," Sarah said. "Okay, this house is actually off the market, and it's empty, and the seller's moved to Florida." She gave him the combination to the front-door security lock.

"Sarah, don't meet me there. It's not safe for you to be around me. Okay?"

"I wasn't planning to drive out to Concord, come on."

"Just wanted to make sure. Actually, hold on a second. You have our ATM card, right?"

"Sure."

"I need cash."

"You have the card, too, right?"

"Sure. But I can't use it." It would set off an alarm, just like a credit card, and they'd locate him quickly.

"How can I get you the money? I suppose I could hide it in the house somewhere."

"You'd drive out to Concord after all."

"Late afternoon I can do it."

"Thank you. But I don't want you to do that. They might be tracking you to find me." He also didn't want anything to happen to her, but he didn't want to scare her by saying it. "Maybe you could bring it over to Lucy at the office and I can make arrangements with her."

"Okay. How much?"

"Whatever you can withdraw from savings. A thousand, two thousand, whatever." Cash wasn't crucial, but it would help.

Near the Dunkin' Donuts was a Starbucks. They had Wi-Fi, but Tanner needed a computer. He passed a funky-looking coffee shop that he knew served excellent coffee. Karen had tried them, but they used Counter Culture out of Durham. At the intersection of two main streets he found the Concord Free Public Library, a handsome Georgian building with white columns.

Exactly what he needed. He entered the library and found his way down a hallway to the reference desk. Nearby were a number of computer terminals for the patrons' use. He sat down in front of one and opened a browser and then pointed it to Gmail. He entered his personal e-mail address, "TannerRoast@gmail.com"—more evidence, as if he needed it, that he worked too hard, that he'd let his business take over his personal life. He clicked the "Next" button, and a red error message popped up:

SORRY, GOOGLE DOESN'T RECOGNIZE THAT EMAIL.

Certain that he must have typed it in wrong, he typed "TannerRoast" carefully and got the same red message.

SORRY, GOOGLE DOESN'T RECOGNIZE THAT EMAIL.

He sat back in his chair, perplexed. He hadn't typed it in wrong twice. Gmail didn't recognize upper- and lower-case in your e-mail address, so that wasn't it. He entered it again, all lowercase, just in case that made a difference.

SORRY, GOOGLE DOESN'T RECOGNIZE THAT EMAIL.

The burner in his pocket rang. A few people looked around at him disapprovingly. He pulled the phone out. Sarah calling from the burner he'd given her. He answered it softly, while striding out of the room and into the hallway. "Sarah," he said.

"Did you change the password?"

"What are you talking about?"

"The bank card doesn't work. The ATM. It locked me out—it swallowed the card!"

"I didn't change anything, Sar. Maybe you could call the bank and see what's wrong."

"Yeah," she sighed. "I will. I'm sorry about this."

"I don't get it," he said.

But maybe he did. He returned to the computer he'd been using near the reference desk. Once again he entered his Gmail address, and once again he got an error. *Google doesn't recognize that email.* It wasn't that the password had been changed. He couldn't even get that far.

There was no such e-mail address.

Just like his ATM card didn't work.

He went to Yahoo.com and signed in to the account he'd just created the day before, at Carl's house. It was a fake name and the number 322, which was his house number when he was a kid. This time it opened. Two e-mails in its inbox: one was the video automatically e-mailed from the wireless camera Scott had set up in the woods. The other was an invoice from Scott for a little over a thousand bucks.

Then he opened another browser window, Facebook .com. It was the sign-in page. One blank was for e-mail or phone; the other was for the password.

A red box popped up. *The email you've entered doesn't match any account. Sign up for an account.*

As if no such account ever existed. He had an account, a Facebook page, which he rarely visited. He tried it twice, got the same error, and didn't need to try it again. He couldn't get into Facebook. His account no longer existed.

With increasing disbelief, he opened up Amazon.com. He clicked on "Sign in," which took him to another screen where he was supposed to enter his e-mail address and password.

A red-outlined box popped up, a caution sign, and the words:

There was a problem.

We cannot find an account with that email address.

He opened Netflix.com and got:

Sorry, we can't find an account with this email address. Please try again or create a new account.

What other accounts do I have? he thought. Oh yes: the bank. He opened BankofAmerica.com.

A pink box with a big red triangle with an exclamation point on it. *We don't recognize your Online ID and/or Passcode. Please try again or visit Forgot Online ID & Passcode.*

One after another after another, he was unable to log in to any of his online accounts. Accounts weren't found. *We don't have a record of any account with that e-mail.* Even CraftBeerTemple.com greeted his log-in with an uncomprehending stare. He didn't exist.

It was unnerving to the point of terrifying. In the Internet-dominated world, Michael Tanner had become a ghost.

62

Tanner's entire digital existence had been wiped out. As if the whole Internet had been hit by a power surge. Or someone had flipped a switch.

How was this possible?

He had to get money soon, if he was going to stay "out here," as he thought of it—outside the ambit of his regular life. And he had a queasy feeling that the NSA might have gone even further than erasing him online. *What if they've seized my assets?* Did they have the power to do that?

Heart thudding, he looked up his bank's customer service number and entered it into his phone. Then he walked back out to the library's hallway and out the front door. A series of voice-mail prompts came up, telling him to listen carefully "as our menu options have changed."

He barked out, "Customer service," and after a few minutes of advancing through the phone tree, a distracted and squelched young male voice asked how he could help.

"My online account isn't working," Tanner said. He explained.

It took a long time for the distracted kid to understand, but he finally decided to bump Tanner's call up to a supervisor.

A woman came on the phone who sounded much sharper. "This is Audrey Jones, may I help you?"

Tanner explained.

Audrey answered without hesitation. "Certainly, sir, it looks like there was some sort of a security breach on your account, but I'm sure we can straighten this out easily. You just need to come into our offices on Boylston Street in Boston." She gave a street address.

Tanner hung up immediately.

Come into our offices. That sounded wrong.

They thought he was simpleminded and trusting, and that he'd surface in order to walk into an NSA ambush, a setup.

No sooner had he punched off the burner than it rang again.

"There he is," said the smooth baritone, that hard-to-place southern accent.

"What do you want?" Tanner said.

"Sucks not having the Internet, doesn't it? I mean, I always hear people complaining about the tyranny of the Internet and I feel like saying, *Try going without it.* You know?"

"The bank idea was great, by the way. I almost fell for it."

Earle laughed, a smoker's hoarse laugh. "We had a deal, you and me. By my watch, it's more than twenty-four hours. What happened?"

"Let me be clear," Tanner said. "I know there's classified documents on that laptop, but I haven't looked at them. Because I knew I'd gotten this computer by mistake. Okay?"

"Good citizen, we like to hear that."

"I'm not another Edward Snowden, I'm not a whistle-blower, and I have no interest in giving it to *The New York Times.* But I will if I have to." That wasn't just some bluff. It was leverage. Probably *The New York Times* would require the actual laptop, not just e-mailed files. Go to them with only the files and you're just another tinfoil-hat crazy.

"And you think *The New York Times* will do anything with it? You think they're gonna put it online? Times like these, newspapers are a lot more circumspect about what they print. Those few newspapers that still exist, I mean."

Tanner wondered: Did they have some way to locate him physically via the burner phone? He didn't know, of course. But it didn't seem likely. Not with a disposable mobile phone. Anyway, if they could have found him that way, they'd have found him already. So maybe he was safe talking on this burner after all.

"That's not all I got," Tanner said.

"I've seen the video. You got nothing, my friend."

"Oh, yeah? According to the NSA charter, you guys aren't allowed to operate domestically."

"It's not that simple, Michael."

"We'll see how simple it is when the ACLU gets a copy. And *The New York Times.* That video captured at least three faces very clearly. This is evidence you are operating within the US in violation of your charter. Plus, if any of them are undercover guys, their cover is now blown. Or burned, or whatever you say. I could post it myself, on YouTube."

"And it would disappear within seconds, I promise you."

"Not if I give it to a journalist. It's a big story."

"I don't know if there's a newspaper ballsy enough to damage our national security by running it. Anyway, the video is no longer in your inbox."

"That's not the only copy," Tanner took pleasure in saying. "There are plenty of backups." There was one, anyway, in his new Yahoo e-mail inbox. They still hadn't gotten to that one yet.

Earle sighed noisily. "I wish to hell you wouldn't do that. But what does it show, really? A bunch of guys in the woods? Are they geocachers? Are they *Pokémon Go* fanatics? Who's to say? Oh, maybe you'll spark some subreddit conspiracy group, with the kinda guys who believe that pizza parlors in DC keep child sex slaves. But what you're peddling to the ACLU and *The New York Times*? Hate to break it to you, Michael, but it looks more like an outtake from *The Blair Witch Project 2* than, I don't know, the Pentagon Papers."

Tanner didn't know how to reply, so he didn't.

"We're going to find it, you know," Earle said. "We found your company safe, by the way. In the kitchen. Clever."

"Thank you."

"Sorry we had to break it to get it open. We'll reimburse you. Anyway, you didn't leave it there, which was smart. We'll find it soon enough. And you too, Michael. It's actually not possible to hide from the government anymore. The longer you stay out there, the more we're gonna have to push, and you don't want us to push, believe me. Maybe we freeze Tanner Roast's assets, right? You know, with all the importing and the sales trips around Central America and Africa, your business might well be an entity of concern. And when we—"

Tanner disconnected the call. He'd heard enough. He had to get out of here.

63

Tanner went back into the public library and Googled for a few hours, took some notes on a scratchpad, made a list of what he'd soon need. Midafternoon, drained and in need of a caffeine fix, he went to McDonald's. He was afraid to go into the groovy indie coffee shop, in case the owner, who knew him, was there. He didn't want to be recognized.

Outside, on the next block, he found a hardware store. He took out his list and picked up a number of items: a flathead screwdriver, a Phillips-head screwdriver, a length of wire, a hammer, a little LED flashlight and batteries, wire cutters and strippers and electrical tape, a pair of insulated gloves. Then a jobsite backpack to carry it all around in. The total purchase was close to a hundred bucks. He paid cash, of course, and as he was waiting for everything to be bagged up, he counted the money in his wallet. He didn't have a lot left. He needed more cash.

And with his account frozen, he was stuck. He couldn't withdraw money. He couldn't even try to use his credit cards or else Earle's team would be immediately alerted, would see where he was. What did that leave? He could borrow from a friend, someone who knew he was good for it. Most of his friends, he imagined, would gladly lend him money. But who was it safe to contact? That was the problem. The friends he saw most often—the beer buddies—had to be ruled out. Or anyone he'd recently called, on any phone.

Or anyone he e-mailed. Unfortunately, by the time he ruled out anyone he'd been in touch with in recent memory, even the gang of buddies he went to Red Sox games with, he was left with a tier of friends he'd lost contact with. They were still friends, yes, but they were drifting away. He thought of a college friend, who like him had worked in a café in Boston during college to make money. Theo Oliveira. In college he was a musician, a keyboard artist, and he sometimes got paying gigs. A stoner, back then, and a bit of a flake. But a talented, nice guy. Last time they'd talked, which must have been at least five years ago, Theo was married to a fellow band member and lived somewhere in Acton, or thereabouts.

He mentally filed away Theo's name. He had the impression that Theo was just scraping by, so maybe he wasn't the best person to beg money from. But Theo would do what he could, Tanner was sure.

He returned to the library and located Theo Oliveira online, found his street address and phone number. He was living in the town of Carlisle, next to Concord. Then he watched a couple of YouTube videos on how to hot-wire a car, to remind himself. Apparently, hot-wiring a new car required a degree from MIT. The wires were hidden now, and there were immobilizer technology and smart keys. No, he'd have to find an older car.

As uncomfortable as he felt about stealing some poor guy's car, he didn't really have a choice: he needed to get around on not much money, out here where everything was fairly far apart, compared to Boston. Truth was, he didn't have enough money for gas.

But there was the moral thing: Tanner wasn't a thief. In all of his dealings with Tanner Roast, he was always scrupulously honest. To him, it was a matter of honor. And now he was going to break into someone's car and steal it? Hard to justify. Except that he couldn't see any alternative. The survival instinct made his moral qualms seem dispensable.

He hadn't even stolen a car yet and he was already feeling guilty about it.

According to his library research, modern cars had become quite difficult to steal. Cars made since the mid-1990s had all sorts of antitheft devices like engine immobilizer technology. Video games like *Grand Theft Auto* made it all look so easy.

By the time he was finished with his research, it had grown dark. He grabbed a wire coat hanger from a coat closet. That was an easy theft.

It had gotten cool outside. The blazer he was wearing helped, but it wasn't really enough. He felt cold and miserable.

He went down Main Street looking for a suitable target. He went right past shops and businesses that appeared to be open and operating. He found an old gas station that was apparently out of business, with a couple of cars parked in a lane in front. But that was right in view of vehicles and people passing by, so that was out. Behind a strip mall (a bridal shop, a small insurance firm, a bakery) a few cars were parked, but they were newer models, couldn't have been more than five years old. Too new to steal. When he passed a supermarket, he went in and bought some more cheap mobile phones.

The supermarket's parking lot was far too busy. He moved on, bypassing car after car, ruling them all out on various counts: too visible, too new, alarmed. It was dark and he was hungry and cold and lonely. He passed neighborhoods where he could see lit-up kitchens, people eating, watching TV, quarreling, and he felt isolated.

He was beginning to put together a plan, a way out of all of this, a way he might survive . . . and return to a normal life. Those few hours in the library had given birth to an idea.

He just needed to think it through.

But as of now, he needed to find a car to steal.

He found it after a few minutes. Another insurance company, a long, low, 1950s-era brick building. No night watchman there; it was dark and shuttered. A couple of cars were parked, presumably overnight, in a lot behind the building. The lot was deserted but also apparently unobserved. You couldn't see anyone or anything from back here except a closed auto dealership on one side.

One of the cars was a fairly late-model Mercedes, which was out.

The other was a stubby little yellow Ford Festiva that had to be almost thirty years old. Made in the late 1980s or 1990s, he was pretty sure. Looking around—there was no one in sight—he took the coat hanger out of the backpack and straightened it. At one end he left a little bent hook. He slid it under the little black flap of weather stripping at the bottom of the driver's side window, wiggled it around, felt something catch. Lost it. Wiggled it some more, felt it catch against some piece of machinery inside the door-locking mechanism, then yanked it up.

The door unlocked.

He looked around once again, just to be sure. Then he climbed in. The car smelled like the inside of an ashtray. He almost heaved. He felt around under the steering wheel for stray wires, but no. That would be too easy.

Try number one: he inserted the flathead screwdriver into the ignition slot, pounded it in with a hammer, then turned the screwdriver handle to start the car.

But of course it didn't work. That, too, would have been too easy.

He shone the flashlight around, located the screw holes in the molded plastic kick panel beneath the steering column. Then, flashlight gripped between his teeth, he unscrewed the panel and, with difficulty, pulled it off.

There it was, the guts of the starter, a rat's nest of bundled wires, slathered in thick dust.

Finding the bundle that led to the ignition cylinder in the steering column was quick. Finding the battery voltage supply wires was almost as quick: they were the two thicker-gauge wires, both conveniently red. He put on the insulated gloves—the wires were live—and snipped both. Then he stripped them a half inch or so. He put the ends of the two wires together and the car came to life—the radio blared on, the dashboard lit up. Success. Part one, anyway.

He snipped another couple of wires, both brown, and both live too. He stripped the end of each and then touched them together. They sparked, and the starter cranked at once. The car fired up, a good, healthy, throaty ignition, and once it had caught, he pulled the two starter wires apart and taped up both ends.

Success, part two.

Sighing with relief, he revved the engine a bit, turned on the headlights, and familiarized himself with what was where. Foot on the brake, he turned the wheel—and the steering wheel wouldn't move. It was locked. He turned the wheel back and forth a few times, but it was stuck.

A wheel lock. He had been afraid of that. You couldn't tell by looking a car over whether it had a wheel lock.

Shit.

He had to move on. He passed up car after car, all too modern. Car thief was apparently now a skilled profession.

Behind a closed restaurant-supply shop he finally found an old, well-maintained Mazda that also had to be vintage 1990 or so. He got into the car quickly and managed to get it started in less than five minutes. He was learning.

The Mazda ran well and smoothly, and it had about a quarter tank of gas. He'd written down the address of a house in Concord where Sarah had said he could stay. When he was about to reach for his iPhone to punch the address into his favorite navigation app, he suddenly remembered he didn't have it; he'd deliberately left it back at the office.

And couldn't use it anyway. Not anymore. *How did people navigate before navigation apps?* he wondered.

The library was probably closed by now. So much for Google Maps or whatever. What he needed was a gas station, but he learned quickly that not all of them sold maps anymore. He stopped at a McDonald's and picked up a fast-food dinner, which he ate as he drove.

Eventually, by stopping and asking for directions the old-fashioned way, he found the right street in Concord. He parked on the street, not in the driveway. He pulled a wire from the ignition assembly to shut off the car and got out. Halfway down the block was a stuttering streetlamp; the dim light flickered.

This house was immense and modern and angular. From the front it looked like a Lego construction, but pleasingly so: a ziggurat of glass and concrete. He punched the code into the burglar alarm and disarmed it. Then he entered the combination on the front-door padlock and got the door open.

He could smell something faintly lavender, probably from a sachet placed in the front hallway by the listing agent. He pointed the mini-flashlight's beam up and down, side to side, so he could see which way to go. Honed marble tiles on the floor, a small black table that bore a single orchid in a white vase, and—

—the door opened, and an angular man loomed in the entrance, a woman just behind him.

"Hello?" the man said.

"Can I help you?" said Tanner.

64

The man, who looked around forty, had short brown hair and a smudge of lipstick on his left cheek. He reeked of booze.

The woman right behind him was a pale blond whose lipstick was a mess. She was blushing a violent pink.

"N-no," the man said. "We're—we're fine, we were just—I'm with Century 21—are you from Coldwell Banker?"

Tanner shook his head.

"Sorry, I thought it was off the market," said the man.

"No," Tanner said. "I've got a buyer who's going to show up at any second." He tugged the backpack off his shoulder and set it down. "Sorry about that."

The disappointed horny couple turned and stumbled down the broad concrete front steps into the night.

Next to the orchid on the black table stood a square white envelope with his last name on it, in Sarah's neat printing. She must have come by.

On the card inside it said only

Goes right to your hips
xx

"Huh?" he said aloud.

"Goes right to your hips"? Was that some kind of joke he didn't get? Some women talked that way, about ice cream and slices of pie, but fortunately that wasn't Sarah's style. The only time she'd say something like that—actually, now he remembered—was quoting her mother explaining why there was never a cookie jar in the house. *You eat that, it goes straight to your hips,* her mother warned her. Which only made Sarah more fond of cookies. Because no one wants to be told something like that.

Cookies. She was talking, for some reason, about cookies.

He shone a path down a short hallway to a giant industrial kitchen with high ceilings. The inevitable Sub-Zero fridge and freezer, the obligatory Wolf range, a half-mile of white granite counter. The place was big and well equipped enough to service a bustling restaurant.

There, on a stretch of granite counter on his right, was a large white egg-shaped canister on a low metal stand. On the front of the egg it said COOKIES.

He lifted the lid. Inside was another white envelope. This one was fat. It was scotch-taped closed. He tore open the flap and saw a thick bundle of bank notes.

"Jesus."

He counted out the hundreds and fifties and twenties. Three thousand five hundred dollars.

"Sarah," he said aloud, chidingly, to no one. She must have taken out her own money, from her own, neglected account, and there sure wasn't much. This had to be most of what she had. She shouldn't have done it.

Still, he was relieved she had. He needed the money.

Tanner awoke early to make sure he wasn't surprised by another Realtor. Since the house was temporarily off the market, he didn't need to be quite as fastidious as at the last house. He bathed in an amazing glass-walled shower that produced steam and jetted water at him from all around.

He dressed in the new clothes and made a mental note to find a Walmart and buy some inexpensive ones. The shower had woken him up, but he still needed coffee, and badly. Like a lot of people, Tanner was a caffeine addict. Being in the business, he was used to having coffee throughout the day, an occupational hazard.

The walls of the front of the house were glass. He found the right button to electrically lower the blinds to provide some privacy. He peered outside through the slats, spent a good ten minutes that way, looking for watchers. Saw nothing, no one walking by. It was early, still dark out.

He left the house, locked it up and the padlock as well, and got into the stolen Mazda. Then there was another consideration: What happened when the car was reported missing? How long would it take for the police to do something about it? He didn't know. He didn't want to be pulled over and asked for license and registration. Yet he couldn't imagine its owner was paying very close attention, since it had been left overnight behind a building. It wasn't as if he'd stolen someone's Ferrari. It was a cruddy old Mazda.

Connecting the wires to start the car took a matter of seconds. He wanted to get out of town, find another library—an analog solution to a digital problem—and figure out his next move. And call Tanner Roast to check in. Yesterday's research had told him that you could buy bus tickets with cash, no ID. Traveling by bus was one way to stay under the radar, one of the few ways left. But he'd decided that today he would buy a used car with some of Sarah's money, and ditch the stolen one.

In Framingham he found a diner that looked good. It was nothing like the one in Southie where he and Lanny sometimes used to meet. Didn't have that abandoned-railroad-car look. But it already had customers, and it was before six.

It was a cash-only place, which was fine with him, because he now had lots of it. He sat at the counter. The waitress poured coffee without asking, as if she knew. It was not bad. A little watery, but freshly brewed, good beans. Everything at this diner was supersized. Pancakes were the size of dinner plates. Hash browns were heaped up high. Even the coffee mugs were unusually large.

He thought of Lanny—he couldn't help it—and felt guilty. His mistake, picking up the wrong computer, had led directly to Lanny's death. A good person had lost his life.

There was no way to undo what he'd done.

The counter filled up with customers. He had more coffee, ate eggs and bacon and buttered toast, with pancakes on the side. Nothing healthy. He was risking his life, being out here, on the run. Watching what he ate seemed pointless.

The guy at the counter next to him smiled, watching Tanner eat ravenously. "Good stuff, right?" the guy said.

Tanner smiled.

"Coffee's okay too, huh?"

"Yep, it is."

"But it doesn't compare to yours," the guy said.

65

Tanner felt jolted by a shock of electricity.

They've found me.

But just as quickly, he thought: *Don't freak out, maybe the guy recognizes me from a trade show, a sales call, something like that.*

The man on his left was soft and middle-aged, with a round belly under a loudly patterned, acid-trippy red-and-black-and-green sweater. He wore steel-rimmed aviator glasses, had deeply inset eyes like raisins and a bristly gray mustache. He did not look like one of the members of the NSA team he'd filmed in the woods. He was professorial, physically unprepossessing.

"Do I know you?" Tanner asked.

"Seattle, wasn't it? The coffee expo?"

Tanner stared. He slowly shook his head. "I wasn't there."

"Too much of a coincidence?" The man shrugged. "When something seems that way, it usually is."

"What are you saying?"

"I'm saying you're a man who needs help," the man said quietly, "and I'm offering mine."

"What?" He felt the adrenaline start to course into his bloodstream.

"You're a hunted man, Mr. Tanner. But you need to know I'm not one of the hunters. I'm your friend. I'm an admirer."

Tanner sat back. "Who are you?"

"Call me Gregory." The man spoke with a barely detectable accent of some unidentifiable kind. He flattened his *A*'s too much, a foreigner trying hard to mimic an American accent.

"But that's not actually your name."

"Close enough."

What was the man's real name? *Gregorio, Grigor, Řehoř* . . . ? Where was he from? His American accent was extremely good. But he wasn't American; of that much Tanner was sure.

"Mr. Tanner, you're a man who, through no fault of his own, has made a lot of enemies. Now they're trying to run you off the road. But I look at you and I see someone who's incredibly brave. Someone who's been given an extremely rare opportunity to change the world. And I want to help."

The waitress refilled Gregory's coffee mug and then Tanner's, moving away quickly, discreetly. She could see the men were talking about something heavy.

"Help how?"

"You know, there's a great tradition. Men of conscience who expose terrible abuses. Like it or not, you've been thrust by history into an extraordinary position."

"To do *what*?"

"All you need to do is share your documents with my people. They'll know what to do with them. You know the saying, 'Sunlight is the best disinfectant,' yes?"

"And who are 'your people'?"

"My associates, I should say. An organization devoted to that disinfecting sunlight. We believe that secrets, especially government secrets, must be disclosed whenever it's within our power."

"You mean like WikiLeaks?"

He nodded, smiled. "I work with them, yes."

"You work 'with' them?"

"But let's not get caught up with prepositions. *With, from, of;* the filaments can get pretty tangled. The bottom line is this: we want to help you. What I want you to know is, there are people who are rooting for you. People who care about openness and transparency."

"And then what happens to me? Do I get killed?"

Gregory shook his head slowly, soulfully. "This is what I'm here to tell you. When it comes to threats on your life, we have some powerful assets. We can give you as much protection as you need—and I'm talking about the full resources of a rather powerful state."

Now he understood. "You're talking about Russia."

Gregory didn't reply.

"Wait, so you're in a position to offer full protection of the Russian security services?"

"I am."

"Are you Russian?"

He shrugged, said nothing: a simple acknowledgment.

"Are you WikiLeaks or are you—Russia? Which is it?"

"Do I have the support of certain Russian assets? Distinctions like that have become meaningless these days, really. There's no clear line, and it doesn't finally matter. It's complicated, but the world is a complicated place. What *does* matter is—I can help you. I can protect you."

"In *Russia*."

"We're talking a luxury apartment, a dacha—the life. You're not going to be like Philby, drinking yourself into obscurity. We're a capitalist paradise now. And I've had your coffee. It's great. Your coffee could be huge over there—it's an untapped market. Point is, we can protect you. You can have any kind of life you want."

"And, what, I have to move to Moscow for the rest of my life?"

"May it be a long life. Which I wouldn't put odds on over here."

"I'm still alive," he pointed out.

"I'm impressed; I really am. You've done well in the last few days, staying out in the cold as long as you have. You are an amateur, after all. Not a trained operative. Clearly, some combination of resourcefulness and luck has served you well. But how long do you think you can keep going? Even a hot hand cools eventually."

Tanner shook his head.

Gregory picked up a fork and traced a pattern on the

countertop. A windy sigh. "Mr. Tanner, listen to me, please. You go back out there, and they'll grab you. It's only a matter of time. Now, will they *kill* you, an American citizen? I don't know. Then again, they have ways to do that untraceably these days."

"Well, you've got the wrong guy."

"The wrong Michael Tanner?" Gregory asked with a glint of amusement.

"I'm not a whistle-blower, and I'm not a hero."

He set down the fork carefully, like a surgeon handing off his instruments. "You know, Ed Snowden didn't plan to be a hero either. One day he just woke up and realized, *enough is enough.* That's all. He did the right thing. He listened to his conscience."

"That's got nothing to do with me."

"You can decide to be a hero. And change the world. Do you realize how powerful you are? If we're right about what you've got, this could change everything. Mr. Tanner, there are moments in history—hinge moments, they're called—when the world suddenly changes. This is where we are, I think. Will America become a surveillance state, eventually a dictatorship? Or do you have it in your power to stop all that in its tracks? See, you can become the Nathan Hale of our time. Nathan Hale could have remained a schoolteacher, but he made a decision and he became a hero. To save the American Revolution."

"Wasn't he executed by the British?"

"Well, he's probably not the best example. But you can become someone truly important. You probably think of yourself as just a common man, a small man now. But you've proven yourself to be a brave man—and a man of conscience. A righteous man who's about to become someone truly important in the history of our world. You alone can stop the abuses. Turn over the rock and reveal the . . . the writhing maggots. Let the sun shine in. Save your country."

"I'm not handing classified documents over to *Russia*. That's not who I am."

"Because, what, you love your country? Given what your country has done to you? Look, the Cold War was over years ago. Russia isn't the enemy anymore."

Tanner shook his head mutely.

" 'The only thing necessary for the triumph of evil is for good men to do nothing.' Someone wise said that once." Gregory looked up, cocked his head. "Mr. Tanner, the time to decide is now. You have very little time left."

Tanner said nothing.

Gregory turned away. Something in the window seemed to have caught his eye. He turned and looked outside, squinting. Tanner looked where Gregory was looking. He saw a black Chevy Suburban pull into the diner's small parking lot.

"A Suburban weighs five thousand pounds," he said. "An armored one weighs ninety-five hundred. It tends to sit low on its run-flat tires." Suddenly the man sprang from his stool and stood. "Oh dear. I told you that you have little time. In fact, you have no time."

Trailing behind the Suburban were two, no, three

smaller black four-wheel-drive vehicles. Tanner heard the loud squealing of brakes.

Gregory put an urgent hand on Tanner's shoulder. "There's no time! I know a way. Come with me."

Tanner glanced outside again, at the team that he knew was forming to apprehend him. He thought for a moment. "No, thanks," he said.

66

Tanner had lost track of time.

For a long time, he had been sitting at a steel table bolted to the floor in an all-white room. He'd been in the small, windowless room for more than an hour. He had nothing to read, no phone, no way to entertain himself. He just examined the dense white foam on the walls, the small camera lenses in each corner of the room. The metal-halide lights inset into the ceiling, with their constant high-pitched hum, like tinnitus.

He had been taken to this room about an hour ago, he estimated, from the windowless room where he ate and slept. Which was not much different from this room, except that it had a bed and a chair and a toilet. All were steel and bolted to the floor too. On the bed, a thin mattress.

He didn't know where he was. His captors did not talk to him. All he knew was that he was in solitary confinement somewhere.

He wasn't entirely sure how long he'd been here, but he thought it had been around two days. He had determined that by how many meals he had been given. Which was complicated by the fact that the meals had mostly been the same: a brown brick of something he was pretty sure was nutraloaf. Which he'd once read was given to prison inmates only as punishment. It was inedible, a flavorless neutral-tasting substance, like chewing Styrofoam. He tried a few bites at first and spit it out.

So it had been two days and two nights since four black vehicles had slammed to a halt on either side of the diner in Framingham. Agents swarmed out of the Suburbans: men in plain black windbreakers and unmarked green military uniforms, with black helmets and black vests. A few of them toted assault rifles. Two agents grabbed him and yanked him out of the diner. Behind him, he could hear a few patrons scream.

He didn't resist. What else was he to do?

They whisked him into one of the Suburbans and put the blacked-out goggles over his eyes and headphones over his ears.

He was driven somewhere for about thirty minutes and then the Suburban came to a stop. The doors opened and cold air entered.

He said, "Is someone going to tell me what's going on?"

He'd begun to sweat profusely. He must have sat there in the middle row of the Suburban for ten minutes. He detected aviation fuel, which smells very different from gasoline, and he knew he was on the grounds of an airport.

Then he was hustled across a broad expanse and up a flight of stairs into what smelled like a plane. They locked his handcuffs to the arms of a seat.

"Is anyone going to tell me what's going on?" he said again. "Anyone? Or where you're taking me?" He raised his voice. "Or what all this is even *for*?"

But even if someone did reply, he couldn't hear.

The plane taxied and then took off. The flight was short, maybe an hour or an hour and a half. He found himself disappearing into his thoughts.

After another drive in some kind of vehicle, he was trundled into a building. He still had no idea where he was, just that it was about an hour from an airport, by plane. When the goggles and headphones were finally removed, he was in a brightly lit white windowless room. Two guys in unmarked khaki uniforms had brought him there.

He saw a folded orange garment on the bed.

"Please change into your jumpsuit," the man said.

"Where am I?" Tanner said.

The man closed the door behind him without answering Tanner's question.

He examined the room, which was really a prison cell. There was a pinpoint hole in the door. Probably a peephole that let them look in at him, one-way.

"Aren't you going to read me my rights?" Tanner said.

No one answered.

He was alone.

That was around midday, he later figured. Based on the meal pattern, two days followed.

After a nutraloaf supper, he was left alone for a long

stretch, probably six or eight hours. It was probably bedtime. But the metal-halide lights in the ceiling were not turned down.

He tried to sleep in the blazing light, managed to drift off a few times, not for very long. When that stretch was over—Tanner believed it was morning—he was handed a long cardboard tray with nutraloaf again, nothing else.

It was the pure isolation that eventually made him desperate.

He examined every inch of the white room. He listened to voices going past.

He assumed he was in a government facility. He didn't think it was the army, because the uniforms didn't say so. NSA, probably. But wasn't the National Security Agency part of the military? He didn't remember.

Anyway, it made no difference where he was.

The hours dragged by. He thought about the goddamned laptop and wondered if it was still where he'd put it. He drafted imaginary conversations he would have with his jailers.

He examined the orange jumpsuit he was wearing. It was made of some nontearable kind of synthetic fabric, with Velcro closures.

At supper the first day, he said to the guard who handed him the nutraloaf, "Is there anything else to eat besides this crap?"

The guard said nothing. He seemed to smile, not unkindly.

"You ever taste it, pal?"

"It's got all your daily nutrients," the guard said, and he closed the door as he left.

"Don't I at least get a phone call?" he said to the door.

Being alone in his head, with all his thoughts, was dismal.

The terrifying notion occurred to him that this might go on for the rest of his life. Locked up here, isolated from human contact. No one would know where he was. Truly a nightmare scenario.

What would happen when his employees at Tanner Roast began to wonder where the boss was? When Lucy Turton called with problems for him to solve and couldn't reach him? Even Sarah, who knew he was on the run, began to worry that she hadn't heard from him, that something must have happened.

Michael Tanner had just vanished.

On the afternoon of the second day, the door to his cell opened, and a different bullet-headed guard came to escort him to the white-walled room down the hall that had the steel table in it, bolted to the floor.

And now he waited, hungry and light-headed.

He sat in one of the four steel chairs bolted to the floor around this table, and he waited.

When it finally came, the sound of the door unlatching startled him.

"We meet again," said Earle Laffoon.

67

The man from the NSA was wearing a red-checked flannel shirt, faded jeans, and tooled Western-style boots. Weekend attire. He grinned as he sat down, sprawled in his seat, legs splayed.

"Long time no see," Earle said.

"Well, you found me," Tanner said. "I don't know how, but you found me. I'm sure it was child's play for you guys."

"Give yourself a little credit, man. Our busy beavers back at Fort Meade have been assembling an incredibly exhaustive profile of you—all your electronic communications since forever, everywhere you ever went, every friend you ever had, and there's a lot of 'em. Every digital trace you've ever left. We now know more about you than your wife does. And it's not very interesting, I'm afraid to say. But if we didn't have the satellites, man, we still would never have found you. You're too good. And an amateur, to boot. Hell, man. You should work for us."

"Am I under arrest?"

Earle shook his head. “Nope.”

“Then I’m free to go.”

“Nope.”

“This is illegal. You haven’t even read me my rights!”

“That’s because you really don’t have any to *read*, I’m afraid.”

“Well, to start with, I’m an American citizen and we have something here called the Bill of Rights,” Tanner said indignantly. He didn’t actually remember what those rights were. Was one of them search and seizure? Maybe so. The right to bear arms, there was that. Speech too.

Earle shrugged, smiled sadly. “Not in the situation you’re in. Now, I’m not saying that’s right or wrong. I’m just saying that’s how it is. You or me, we might have designed the system differently, but this is the system we got.”

“Bullshit.”

“See, here’s the deal, Michael. You are a material witness in an extremely high-priority leak investigation, in illegal possession of classified material, and we have been unable to secure your cooperation without detaining you. So—we’re detaining you. That’s how it is.”

“For how long?”

“Until you start cooperating.”

“You can’t do that.”

“I’m afraid we very much can. It’s all legal. It’s called the material witness statute. Eighteen USC 3144. Check it out, next time you’re in a law library.” His face folded into a sort of corrugated grin. “Or a prison library.”

“So you’re a lawyer as well as an NSA agent?”

"Thank you, but no. Though I did go to law school, smartest move I ever made for my career. So I'll tell you a little story about a guy from Brooklyn, New York, named Jose Padilla. Right after 9/11. Name sound at all familiar to you?"

Tanner shook his head.

"So we think he may be connected to al-Qaeda. But we don't know for sure. We—I don't mean us, the NSA, but I mean the US government—we arrest him on what they call a material witness warrant. So what happens next? He lawyers up? He's brought before a judge? Nope. None of that. We lock him up in solitary for a month while we decide how to charge him. Military trial? Civilian trial? That's a tough one. We're at war, right? Anyway, he's pounding on the bars of his cell, demanding to see a lawyer; we say nada."

"That can't be legal."

"It is now, good buddy. We detained him for a month. Statute doesn't say how long we can keep you. Could be longer."

"And what happened to Padilla?"

"He's in solitary in supermax prison in Colorado, ADX Florence, for twenty-one more years."

"So he's a terrorist. What does that have to do with me?"

"You," Earle said through a yawn, "are in legal limbo."

"What the hell does that mean?"

"Gosh, it could be a couple more weeks, a month, maybe longer, before you see a judge. Or a lawyer. Depends on how long it takes you to realize it's time to hand over that laptop. To start cooperating with us. The time for games is over." Earle gave another one of his sad smiles. Tanner saw teeth stained, probably by chewing tobacco. "We're at what you'd call an impasse."

"You ever see the movie *Midnight Express*?" Tanner asked.

"No, but I heard about it plenty."

Tanner remembered the movie about an American college student who tries to smuggle drugs out of Turkey and is thrown in prison, where he's tortured sadistically. It must have been lousy for the Turkish tourism business. He felt sort of like that college student.

"Isn't that the one where the hero gets into a nasty fight with his guard and ends up spitting out the guard's tongue?"

Tanner nodded.

"Won't be anything like that here, I promise. Just between you and me and . . . the table, I think they did torture Mr. Jose Padilla. But those were tough times for the country. Compared to him, you're being treated like a king."

"Yeah, that's pretty much what I'd call it. Treated like a king."

"The problem is, Michael, that you've broken the law, and a damned serious law it is. The Espionage Act. Whether you know it or not, it's against the law to possess classified information without the proper authorization."

"I don't possess it. It's not *my* laptop, it's . . ." He thought a moment. "Someone else's."

"Whose?"

Tanner shook his head. They didn't know the laptop belonged to a US senator. That was a fact he might be able to use as leverage. Something to hold on to, at least for now.

And then it came to him, like two puzzle pieces clicking perfectly together. They didn't know it was Senator Susan Robbins's laptop because they weren't working with the senator's chief of staff, Will Abbott.

They don't know about him. "I'd feel a lot more talkative," Tanner said, "if I was back home, in my own house."

Earle crossed his arms, gave a crooked smile. He wasn't buying. "Check out 18 USC 793. About the 'willful retention of information relating to the national defense.' " He made little scare quotes, two fingers on each hand twitching in the air. "Whoever has unauthorized possession of information relating to the national defense and blah blah blah. That's you, pal. You also knowingly passed classified information to a reporter."

Tanner shook his head but didn't argue.

"Maybe we should talk about your friend Lanford Roth."

"Landon."

"I always screw that up. Landon. We know he had documents on a whaddayacallit, a mini-thumb-drive thingo. Meaning you made a copy of those top secret documents and gave them to a reporter. To the news media. So please don't feed me this line about *You didn't know what you have and you didn't even look at it.* You knew you had top secret national security documents, and clearly you read through them enough to decide to notify the press." He shrugged. "I mean, you see where I'm coming from, right? And then there you are, playing *Let's Make a Deal* with someone from the Russian GRU over flapjacks and coffee. You beginning to see why we might be concerned?"

"I didn't know that guy was a Russian until—"

"I know, I know, I know. We heard it all. But it's not going to look good to a grand jury, I don't think."

"I wasn't even arrested or charged!" Tanner said.

"We're back to that? There's no shortage of lawyers in the national security division of the DOJ. We'll get you arrested when the time is right."

"Are we in a police state now? Is that what's happened?"

"Lucky for you we're not a police agency or we'd get you for killing a man. On Mayfield Street in Boston, right?"

Tanner smiled furiously. "Yeah, the man you sent to kill me."

Earle looked as if Tanner had slapped him suddenly. "Aw, now, come *on*."

"You sent that guy to kill me."

"No, sir, we did not. Most certainly did not. What you're suggesting is an affront. We are a highly professional operation with a headcount of sixty-five thousand and about that many contract employees. You think we're going to outsource to some Boston hit man? With a goddamned police record? You don't seriously think we'd hire some third-rate *mobster*, now, do you?"

Tanner just looked at him. He had a point. Maybe it wasn't the NSA that had tried to have him killed.

"I mean, hell. That's crazy. I got people on staff that'd do this. We send somebody to take you out, you'll be *out.*" He folded his arms, sat back again. "No, sirree, if we sent somebody to kill you, we'd be meeting at a cemetery and you wouldn't be doing much talking."

"And Lanny Roth?"

Tanner waited for the inevitable denial and was surprised when Earle offered, after a few seconds, "The reporter."

"His murder set up to look like a suicide," Tanner said. "Pills and booze all around him when he died. Probably in his bloodstream too."

Earle looked thoughtful, maybe even a little distraught. "Yeah, that sounds like something the Theta team would do." He said it matter-of-factly, but not approvingly. Almost as if he were processing it. "Which is not a confirmation of anything. It's a hypothetical surmise about a hypothetical entity."

"Theta?"

"Never mind. Can't change the past. Let's talk about your future."

"I demand to see a lawyer immediately."

"Sure. All in good time. You got a problem with this? Welcome to life after 9/11."

"I'll tell you something else," Tanner said. "I'm supposed to e-mail a buddy of mine every day by two o'clock in the afternoon. If he doesn't get any e-mails from me after four days, he's going to start e-mailing documents to a list of people. Including *The New York Times*."

"Ye olde dead-man switch. Right? Clever. But I'm calling your bluff." Earle smiled delightedly, a kid playing a game. "We're keeping a pretty close watch on a whole lot of people you know. Including people you forgot you knew. You've got a lot of friends, I'll give you that."

Tanner shrugged as if it didn't make a difference whether Earle believed him or not. Unfortunately, Earle had called it right.

"So that's where we are, Michael. Without that laptop, there's really nothing I can do to help."

"Are you at least going to give me one phone call?" Tanner said.

"You want a phone call? I'll give you one phone call, 'cause I like your coffee." Earle looked up and spoke to the wall. "Please bring in a landline for my friend here." Turning back to Tanner, he said, "Mobile phone signals are jammed in here, sorry."

The door opened about a minute later, and a large bulky black touch-tone phone on a cord was brought in by one of the bullet-headed guards. He placed it on the table in front of Tanner. Its wire ran across the floor of the cell and into the hallway. Then the guard left, closing the heavy-sounding door behind him.

Tanner looked at the phone, picked it up, heard the

dial tone, then replaced the handset in its cradle. Calling Jamie North was pointless; the lawyer had made it clear he would never represent Tanner. Call *The New York Times* or the Associated Press or something? His call would be ignored. He wanted to call Sarah, wanted to talk to her, hear her voice. But he knew there was one call that could get him out of here.

Earle saw Tanner looking at the phone. "You want a phone number, we'll get it for you in a jiffy. No shortage of computers here. You remember when they used to give out those big thick phone books? Man, those days are gone, huh?"

"Yeah, I need a phone number," Tanner said.

"What's that?"

"There's a guy I know in Washington, went to school with a friend of mine." He spoke mostly to himself. "What's his name? . . . I met him a few times . . . He's the chief of staff to Senator Roberts—*Robbins,* that's it. Chief of staff to Senator Robbins. I don't remember his name, but I bet he could sort this out. Just connect me to the senator's office."

68

This is Senator Robbins's office."

"William Abbott, please."

"May I ask who's calling?"

"Michael Tanner."

Will Abbott picked up the line instantly. "Mr. Tanner—"

Tanner cut him off. "Yes, I don't know if you remember me, but we met through Seth, in Boston—?"

"Tanner—"

"Hold on. I need your help. I'm being held at, uh . . ."

Tanner looked at Earle, who said, "The new federal detention facility right outside Waldorf."

"At the new federal detention facility outside Waldorf, Maryland. By the National Security Agency. Now, I'm sure you'd like me to cooperate with them. But before I do, I was hoping you might be able to talk sense into our friends here. Thanks."

He handed the phone back to Earle. "I think he wants to talk to you."

* * *

"Is this Deputy Director Lash?" Will said. "Yes, this is Will Abbott. I'm the chief of staff to Senator— Right. Will Abbott." Will stood up and, stretching the phone's curly cord, he walked over to his office door and pushed it closed.

"Well," he continued, "I don't know what the hell your agency thinks it's doing, but this isn't some . . . Abdul Mohammed you've got locked up. This is a respected Boston businessman, a well-known member of my boss's . . . support community. I mean, there have been articles written about this guy. Right. Michael Tanner. He's at your detention complex near Waldorf."

Will was trying not to sound panicked, which he was.

NSA had grabbed Tanner! Did they have the senator's laptop too? Had Tanner told them whose laptop he'd accidentally picked up? If so, they already knew where the leak had come from. And her career was over. As was his. All Tanner had to do was answer their first question.

Tanner, who was obviously calling from a monitored line and knew it, had figured it out. He knew that Will was desperate not only to get the boss's computer back but to keep secret whose computer it was. And to keep that compromising information secret from the NSA in particular.

So Tanner was making an unmistakable, implicit threat. *If you don't get me out of detention by the NSA, I will tell them whose computer I ended up with. And you sure as hell don't want that.*

No, Will sure as hell didn't want that.

"This is very *much* an oversight matter," Will said crisply. "You're holding an American citizen in detention for what exactly? We find this highly troubling."

He listened for a minute and then broke in: "And now your agency is asking for another ten billion dollars in black-box allocations? Well, the senator is going to have to take a very careful look at that. Especially if you persist in holding a noncharged US citizen in a prison cell. Do we need to get the entire committee involved in this?"

Will listened a bit longer. "Okay," he said. "I'm glad I'm getting through to you."

"Yes, sir, absolutely. The very next thing I do." Earle put down the phone.

He swiveled around in his chair, which emitted a moan. "Well, Michael, I sure underestimated you. You obviously have some kinda juice in this town. I don't know who you know, but you sure pushed the magic button. That was the deputy director. My boss. And you, my friend, you are free to go."

Earle shook his head with what looked like disbelief.

69

Mr. Tanner," Will said.

Michael Tanner emerged from the side entrance to the federal detention facility, a hulking brick windowless structure the size of a city block, built on the site of an abandoned strip mall. Tanner looked around uncertainly. The man looked wearier since Will had last seen him in Boston. He had obviously been through a lot.

Well, so had Will.

He offered his hand, and Tanner shook.

"Good to see you again," Will said.

"Glad we could do business."

"Me too." Will gestured with a hand. "My car is right outside."

The NSA had offered to convey Michael Tanner to Washington National Airport. But Tanner had apparently decided that the less time spent in the company of the NSA, the better. He'd get a ride with Will.

Will unlocked the car doors, and when Tanner got into Will's Audi—technically Jen's, but she never used it;

she almost always took the Metro—his knees touched the dashboard. He was a much taller man than Will. He pulled back on the seat-adjustment lever to slide the seat back. Then he shut his door.

Once they'd pulled away from the curb, Will said, "Did you tell them whose laptop you have?"

"Of course not. You were my secret weapon. I wasn't going to give it away."

"Secret weapon? How do you figure?"

"It was a simple calculation."

"Oh yeah?"

"The same calculation you're making too. See, I had a lot of time to think. And I figured something out."

"Like what?"

"The NSA doesn't *know* whose laptop is missing. And you really don't want them to know."

"Why not?"

"Because then they'd learn that your boss had classified information on an unsecured laptop. And that's probably a major no-no."

"Huh," Will said.

"I know I'm just a coffee guy, but I'm pretty sure you're not supposed to keep classified information on a regular old computer. And I'm thinking, if the NSA ever found her laptop, your boss, the senator, would be in deep doo-doo."

"Huh."

"You don't want them to find the laptop. And I'm happy to be rid of it."

"And where is it?"

"In a safe place in Boston."

"Then we're going to Boston."

"We?"

"Part of the deal. You'll notice I've put my trust in you that you're going to keep your end of the bargain and give me that laptop back without any more games."

"Then again," Tanner said, "you did try to have me killed."

Will stiffened, felt his body go alert: a physical sensation. He looked at the road, compressed his lips while he considered how to reply. He glanced to his right and was surprised to find Tanner smiling.

"At first I thought it was the NSA that sent the guy," Tanner said. "But it wasn't. By process of elimination, I figured it out. It was you."

Will let out a breath, shook his head. "He wasn't going to kill you or anything like that," he said. "He was only going to put a scare into you."

"The guy was a goddamned hit man," Tanner said.

There was a long pause. "You think I'm some kind of ogre, because you don't know me. I get that. What makes it so strange for me is that I know you—"

"Except you don't."

"I'm not even talking about the file we put together, the bio stuff. I look at you, and yeah, I *know* you. You're the high school star, the scholar-athlete, the center of the high school universe. Guys like you, we used to call you the barbarians. The warrior class. You could get anything you wanted, any girl you wanted."

"Yeah, right," Tanner said.

"Everyone always sucked up to you, even the teachers. Everyone wanted to get on your good side. Whereas I didn't *have* a side. I was the kid you never looked at twice. I mean, Dad was dead by the time I was fourteen. Mom worked as a receptionist for a dentist—she sold houses on the side to keep us afloat—but there was a lot of coupon clipping going on. Maybe I had the wrong brand of sneakers. Or my clothes didn't fit the way they were supposed to. Or maybe I'm just making excuses. I was the guy who ran for class treasurer in college and got his ass handed to him. But you know what? It took me a while, but I found a place."

"Good," Tanner said. "I'm glad."

Will looked uneasy, as if he'd talked too much. Then, crisply, he said: "I suggest we take the Acela back to Boston." That was the relatively high-speed train between Washington and Boston.

"Isn't flying faster?"

"I have a problem with flying."

"Well, I don't mind the Acela," Tanner said.

A moment of silence passed while Will turned onto Route 301 heading north to DC. Tanner was looking at something on the right of the road. Then he turned back to him and said, "So how'd you convince them?"

Will smiled. "I speak with the authority of a powerful

US senator. The higher-ups listen. They get it. Isn't that why you called me?"

"Partly."

"As long as we're clear."

"I'm clear. I give you the laptop and we never have to see each other again." Tanner said it in a not unfriendly way, though.

"You also have agreed not to talk about whose laptop it is and what's on it. In return I ensure the NSA leaves you alone."

"Okay. As agreed."

"From now on you're protected. But no more passing documents on to reporters. You go back to your life. And don't look back. Don't turn into a pillar of salt."

"Got it. So why are you so desperate to get this laptop back?"

"Desperate? I'm not desperate. This is Washington, man. I can't let them own me."

"Own you?"

But Will just shook his head. *Because I don't want the NSA to make Senator Robbins their bitch; that's why. Because that's how the game is played here. Once they own us, the NSA will basically be able to ram through Congress whatever program they want.* Senator Robbins was the most powerful, most respected member of the committee. Of course they'd want to own her.

He could feel his throat start to pulse. "So let me ask you something," he said. "Why?"

"Why what?"

"Why didn't you tell them how we know each other?"

A long silence passed, and Will began to worry about what Tanner might say.

"Because I think we have a common interest," Tanner said. "You don't want the NSA to get the laptop, and I want to stay alive. And out of prison."

Will nodded.

"I knew if I told them everything I'd never get out of that damned prison," Tanner said.

He looked like he meant it.

"So did you look at the documents?" Will asked.

"Yes."

"You read them?"

Tanner nodded.

"Understand now you've picked up a hornet's nest?"

"Yes," Tanner said.

"You understand, I hope, that if you leak any information regarding CHRYSALIS, you'll be arrested. That's not a threat. That's just— That's what would happen, and you should know it."

"Is this a program that's already in existence? Or is it . . . being debated?"

Will hesitated, looked like he was about to say something, then shook his head.

"You don't know, but you won't tell me?"

Will didn't respond.

"Holy shit," Tanner said.

70

The train ride to Boston took six hours and forty minutes. The two men sat across from each other, a table between them.

Will Abbott spent most of the first hour busily tapping away at a laptop and complaining about the agonizingly slow Wi-Fi, drinking Amtrak coffee, eating mini-pretzels, and talking on his cell phone. At one point he seemed to be talking to his wife, about a baby. Abbott's wife was apparently upset that he wasn't coming home tonight.

Tanner, who missed having an iPhone, used one of his new disposable phones to check in first with Sarah, and then with Lucy at the office. When he'd finished, he sat and watched the scenery race past. And he thought.

He was sitting across from a man who'd tried to have him killed.

It was sort of like enemy spies being traded on the Glienicke Bridge, the Bridge of Spies, in Berlin. It had that weight. A kind of mutual wariness. He was sitting close enough to smell the man's Drakkar Noir. Very high school.

Will Abbott was a balding man around Tanner's age who looked as if he spent all of his time hunched over a computer, like so many other people these days. But at the same time there was something about him, a red thread of desperation, that could make him a dangerous adversary.

He thought about what Abbott had said.

So how'd you convince them? Tanner had asked.

I speak with the authority of a powerful US senator. The higher-ups listen. . . .

"So I'm getting some pressure to release you," Earle had said to him. "From your friend on Capitol Hill."

"Pressure?"

Earle smiled. Deep vertical gullies creased his cheeks. "We're going to make a deal, you and me."

"What kind of a deal?" Tanner had said.

"I believe William Abbott is the owner of the laptop you accidentally grabbed. That's why he's calling in his chips."

"Just to be clear, I didn't say whose laptop I have."

"No, you didn't have to. But that's fine. I'm letting you go. And here's what you're going to do. If you want your troubles to go away permanently, anyway. You're going to hand the laptop back to its rightful owner. And if we're able to grab him with the laptop, why, then, you and me, we're good. *Vaya con Dios.*"

It was strange: Tanner's instincts told him to trust this guy Earle. Even though he'd had him abducted, had threatened him—at the same time, he'd never offered false assurances or fake comfort. He was basically a straight shooter.

"Deal," Tanner had said.

Earle offered his hand, and the two men shook.

Finally, Tanner had thought, *a way out.*

After they'd been in the train for an hour, Abbott put down his phone, and the two started to talk. Tanner was too social a man to let the entire journey pass in silence. He said, "So you have a baby? I couldn't help but overhear."

"Uh, yeah. Eight weeks."

"Tough gig, being chief of staff to a senator and having a newborn."

"It is."

Tanner kept mulling over Abbott's cryptic words.

This is Washington, man. I can't let them own me.

No wonder Abbott was so desperate.

"Boy or girl?" Tanner asked.

71

In the late afternoon, the train pulled into Back Bay station in Boston. The two men got off. The station stank of diesel. The platform was crowded with people who were just getting back to Boston from meetings in New York or maybe Washington. Like a herd of cattle, they all migrated in close pack formation toward the exit doors, the escalator up to the station's main level, and then the inevitable Darwinian struggle to hail a cab outside on Dartmouth Street, where there seemed to be no cab stand, just the occasional passing taxi.

Tanner wanted to go home and collapse and be done with the insanity of the last two weeks. But he had just one more stop to make.

After five minutes of trying to flag down a cab, Tanner gave up. He turned to Abbott, pointing down the street toward the South End. "Just a couple of blocks that way and then to the left."

They set off for Tremont Street, Tanner with his dirt-flecked knapsack and Abbott with his briefcase. They walked in silence. That spot on his lower back, the wound that had been bandaged, was throbbing again. It was probably infected. He'd have to take care of it when he had a little time.

In about ten minutes they'd reached the great granite-and-glass insurance company skyscraper that had the SportsClub Boston occupying the northwest corner of its street level with its familiar blue-and-red logo. On the way in Tanner glanced over at the fruit stand, saw Ganesh, and exchanged greetings.

He pulled open a glass door for Will Abbott and followed him into the gym. At the front desk, where members had to swipe their bar-coded card or key fob to gain entry, Will said, "I'm going in with you. Swipe me in as your guest."

They passed a row of glass-walled offices, the manager and the membership director and so on, and then a kick-boxing class or maybe it was a Zumba class; Tanner wasn't sure of the difference. Music blasted inside the room, but it was muted by the glass walls. They took the stairs down to the men's locker room.

"*Buenas tardes,* Mr. Tanner," said a short, swarthy man wearing a red SportsClub Boston uniform shirt, pushing a cart full of used towels.

"Hey, Ramon," Tanner said.

In the second bank of lockers he immediately spotted his locker.

"Right here," he told Abbott.

It was smuggling the computer out of his office in the

gym bag that had first given him the idea. They'd already searched his home, and they'd surely search every inch of Tanner Roast's offices for the laptop. Leaving it in the office safe—even hidden as it was—wasn't a good idea.

But the one place where you wouldn't stash anything of value was a gym locker. He'd gone in with the laptop in his duffel bag and came out with a bag that was about three pounds lighter.

Tanner had found his locker, but the brass combination lock was no longer there. He pulled the door open.

The locker was empty.

72

For a moment everything felt unreal. Like the world had abruptly flipped upside down. Tanner felt lightheaded. He just stared into the gaping maw of the locker.

Everything was gone. Not just his ratty old gym clothes and his deodorant. Everything.

This couldn't be happening.

"Is this a joke?" Abbott snapped.

Tanner said nothing. He raced out of the locker room and thundered up the stairs, Abbott following right behind him.

They passed the Zumba-or-kickboxing class, and then Tanner stopped at the manager's office. The manager was a tall, blond young woman with a strong Polish accent named Agnieszka.

"Can I help?"

"My locker—my locker is empty."

"Pardon?"

"There's stuff missing from my locker." Tanner stared.

"You didn't see notice?" the manager replied. "I post

at entrance to men's locker. Everyone must to remove contents of lockers by yesterday twelve noon for clean of locker area. Anyone who did not, we remove for you. We cut locks."

"You removed—where?—where did you put stuff?"

"In lost and found." She pointed out of her office and down the hall.

Lost and found was just an unmarked closet containing steel-wire shelves heaped with items: a shelf of locks that had been left behind, smelly sneakers, gym clothes. One shelf had some mini iPods and several sets of earphones. Tanner found a pile of his gym clothes and pair of running shoes.

No laptop. No computer.

"No?" Agnieszka said.

"It's not here," Tanner said, swallowing hard. "Could someone have put it somewhere else? Like, because it's a computer, it's valuable, all that?"

"Everything here," Agnieszka said. "Valuable, not valuable, all here. No other place."

"But it's gone. It's missing."

"We don't assume the liability for the lost or stolen items. Sign says this."

"Right, I know, but where might someone have put it?"

Agnieszka shrugged. "This is only place. Maybe someone took? I lose two employees last week. I can't keep cleaners, some reason. Always leaving."

Will Abbott whirled around to look at Tanner. "You son of a bitch," he said.

Agnieszka closed the door to the lost and found.

"Sorry," she said. "Maybe someone steal?" She shrugged as if it didn't make much difference to her. Might as well have been some pilfered, dirty gym socks. As she walked away, she muttered, "Is not good."

73

William Abbott, his face gone red, grabbed Tanner's arm, gripping it hard. "You goddamned son of a bitch, do you have any *idea* what you're doing?"

"It was in my locker," Tanner said numbly.

"What the hell kind of long con do you think you're running? Let me tell you, you've just made a very dangerous enemy."

"Get your hands off me," Tanner said. Abbott—though several inches shorter—was trying to hurt him.

"You're a dead man," Abbott said. Veins at his temples were throbbing visibly.

"It was in a gym locker," Tanner said. "I mean, who the hell robs a gym locker?" He glanced out the window onto Tremont Street. He looked over at the Nepalese fruit stand, where he usually bought bottled water, and realized something was off.

He looked for the proprietor, Ganesh. But he wasn't sitting there. Instead, it was a young white guy with a clean, hard look.

Ganesh was gone.

Ganesh never took time off. He sent more than half his earnings to his sister and her kids back in Nepal. Tanner always made a point of greeting him. Ganesh was always there. Something wasn't right.

A guy in a baseball cap was sitting in an idling car, window open. Two guys in their thirties were standing in front of the entrance to the sports club, talking to each other, or at least pretending to; he wasn't sure.

These were Earle's men. They were waiting to grab Will once he exited the sports club with the laptop.

Now that plan had been dashed.

He knew how the conversation with Earle would go. Nobody would believe the laptop was truly lost or stolen. Without the laptop, Earle was not going to be in a forgiving mood. Abbott suspected him of playing a trick, and Earle would think the same way.

Earle's men would grab Abbott, and once they learned he didn't have the damned laptop, they'd come for Tanner. They'd detain him in the white facility, for who knew how long, and Tanner would be powerless to do anything about it.

No. He had to find a way out of the situation.

"You need to take your hands off of me," Tanner said.

"You bastard, where the hell did you put it?" Abbott swung a fist at Tanner, who dodged, but the fist connected, cracking into Tanner's upper chest around the breastbone. It was painful, and it pissed Tanner off. He let loose, shot a fist into Abbott's solar plexus.

Abbott instantly doubled over and collapsed onto the floor.

Tanner raced down the hall.

He descended two floors to the custodial area, where he saw Ramon, the Guatemalan attendant, folding and stacking gym towels.

"Hi, Mr. Tanner," Ramon said, surprised to see him there.

"Ramon, I need to ask you a favor. A big one."

Will gasped. He couldn't breathe. The wind had been knocked out of him. He was on his hands and knees and he felt like he was dying.

Some big muscled black guy in a blue polo shirt that said "SportsClub Boston" and "Trainer" loomed over him. "You okay, dude?"

"Yeah, I'm fine," he mumbled.

"Gotta pace yourself, man." The trainer put out a hand and helped Abbott up. "Have some water."

Michael Tanner had slugged him just below the chest, right in the solar plexus, and it was breathtakingly painful. He didn't know anything could hurt this much. He wondered if there was internal damage to organs and blood vessels. How was he going to explain this to Jen? He teetered, and the trainer steadied him by grasping his shoulder.

"Whoa, there, big guy, you need to sit down."

Abbott leaned over, head down. His stomach was

spasming. "I'm okay, thanks," he gasped, waving the trainer away.

He didn't know which way Tanner had run—he'd been too busy gasping for air—but he knew that, whichever way he went, Tanner was heading for the exit. Was there more than one? He walked, stumblingly, in the direction he'd come in from.

"Excuse me, sir?" said a small young woman with a pixie haircut and a gymnast's build, a low center of gravity. "Weren't you just swiped in?" She was wearing a blue polo shirt that said "Membership Director."

Will turned. "Yes." A red-shirted custodian passed by, pushing a laundry basket full of wet, dirty towels.

"I'm sorry, sir. Guests are required to be accompanied by their hosts at all times. Is your host nearby?"

"I'm looking for him, actually."

"I'm sorry, sir. I'm afraid you can't be here."

But Will kept walking.

74

It was five thirty, and Tremont Street swarmed with people leaving work. Tanner had caught a break. Lots of people around meant plenty of distraction for the watchers. Also, they wouldn't be looking for someone wearing a red SportsClub Boston polo shirt pushing a heaping laundry cart.

Pedestrians bustled past. He abandoned the laundry cart where he'd told Ramon he would and continued down the street, like an employee let out for the day. He walked toward Clarendon Street and turned right toward Back Bay station, where he could get on the subway on the orange line.

Somewhere.

He didn't know where. He just knew he needed to be someplace underground. He was testing out a theory about why the NSA's team—Theta, Earle had called them—always seemed to know where he was at any moment.

Tanner paid two dollars and twenty-five cents for a

ticket, passed through the gate, and descended the steps. Arbitrarily he decided to take the train in the direction of Forest Hills, a place he'd never been and didn't know where it was, and he took some more steps down to the platform.

He was sure he hadn't been followed.

Tanner needed to think. The goddamned laptop was gone and had probably been stolen. And that laptop was his salvation. It bought off both the NSA and Will Abbott. The deal he'd made with Earle had seemed solid and logical: he'd give the laptop to Abbott, and the NSA would immediately apprehend him. They'd have the proof they needed that Abbott was the source of the leak. And Tanner would be left alone.

But now, without the damned thing, he was sunk. The deal fell apart.

His lower back throbbed.

A couple of guys who could have been lawyers or bankers were talking. They each had a local accent. Tanner couldn't help but listen.

"I said no way in hell are you getting a tramp stamp," one of the guys said. "She's like, no, I'm talking about piercing. Gauging, she says. I'm like, what the hell's gauging? You ever see how people have these big-ass holes in their earlobes?"

"Oh Jesus," the other guy said. "No one's sticking a razor blade in my earlobes, no thanks. Or a scalpel."

"It's crazy, man, the shit people do to their bodies. They call it body modification. It's, like, disgusting. So she comes back with a tattoo of a *turtle* on her arm and I'm friggin' *grateful.* She played me, man."

The two men laughed gustily as a train came into the station and you couldn't hear anything else.

And Tanner found himself thinking about razor blades and scalpels and body modification, and he had an idea. He realized suddenly what he had to do.

He turned around and left the platform and ran up the nearest exit steps. He had to catch the green line.

As far as he could tell, no one followed him.

Half an hour later he exited the subway aboveground in Allston.

The tattoo parlor was where he remembered it being, on the second floor of a prominent rounded-front building at the busy, windswept intersection of Harvard Avenue and Cambridge Street. The name, Mustang Creations Body Art, was painted in circus-style lettering.

Inside it was surprisingly big and well lit. The walls were lined with framed designs for what Tanner assumed were tattoos. There were wooden cases of body jewelry. In one corner was an ATM. Seated at the counter was an attractive woman of around forty with a head of blond curls.

She was talking to a young black woman who said, "I'm here to get a new nose ring put in."

"You want an actual hoop? Or just a stud?"

"A stud."

"A little gem or something?"

When it was his turn, Tanner said, "Is your piercing guy here?"

"Stefan is in and he should be available in about . . . five minutes. Have you decided on what kind of piercing you're interested in?"

"I want to discuss it with Stefan."

He sat on a small couch and looked mindlessly through a loose-leaf binder of tattoo photos. He wondered whether the NSA had already grabbed Will Abbott, whether they'd found out by now that he didn't have the laptop with him. And how soon it would be before they came for Tanner.

The door to a small office came open and a small man, a young guy with a spiky punk haircut and a ring in his nose, emerged. "Michael?"

The piercing room was immaculate and surgical-looking: a hospital bed covered with white paper, a rolling metal table with packaged needles on top, a metal sink.

He introduced himself as Stefan and said, "So what holes of happiness are we putting in you?" He smiled, showing a large gap between his front teeth.

Tanner explained what he wanted.

"I'm not allowed to use a scalpel."

"But do you have one?"

Stefan said nothing.

Tanner took out a fifty-dollar bill from his wallet. "Can we make this a cash transaction?"

Stefan closed the door and then removed a sterile packaged scalpel from a desk drawer.

Tanner, sitting on the hospital bed, took off his jacket and then his shirt and turned around.

"Pretty bad infection," Stefan said.

"That's the spot," Tanner said.

"This is going to hurt a little. Are you okay with pain?"

"I'll be okay."

Stefan deftly sliced a small cut in the infected area on his lower back. Tanner winced. The pain, white-hot, surprised him.

"There *is* something back here," Stefan said.

Tanner felt Stefan dig something out of the throbbing wound. Quickly, Stefan placed a small, bloody object on the metal table. "This must be what caused the infection. What do you think it is?"

A GPS tracker. A micro-transponder. "Who knows."

Stefan's eyes widened. "Whoa. How'd it get there, man?"

"I don't know," Tanner said. But he had an idea. He remembered when Earle's men grabbed him and he fought back and broke one of the guy's noses. They'd jabbed him with something, some kind of tranquilizer that had knocked him right out. That was when they'd done it, inserted the GPS chip or whatever it was.

Tanner picked it up. It was a cylinder, not much longer than an inch, made of some kind of light-colored metal. This explained how the Theta team always seemed to know where he was, even though they weren't nearby. He didn't know how it worked, but it must have sent out a signal they were able to track.

"What do you want me to do with it?" asked Stefan.

75

The house had been on the market for almost a year. According to Sarah, no one bothered to show it anymore. It was an ugly little wood-frame hovel on a spectacular piece of land, right on the ocean, northeast of Boston. It was vastly overpriced, something to do with a brother and sister who had jointly inherited it and were at a standoff about whether to sell it or not. No one had lived in it since the original owner, the mother, had died, two years ago.

It also smelled bad, like a dead animal. Maybe a mouse had died somewhere inside the walls. He opened all the windows to let it air out, to let the bracing sea air in.

He had several hours to kill, and he knew he should grab sleep when he could. But for a long while he was too revved up. He needed to distract himself from what was about to happen: there was simply nothing more he could do about it. So he thought about Blake Gifford and City Roast, and he decided to make a call to his sales director.

"Karen," he said, "I need you to listen really carefully

to what I'm about to tell you. I want you to call the Lockwood Hotels Group in California and offer them the following deal."

"But Lockwood isn't bidding their coffee out. City Roast has it—"

"Just listen," he said.

She did. When Tanner was finished, Karen said, "But . . . we'd lose money on that!"

"I don't care. Do it."

"Michael, that's crazy. In six months we'd go bankrupt."

"Just do it," Tanner said, "and text me when it's done."

He ended the call. Then he called Sal Persico, his roaster, to see whether he'd done the errand.

Sal had met Tanner at the tattoo place in Allston and had taken the tracker to the last house for sale Tanner had stayed in, the mansion in Chestnut Hill.

The NSA would probably figure Tanner was staying at a friend's house. If Tanner was right, anyway, that he'd found a tracker and removed it. Because if he was right, and he'd temporarily disappeared from the NSA's radar screen, that would explain why they hadn't yet grabbed him. He needed more time to get them what they wanted. It was a low-trust situation. He'd have to have something solid to hand Earle or they'd just lock him up. Or worse.

It wouldn't be much longer.

He was about to call Sal when his burner phone emitted a musical sound. He'd received a text message.

It was from his sales director. It said only, Done.

He called Sal and asked him how it was going. "You're all set," Sal said.

"Thanks. And I'm sorry to bother you with this at night."

"Not a bother at all," Sal said.

He finished making calls about an hour later. Then the burner rang: it was Lucy Turton. "There's a guy who's, like, *desperate* to reach you."

"It's after business hours."

"Not in California."

"Who is it?"

"Blake Gifford with City Roast."

"Ah."

"Is it something I can handle, or . . . ?

"Did he leave a number?"

Tanner had disappeared, but Will had an idea about how to find him.

He'd been thinking about when he first made contact with the NSA, a couple of days ago. The NSA had been keeping close tabs on Michael Tanner's whereabouts when he was on the run, but they were puzzled. They couldn't see a pattern in where he was staying. He didn't stay at his home or office, of course, or with his wife—they were separated—or even with any known friends, relatives, or associates. Basically, he was staying at a succession of unoccupied houses in the Boston area.

When Will heard that, he had smiled to himself and said nothing. He guessed immediately what it meant. Tanner's wife, like Will's mother, was a real estate agent. She sold houses. Tanner, with the help of his wife, was being clever.

He was staying in *unoccupied* houses for sale. Where else could he spend the night without using his credit card?

Twenty minutes later, Will was sitting at his laptop in a Starbucks, browsing through house listings. He'd called his mother at the dentist's office and asked for her ID number to use MLS, the database of houses for sale. She still sold houses and was delighted to help. She'd been campaigning for Will to move his new family out of a condo and into a real house anyway.

He scanned the list of unoccupied houses for sale in the Boston area. But there were too many; he needed to narrow down the search.

Michael Tanner was probably going to do what frightened mammals do: seek solitude. Seek safety through isolation. He wouldn't want to stay in an apartment in the city, nor a house that had neighbors nearby. Instead, he would want . . . Yes, here we were.

A house for sale on a secluded bluff in Nahant. In the photo the house looked lonely, all by itself on the edge of a cliff overlooking the ocean.

Nahant was a small resort town north and east of Boston, located on an island on a spit of land that jutted into the Atlantic. About a half an hour drive away.

It was perfect.

* * *

Tanner called Blake Gifford in Santa Barbara, California.

Gifford answered the phone after the first ring, and he did not sound friendly, barking: "Dude!"

"I got a message you called."

"Hey, ol' buddy, ol' pal, I don't think you quite know what you're doing. That's some crazy-ass deal you made."

"Which deal is that?"

"You know damn well what I'm talking about. Lockwood, dude. I'm saying this as a friend: you're gonna screw your company six ways to Sunday if you take on an obligation like that. No way can you sell him beans at that price and stay in business. I mean, it's totally—"

"It's totally kamikaze," Tanner said. He'd offered Lockwood Hotels a price so low they couldn't resist switching coffee providers. They'd dumped City Roast and signed with Tanner Roast. Gifford had just lost his biggest customer.

"Exactly!"

"And I'm flying my little plane right into your ship, so I hope you're a real good swimmer, Blake."

"Just to sabotage my IPO?"

"Yeah, it's a shame about that, isn't it?" Tanner knew that the Lockwood Hotels Group represented fifteen percent of City Roast's revenue. He knew this from the form S-1 he'd asked Karen to get. He also knew that, until that moment, City Roast was growing thirty percent a year. Which made the initial public offering worth 550 million dollars. Trend lines were everything for stock analysts, and the trend was now bad.

Very bad.

Now, without Lockwood Hotels' business, the IPO would fall apart for sure. Their year-to-date business would plummet. Whatever they'd priced their stock at would suddenly be way too high. It would be a disaster.

Gifford used a colorful expletive. Then he added, "You'll go bankrupt."

"I may, but I don't care if it means screwing you, you son of a bitch."

Gifford used another expletive.

"Also," Tanner said, "you're not going to have much time to tape your TV show. You'll be spending all of the next two or three years fighting off lawsuits from your investors." Lots of people who might lose money in the IPO would go after Gifford, sue him for millions. All these big, scary investment banks like Goldman Sachs and JPMorgan Chase. He smiled. "Enjoy explaining your new trend line to the boys at Goldman Sachs. But, hey—it's just business. Nothing personal."

"All right!" Gifford roared. "You can have your damned Four Seasons back."

"I'll await a call from Liam."

"What the hell's gotten into you?"

"You kill my dog, I kill your cat," Tanner said, smiling. A weird expression that one was: he wondered if people actually did that sort of thing.

"This isn't like you, Michael!"

"It is now," Tanner said. He hung up. He grinned. Then he called his office manager.

"Lucy," he said. "Tell Connie Hunt to pack up her cubicle."

He was pretty sure he'd just saved his company.

He wanted to call Sarah and tell her, but he couldn't risk it. Someone might be listening.

For a long while, he sat outside in a rusty lawn chair, staring at the sea, listening to the crash of the surf. It was lulling. He was exhausted.

He went inside, stretched out on the sofa in the front sitting room, and quickly fell asleep. He had vivid dreams about being chased on foot by someone driving a car.

He heard a man's voice. In his dream someone was yelling at him, and he didn't understand what the man was saying.

Then he realized that the man's voice was in the room where he'd been sleeping. He jolted awake.

"Get up."

A man was standing in the middle of the room, in shadows, illuminated faintly from behind by moonlight.

Will Abbott had found him.

He was pointing a gun at Tanner.

76

"Move it," Will said, a little louder.

Tanner sat up abruptly and stood up. Was he about to jump at him? No. Will kept the gun leveled to make sure he didn't do anything.

"How the hell did you find me?" Tanner said.

"Hands in the air."

Tanner obediently put them up. "Look," he said, "I already told you, I don't know where the hell that laptop is. It's gone!"

"No," said Will. "It's not lost or stolen. Don't bullshit me. Where'd you hide it?"

"Put the damned gun down."

"Where is it?"

Tanner inhaled and exhaled noisily. He looked tired, defeated. "Okay," he said quietly. "This is not worth my life. I just need a guarantee that my wife and I are protected."

Finally. Will almost smiled. "Excuse me," he said. "Who's got the gun?"

Tanner shook his head. "I need a guarantee."

"If it's the senator's laptop and you maintain absolute silence on what you saw, we're good. Where is it?"

"It's in my office."

"Wrong. The NSA already broke into your safe."

"I didn't put it there. That would have been too obvious. It's hiding in plain sight."

"Where?"

"On the desk of one of my employees."

"Which one?"

"Sal Persico, the name is."

"All right," said Will, "you're taking me to your office. Move it."

"Why do you need me there?" Tanner said. "Here's the keys."

Will shook his head, kept the gun leveled at Tanner, and made sure he stayed a comfortable distance away. "Let's go."

Tanner looked athletic. He looked like someone who would do something crazy, like try to grab the gun off him.

When Arthur Collins had loaned him the gun, he'd told Will it was a Philippine knockoff of a 1911. It didn't have any serial numbers cast into it. Therefore untraceable. Will had bought some ammunition off of Arthur, a handful of .45 cartridges, as big as thumbs. If he needed more, he knew he could buy ammo without a license anywhere in Virginia. But he had a feeling he wouldn't need any more after tonight.

He thought about the .45 cartridges loaded in the pistol.

A bullet that big and powerful would tear an immense hole in a person.

77

Will's rented Toyota was parked right in front of the house. Once Tanner had gotten in behind the steering wheel, Will came around and got into the front seat. "I've got the fob," Will said. "This car is push to start."

Tanner pushed the starter and the car came quietly to life. He drove in silence. After a few minutes, he said, "So how *did* you find me?"

"You're not the only one who knows the tricks. Like I said, my mother sold houses."

Tanner remembered Will mentioning that on the train ride to Boston. His mother sold houses on the side. To keep them afloat.

"Is that right?"

"This is going to be very simple. You'll hand me the laptop, I verify it's the senator's, I take it, and I'm gone. It's over."

"Am I supposed to believe you'd fire that gun at me?"

"Try me and find out."

Tanner half smiled. After a minute or so, he said, looking straight ahead, "You'd kill for a laptop? Really? For a *laptop*?"

"'Kill for a laptop'?" Will said. "That's not the way to think about it. "Would I kill to protect the country? Would I kill to protect a future where a truly remarkable woman has a decent shot at the Oval Office? Kill to protect a transformative political career that could mean so much more than either of our lives? Are you telling me there's nothing you'd kill for?"

Tanner said nothing.

"If you don't have that, that one thing you'd kill for, or die for—your life is meaningless," Will said.

But Tanner kept staring at the road and said nothing.

This was not a game, Will thought. Not a sport. This was serious business.

Will found himself thinking about Peter Green, the student president at Miami of Ohio he'd gotten elected. He'd had to resort to *certain measures* back then too. Otherwise it would have been a squeaker—no, actually Peter would have probably lost, based on his own informal polling—had it not been for those certain measures.

Thanks to his clerical job at the admissions department, he had access to his classmates' folders. One day, during the election campaign, he pulled the admissions folder of Jake Califano, Peter Green's opponent, where he learned that Jake had been suspended for a semester at Groton because of a disputed, hushed-up rape accusation. He made a furtive copy and offered it as a leak to *The Miami Student.* But they wouldn't run it, so he told a few people, and of course the rumor spread. In a matter of days, everyone knew about it. He didn't ask Peter's permission to do this, because frankly, Peter didn't take the campaign as seriously as Will did. But somehow the word got around to Peter, about how Will had tried to slip the damaging information to the student newspaper. And Peter tracked him down at the dining hall, clapped a hand on his shoulder, and said, "We've gotta talk."

Peter asked if it was true what Will had done, and Will, anticipating Peter's gratitude for winning the election for him, happily fessed up.

Peter replied, "Kind of a douche move, Penguin."

The memory pained him. But it was also an important reminder that you didn't get into politics to be appreciated. It was a dirty game. The ones who operated at any serious level did whatever it took.

For Susan, he would do whatever it took.

78

Two thirty in the morning and Tanner Roast was dark, the alarm on. Tanner punched in the code. Will stood a few safe feet behind him. Tanner opened the heavy steel interior door and then clicked on some lights. Will saw a large warehouse with high ceilings and a couple of large machines in the front area that had to be coffee roasters. To his surprise, the place didn't smell of coffee.

He followed Tanner across the floor of the warehouse and into the smaller office area. Tanner stopped in the middle of an aisle of cubicles and turned around. Will raised the gun. "Don't even think about it," he said.

"It's in the cubicle behind you."

Warily, and slowly, Will half turned. "Hand it to me. Please don't give me an excuse to fire this."

He backed up to give Tanner room to move. Tanner reached over to Sal's cubicle. A MacBook Air sat in the middle of an otherwise empty desk. He handed it slowly to Will.

Will took it with his left hand. The first thing he did was turn it over and look for the long scratch.

It was there.

This, finally, was the boss's computer.

Still, he had to be certain. But he couldn't put down the gun, so he handed the laptop back to Tanner. "Open it up and turn it on," he said.

Tanner did so. It took a long time, more than a minute to boot up.

It was jarring. Will didn't recognize the image on the screen. It was a full-screen photograph of what was probably a coffee bush, with red berries. On the top right of the screen, in that little white band up top, it said SALVATORE PERSICO LAPTOP.

This wasn't Susan Robbins's laptop. Yes, it had a scratch in the right place, but—

"You goddamned—"

But then something scuffled, something behind him, and, scared, he whirled around and squeezed the trigger and fired into the darkness.

79

A man screamed.

The gun bucked and danced in Will's hand. The explosion was so loud it momentarily deafened him. A high-pitched note rang in both his ears.

A man screamed, "Augh!" and then the shape tumbled to the floor, and Will saw that he had shot a man, a large man, who now lay sprawled on the floor in the shadows. He had shot a human being for the first time in his life, and what he felt most of all was fear. He was terrified that the man he'd just shot would die. A few seconds ago he'd fired at a motion, a potential threat, a disturbance in the field, nothing. Now he knew he'd wounded someone, probably killed him. He didn't know if the man was dead or not, but he was sprawled on the concrete floor, not moving.

Then Tanner lunged at him.

The plan had worked perfectly until it hadn't.

Tanner had expected William Abbott to come after

him. It was a certainty. He just had to make it plausibly difficult. Too easy to track him down, Abbott would be suspicious. On guard.

When he heard that Abbott's mother sold houses, Tanner thought it—well, not likely, but *possible*—that Abbott would figure out where he was hiding. Because Abbott seemed smart and strategic.

Abbott had impressed him. He'd found him after all. The NSA couldn't find him, but William Abbott had.

But if he hadn't, Tanner would have simply called him and told him they had to meet, they had to come up with an arrangement, a truce. And Abbott would have met him, though much more warily.

And now Sal Persico—who'd instantly agreed to bring his own MacBook Air, just like Tanner's, to the office, even agreed to put a long scratch in its case—was probably dead.

Rather than dropping the laptop and immediately leaving, as Tanner had asked him to do, Sal Persico had decided, on his own, to lie in wait for Abbott in the dark office.

And Abbott had probably just killed him.

Sal, who'd done a kindness for Tanner. Who'd overcome so much and had such a gift. If he wasn't dead, he was gravely injured.

It was as if someone had pulled a switch inside Tanner and he was suddenly flooded with white-hot anger, a fury he'd only guessed was there, beneath the surface of things, something he'd fought against all his life. With a guttural snarl he launched himself at Abbott, body-slammed him against the concrete wall. Something clattered on the floor: the gun, skittering a couple of feet away. Abbott's face came away from the concrete and Tanner could see blood sluicing from the man's split lip. Tanner body-slammed him again, and Abbott sank to the floor, his right hand extended, grappling for the pistol. Tanner saw this a moment too late. Abbott sprang to his feet, the gun gripped in his hands. Tanner was about to try to grab the gun when it suddenly went off, incredibly loud. His ears rang.

Abbott must have accidentally pulled the trigger, fired into the air. The bullet pinged against something hard and metallic.

Tanner flinched, but at that moment, Abbott jammed the gun against the side of Tanner's head, right against his temple.

"No!" Tanner said, and he froze.

He could smell that acrid gunpowder smell. He could smell Abbott's perspiration too. He felt the hard metal muzzle grinding painfully into the skin of his temple.

A trigger-happy man who'd just fired twice, once by accident, now held a gun a quarter inch from Tanner's brain. He might pull the trigger even if he didn't mean to. He'd just done it. He could do it again.

Tanner's mind went blank for an instant.

He was about to die.

80

Everything fell away from Tanner's world. There was just the grinding pressure of the gun against his temple and the gleaming, wild eyes of the man holding that gun.

Tanner could feel an odd vibration and realized that the gun was shaking in Abbott's hand. Abbott was probably jacked on adrenaline. That was dangerous.

"Are you sure you want to kill me?" Tanner said.

"Where's the goddamned laptop?" Abbott ground the muzzle into his temple. It felt like he'd broken through the skin.

"I know you don't believe someone stole it from my gym locker, but that's the sorry truth."

"Then what was this whole damned charade about?"

"I'm sorry," Tanner said. "I thought you'd take it and go away."

"Bullshit."

"Why the hell would I want to keep it?"

"Why? You know damned well why. You're keeping it

for leverage, or maybe you plan on selling it. Your business is tanking, and you need the money."

Tanner heard Sal groan and shift on the floor.

"Put the gun down," Tanner said.

He felt the pressure of the muzzle against his head and he thought about whether this would be the last night of his life. "If you put down that gun, everything can go back to the way it was."

"Everything changed when your friend came at me like a goddamned idiot," Abbott said.

"You've got a life out there," Tanner said, "and it's yours if you want it. You know that?" He wondered whether he could snatch the gun away from Abbott without causing him to fire. He didn't think so.

"Shut the hell up," Abbott said, and the pressure of the steel on Tanner's temple increased.

Will's heart was jackhammering. He found himself staring at that one spot on Michael Tanner's temple, the indented skin where it met the black steel muzzle. He couldn't look at the face of the man he was about to kill. Maybe he'd killed someone already, maybe the guy on the floor, the guy who'd tried to take him down; maybe that was number one. Maybe Tanner would be number two.

He was in a long tunnel, and ahead of him was just that patch of skin and the muzzle of the pistol.

His index finger touched the cold steel of the trigger. Just touched it, tickled it. It didn't take a lot of pressure to fire this gun. Artie Collins had told him he'd done a trigger job, modified the sear, reduced the trigger pull to near zero. You just had to give it the slightest pull.

"No more games," he said. "Where the hell is it?"

This man, Tanner, was for some reason hell-bent on destroying him. And more important, on destroying the boss.

And ultimately it was Will's fault. For agreeing when Susan Robbins told him she wasn't going to sit in that SCIF all day, *Could you please make me a copy?* For giving in to pressure. He should have refused, for her sake.

But he hadn't. He'd made a mistake. This all wouldn't be happening if he hadn't done it. It was his responsibility to fix things.

He couldn't let Tanner torpedo Susan's career, her future presidency. Or his own future as chief of staff to the president.

The intelligence bureaucracy would not want any of this made public. Tanner's death would be swept aside, along with any public mention of CHRYSALIS, into the black memory hole. Theta, the NSA's action component, would make sure of it. Make sure it looked like a suicide, or a struggle between Tanner and the guy on the floor beside him. They'd fix it up. The gun was untraceable. This could all be made to go away.

"Did you ever seriously think you were going to survive this?" asked Will. "You think they were going to let you walk this earth knowing what you know? I hate like hell that this is where it's going, but this is where it's going."

He thought of the maddened raccoon in the garage that day long ago, and he knew how to switch to that place deep inside, and he knew he had it in him to finally pull the trigger.

Tanner forced himself to take a breath.

He said, "You're the chief of staff to a major politician; that makes you a Washington power broker, okay? And the father of a beautiful little kid. Don't you want to keep that life? You need to ask yourself that. Because if you squeeze the trigger, it all goes away. This *will* get traced back to you. Our friends at the NSA will know what happened. It will hang on you like a big black lizard perched on your shoulders. And you'll never be safe. Your life as you know it will be over. Your worst enemy, Will—"

"Shut the hell up."

"Your worst enemy isn't me, Will. It's you. Right now you're your own worst enemy. But you can make the right decision. You can decide to put that gun down and save the life you have."

Abbott said nothing.

"Listen to me when I tell you—it isn't too late for you," Tanner said. "And here's what you need to know, Will. You're being recorded right now. You're on video."

Abbott said nothing.

"That's why Sal was here. He brought in this home security device he has. It's on his desk—that black thing. It records audio and video, it's got an HD camera, and it's got a motion-sensor in it, and it's been recording everything you've been saying. You're on *Candid Camera*, Will. You kill me and the evidence is recorded and your life is over."

A few seconds later he felt the pressure against his temple ease up. Abbott had pulled the gun away from his head. Tanner turned slightly toward Abbott and could see him lowering the gun. Abbott's eyes shone with tears.

"You made the right—" Tanner began, but then something warm misted his face, and he heard Abbott say, "Uh." Tanner blinked and turned and saw a small red oval on Abbott's throat explode, an instant later, into a jagged gash that gouted crimson. Abbott's face looked stunned and then slack, the head lolling ridiculously, the eyes staring, unseeing.

81

Tanner stared in shock. Men in black tactical gear were swarming the warehouse floor, in helmets and bulletproof vests and shin guards. Two of them were rolling a gurney carrying Will Abbott's body. Another couple of guys were strapping Sal Persico onto a stretcher. He was struggling, but at least he was alive. He appeared to have been shot in the shoulder or chest and to be in a great deal of pain.

Will Abbott, he realized, was dead.

A man approached, and Tanner recognized Earle Laffoon, also in SWAT attire.

"He lowered his gun," Tanner said.

Earle's reply came slowly, softly. "You were in danger; that's what I saw."

"You guys—you killed him." Tanner panted, crackling with adrenaline.

"It was a judgment call," Earle said crisply, "and I'd do it again in a heartbeat."

"Jesus," Tanner said. He caught his breath and

thought for a moment. "And what's the world going to know about why Abbott died? Doesn't he have a wife and a newborn?"

"There's any number of ways we can go. I like keeping it simple. A congressional staffer is killed in a plain-vanilla mugging in Boston."

"That way you own the senator, don't you?" The real story of what William Abbott had done, copying classified information onto his boss's laptop, would never come out. But for years the NSA would have their hooks in a powerful US senator.

"Let's just say, how I report this is going to be a matter of some discussion among the interested parties." His eyes drifted toward Sal's cubicle; then he took a few steps in that direction. He picked up the squat black cylinder. "It's all here? Audio and video both?"

"It's a whole new world, Earle."

"More than you know."

"My only worry is whether, with all that gunfire, the recording devices got hit."

Earle grinned, creasing his face. "Oh, I wouldn't worry about that, Michael. I'm sure I can turn up a recording somewhere. We're the NSA, after all."

For a long while, Tanner was silent. His mind raced. He was flooded with relief, a sudden sense of calm. "So we have a deal?"

"Works for me. An understanding. We go our separate ways. End of the story. We're good, you and me. You know, in another world, we could have been friends, Michael. Texas Hold'em and some Pappy Van Winkle, or a good IPA. But it wasn't to be. These are the hands we've been dealt."

Tanner nodded. He didn't want to say it, but he'd actually come to like Earle. *The guy kidnapped me off a Boston street and stuck a tracker in my lower back, and yet somehow it feels like I owe him something.*

"I will say, I've tracked quite a number of people in my day, but you're better than most of 'em."

"How so?"

"You're not a true believer. You're not a fanatic, not a nut job."

Tanner shrugged.

"You got yourself off the radar screen. You went low-tech on us. Then you found the implant. Well done. And you fooled us with that little game you played with it. You lost us for a while. And then you go and get Mr. Abbott on tape, admitting to everything."

"Huh."

"You're just a smart guy who made a couple of bad decisions."

"Maybe. So tell me something—tell me if I'm wrong. If I'd given you that laptop when you first asked for it, would you have . . . disappeared me?"

Earle gave him a long look. "My colleagues misunderstood you."

"Is that what would have happened to me?"

Earle shrugged. "No comment. You get your whole goddamned life back. Isn't that enough?"

Tanner just smiled.

"So tell me. What'd you really do with it?"

"With what, the laptop?"

Earle nodded.

"It got stolen. Like I said."

"That defies belief. Yet I'm inclined to believe you."

"Do you? And how do you know I don't have a copy of the documents, somewhere in the cloud, that I'm planning to send on to *The Washington Post*?"

Earle smiled, his face creasing. "Two reasons."

"Yeah?"

"One, I know you're a smart guy, and you've got this all figured out. You have a good life and you want to go back to it. We patrol the cloud pretty thoroughly. We see a leak, we'll immediately know it's you, and your life is over."

"And what's the second reason?"

"In this era of fake news, you don't have that laptop, no one's gonna believe you. You say you have classified documents, huh? Well, I have photos showing the moon landing was faked. I have Obama's Kenyan birth certificate. You'd just be laughed out of town. You don't have that laptop, you don't have shit."

"Maybe."

"Sure, there's always going to be some people who believe you. Maybe there'll be some conspiracy theories. A whole website about it. But we live in a post-truth era. The only thing people believe is "you can't believe what you hear." We've all gotten jaundiced and cynical. The truth these days has been devalued like Weimar currency."

"Huh."

"No, I don't think you'll say anything. Anyway, CHRYSALIS looks like it's getting shelved."

"Shelved?"

"Canceled. The Senate intel committee was on the verge of signing off on it before all this happened. Now, cooler heads have prevailed. Into the deep freeze it goes. Lot of midnight of the soul. My higher-ups realized how hard it would have been to defend to the public. It couldn't stand the scrutiny. You helped us see that."

"Uh-huh."

"I think we owe you something for that."

"Just leave me alone," Tanner said. "That's all I want."

Earle stuck out his hand. After a few seconds, Tanner took his hand and shook. "Hope we never see each other again."

"I think we're done here," Earle said.

"Okay, good," said Tanner. "Because I've got a business to save."

82

Six months later

The guy on the speakerphone was the head of a company that supplied glass bottles for Tanner Cold Brew, which had really taken off and was now distributed throughout the Northeast. Orders had been insane. A national distribution deal was in the works. They needed a lot more amber Boston round glass bottles all of a sudden.

The guy on the phone knew that Tanner Roast had an urgent need for bottles. That was probably why he was being so intransigent on the price. Normally, Tanner wouldn't get involved in negotiations on supplies, but Ken Jones refused to budge. So his new production manager had called in Tanner, who called Ken Jones directly.

"I gotta ask myself," Jones was saying on speaker, "can I cover my expenses at that price point?"

Tanner picked the phone up. "You're asking the wrong question, Jonesie. Question you should be asking is, do you ever want to do business with us in the future?"

The guy sighed loudly. "We'll make it work."

"Good," said Tanner. "We're back in business."

Then Sal Persico knocked on the doorjamb to Tanner's office with his left hand. His right arm and shoulder were still stiff. His right hand was especially stiff in the morning. The bullet had gone through the clavicle, the top of the shoulder, just missing the dome of the lung and the subclavian artery. It had left a large divot in the trapezius muscle, the exit wound. Only recently had he stopped wearing the sling. The doctors told him it might take a year before he regained full use of his arm.

"We're ready," he said.

The morning cupping was on. It was Costa Rican day.

"Be right there," said Tanner.

He'd been reading résumés. Actually, he was *supposed* to be reading résumés. There were a lot to read, and six new employees to hire, including another roaster and an assistant sales manager. Plus he was looking at larger office/warehouse spaces. They'd already outgrown the old space. They were moving a lot of coffee, and the one that seemed to be the biggest seller was their new, light roast, the Lanny Roast.

Business had taken off after the Four Seasons deal went public. That had generated a number of major copycat hospitality accounts that wanted the same coffee as you found at Four Seasons hotels.

Instead of reading résumés, though, Tanner found himself distracted by a news article about how the National Security Agency's budget was about to double, to twenty billion dollars. The biggest proponent for that increase, according to the reporter, was Senator Susan Robbins, chairman of the US Senate Select Committee on Intelligence.

He wondered for a second about whatever had happened to her laptop. Maybe it was reformatted and being used by some drug dealer, someone sketchy. Or maybe it was at the bottom of a pile of scrap metal at a dump somewhere.

Another knock at his doorjamb. "I'm coming," he said, but then he saw that it was Sarah. He beckoned her in and got up.

His phone buzzed, and he heard Lucy's voice. "It's that biz-dev guy from Starbucks again."

"Tell him I'm in a meeting."

"Again?"

"Isn't he bound to get the point? I mean, I've already told his boss I don't want to sell. I gotta go." He came around and gave Sarah a kiss.

"There's a bid on Brattle Street," she said. "I think we should counter with the asking."

She was talking about the big clapboard house on Brattle Street in Cambridge they'd made an offer on. It had just gone on the market. She'd been on a hot streak for three months, since selling that mansion in Chestnut Hill he'd stayed in to a Russian oligarch. Sarah had always considered their South End house too damned vertical, too many stairs to climb.

"It's a lot of house," Tanner said. "Six bedrooms."

"We each get a study, and there's a guest room, and . . . room for expansion."

Tanner smiled. They'd talked. "I'm liking the idea of expansion."

Sarah's face lit up, and she threw her arms around him. She came in for a kiss. Tanner glanced at the laptop on his desk, then reached one hand over and pulled it shut.

Epilogue

It's gotta be the laptop," said John Thomsen as he held aloft the heavy oblong cardboard box. He was a second-year graduate student in classics at Princeton. He and his roommate and fellow grad student, Matt, were standing at the counter of the Frist Campus Center Package Room, where you picked up parcels.

"That piece of crap you bought on eBay for a hundred bucks?"

"Hundred twenty-five. Plus shipping."

"For a MacBook Air? Dude, it's gonna be a brick."

"No way." Matt was obviously jealous. He was complaining last week about how much he'd had to spend on a new Acer laptop—almost six hundred bucks!

By the time they returned to their town house on Prospect Avenue, John was beginning to wonder himself whether he'd just bought a dud.

"Hey, it works," he said to Matt, who was sitting on the couch with his laptop on his lap, but really concentrating on the football game. "Booted right up."

"Huh," said Matt, uninterested.

"Oh my God, it's got the last owner's sign-on screen. They didn't even reformat it!"

Matt laughed. "Without the password, you're totally screwed."

"It's right here. On a sticky note."

"Jeez. No wonder it was so cheap. They didn't do shit to it. How many owners did it have?"

"I don't know," John said distractedly as he entered the numbers and letters into the passcode blank. "The thing's only like a year old. Can't be more than one owner."

A commercial came on, and Matt muted the volume. "Where do you think this seller gets his laptops? You think they're hot? Wouldn't that be funny? You get in trouble 'cause you have someone else's stolen laptop?"

John looked up from his computer. "It might *be* hot," he said.

"Who's the owner?"

"S. Robbins. That's all it says. And most of the documents—wait . . . Huh, now, *this* is interesting."

"What?"

"Check this out. 'Top secret' and 'classified,' it says. Check it out." He handed the computer over to Matt.

"Dude, are you sure you should be looking at that?"

"Seriously?" said John. "What's the harm?"

Acknowledgments

I'm grateful to a number of people who so generously helped me in the preparation of this book, including a number of current and former chiefs of staff and aides to US senators, all of whom exhibited more spine and heroism than Will Abbott: Clarine Nardi Riddle (Joe Lieberman), Dan Geldon (Elizabeth Warren), Jeff Duncan (Ed Markey), Travis Johnson (David Vitter), Mark Kadesh (Dianne Feinstein), Allison Herwitt (Chris Murphy), and especially Andy Winer (Brian Schatz). My thanks to James Bamford, dean of NSA writers (with apologies for my fictional conceits). Also in DC, I'm grateful to Dan Jones of the Daschle Group, my terrific researcher/editor/assistant Clair Lamb, and Doyle Bartlett of the Eris Group. (Note: For dramatic purposes, I've taken creative liberties with the Senate Intelligence Committee's security protocols.)

For legal assistance, I thank Charles Sims of Proskauer Rose, J. Patrick Rowan of McGuireWoods, Stephen Vladeck of the University of Texas School of Law, Alex Abdo of the ACLU, and Mark Zaid. My coffee experts included

Corby Kummer, Jaime van Schyndel, and particularly George Howell.

In Boston, thanks to my friend Jay Groob of American Investigative Services, Bruce Irving, Larry Roberts, Eric Boutin, Chris Keller, Marc Davis, Sean Murphy of *The Boston Globe*, and my unindicted coconspirator, Giles McNamee. For medical help, Mark Morocco of the UCLA ER, and for some baby details I'd forgotten, Matt Miller of Stories Bookshop. At Dutton, my thanks to Christine Ball, Amanda Walker, Abigail Endler, Carrie Swetonic, Jess Renheim, and Ben Sevier. At my office, many thanks to Laura Jaye and Marilyn Saks Goldstein. Finally, I'm grateful to my agent, Dan Conaway, and most of all to my brother, Henry Finder.

Being a judge was a kind of performance art, Juliana had often reflected. Every word you said was being recorded, so you had to be absolutely fair and make sure to sound that way. You had to act and talk with dignity. You had to look and sound engaged.

You wore a costume: a black silk robe—actually 100 percent polyester and made by a company that provided caps and gowns to graduating seniors in high school and college. No one could see what you were wearing underneath the robe. On the other hand, at least in the American system (unlike judges in France or the U.K.) you didn't have to wear a white wig. When she first started as a judge, she walked out into the courtroom without her robe a number of times, forgot to put it on. On some level she disdained the formalities. But eventually she decided there was a purpose to the robe. It showed respect for the legal process. That was important.

And you had to live your life with probity. Juliana

never drove above the speed limit. She never broke the law. She was scrupulously honest about her taxes.

That requirement extended to her family as well. She couldn't have a son arrested for marijuana possession, and at his age he could be arrested. Yes, he would resent it, and yes, he'd be oppositional, but tough luck. That was the reality. Judges' kids had to be better behaved than other kids. That was the deal.

You also weren't supposed to let your mind wander during a hearing, but it was happening this morning anyway. She found herself listening to the defense attorney in the medical malpractice case, trying to focus, when she realized: *she had to recuse herself.*

It had been a perfect May night, warm but not quite balmy, with a soft breeze coming in off the lake, carrying with it the faint sounds of traffic from Michigan Avenue twenty floors below. Juliana was sitting alone on one end of a couch on the Peninsula's rooftop terrace, still wearing her conference lanyard, still wired from her speech from two hours ago. She'd delivered a talk on the rules of evidence in front of five hundred people, and it had gone really well. She tended to be self-critical, but she also knew when she'd hit a home run. *Rules of evidence* wasn't exactly a sexy topic, but she had her own take on it, and people seemed to respond.

She'd just had a drink with six fellow attendees, all judges from Indiana, and she was all talked out. Mostly she'd been the center of attention, which was flattering for a while, and then just exhausting. For now, she wanted to sit by herself—not in her room, with CNN keeping her company, but out there on the terrace in the refreshing breeze off Lake Michigan. Be in her own head. She dropped her lanyard on the glass-topped coffee table and scanned an array of magazines fanned out in front of her. One caught her eye—a travel magazine with a cover story about Spain—and she started leafing through it, keeping one eye out for a server. Another drink? Or maybe a cup of coffee—luckily, caffeine at night usually didn't prevent her from falling asleep.

No server was on hand, so she went back to her magazine—"The Unknown Mallorca," the piece promised. She felt someone's eyes on her, and she looked up; when she saw nobody looking her way, she felt a little silly. *Too much time in the spotlight,* she told herself with a laugh. *Having delusions of grandeur.*

Again she felt that strange sensation of being watched. She glanced up to see a man in a charcoal suit making his way in her direction. He was tall, early thirties, an olive complexion and wavy dark-blond hair that fell below his collar. She didn't recognize him. Maybe he was attending the legal conference too.

"Is this seat taken?" he asked. "Or am I interrupting?"

She gestured noncommittally to the chair by the couch—*suit yourself.* Her gaze could sometimes be stern and intimidating. "I'm not here for much longer, but help yourself."

Something about him gave off a slightly melancholy air, but he was a good-looking guy.

"Long day?" he asked.

She nodded. "And for you? Are you here with the law conference?"

"V.C. I think there's three conferences going on here this weekend." He paused, took in the magazine. "Planning a visit to Spain?"

"Looking at rentals in Costa Brava. In my dreams, mostly." She drained the last few drops of her Sancerre.

"You should go for real."

"Oh, Spain is my favorite place on earth."

"I just got back from Mallorca yesterday."

She tipped her head. "Nice vacation."

"Business, but still nice."

She put down the magazine. "Never been to Mallorca. I hear it's beautiful but overrun by tourists like me."

"Not if you know where to go."

She put out her hand. "Juliana Brody."

He shook it firmly. His hand was dry and smooth, his nails neatly trimmed. "Matías Sanchez." Just the faintest accent.

"You're Spanish?"

"Argentine. Spanish and Argentinians, we're like cousins." He shrugged.

"But you know Mallorca."

"Quite well. I travel a lot."

"So where do I have to go in Mallorca to escape the crowds?"

He paused briefly. "The most spectacular sunset you'll ever see at Cap de Formentor. You've got to drive up a terrifying little winding road, but by the time you get there it's worth it."

"Yeah?"

"Oh, and there's this great little restaurant in the old town called La Boveda; nothing fancy, but their tapas are to die for. And you can have a drink next door at Abaco, this fourteenth-century house filled with flowers and baskets of fruit. You tell them Matías Sanchez sent you, they'll take care of you right."

"Okay, I'm sold." She laughed lightly. "I'm easy. When it comes to Spain." She flushed. Then, to cover her embarrassment, she gestured for the server, who'd miraculously appeared. "Another Sancerre?"

He ordered an Ardbeg, ten years old, on the rocks.

"I'm afraid I was staring at you before. It's just that you remind me of someone I used to know." He smiled again, a nice, frank smile. One of his front teeth was crooked.

"It happens with me a lot," Juliana said. She used to remind some people of a movie actress named Amy Adams. *Used to* being the operative phrase.

And she thought: *Is this guy actually hitting on me?* It had been a while since she'd felt that particular buzz. This fellow—Matías—was easily ten years younger. And unnervingly handsome, she had to admit.

This is exactly the kind of thing I don't do, she thought. Would never do.

She wanted to say to the guy: You've got me all wrong. She'd say, If you knew anything about me, you'd know I'm not your 'live in the moment' kinda gal. You are wasting your time, buddy.

He tilted his head as if assessing her anew. "What's weird? Up close you don't look anything like her. It's just—I can't put my finger on it; it's something in the way you hold yourself. A kind of self-confidence, or maybe it's elegance, or both."

"So who do I almost look like?"

"The woman I used to be married to."

"Oho, I see. Nothing quite like being compared to a person's ex!"

Matías averted his gaze. "It's not like that . . ."

"I was only teasing. And anyway, I'm sure you have a girl in your life already."

"I do! An amazing, beautiful girl. She's everything to me."

He took out his phone and swiped at it.

She leaned in close to him and looked. A blond girl, maybe seven or eight, a gap-toothed smile, sitting in a rowboat. A red-and-white-striped T-shirt. Not what she expected.

She caught him watching her and smiled.

"She's a darling," she said. "Is she with her mother?"

"She . . ." He looked away, put the phone back in his jacket's breast pocket. She noticed tears in his eyes.

"Hey," she said, touching his wrist. "I didn't mean to . . ."

"No, it's . . . We were swimming in Costa Rica, a place called Playa Hermosa, and she . . ." He compressed his lips. "She was a terrific swimmer, but the riptide was too strong, and by the time . . ." His face seemed briefly to crumple in on itself, then just as quickly he recovered.

"I'm sorry," he said. "I thought this part of it was behind me." He got up, bowing his head in apology. Juliana reached out a hand, took his forearm, beseeching him to stay.

"Sit, please," she said. "How long—?"

He picked up his drink, sipped, put it down. "Two years." He slowly sat back down. "I still can't really talk about it. I shouldn't have tried. I—I never do this. This isn't me."

"It's quite all right—Matías, is that right?"

"Yes. And—Juliana?" She nodded.

"I don't know you," he continued. "But I feel as if I do; that's the weird thing. Just something I saw when I looked at you. Don't ask me to explain."

"Okay, now you're going to have to explain."

"Well, I can try. You're beautiful, of course. But so many beautiful women have this icy reserve—they have to, it's how they protect themselves, keep people out of their swim lane. But you—this is going to sound crazy. I saw a sense of a light inside you."

She blushed again, hoped it wasn't visible. "LED, I'm sure."

"You're making fun of me, and you should."

"No, I'm sorry, go on. What else did you see?"

"Honestly?"

Juliana reached for her wineglass, took a steadying sip. "Sure, why not?"

"I see a kind of . . . loneliness. Not by-yourself lonely; but lonely. Maybe because . . . well, didn't you say you're a judge? Perhaps people are intimidated? And maybe because the ones who should love you don't love you like they should."

Juliana was momentarily speechless.

"I am so sorry," Matías said. "I swear I'm not normally like this. Let's blame the Ardbeg." He put his hand on hers briefly and she felt the heat. "Four hours ago I was deciding whether to do an equity arb deal with a binational real estate investment trust. Now, that's where my instincts are good."

She gave him a long look. "Maybe not just there," she admitted, and she finished the Sancerre.

They kissed leaning against the door to his suite. She could taste the single malt. She leaned back, took a breath. He found a tendril of her hair and ran his fingers under it, along her cheek. His eyes met hers for a moment. "I wonder if you know how beautiful you are."

She could feel the heat radiating off his body. "Tomorrow I'm flying off. Back to my life. This . . . this can't mean anything."

Something was happening inside her. Like a wave that suddenly, startlingly forms in a usually placid lake. A wave formed by that surprisingly good French Sancerre and some kind of reservoir of resentment at how goddamned predictable she'd become. Everybody knows she'd never do this. But shouldn't there be more to her than what everybody knows?

For just one night, she'd pretend to be that woman she's not. For just one night, she'd do what she never does. For just one night, she'd live a life that isn't the one she so carefully mapped out.

Just one night.

He found his key card and the lock beeped open and he held the door for her.

That was when it all had unraveled. When he had reappeared in her courtroom with the threat. With the video and his demands about her judgment of the case over which she was presiding right now.

She had to recuse herself.

Otherwise, she was trapped . . . and that blackmail video would go public.

She took the elevator up to the thirteenth floor of the courthouse building and stopped by the office of Sam Giannopoulos, the deputy court administrator, a few doors down the corridor.

"Justice Brody," he said, looking up from his crowded desk. He was a small, gaunt, bald man with heavy black-framed glasses, around sixty. "What brings you up here?" Giannopoulos's shoulders were stooped. He was an affable introvert, always pleasant to deal with, probably something of a clock-puncher. He was there to serve out his time until retirement.

"A scheduling thing. I have a question about the calendar." She sat down in the chair next to his desk.

He gave a nervous smile. In front of him was a half-eaten sandwich, which he was slowly pushing away.

"Okay. What's the question?"

"I'm considering recusing myself from a case I'm presiding over. And I'm wondering if it's going to be a problem to assign it to another judge."

She expected little more than a shrug. Judges recused themselves fairly often. Another judge could be assigned. It happened.

Instead, Giannopoulos looked wary and tense. His brows furrowed and his mouth jutted open. "But is—is there a problem? Something I should know about?"

She was surprised at his response. Giannopoulos took care of the court's calendar, but he didn't normally get involved in judges' decisions on whether to step away from a case.

"A possible conflict with a member of the defense team." She couldn't say much more than that, and she'd already told him more than she was required to.

But others would ask, other judges on the circuit. And what could she tell them? That she'd once had a drink with one of the lawyers on the case? That again. How could she possibly justify recusing herself if she was pressed for details? In fact, she couldn't. Not honestly.

Giannopoulos's face was slowly drained of color. "Everyone else has crowded schedules," he said, taking off his glasses and polishing them with his tie. "This wouldn't be easy for another judge to take over after—how many months?"

"Four."

"Four months. Wow. That's a lot of water under the bridge. You recuse yourself at this point, you could have a mistrial. I'm not—I'm not so sure it's a good idea. You should think seriously about this."

"Which is exactly what I've done." Something was off about him.

Giannopoulos seemed to study his desktop. "For a number of reasons, I think it would be better if you made no changes to your schedule."

"I understand that," she said. "But there are also strong reasons to recuse." She said it as much for herself as for Giannopoulos's benefit. She didn't *have* to give a reason if she decided to withdraw from a case and pass it on to another judge. She could just do it.

A long silence passed.

Finally, Giannopoulos said softly, "I think you'd be well-advised to see this through." He quickly looked away, glancing down at his keyboard.

Juliana felt ice freeze in her abdomen, dripping coldly into her bowels.

See it through.

Matías had said the same thing, hadn't he? *I advise you to see it through.*

"What's that supposed to mean?"

Giannopoulos wouldn't meet her eyes. He got up and closed his office door. Then he returned to his desk, his face now chalk-white. He folded his hands, interlacing his fingers. He cleared his throat nervously. "Just—just see it through. It's better this way." He repeated: "Just see it through."

"Sam, what's wrong—what happened to you?"

He shook his head slowly. "All I can say is, see it through." His phone rang, and he lunged for it, seemingly grateful for the interruption. "Will you please excuse me, judge?"

In the elevator down to the ninth floor, she could feel her heart thudding in her ears. She was still numb from her encounter with the court administrator, his tone thick with warning. *Just see it through*, he'd told her. *It's better this way.*

She felt queasy, her stomach tight. She remembered, too, how Sam himself had seemed frightened, even as he was warning her. They'd gotten to him, that much was clear. Whomever *they* were. They'd scared him somehow.

Shakily, she returned to her office, her lobby, and keyed open the door, glanced at her watch. Twenty minutes before she had to be back in court for the afternoon session. . . . She tried to focus on the document that was on her monitor, but her brain felt scattered; she couldn't concentrate, her mind flitting from the videotape she'd seen to Sam's blanched face.

Her life was balancing on a tiny fulcrum. It was on the verge of being ruined. One wrong move, one mistake, and it was over. She was petrified and couldn't think clearly.

Suddenly her cell phone rang. Not many people had that number. Duncan, Jake, a few other people. The caller ID said Private Caller. Apprehensively, she picked it up.

"Listen to the man," the caller said. "See it through."

She recognized the voice.

"You are not to recuse yourself. That would be a serious mistake. I've already told you what will happen. The video goes public, and your career is over. Thousands, maybe millions will watch it. Your life will be over."

The line went dead.

JOSEPH FINDER

"A master of the modern thriller."
—*The Boston Globe*

For a complete list of titles,
please visit prh.com/josephfinder